WRESTLING WITH DEATH

A Zoey Wilde Mystery

Book one

RANDEE GREEN

CAMEL
PRESS
Kenmore, WA

A Camel Press book published by Epicenter Press

Epicenter Press
6524 NE 181st St.
Suite 2
Kenmore, WA 98028

For more information go to:
www.Camelpress.com
www.Coffeetownpress.com
www.Epicenterpress.com
www.randeegreen.com

This is a work of fiction. Names, characters, places, brands, media, and incidents are either the product of the author's imagination or are used fictitiously.

Wrestling With Death
Copyright © 2024 by Randee Green

Library of Congress Control Number: 2024931749

ISBN: 978-1-68492-197-3 (Trade Paper)
ISBN: 978-1-68492-198-0 (eBook)

To Matt and Jeff Hardy

ACKNOWLEDGEMENTS

LIMITLESS THANKS AND SMOOCHES to Daisy, Molly, and Snookums for the love and support that only pets can provide.

Thank you to my mom for (mostly) not complaining every time that I've handed you a new manuscript with the expectation that you find and correct all of my grammatical and punctuation errors. And thank you to my dad for subjecting me to professional wrestling at such a young age and for taking me to all of those events. The cage should remain standing . . .

Huge thanks to Nick "Sicend" Taylor of Riot City for giving me an insider's view of the business and for answering all of my pro wrestling questions over the years.

And to all the professional wrestlers who have inspired me . . . None of this would have happened without you.

ONE

Saturday August 18, 2018

"WHERE'S ZOEY? Where's my soon-to-be first ever Women's Champion?"

The shout echoed throughout the VFW Hall's cavernous banquet room, causing Zoey Wilde to flinch. Beneath her, the six-foot-tall stepladder wobbled on the old, uneven floorboards. Zoey shifted her weight and steadied the ladder.

"I'm right here," Zoey muttered. "How can you possibly miss seeing me?"

Ignoring the person looking for her, Zoey carried on with hanging up a gigantic vinyl banner. Printed along the top of the banner in red, two-foot-high block letters was "Linville Association of Wrestling." Lined up along the banner were some of the wrestlers who had appeared at LAW events throughout the past year. Tacked on the end like an afterthought, Zoey was the only woman pictured: a tattooed, leopard print-clad Beauty alongside a half dozen shirtless, speedo-clad Beasts.

After securing the banner, Zoey pivoted so that she could look around the banquet room. Her movements caused the ladder to totter to the side.

"Don't fall!"

Hannah Stoltzfus—Zoey's twenty-year-old protégé and her opponent for later in the evening—grabbed the swaying ladder. Despite her best efforts, the ladder continued to wobble.

With the ladder threatening to tip over, Zoey fumbled along the wall for something to hold on to. With one hand, she clutched the bottom edge of the banner. With the other, she accidentally tore down a string of half-burnt-out twinkling Christmas lights. Zoey didn't feel too bad about tearing down the lights—it was August after all.

"I told you the top step is not really a step," Hannah scolded as she finally steadied the ladder. "There's a big sticker that says you should never stand on the top step. But, no . . . You insisted on standing on it anyway."

"Well, you know me . . . I'm not just *a* wild woman. I am *the* 'Wilde Woman,'" Zoey said, referring to her professional wrestling personae. "I like to live dangerously. After all, what's life if you don't occasionally ignore the warning labels and break a few rules?"

"Oh please, you hardly live dangerously. You're just barely living," Hannah said. "All you do is go to work and wrestle. I mean, yeah, wrestling can be dangerous but—"

"Hey, I also go to the gym."

"And that's positively life-threatening." Hannah managed to look stern for a second or two before she ruined the effect by giggling. "Seriously, Zoey. You don't date. You don't go to parties. You don't jump out of airplanes—"

"When was the last time you jumped out of an airplane?" Zoey clenched her hands into fists and jammed them against her hips. She glared down her nose at Hannah. "I'm sorry my life isn't exciting enough for you. But I'm perfectly happy with it."

"I'm just saying . . . You need to get out more. Live a little."

"And you need to mind your own business."

Zoey hated being lectured to—especially by someone who was a decade younger than her and didn't have a fraction of the life experience that she had.

Above Zoey's head, a speaker crackled and screeched. The sound left her ears ringing.

"Zoey? Where are you? Are you even in here?"

"I'm right here, Uncle Leland." Zoey pivoted towards the stage that was at the other end of the room and waved her arms to get Leland Freeman's attention.

Leland was not Zoey's biological uncle, but he was considered family because he was her dad's closest friend. Leland and Marlon Wilde had also been tag team partners back when they had wrestled on the independent circuit.

"Oh, there you are." Leland waved as he continued speaking into the microphone. "What are you doing on top of that ladder? Get down from there. The last thing I need is for you to fall and break your neck this close to showtime. Who told you to climb up there anyway?"

"You did."

Leland was the man behind the curtain at the Linville Association of Wrestling. As the owner, operator, CEO, promotor, and booker, he wore many hats. Among numerous other duties, he created the storylines, booked the matches, and decided the winners.

Back on solid ground, Zoey yelled, "Where's my title belt?"

"It's right here!" Leland held up a fabric wrapped bundle. "Get on up here if you want to see it. And bring Hannah with you. I need to talk to both of you."

"Are you excited about winning the title tonight?" Hannah asked.

"I'm always excited to win a title," Zoey said. Throughout her twelve-year wrestling career, she had worked for various promotions up and down the East Coast. She had won so many Women's Championships that she had long since lost count. "But tonight is going to be extra exciting since I'm going to be the first LAW Women's Champion."

"Plus, this is your hometown," Hannah said, as if Zoey needed a reminder that she was a lifelong resident of Linville, Pennsylvania. The small town was located in what was known as Pennsylvania's Amish Country, and was about halfway between Harrisburg and the city of Lancaster. "I hope I get to win a championship someday."

"Your career is only just getting started. You've got plenty of time to win a championship or two." Zoey linked arms with Hannah and pulled her towards the other side of the banquet room. "Now let's go see this title belt."

The VFW Hall was housed in an old church that had been built in the early 1800s. About forty years ago, the VFW took over the building and turned the former chapel into a banquet room. The wood floor was the original, and the marks left behind by the pews were still visible.

The banquet room was not the most attractive of venues—too much old, dark wood and not enough natural light—but it served its purpose.

Residents of Linville had rented the hall for everything from receptions to rummage sales and bingo tournaments to community theater. For the past year, the VFW Hall had hosted the Linville Association of Wrestling for monthly events.

"Let's see the title belt," Zoey said as she bounded up the five steps to the stage. "I've been waiting a long time for this."

"Hold your horses. We'll get to the title in a minute," Leland said as he placed the fabric wrapped bundle on a podium that was off to the right side of the stage. "First, we've got to go over my plan for opening the show. I want to make a big deal out of unveiling the title."

"Maybe you should make a big deal out of the match," Zoey mumbled.

Earlier, Zoey had seen the match card. She knew that her match against Hannah was the fourth out of eight matches. Leland had allotted them a measly eight minutes—and that included the time it took for introductions and for them to walk to the ring.

"Yeah, I vote you change up the card," Hannah said. "Put us in the main event."

"No." Leland twisted the ends of his handlebar mustache. "The Heavyweight Title match always gets the main event."

"Then give us more time. We could make it a two-out-of-three falls match," Zoey said.

"As of now, the card is set. I refuse to make any more changes to it," Leland said to Zoey. "It's bad enough I had to make a last-minute change this morning. The guy I had booked to wrestle your brother cancelled on me."

Before Zoey could point out Leland's irritating habit of making changes within minutes of showtime, he emitted a shrill whistle. He then called for the two dozen or so people in the banquet hall to gather around the stage.

Once all the wrestlers, referees, and volunteers were in front of the stage, Leland said, "As many of you know, I always open the show by welcoming the audience and thanking them for coming out. I'll then go over the rules. Including the most important one of—"

"Don't try this at home," Zoey said. "We all know the rules. You don't need to tell us."

"No, but it bears repeating." Leland gave Zoey the stink eye. "I don't need some dumb kids getting the idea that they can put on wrestling matches at home. Then they get hurt, and their parents try to sue me."

"Kids are going to try it at home whether you warn them or not," Zoey said.

"Yeah, Zoey, Zack, and I did," Justin Wilde added as he climbed onto the stage. With his muscular frame, long hair, scruffy beard, and a copious number of tattoos, Zoey's little brother was a fan favorite among women of all ages. "And we almost never got hurt."

"Your dad was also a pro wrestler, and he started training the three of you before you could even walk," Leland said to Justin. "But safety is the most important thing. Not only the safety of the people who come out to the shows, but the safety of all of you who wrestle for me. Which leads me to the second rule—"

"Don't throw anything other than streamers at the wrestlers or into the ring," Hannah said, following Zoey's example and cutting Leland off.

"Thank you, Hannah." Leland's nostrils flared. "Now, I know all of you are aware of those rules. But not all of you know that I've had to establish a third rule since the last event."

"Don't jump over the fan barricade and try to get involved in the matches," Zoey's grandmother, Vivian Wilde, said as she stepped through the curtains.

The elderly woman wore skintight, snakeskin capris that hugged her scrawny legs. Her rhinestone-studded t-shirt implored everyone to ask her about her grandchildren. On the back of the shirt was a picture of Zoey and her brothers. Vivian had completed the outfit with a lime green feather boa, chunky bracelets, and a pair of orange eyeglasses.

Vivian was a lot of things. Subtle was not one of them.

"I'm glad you know the rule since I had to make it specifically for you, Vivi." Leland sighed. "You know, since you decided to get involved in Zoey's match last month."

"It was all part of the storyline," Vivian said.

"Oh, no, it was not!" Hannah hissed at Vivian. "You know you, like, tweaked my neck and my back. I had to go to a chiropractor, and my neck still hurts."

Making her debut at last month's show, Hannah attacked Zoey following her match against a wrestler who went by the name Beverly Hill.

Despite knowing what was going to happen, Vivian decided to come to Zoey's rescue. After climbing over the barricade, Vivian jumped on Hannah's back and put her in a headlock. It took a combined effort from Zoey and the referee to pull Vivian away from Hannah.

"You're just a whippersnapper. You'll recover. Besides, it added some extra excitement to the show." Vivian gave Hannah a grandmotherly pat on the cheek. She then turned to Leland and said, "I'll follow your new rule. But you need to promise me that you will never make up a rule that says I can't heckle the wrestlers."

"I would never do that, Vivi. I love it when you hassle the wrestlers and give them a hard time," Leland said, causing some of the wrestlers to grumble. "It's the best part of the show."

Leland was not in the majority when it came to positive opinions on Vivian's loud and obnoxious heckling. Zoey was immune to it, but Vivian's antics embarrassed Justin . . . and she annoyed most of the other wrestlers because they did not appreciate her stealing the spotlight.

"Now, like I was trying to say before all of you started interrupting me . . ." Leland said, bringing the attention back to himself. "I'm going to start off the show like I always do. I'll welcome the audience and go over the rules. Then I'll tell everyone that tonight we will be crowning the Linville Association of Wrestling's first ever Women's Champion. I'll have Zoey and Hannah come out on stage with me. Then I'll say something along the lines of . . . 'Ladies and gentlemen, as the owner and operator—'"

Zoey had had about all she could take. "I don't care what you say when you unveil the title. I just want to see the title. And I want to see it now."

"I'm with Zoey. Let's get this show on the road," Justin said as he pretended to crack a whip. "We've got less than three hours until the doors open. If you drag this out any longer, they'll be letting the fans in and we'll still be standing here."

"The ring is up." Leland wandered towards the edge of the stage. "What else needs done?"

"We need to finish putting up the chairs around the ring," Leland's stepson, Terry Gibbs, said as he leaned against the front of the stage. "We're estimating around four hundred people coming out tonight. They ain't gonna be happy if we make them sit on the floor or stand."

"And I need to get the concession booth set up," Leland's wife, Kimberly

Gibbs-Freeman, said. "Unless you want me serving lukewarm beer and cold nacho cheese to the fans."

Despite having known each other for years, Leland and Kim had never shown any interest in each other—or even seemed to like each other all that much—until they began dating three years earlier. Before any of their family or friends had the chance to get used to them dating, suddenly they were married. No one thought that the marriage would last very long, but, so far, Kim and Leland had proved everyone wrong.

Kim was twice as old as Leland's former girlfriends, her hips were twice as wide, and her IQ was probably twice as high. Before Kim, Leland only dated well-endowed women who were roughly Zoey's current age or younger.

Kim was also the only person who Zoey knew that was more obsessed with pro wrestling than the Wildes. For Kim, it wasn't just a hobby or a passion. Pro wrestling was her religion. She preached the gospel of pro wrestling the same way religious fanatics preached about Jesus. The only thing Kim loved more than pro wrestling was her son.

"If there is so much that needs set up, why are you all standing here?" Leland asked.

"Because you told us to, Uncle Leland," Justin pointed out. "You're the one who made everyone gather around so you could show off the women's title belt."

"Yeah, old man, you're the one wasting our time. Now hurry up and show us the title," said an extremely hairy man who was known almost solely as Sasquatch.

"Yeah, let's get on with it," Zoey said. "Some of us still need to change into our ring gear and set up our merchandise tables. I'm sure I'm not the only one who would like to make more money than the few dollars you throw our way."

"Well, I don't have anything to do before the show starts. But I'm also not getting any younger," Vivian said as she pushed past Leland. Her blinged-out, gold orthopedic shoes squeaked on the stage's old wood as she shuffled towards the podium. Vivian grabbed the sparkly piece of fabric and whisked it away from the title belt. "Ta-da!"

"Oh . . . my . . ." Zoey whispered as she took in the monstrosity of a title belt.

The strap was made from hot pink artificial leather, and most of it was covered in a jumble of black and clear rhinestones. At the center was a plastic silver disc the size of a dinner plate. Written across the disc in sparkly, black paint were the words "Women's Champion."

"What do you think, Zoey?" Leland asked as he picked up the belt. "Do you love it?"

"No, I can't say I love it," Zoey said as she struggled to come up with something to say. For as long as she could remember, her mother had lectured her about keeping her mouth shut if she did not have anything nice to say. And she was having an exceedingly difficult time coming up with something nice. Settling for tactful, Zoey said, "But it is unique."

"Yeah, it's uniquely ugly," Justin said. Clearly Roxanne Wilde's lectures had been in one ear and out the other when it came to her youngest child.

"It reminds me of the plastic title belts you can get at the toy store." Zoey picked up the belt. "And . . . ummm . . . Why is it pink?"

"I did that for you," Leland said. "Because I know pink is your favorite color."

"Uhh, no. Pink is definitely not my favorite color."

Zoey wondered how Leland could have known her for her entire life and not know that her favorite color was purple. Over half of Zoey's wardrobe was purple. Heck, even her Jeep was purple.

"Oh . . . I thought you liked pink." Leland shrugged. "Personally, I like the belt."

"You would considering you have horrible taste. Case in point is that ridiculous mustache." Vivian grabbed the title belt and yanked it away from Zoey. "You know, I don't have many regrets in life. But never winning a women's championship is one of them."

"I know, Nana."

Zoey steeled herself for another one of Vivian's talks. Every time Zoey won a championship, Vivian had to remind her granddaughter that she had never won a title during her career as a professional wrestler in the late-1950s and early-1960s.

Wanting more than small-town life in southcentral Pennsylvania, a young Vivian had decided to pursue a career as a professional wrestler. She was only sixteen years old when she left home and moved to Columbia, South Carolina, so that she could train at Fabulous Moolah's wrestling school. After a year of training, Vivian hit the road.

Calling herself Vivacious Vivian, she traveled up and down the Eastern seaboard and wrestled for any promotion that Moolah could get her booked at. At one of her first events, Vivian met a man named Kazimir "The Wilde Man" Wilde. It was love at first sight, and they soon married. Vivian then parted ways with Moolah—something that didn't exactly help her career. At the time, Fabulous Moolah essentially controlled women's wrestling.

A few years after getting married, Vivian and Kazimir had a son. For the first few years of his life, Marlon traveled around the country with his parents. When he was old enough to start school, Marlon was sent back to Linville, Pennsylvania, to live with Vivian's parents. Vivian continued to wrestle for a couple more years, but then she mostly gave it up so that she could be with her son. Vivian swore she had no regrets about choosing her son over her career, but that didn't stop her from lamenting that she had never won a championship.

"You know what I think I should do?" Vivian asked Zoey. "I should come out of retirement and challenge you for the LAW Women's Championship."

Vivian had been threatening to come out of retirement for as long as Zoey could remember. The older Vivian got, the more determined she became to follow through.

"I hate to break it to you, Nana, but I think you've waited a bit too long to come out of retirement. You're too old to be getting back into the wrestling ring."

"You want to come out of retirement, do it at someone else's promotion," Leland said. "Because it ain't happening at mine. You'd probably break a hip or something."

"I'm not some brittle-boned, ready for the nursing home, 'help I've fallen and I can't get up' old lady! I might be a bit long in the tooth, but I'm not knocking on death's door quite yet. I'm not too old to get back into a wrestling ring. Mae Young was almost my age when she got powerbombed through that table on *Raw is War*. And she was pushing ninety when she had her last match." Vivian jabbed Zoey in the chest with an arthritic finger. "Besides, my girl, it'll barely be a wrestling match. Everyone knows you would never hit an old lady. You'd just lay down and let me pin you."

"We've talked about this on countless occasions, Nana . . . I'm not taking a dive just so you can be a champion," Zoey said as she struggled to maintain a straight face. "Besides, you getting back in the ring at your age would have Pop-Pop spinning in his grave."

"Didn't we have Kaz cremated?" Justin asked.

"It's just an expression," Zoey said.

"If your grandfather was still alive, he would support me—"

"No, he wouldn't," Zoey and Justin said in unison.

"I think I knew your grandfather a little better than you two. I was married to Kazimir for fifty-five years, after all." Vivian let the belt slip off her knobby shoulder and handed it to Zoey. "I guess some dreams just aren't meant to come true."

"Do you really hate the belt, Zoey?" Leland asked.

"If you had let me design it like I asked . . . Well . . . This is definitely not what I would have come up with." Zoey scrutinized the title belt that she cradled in her arms. It was not getting any more attractive the longer she looked at it. In fact, it was getting worse looking as she came up with more and more reasons to hate it. "I just don't understand why you couldn't design a simple, classy-looking title belt like you did for the Heavyweight and Tag Champions."

"Because simple and classy is boring. I wanted something flashy for you girls."

"Well, the lights flashing off the rhinestones will blind the fans." Zoey handed the title belt to Leland and then backed away. "Let me know what you finally decide to do to open the show. Meanwhile, I need to grab my stuff out of my Jeep and get my merchandise table set up."

"Need any help?" Terry asked. He was the only person still lingering around the stage aside from Zoey, Justin, and Leland. Everyone else had gone back to setting up for the show.

"Yeah, sure. Thanks," Zoey said, accepting Terry's offer.

Terry scampered along at Zoey's heels like an exuberant puppy. In fact, with his shaggy blonde hair, brown eyes, and happy-go-lucky attitude, Terry reminded her of a golden retriever, albeit not an extremely cute one. At least he was no longer following her around like a love sick puppy.

For years—starting when Justin befriended Terry in second grade—Terry had had a crush on Zoey. Zoey, who viewed Terry as just another brother, did nothing to encourage him. His adoration had actually made her uncomfortable and she did everything she could to dissuade him. As he got older, Terry finally got over his crush and now treated Zoey like a sister.

"Sorry about the crappy title belt. I have no idea what Leland was thinking."

Zoey was about to respond when she heard Justin yelling. She glanced over her shoulder and watched as her brother shook his fist under Leland's nose.

"Any idea what that's about?"

Terry shrugged. "The guy booked to wrestle Justin had to cancel. I know Leland was scrambling to find a replacement. Maybe he had to cancel Justin's match."

"That would make Justin angry."

Justin had a history of being hotheaded and for overreacting. But he was relatively harmless. Because of that, Zoey wasn't concerned about what was going on.

Stepping through the side door, Zoey and Terry headed towards where she had parked her purple Jeep Grand Cherokee at the back of the VFW's lot. While Terry grabbed Zoey's box of merchandise out of the rear cargo area, she opened the passenger side rear door and reached for her gym bag full of wrestling gear.

"I'm missing a boot. I swore they were both in here when I left my apartment," Zoey mumbled to herself as she dug through the bag in search of her other purple and black combat boot. She'd worn the boots last night at a show in Scranton, and she was positive both boots had been in the bag earlier today when she'd gotten her gear together. She handed the gym bag to Terry. "Take that and my merch inside. I'll be in as soon as I find my other boot."

While Terry headed inside with her things, Zoey climbed into the back seat. She was typically a neat person, but she had not bothered to clean out the Jeep in a while. That turned searching for the missing boot into a treasure hunt. While Zoey sifted through the detritus, she came across a wadded-up blanket, a snow scraper, a pair of mismatched socks, a six-pound sledgehammer, a plastic pink flamingo yard decoration, and a pacifier that her niece must have lost during a rare occasion when she had Paige in her Jeep.

Zoey finally located the boot wedged under the passenger seat.

With the boot in hand, she was about to slide backwards off the seat when someone smacked her on the butt.

TWO

"WHAT THE—!"

The force of the smack to her butt sent Zoey sprawling. Her nose slammed into the heated, black fabric of the back seat and brought tears to her eyes.

Zoey hated getting manhandled. Unfortunately, because it happened fairly often at wrestling events, she was almost used to it, but that didn't mean she accepted it. Over the years, Zoey had blackened a few eyes and bloodied a couple noses of other wrestlers, promoters, and fans who had been dumb enough to try groping her.

There were three people who Zoey knew were currently on site at the VFW Hall that she would tolerate manhandling her. Vivian would give her grandchildren a solid smack on the bottom regardless of how old they were. Zoey could tell by the size of the hand and the force of the blow that the culprit was not Vivian. It also ruled out Hannah, who would have snuck up on Zoey and smacked her butt just to be funny. That left Justin—who was under the misconception that it was humorous to manhandle his sister—but Zoey knew her brother's laugh, and whoever was chuckling did not sound like Justin.

"That wasn't funny!"

Zoey pushed herself up into a sitting position and then spun around so that she could confront her assailant. She was about to verbally tear into the person, but the words died when she recognized the man leaning against the Jeep's open door.

Zoey opened her mouth to scream, but the sound that came out was a whimper.

"Hey, Zoey."

"Devon . . ."

Zoey could barely whisper her ex-boyfriend's name as her lungs seized up. She had to force the breath down into her chest, causing her lungs to painfully expand. Zoey hadn't had a serious anxiety attack in years, but she could never forget how they felt. The pounding heart, the crippling chest pain, breaking out into a cold sweat—all three symptoms hit her full force. For a second, her head spun, and she saw black.

Almost seven years had passed since Zoey last saw Devon Isler.

Almost seven years had passed since the night he almost killed her.

The bruises and broken bones had long since healed, but the memories of the assault continued to haunt her.

Zoey had been dating Devon for almost a year before she packed up her things and moved with him to Florida. Almost as soon as they crossed the state line, Devon's real character began to show. After suffering in the now toxic relationship for another six months, Zoey gathered up the courage to leave him. Devon refused to let her go. The assault started with a backhand across the face. It ended with Devon straddling Zoey's chest and pinning her flailing arms down with his knees. Zoey had struggled to buck him off, but he outweighed her by at least a hundred pounds. While laughing at Zoey's failure to fight back, Devon wrapped his hands around her throat and squeezed. As Zoey ran out of oxygen and her vision faded, she was terrified that Devon's rage-contorted face would be the last thing she ever saw.

The reason that Zoey wound up in the ICU and not in the morgue was because the next-door neighbors overheard the fight, broke into the apartment, and saved her.

"Come on out of there, Zoey." Devon reached into the back of the Jeep, grasped her wrist, and yanked her towards the open door.

"Let go of me!"

Zoey snatched up the boot that she had dropped and used it to smack Devon's hand away.

He was real! He was really here! He wasn't a figment of Zoey's imagination. This wasn't a nightmare—another version of the same nightmare that she'd had almost every night since he almost killed her. Devon was back. Zoey's nightmares were now reality.

"Go away!"

"But, Zoey . . ."

"No!" Zoey screamed as she scrambled across the seat. She barely felt it when her head and back collided with the window and door. "Get away from me!"

Keeping her eyes on Devon, Zoey reached behind her and fumbled for the door handle. She had to get out of the confines of her Jeep. She had to get away! After her trembling fingers wrapped around the handle, she shoved open the door and tumbled out. If she hadn't been clinging to the door, she would have landed on her head; but, thanks to the door, Zoey kept herself upright while she swung her feet off the seat and to the ground.

Turning to run, Zoey crashed into Devon. He had come to stand between her Jeep Grand Cherokee and Justin's lime green Rubicon. She was trapped. Devon was in front of her. There was a Jeep on both sides. Behind her was the backside of the Linville Community Park office building. Zoey backed up, putting some distance between herself and Devon. He didn't recognize Zoey's need for personal space and moved along with her.

Backed up against the office building, Zoey had nowhere to go. If she wanted to get away from Devon, she would have to squeeze between the building and the front end of either Jeep.

Where the heck is everyone? Zoey thought as she looked around what she could see of the parking lot. There were at least two dozen cars in the lot, but she couldn't see or hear any people.

"After all these years, is that any way to greet me, Zoey?" Devon held out his arms and gestured for her to come closer. "I think I deserve at least a hug after what you did to me."

"After what I did to you?" Zoey asked, spitting out the words. Yes, she was still in the middle of an anxiety attack, but pure rage was beginning to take control and that overrode the anxiety for the moment. "Tell me, Devon. What did *I* do to *you*?"

"I wasted years in prison because of you." Devon smacked his arms against his sides. "The least you could have done was answer the letters I sent instead of getting the prison to cut me off. You owe me."

"Letters? What letters? I never got any letters from you."

"I sent a few right after I went to prison. Then the warden told me I could write to you all I wanted, but he wasn't going to let the prison mail any of the letters."

"Well, I never got any letters," Zoey said. "And you put yourself in prison because you almost killed me."

"I wouldn't have done that had you not tried to leave me."

Devon could never take responsibility for anything he had done. Instead, he shifted blame to an innocent party. Zoey had allowed Devon to blame her for almost everything during their relationship. In Devon's opinion, every little thing that had gone wrong had been her fault. Zoey would not let him blame her for anything else.

"Oh, no. You're not going to blame me. I'll take the blame for sticking with you for as long as I did. Had I been smart, I would have broken up with you long before that. Then it never would have come down to you almost killing me."

"You caught me by surprise that night. I thought you loved me, but, instead, I come home to find you packing your stuff," Devon said, sounding hurt. "But, darn, girl, you look good. Though you could be skinnier."

Zoey huffed in annoyance as she looked over Devon. She wasn't going to let his insults bother her. "What about you, Devon? Looks like you've let yourself go. When was the last time you went to the gym? And what happened to your hair?"

When Zoey had first turned around, she almost hadn't recognized Devon. Physically, he had changed a lot in the past seven years. He was nowhere near as muscular as he used to be. His once tanned and sculpted arms were now pale and flabby. He also used to have long, flowing, bleached blonde hair that he flung around like a certain Canadian wrestler that Zoey'd had a crush on since she was a teenager. His hair was now short, and his hairline was beginning to recede. Zoey spotted gray hairs mixed in with the brown. Devon had loved his hair—loved it more than Zoey, in fact. To have it short, graying, and receding must be a blow to his ego.

"Sometimes a man needs to change his look." Devon ran his hand over his head. "But, speaking of appearances, didn't we agree you wouldn't get any more tattoos?"

"No, you told me I wasn't *allowed* to get any more tattoos. I never agreed to it," Zoey said. She'd had five tattoos when she started dating Devon, and he told her that those five were more than enough. In the past seven years, Zoey had gotten more tattoos—covering both arms from shoulder to wrist, as well as on her legs.

"Had I not been wasting away in prison; you wouldn't have been out here running wild and defiling your body."

"It's my body—"

"But I think tattoos look trashy on women. And, as my woman, I don't want you to look trashy." Devon ran his fingers along the black lace garter belt that encircled Zoey's right thigh. "I do like this one, though. I just wish you wouldn't wear such short shorts that allows everyone else to see it."

"Don't touch me!" Zoey smacked Devon's hand away.

Zoey wouldn't lie—getting tattoos can be painful. But the pain she had felt when getting the tattoos was nothing compared to the pain of having Devon touch her again.

"There was a time when you liked it when I touched you," Devon said.

"That was a long time ago."

"I can remind you what it was like." Devon pushed his sunglasses on top of his head so that he could wink at Zoey. "Maybe you'll still like it."

"Keep your hands to yourself. And stay away from me."

Zoey planted her palms on Devon's chest and shoved him. As she did so, the collar of his shirt shifted, and she caught a glimpse of a tattoo on his chest. From what little she could see of it, she could tell that it was done in poor quality ink. Not only did she have multiple tattoos, she also managed her twin brother's tattoo shop. Zoey knew bad tattoos when she saw them.

Slipping her fingers under Devon's collar, Zoey yanked the shirt down to reveal her name tattooed across his chest. It was shocking enough that Devon had a tattoo—after all, he had sworn he would never sully his body with ink. But to have gotten her name! She was looking right at it, and she almost couldn't believe it.

"Do you like it?" Devon asked as he grinned at Zoey. "I got it right after I went to prison. My cellmate did it."

"No! No, I don't like it at all. Why do you have my name tattooed on you?"

"Because I wanted a reminder as to why I was in prison." Devon stepped closer to Zoey, looming over her in a way that would have intimidated her years ago. He was shorter than Zoey remembered—but that was because he had her so worn down in the end that she hadn't been able to stand up straight. "And because I'm not done with you . . ."

Zoey shook her head. "What are you doing here?"

"I'm here for the same reason that you are. To wrestle."

"No, you're not. I know the card for tonight, and you are not on it."

"I wasn't on it until Leland called me this morning and asked if I could fill in for a wrestler that had to cancel at the last minute."

"Oh, no . . ." Zoey had forgotten that Justin's opponent canceled, forcing Leland to get a replacement. "How did Uncle Leland know you were back?"

"I ran into him earlier this week. Told him I was around and that I was ready to get back in the ring. He told me he'd call if he needed me. This morning, he called."

"I know you were released from prison about a year ago. Someone from the Orange County State Attorney's office called to warn me you were a free man," Zoey said. " But when did you move from Florida back to Pennsylvania?"

Zoey had been spared from having to sit through a trial when the prosecutor agreed to drop the attempted homicide charges and offered Devon a five to ten-year sentence if he pled guilty to the aggravated assault. He accepted the deal and was sentenced to five years in prison. The judge had given him the minimum sentence since it was his first offense.

"I moved back home earlier this week—"

"You didn't come back because of me, did you?"

"You're the main reason I came back. Mom was also begging me to come home. You know how she is . . ."

"But why me? Don't tell me you spent the past seven years pining over me—"

"No. I spent that first year hating you. But, thanks to the anger management classes the judge forced me to take, I finally forgave you."

"Forgave me for what?"

"For putting me in jail. If you hadn't . . . . But that's all in the past." Devon pressed both hands over his heart. "Those anger management classes taught me to accept my faults. I've changed my ways, Zoey. I'm a new man."

Zoey snorted. "Part of me finds that hard to believe."

Devon shrugged. "Believe what you want, but it's true."

"So now what? You want to get back into wrestling?" Zoey asked.

There was no way Devon had been involved in wrestling since getting out of prison. Zoey would have heard about it. She had plenty of friends in the pro wrestling community throughout Florida. If Devon had shown his face on the wrestling scene in the Sunshine State, someone would have let Zoey know.

"I lost interest in wrestling while I was in prison. My dream of wrestling for the WWE died," Devon said. "I didn't care about it at all until about three weeks ago when I saw a poster promoting a show outside of Orlando. Any guesses who was pictured on that poster?"

"Me," Zoey said. She'd wrestled at an event in Kissimmee, Florida last Saturday. It was the first time she'd been back to Florida in almost seven years. "I'm guessing you came to the show."

"I even got my picture taken with you."

Zoey's knees wobbled and she fell against the side of her Jeep. How could she have not recognized Devon? Even with his short hair and transformed appearance, how had she not recognized him?

She was so caught up in her thoughts that she had tuned out what Devon was saying. She tuned back in when she heard him say something about second chances.

"What did you say?"

"I said that I'm still in love with you. I didn't realize it until I saw you at that show," Devon said as he clutched Zoey's hand between both of his. "Maybe I wasn't the best boyfriend years ago, but I'm ready to be one now. I realize I wasn't perfect, and I didn't treat you the way you deserved. But I'm a changed man. I want to start over with you, Zoey. Give me a second chance."

"Second chance? I already gave you a second chance years ago. And a third, and a fourth, and a fifth. So . . . no thanks. I'll pass."

"I'm not going to take no for an answer. I want another chance, and you're going to give me one." Devon dropped Zoey's hand and leaned closer to her. Reaching up, he wrapped one of his large hands around her narrow throat and squeezed. "You will get back together with me. Or I'll ruin your life just like you tried to ruin mine. Don't think I can't."

Zoey refused to panic or show any fear. Instead, she opened her mouth to tell Devon to get his hands off her. But, before she could tell him what she thought of his threats and what he could do with them, she heard someone shouting.

"Zoey, are you out here?"

"Where are you?"

Zoey knocked Devon's hand away from her throat and breathed out a sigh of relief.

"Justin. Terry." Zoey screamed. "I'm by my car."

Zoey could hear their feet pounding on the pavement as they raced across the parking lot. Even on their best days, neither of them would qualify as a knight in shining armor. But, today, they were her heroes.

"Zoey, you're not going to believe this but—" Justin rounded the side of her Jeep and crashed into Devon.

"Devon's here," Zoey said, anticipating that was what Justin was going to say before he collided with the man. "I already know."

"You! What are you doing to my sister? Get away from her."

Justin grabbed Devon and threw him against the side of his Jeep. He then took a wild swing, and there was the sickening sound of flesh striking flesh as Justin's fist connected with Devon's jaw.

"Cool it!" Terry said as he wrestled Justin away from Devon.

"Well, if it isn't Tweedledee and Tweedledumb. All grown up, and still attached at the hip. Why am I not surprised?" Devon said as he worked his jaw back and forth. "Hey, Terry, do you still have that pathetic crush on Zoey?"

"I . . . I . . ." Terry stuttered as he glanced at Zoey.

"I thought so. Like Zoey would ever date a dork like you. You are nowhere near her league." Devon shoved past Justin and Terry. He then bumped into Vivian who had snuck up and joined the party. "Vivi . . . You still don't look a day over sixty-five."

"Don't try to sweet talk me you silver tongued devil."

Muttering a curse, Vivian let her tote-bag-sized straw purse slide off her shoulder. Gripping the purse by the handles, Vivian swung it up and caught Devon under the chin with it. The force of the blow snapped his head back.

"Nice job, Nana," Justin said.

"Still a spitfire, I see. What have you got in that purse, Vivi? A bowling ball?" Devon asked as he ran his fingers over his chin. The rough straw had scraped a couple layers of skin off his chin and neck. He sidestepped Vivian and headed towards the VFW Hall. Over his shoulder, Devon called out some parting words, "I'll see you later, Zoey. And remember what I said . . . I know you'll make the right choice."

"What is Devon talking about?" Justin grabbed his sister and pulled her in for a hug. "What happened? What did he say to you? Did he hurt you?"

"I'm okay," Zoey whispered as her knees gave out and she collapsed against Justin. "Or I will be. I just can't believe Devon is back. And he wants . . . He wants to get back together . . ."

"I always said that boy had a nice house . . . But he ain't got much furniture," Vivian said, using one of her favorite phrases for someone who didn't have much common sense or smarts.

"You don't want to get back together with Devon, do you?" Terry asked.

"I barely survived Round One. I'm not dumb enough to go back for Round Two."

"But you know why Devon's here, don't you?" Justin asked. Before Zoey could respond, he continued, "Uncle Leland is making me wrestle him tonight. And he's decided Devon is going to win the match."

"Leland has gone and lost his dang mind. Not that he's ever had much of one," Vivian said as she rummaged in her purse and pulled out a knitting needle. "You think I could stab him through the jugular with this?"

"Nana . . ." Zoey said. She wondered who it was Vivian wanted to stab. Leland or Devon? Knowing Vivian, it was both.

"I'm sorry," Terry said as he patted Zoey on the back. "I had no idea my stepdad called Devon. I have no idea how Leland even knew Devon was back in town."

"I need to talk to Uncle Leland. He owes me an explanation."

Zoey pushed away from Justin and stomped on wobbly legs towards the VFW Hall. Her anxiety was fighting to take control and send her into a ball of anxiety. Zoey clung to her anger as it drove her forward, steadying her legs and carrying her towards the VFW Hall's back door.

Wrenching open the door, Zoey went from the blazing sun to the dim backstage. She stepped inside and allowed her eyes to adjust to the change in light. Vivian, Justin, and Terry crowded in behind her.

There wasn't much to the VFW Hall's backstage area—it was nothing more than a hallway with bathrooms on one side and a storage room on the other. At the far end of the short hallway, a ramp led up to the stage.

"Leland!" Zoey ripped aside the curtains and stomped out onto the stage. Her eyes swept over the banquet hall until she spotted Leland and Devon standing next to the ring. Leland had his arm around Devon's shoulders, and the two were laughing. "I need to talk to you."

Leland waved at Zoey before gesturing towards Devon. "Look who's here."

"I know. That's what I need to talk to you about." Zoey jumped down the steps and hustled towards the ring. She grabbed Leland's wrist and yanked him towards where his wife was hanging soft pretzels on the rack at the concession stand. "How could you?"

"Jeez, you don't have to yell." Leland stuck a finger in his left ear and jiggled it. "And how could I do what?"

"Devon," Zoey said. She was still shouting, though not quite as loudly.

Leland shrugged. "I needed a wrestler, and I knew Devon was available. So, I called him this morning and asked if he wanted to come out tonight."

"That's not what I meant." Zoey stomped her foot. "How could you have known that Devon was back in the area and not tell me?"

"Calm down. You're carrying on like a drama queen. And you know how I feel about drama queens," Leland said, scolding Zoey like she was a little kid. "The reason I didn't say anything to you is because I figured you already knew Devon was back. And, if you didn't know, it wasn't my business to tell you."

"Oh, yes, it was," Vivian said as she whacked Leland on the arm with her purse. She and Justin had followed Zoey and Leland to the far side of the room. Terry had stayed ringside with Devon. "You're the closest thing Zoey has to an uncle. Of course, it was your business to make sure she knew that Devon was back. But you went behind Zoey's back and hired Devon to wrestle for you."

"Hey, I've got no beef with Devon." Leland held up his hands in a placating gesture. "I'm not going to punish the man just because Zoey had a little spat with him a few years ago."

"Little spat? Did you just refer to Devon almost killing me as a 'little spat'?"

Pain tore through Zoey's chest, shooting down to her left hip and up to her shoulder. The pain radiated down her left arm, leaving it feeling numb. If she hadn't experienced similar pain during other anxiety attacks, she would have thought she was having a heart attack.

"Here, Zoey, sit down," Justin said as he grabbed a folding chair and shoved it against the back of her legs. He gripped Zoey by her aching left shoulder and pushed her down onto the chair. "Breathe. In the nose. Out the mouth."

"I'm trying." Zoey forced herself to take a deep breath. Her lungs screamed in agony.

"You have any idea how many bad relationships I was in?" Leland leaned over and stuck his face so close to Zoey's that his mustache brushed against her cheek. "And I got over all of them."

"None of your ex-girlfriends tried to kill you," Zoey said.

"No. But a lot of them were crazy. Remember that woman who gathered up all my clothes, piled them up in her front yard, and set everything on fire? And the one who ran over my motorcycle with my truck? She totaled both! But I didn't press charges against either one of those nutcases." Standing, Leland said, "I just moved on with my life."

"Did it cross your mind how I might feel about Devon being here?" Zoey asked. She'd thought the people closest to her reciprocated the same amount of concern that she had for them. Leland had proven that he had zero consideration for Zoey. "What is up with you, Leland, I thought you cared about your family and friends?"

"The show must go on. You need to suck it up and get on with it," Leland said, sounding exasperated with her. His annoyance only made Zoey angrier. "Put yourself in my shoes. I had a wrestler cancel on me right before a show. I needed to find a replacement fast."

"No, you didn't need a replacement," Justin said, getting in Leland's face. "We could have gotten one of my students to fill in. Or you could have broken up the Triple Threat Match and had me wrestle one of those guys. Or you could have cancelled my match completely. I gladly would have sat out this show if it meant sparing my sister from this."

"Exactly," Zoey said. It warmed her heart to hear her self-centered little brother stand up for her. "You did not need to hire Devon as a replacement, and you know it."

"You know what . . . I won't do it. I'm not going to get in the ring with Devon."

"Oh, yes, you will," Leland said.

"Oh, no, I won't." Justin took another step towards Leland so that they were nose to nose. "If you make me get in the ring with Devon, I guarantee we won't have a wrestling match. It's gonna be a real fight. And I'm gonna do the same thing to Devon that he did to Zoey. I'm gonna beat him so bad that he has to spend a week in the hospital."

"You and Zoey need to quit being so selfish," Leland clamped his hand down on Justin's shoulder. "You owe me, Justin. So you're going to wrestle Devon. You're going to lose. You're going to be a professional about it. And, whatever you do, don't break kayfabe."

THREE

"U NCLE LELAND HAS LOST HIS MIND," Justin said as he paced next to the wrestling ring. He repeatedly punched his right fist into his left hand, and the sound got on Zoey's nerves. "It's bad enough I have to wrestle Devon. But Uncle Leland says I gotta lose the match."

"I think he got hit over the head with a steel chair one too many times back when he was wrestling. His brain cells are scrambled," Zoey said. She was seated on the edge of the ring, her feet dangling above the thin mats on the floor.

"He's a self-centered prick," Zoey's twin brother, Zack, said.

Zack, who was younger than Zoey by two minutes, had been her best friend and partner in crime since birth. When they were eighteen, they'd gotten matching tattoos on the back of their right shoulders to honor their unbreakable bond. The tattoos were sugar skulls—Zack's was a masculine version and Zoey's was a feminine version—with the words "from the womb, to the tomb" surrounding the skulls. It was a motto that they lived by.

Less than ten minutes after Leland had put an end to their argument, Zack flew into the VFW Hall looking for a fight. Zack was a tattoo artist, and his shop was three blocks down the street from the VFW Hall. Hearing that Devon was back in town, he had finished up with his client and rushed to join his siblings.

"Oh, no. According to Uncle Leland, Justin and I are the selfish ones," Zoey said.

"People who live in glass houses shouldn't throw stones," Vivian mumbled, speaking up for the first time in a while.

Since she was a chatterbox, Vivian's silence had Zoey concerned. She assumed that her nana was plotting various ways to kill Devon and make it look like an accident. Vivian watched several true crime shows, and Zoey worried that they gave her ideas.

"You know what I still can't believe?" Justin stopped pacing to gather up his long hair and pull it back into a ponytail. "I can't believe that Uncle Leland told me not to break kayfabe."

"Leland is a stickler for the old ways," Vivian said. "You kids know that maintaining kayfabe is important. It's what the industry was built on. But, in this day and age—what, with social media and all that silliness—it's harder to maintain. Back when your Pop-Pop and I were wrestling, breaking kayfabe was considered the eighth deadly sin."

Kayfabe was an old term that wrestlers and promoters had been using for years, and it meant portraying the staged storylines and matches as genuine. In the early days of professional wrestling, the wrestlers were supposed to be in character at all times. The good guys—known as baby faces—weren't allowed to travel around with the bad guys—or heels—because the promoters didn't want them to be seen together. The promoters didn't want the fans to know that the wrestlers were playing made-up roles. What was going on in the storylines that took place in the ring was supposed to be real. To break kayfabe meant to break character or bring up something real life that wasn't part of the storyline.

"Uncle Leland is nuts if he thinks I'm going to come out here and pretend that Devon didn't almost kill my sister," Justin said as he resumed punching his own hand. "He said there is no place for personal drama in the ring. And he wants to portray Devon as the returning hero."

"Does Uncle Leland really think people have forgotten about what Devon did to me?" Zoey asked.

Yes, the assault happened seven years ago in Florida, but fans all across the country found out about it. The dirt sheets—wrestling magazines and websites that covered the real-life perspective of wrestling and the wrestlers' lives—had covered the assault and the aftermath. Since Zoey and Devon were both from Lancaster County, Pennsylvania, the assault had been covered by all the local media outlets. Zoey was sure that some fans had forgotten about it over the years, but she was also sure that there were plenty of others who remembered—and still held a grudge against Devon.

"Oh, Uncle Leland knows some people will remember what Devon did to you, but he's hoping everyone is willing to forget about it and welcome Devon back with open arms," Justin said as he rolled his brown eyes.

"I'll welcome Devon back with my fist to his face," Zack said. He took a seat next to Zoey, wrapped one of his tattoo-covered arms around her shoulders, and hugged her. Seeing them side-by-side, few people would guess that they were related. While Zack's eyes and hair were also brown, they were a few shades lighter than Zoey's. Zack—as well as Justin—also strongly resembled their father while Zoey looked like their mother. It was Zack and Justin that many people thought were the Wilde twins opposed to Zack and Zoey.

"I already hit him. And I would have hit him again had Terry not stopped me," Justin said as Terry walked over and joined them. Justin clapped his best friend on the back. "But I won't have Terry to stop me during the match."

"Actually, you will have me," Terry said. "Leland just made me the referee for your match. He's convinced you'll get out of control, and he's under the impression that I can somehow stop you from getting into a real fight with Devon."

"I'm counting on you to stop Justin from doing something stupid," Zoey said.

"That's easier said than done. But I'll do my best," Terry said. "It's just gonna be hard because I want to kick Devon's ass, too."

"But right here is another sign that Uncle Leland has lost his mind," Justin said as he kicked the metal trash can that was sitting next to the ring. Inside the can was an assortment of weapons—including an orange traffic cone, a kendo stick, and a baseball bat wrapped in barbed wire. "Leland doesn't want the match to turn into a real fight, but then he comes up with the idiotic idea to make it a street fight. Why would he think it's a good idea to put a weapon in my hands when he knows that I want to seriously hurt the guy I'm wrestling?"

"I told you, Uncle Leland has been hit in the head one too many times," Zoey said.

"What's to stop me from, I don't know, bashing Devon over the head like this . . ." Justin picked up a steel chair that was propped against the ring. He then swung the chair down over the metal barricade that separated the front row from the ringside area, bending the back part of the chair. "I could do some serious damage if I hit Devon for real."

"Just get through the match," Zoey said.

"Not gonna lie, Justin . . . If one of us has to get in the ring with Devon, I'm glad it's you and not me," Zack said. "If I was still wrestling . . . Well, there's no way I could get in the ring with him. I don't know how I'm going to sit in the audience for the match."

Like Zoey and Justin, Zack had been a professional wrestler. Almost two years earlier, Zack injured his rotator cuff so badly that he needed to have surgery. The injury had been to his right shoulder, and it prevented him from tattooing for a few months. As a result, Zack decided to give up wrestling so that he could focus on his career as a tattoo artist. Zoey couldn't fault him for retiring. Wrestlers' bodies took a toll in the ring, and they had to consider their lives outside of wrestling and how the injuries jeopardized their physical wellbeing.

"None of us are going to be able to sit in the front row during the match." Vivian yanked her feather boa from her neck. "If Devon comes anywhere near me, I'll strangle him."

"Your boa probably won't be enough to get the job done," Zack said. He tugged on Vivian's boa and accidentally pulled out a couple feathers.

"Then I'll stab him in the eye with this!" Vivian held up the knitting needle that she was still clutching in her arthritic hand.

"Put the knitting needle down, Nana," Zoey said.

"Hitting Devon over the head with this baby . . ." Zack said as he reached into the trash can full of weapons and pulled out a sledgehammer. It was the same sledgehammer that had been in the back of Zoey's car. "This would get the job done in one or two blows."

"Zack . . ." Zoey said, terrified of the evil gleam in her twin brother's eyes. She also didn't like the way he was running his fingers up and down the sledgehammer's long handle.

"What? I can fantasize, can't I?" Zack asked, giving Zoey a sheepish look. "I won't lie to you . . . I want to kill Devon just as badly now as I did back then."

"So do I," Justin said.

"As my daddy used to say . . . I would take him out behind the wood-shed," Vivian added.

"Stop it! All of you, just stop it!" Zoey slid off the edge of the ring. "Devon is not worth going to jail for. All of you need to control yourselves tonight. Because that's all this is. It's tonight. Tomorrow, we will figure out how to . . . I don't know . . . get Devon out of my life again. But, for tonight, no one is going to beat Devon with a chair, bash his head in with a sledge-hammer, strangle him with a boa, or stab him in the eye with a knitting needle. Nor are we going to feed him through a woodchipper."

"Who said anything about putting Devon in a woodchipper?" Justin asked.

"I think that's what Zoey wants to do to him." Vivian cackled. "And I approve. As long as he's alive when we do it."

"But we are not going to do it," Zoey said. She covered her nana's mouth before Vivian had a chance to tell them about some true crime show she'd watched where a killer disposed of a body by pulverizing it in a woodchip-per. Zoey held out her other hand with the pinky extended. "I'm going to need all of you to promise me right now that you won't do anything to Devon tonight. We are not sinking to his level."

Terry was the first one to hook his pinky around Zoey's and swear that he would not retaliate against Devon. With obvious reluctance, Zack and Vivian did the same.

"I'm not making any promises," Justin said as he crossed his arms over his tattooed chest.

"I'm going to say it again. We just need to get through tonight. If I can do it, then all of you can do it." Zoey made eye contact with Zack, Justin, Vivian, and Terry. "It's like . . . it's like when a wrestling storyline takes a really crappy twist. We still tune in to the next show and hope that it improves. So let's just get to tomorrow and move on."

Tomorrow—or, at least, once Zoey was back in the privacy of her own home—she could give in to the breakdown that was threatening to over-take her. But she had to hold herself together for the time being.

"You should see this," Vivian said. "Devon's over there flexing his muscles and a bunch of hussies are hanging all over him. He looks like the cat that got the cream."

"Get off the chair," Zoey said. "And stop spying on Devon."

Vivian was standing on a folding chair that was behind the card table on which Justin and Zoey had laid out their merchandise. The chair was for Zoey to sit on, but Vivian commandeered it so that she could see over the crowd and keep tabs on Devon.

Leland had opened the doors to the VFW Hall's banquet room at six o'clock—which was an hour before the show was scheduled to start. After the fans snagged their seats, they headed over to the concession stand or to the wrestlers' merchandise tables.

Zoey's parents, Marlon and Roxanne, had been the first people through the door. They were followed by Zack's wife and daughter. Since their front row seats were reserved, Marlon, Roxanne, and Arielle headed straight towards where Zoey, Justin, Zack, and Vivian were huddled behind the table. Marlon had himself worked up into a tizzy, and Zack and Justin had to hold him back from going after Devon. Roxanne was in tears—which made Zoey feel even more anxious. And Zoey's best friend and sister-in-law, Arielle Coleman, had joined Vivian in plotting ways to dispose of Devon's body.

The only member of her family who wasn't a ball of nervous energy and pent-up rage was Zoey's eighteen-month-old niece, and that was because Paige was too young to understand what had the adults all worked up. Zoey hoped Paige was too young to understand the swear words that her mother kept muttering.

Zoey and Justin had to send everyone but Vivian away from the table because they were getting in the way of the fans who wanted to buy merchandise. The reason they couldn't send Vivian away was because she was selling old photos from her days as a professional wrestler. She had a couple action shots of herself in the ring, but her most popular photograph was a glamour shot of her dressed in a bright red two-piece bathing suit and a white faux-fur coat. A crown sat atop her head, and she wore diamond rings, necklaces, and bracelets. With her curly, shoulder-length dark hair, Vivian could have been Elizabeth Taylor's stunt double.

"Devon isn't supposed to be out here," Justin said as he signed his autograph for a teenage girl. "Leland told him to stay in the back so his return would be a surprise."

"Devon never did listen to what anyone told him to do. I wonder how he survived in prison," Zoey said as she made change for an older man who had purchased both versions of her Wilde Woman t-shirts. "Nana, I said stop spying on Devon. I'm sure he can see you."

"I know he can see me. He's looking right at me." Vivian made a rude hand gesture to let Devon know that she was watching him. "And I don't care if Devon can see me. I want the scumbag to know that I've got my eye on him."

"I'd prefer if you ignore him and act like he isn't even here," Zoey said while keeping a fake smile plastered on her face for the fans. "Blatantly spying on him like that is going to make him think we care about what he's up to. And we definitely do not care."

"Well someone needs to keep an eye on him," Vivian said. "What if he decides to come over here? At least I'd see him before he got here."

"Devon isn't dumb enough to come over here," Zoey said.

"Don't be so sure about that," Justin said. "Before we came out here, he told me that he knows you'll come to your senses and get back together with him."

"No, I'd have to lose all of my senses to do that."

"Can we get a picture with you, Miss Zoey?" asked a girl who was ten or twelve years old. She and her two younger sisters were dressed in outfits similar to Zoey's ring gear of a black Wilde Woman tank top along with purple and black zebra print leggings.

"Of course, girls," Zoey said. She made her way around the table so that she could crowd in with the girls for the picture. She then looked up at Vivian and said, "Would you get off that chair before you fall and hurt yourself."

"I'm not going to fall." Vivian craned her neck and pushed herself onto her tiptoes. The chair wobbled, and Zoey had to grab her nana around the waist to prevent her from falling. Vivian gave Zoey a sheepish look and climbed down from the chair. "I'm going over there to tell those hussies exactly what kind of man Devon is."

"No, you're not." Zoey held out her arm and blocked Vivian. "Devon is playing the same game he used to play back when we were together. He used to let women hang all over him to make me jealous. It may have worked then, but it definitely isn't going to work now. I'd say those women can have him, but I wouldn't wish Devon on my worst enemy."

"I would," Vivian muttered to herself. "Okay . . . Probably not."

A commotion broke out nearby, and Zoey heard someone shout "fight!" Vivian scrambled back onto the chair, gripping Zoey by the shoulders to help her retain her balance. Meanwhile, Justin shoved a pile of his t-shirts to the floor and climbed onto the table.

"What's going on?" Zoey asked.

"Some guy took a swing at Devon," Vivian reported. She let go of one of Zoey's shoulders so she could wave her arm. "Hit him again! Break his nose!"

"It's JT Perez." Justin said as he accidentally kicked over one of Zoey's neat stacks of photos. "I think he just knocked Devon out."

JT Perez—the JT stood for Jovani Tommaso—was a local videographer who Leland hired to film the LAW events. JT also filmed weddings, baptisms, bar mitzvahs, dance recitals, and anything else that people wanted to record for posterity. Being a videographer had not been JT's original career choice. Years ago, he trained as a professional wrestler and might have had a chance at making it beyond the independent circuit. Then, not long before Devon and Zoey moved to Florida, Devon accidentally broke JT's neck and ruined his budding career.

During a training session, Devon talked JT into practicing the piledriver with him. The piledriver was one of the most dangerous moves in professional wrestling, and countless promotions had banned it. To perform the move, a wrestler holds their opponent upside-down before dropping down into a sitting or kneeling position. In the process, the wrestler drives the opponent headfirst towards the mat. When performed correctly, the opponent's head does not contact the mat. Devon botched the move, and accidentally slammed JT's head into the mat and broke his neck. In the aftermath, JT was forced to quit wrestling and take up videography.

"What's going on?" Vivian asked. "I can't see."

"You can see more than I can," Zoey said. "All I can see are people's heads."

"Fight's over," Justin said as he jumped off the table. "Zack and Dad broke it up and dragged JT off. And JT's brother and cousin are with them. They'll get him calmed down."

"I just want to get this night over with." Zoey turned and found Leland standing behind her. "What do you want?"

"Change of plans," Leland said. "I gotta cancel the women's title reveal. You're still gonna win the championship. But I need the time I was setting aside for the title reveal for Devon. He's got some things he wants to say."

FOUR

"I CAN DO THIS," ZOEY SAID TO HER REFLECTION. "It's just a few more hours. I can hold it together for that long. I am a strong, kick-ass woman. I can do this."

"Ugh! I hate this!" Hannah groaned as she shoved open the bathroom door and trudged inside. She ripped the black bonnet off her head and hurled it against the wall. "I hate my outfit! I hate my character! I hate my life! Why did I let Leland talk me into being an Amish chick?"

Leland had insisted on coming up with Hannah's wrestling personae instead of letting her create her own. Hannah had wanted to play a conceited Valley Girl, but Leland claimed that character was overused by women's wrestlers. He insisted on something that he found unique. Since they lived in Pennsylvania's Amish Country, he thought a rebellious Amish girl was the perfect character. Instead of the shorts and skimpy tops she had envisioned, Hannah wore a long, pale pink dress. She completed the outfit with a black apron and bonnet.

"Blame your parents. They're the ones who named you Hannah Stoltzfus," Zoey said, reminding Hannah of her Amish-sounding name. "And, come on, it's not that bad."

"Oh, yes, it totally is! This stupid dress, like, sucks to wrestle in because it keeps getting tangled around my legs. I wish I could just wear a t-shirt and leggings like you do." Hannah joined Zoey at the cramped double sink and leaned closer to the cracked mirror. "Look at me! My chin is breaking out. I look hideous. And Leland won't let me use concealer or foundation to cover up the zits. He won't let me wear any makeup at all."

"There are worse things in life than having to wear a stupid outfit and no makeup."

"Yeah, I know." Hannah gave Zoey a one-armed hug. "I'm sorry. Here I am getting upset over something dumb, and you're having, like, a totally crappy day. Are you okay?"

"I will be. I just have to get through tonight."

But getting through the night was easier said than done. Keeping it together had left Zoey completely drained. Grabbing the steel folding chair that she had brought into the bathroom earlier, Zoey pushed it up against the wall and had a seat.

"Are you planning to hide out in here until our match?" Hannah asked.

"Yep."

The bathroom reeked of bleach and a pungent vanilla air freshener. Zoey despised the scent of vanilla and breathing it in caused her to feel more nauseous than she already did. It was still better than sitting in the crowded backstage area where Devon would be lurking nearby. In the women's bathroom, she was free of him.

Hannah walked a few feet to the end of the bathroom and shoved open the exterior door. A puff of hot air filled the clammy room. After propping the door open, Hannah pushed a second chair closer to Zoey and sat down.

"I'll keep you company."

"You don't have to. Our match won't be for about an hour. You can go hang out with Justin and watch the show," Zoey said, hoping Hannah would pick up on the subtle hint that she wanted to be alone. She also wanted Hannah to keep an eye on Justin and make sure he didn't do some-thing ill-advised while hanging out backstage—like get into a real fight with Devon.

Hannah had developed a crush on Justin years earlier, and she had finally gotten him to take notice of her a few weeks ago. Zoey had been aware of Hannah's crush on Justin from the start, and she was trying to nip the flowering relationship in the bud. Justin was immature and only looking for a good time. His past relationships rarely lasted more than a couple months. She was worried that Justin would string Hannah along before ultimately breaking her heart. Zoey didn't want that to happen to Hannah—especially because she would get dragged into the drama.

"If you're staying in here, then I'm staying in here. You're my friend, and I'm not leaving you," Hannah said as she had a seat. "Do you want to talk about it?"

"Not really."

Starting with the police officer who had ridden to the hospital in the ambulance with her, Zoey had told and retold her story more times than she cared to. In the days following the assault, she had been further questioned by the police. The doctors and the nurses wanted to know what had happened to her so that they could better treat her physical injuries. The hospital's victim support counselor had been concerned with treating the emotional and mental trauma. Her immediate family wanted to know everything—and then, after Zoey recovered and moved home, she had to deal with her friends and fans wanting all the grisly details. She'd also spent years in therapy and support groups rehashing every detail of her relationship with Devon.

Throughout the past seven years, Zoey had talked and talked and talked about Devon Isler more than she cared to. She had spent more years trying to get over the relationship than she had in the actual relationship. With each retelling, the story got easier. It became just that—a story. She'd learned to tell it in a detached way so that it no longer hurt, a simple, emotionless recounting of facts. Zoey had become numb to it.

Until today.

"I was a little bit older than you when I started dating Devon . . ."

"I remember when you hooked up with him. I was jealous because Devon was so hot."

"Yeah, well . . . He might have looked good on the outside . . ." Despite not wanting to waste any more time talking about Devon, the words came tumbling out of her mouth. Even though Hannah had been her friend for years, Zoey had never talked to her about Devon. "He seemed like a nice guy at first. But I was stupid and naïve, and I only saw what I wanted to see. If I knew then what I know now . . . I never would have said yes when he asked me out on a date."

"You know what they say about hindsight being, like, twenty-twenty." Hannah reached over and patted Zoey's purple zebra-print clad thigh.

"Plus . . . I'm pretty sure you're not the only woman who was fooled by a jerk hidden beneath a good-looking face and body."

"No. No, I'm just one of many," Zoey sighed. "One of way too many."

Devon had grown up about an hour south of Linville, so it was plausible that Zoey had crossed paths with him at wrestling events throughout the years both when he was a fan and when he was wrestling, but she didn't really meet him until right around her final semester of college. Devon, who was six years older than her, had moved to Philadelphia to train not long after he graduated from high school. After four years in Philadelphia, Devon moved to Orlando. About two years later, Devon moved home to Pennsylvania to be with his mom after his dad died. It was a few months after that when Devon first started showing up at the barn that Marlon had converted into a gym to work with other local wrestlers. At the time, Marlon was teaching a wrestling school while allowing veteran wrestlers to also train in the ring.

Not long after he started hanging out at Marlon's gym, Devon asked Zoey out on a date. Zoey, who had only been twenty-two at the time, had had only one serious relationship up to that point. She'd dated her high school sweetheart for over three years before breaking up with him. After that, Zoey went on the occasional date but she was more focused on her college classes and her wrestling career than her love life. Until Devon came along and swept her off her feet, she hadn't shown much interest in dating. In the beginning, Devon had been over-the-top affectionate and attentive. It wasn't until she was in therapy years later that Zoey realized that Devon had "love bombed" and manipulated her. Everything had been an act, and Devon had played his Prince Charming role almost perfectly.

Looking back, there had been red flags from the start. Devon had been arrogant and egotistical. He had occasional anger and jealousy issues. He almost always put himself before Zoey. Devon had also belittled her and made her feel bad about herself. He'd shown countless signs of the mental, emotional, and verbal abuse that would come later. Convinced that she was in love, Zoey had kept her rosy glasses fixed over her eyes. She could not see the numerous red flags.

Almost a year after they had started dating, Devon and Zoey moved to Orlando, Florida—the home base of World Wrestling Entertainment's

developmental program—to pursue their careers as professional wrestlers. The WWE was the preeminent professional wrestling company in
the world. It was the company that Zoey and Devon strived to work for.
Devon had lived there for a few years and had already made connections
with other wrestlers and wrestling companies. What Zoey didn't realize
until after she'd relocated was that Devon had also established a bad repu-
tation, thanks to his arrogance and unwillingness to listen to constructive
criticism. Her alliance with him wound up hindering her career instead
of helping it.

It wasn't long after they had moved that Devon's real manipulative and
controlling nature appeared. His minor jealousy and anger issues became
major. He couldn't handle it if Zoey had any friends—especially male friends
who he accused her of cheating on him with; however, it was Devon who
had been unfaithful to the relationship. He blamed her for his infidelity.

Devon also became emotionally and mentally abusive. The physical
abuse wouldn't come until the very end. The abuse had been detrimen-
tal to Zoey's mental and physical health. She'd lost weight throughout the
six months they lived and Florida. She also developed crippling anxiety
issues. Her self-confidence faded, and she became a shadow of the strong
woman she had been.

Zoey was miserable, yet she believed she was in love with Devon so she
stayed with him. She began to realize that the relationship was never going
to work when only one person was making an effort. Once they'd moved
to Florida, Devon almost completely gave up trying. He did just enough to
convince Zoey to stay with him.

Determined to find the man who Devon had been, Zoey remained in
the relationship for another six months. She wanted to fix the dysfunc-
tional relationship. Unfortunately, the Devon she was seeking had been an
act and the person who he became in Florida was the real Devon.

Then, one day, Zoey woke up and knew she'd had enough. She accepted
that she was miserable and that she couldn't stay with Devon any longer.
There was no point in trying to save a relationship with a man who treated
her so poorly.

She instinctively knew that Devon wasn't going to let her leave. He'd
said on multiple occasions that Zoey was stuck with him. She decided that
the only way to escape Devon was to slip away while he wasn't home.

A few days after she made the decision to leave, Devon was booked to wrestle at an event in Tampa. Zoey was supposed to go with him, but she faked an injury while at the gym to get out of it. Within minutes of Devon leaving for Tampa in the car that they shared, she began tossing her belongings into a rental car. She took her belongings to a long-term motel room where she planned to stay until she figured out what to do next. There were opportunities in Florida for her to pursue now that she was free from Devon, but she also wanted to go home to Pennsylvania.

It was around one in the morning, and she was just about finished with packing her remaining belongings, when she heard the key scraping in the lock. Aside from herself, the only people who had keys to the apartment were Devon, the landlord, and the maintenance man.

Neither the landlord nor the maintenance man had any reason to come into the apartment in the middle of the night. Devon was home early.

She would find out later that their landlord had seen her carrying boxes out to the rental car and had called Devon to ask what was going on. Realizing that she must be leaving him, Devon left the show immediately after his match and rushed back from Tampa to stop her.

Zoey made it clear to Devon that the relationship was over, and that there was nothing he could say or do to change her mind. Devon told her that she wasn't going anywhere and backhanded her across the face.

Zoey had begun to recount the assault when someone pounded on the bathroom door, startling both her and Hannah.

Justin strolled into the bathroom. "You've got about two minutes until your match."

"Seriously? Why did you wait so long to come get us? Zoey and I are barely ready!" Hannah yelled at Justin as she shot to her feet. She clutched Zoey's forearm and yanked her out of the chair. "Are you ready? Don't take this the wrong way or anything, but I need you to, like, get your head in the game and get us through this match."

"I'm ready," Zoey assured Hannah. If there was anything she knew how to do, it was wrestle. It was second nature. Devon might have her distracted, but there was no way he had her so distracted that she couldn't go out there and put on a good show. "You're ready, too."

"Then why don't I feel ready?" Hannah grabbed the pitchfork that was leaning against the bathroom stall and bolted out the door.

"Where the heck did she get that pitchfork?" Justin asked Zoey.

"She found it in the storage room while looking for 'weapons' for your match. Uncle Leland saw her with it and told her to carry it around so she looked more Amish," Zoey said. She walked over to the bathroom door and stopped. "Where's Devon?"

"Some of the guys herded him into the men's room just before I came in here. They've got Devon cornered in there. You won't have to see him."

"Good. Tell the guys I appreciate the support."

Zoey marched out of the bathroom and bumped into a sweaty Sasquatch. He had both hands buried in the thick pelt of hair that covered his lower back, and he was complaining about needing an ice pack and a shot of whiskey. Sasquatch was one of the two wrestlers in the match before Zoey's. If he was backstage, that meant her match really was about to start.

"Ladies and gentlemen . . ." Out in the banquet hall, the poor-quality sound system amplified Leland's voice. "It is now time for the match that will determine the Linville Association of Wrestling's first ever Women's Champion!"

The four hundred or so people crammed into the banquet hall cheered.

"Don't look so panicky, Hannah," Zoey said. "You know we've got this."

"You forgot your bonnet." Justin placed the black bonnet on Hannah's head and tied the strings into a lopsided bow. "And Zoey's right. Try to look confident even if you don't feel it. You're the heel in this match. You can't go out there looking like a nervous wreck."

"Introducing first . . ." Leland continued. "Hailing from just down the road in Strasburg . . . She got here tonight by horse and buggy . . . She is the Amish Rebel . . . Hannah Stoltzfus!"

Hannah gave Zoey and Justin a thumbs-up before using the pitchfork to brush aside the curtain. She stepped out onto the stage just as her entrance music began to play. Though calling it music was a stretch. Since the Amish do not listen to music, Hannah's entrance music was a conglomeration of barnyard noises including roosters crowing, cows mooing, mules braying, and horseshoes striking pavement.

Zoey and Justin watched through a crack between the curtains as Hannah made her way to the ring, threateningly jabbing her pitchfork at the scornful fans. It was a comical sight, and Zoey laughed for the first time since encountering Devon in the parking lot.

"Poor girl looks ridiculous," Justin said.

"Trust me, she knows," Zoey said.

Zoey watched Hannah climb into the ring, joining Terry who would be the referee.

"And now, making her way to the ring . . ." Leland announced after Hannah's entrance music shut off. "Hailing from Parts Unknown . . . Which I know for a fact is right here in Linville . . . She is your hometown hero . . . The Wilde Woman . . . Zoey Wilde!"

Zoey's entrance music blared from the speakers, and her heart raced along with the crescendo of drumbeats. A lightning bolt of adrenaline jolted up her spine, and rode along her nervous system to tingle in her fingers and toes. It was the same reaction she'd had before every one of her matches. And she expected it would be the same feeling she'd have up until her last match—which would hopefully be many years from now.

Zoey waited until the squeal of the electric guitar joined the drums before sweeping aside the curtains and striding out onto the stage.

On this side of the curtain, Zoey was the extroverted, confident, kick-ass Wilde Woman.

Zoey glared at Leland who was resplendent in the ringmaster costume. He claimed that running his own wrestling promotion was like being the ringmaster at a circus, not that he had any firsthand experience at working for an actual circus. But, like his questionable facial hair, Leland was under the impression that the black top hat, knee-high riding boots, and red coat with tails made him look like a refined gentleman. Everyone that Zoey had talked to thought he looked foolish—including his wife.

Pausing at the top of the stage steps, Zoey looked out over the packed banquet hall and acknowledged the fans who chanted her name. Several fans flung purple and black streamers at her or into the ring. Other fans held up various signs that said "We ♥ Zoey" or "Let's Go Zoey!" The unanimous support of the fans gave Zoey the last boost of confidence that she needed.

"Ring the bell!" Terry shouted at his stepfather after Zoey climbed into the eighteen-by-eighteen-foot wrestling ring.

Three crisp pings from the bell signaled the start of the match.

Hannah ripped off her bonnet and lunged at Zoey. "I'm going to beat you worse than my father beats his plow horses!"

Zoey and Hannah locked up in the Collar and Elbow Tie-Up. With their left hands, they grasped the back of each other's necks. With their right hands, they clutched each other's left elbow. The Collar and Elbow Tie-Up was a neutral position, and most wrestling matches started with the move.

"We have got to work on your trash talking." Zoey pressed her forehead against Hannah's and muscled her backwards across the ring. "You remember what we planned?"

"Yeah, I remember," Hannah said. She barely moved her lips so that the fans couldn't see that they were talking to each other. "Please don't tell me you've, like, forgot."

"Nah, I'm good." Zoey shoved Hannah away from her. "Let's go!"

Zoey and Hannah circled each other for a few seconds before Hannah raised her leg and drove her boot clad foot towards Zoey's midsection. Hannah's foot barely made contact, but Zoey doubled over—grasping her stomach and crying out in pain. Hannah then pummeled Zoey's back with her fists before she grabbed Zoey's long hair and yanked her over backwards.

Thrusting her hips and feet forward, Zoey extended her arms to either side, tucked her chin to her chest, and exhaled before she landed on her back. In wrestling, it was called a back bump. And its purpose was to help spread out the surface area on which the wrestler was landing.

Even though Zoey executed the move properly, it felt like she had been involved in a minor car accident. There was only a thin layer of carpet padding between her back and the thick boards that made up the base of the wrestling ring.

As Zoey always said, anyone who believes that professional wrestling is fake has never gotten into the ring before.

Yes, the storylines were scripted.

Yes, most of the matches were planned out in advance.

Yes, the outcomes were predetermined.

None of that made professional wrestling fake.

Zoey could guarantee that everything professional wrestlers did in the ring was real.

The wrestling moves and submission holds they performed were real.

Almost everything they did in the ring hurt.

It might not hurt as much as they pretended it did. But it still hurt.

Zoey was thirty years old. But, after a match, she felt like she was fifty.

So, no, professional wrestling was not fake. It was fixed. Big difference.

While Zoey lay in the middle of the ring, pretending to be hurt. Hannah flounced around the ring, swishing her long skirt as she riled up the crowd.

After taunting the crowd, Hannah dropped down on top of Zoey for the first pinfall attempt. Zoey kicked out just after Terry's hand smacked down on the mat to mark one second.

Zoey and Hannah both bounced back to their feet and sprang at each other. Zoey caught Hannah in the midsection with her shoulder and drove her into the one corner of the ring. She then smacked Hannah hard across the chest.

"Ouch!" Hannah hissed. "Not so hard. It doesn't have to be real to look real."

"Sorry," Zoey mumbled. Hannah always got annoyed when Zoey hit her harder than she thought she should. "But it still has to sound real."

After more slaps to Hannah's chest, Zoey grabbed her by one of her reddish-blonde braids and pulled her out of the corner.

"Running bulldog," Zoey whispered to Hannah. Zoey forced the younger woman to bend over so that she could tuck Hannah's head under her left arm. Zoey then wrapped her arms around the top part of Hannah's head in a modified headlock. Pulling Hannah along with her, Zoey took three steps forward. "Now!"

Zoey jumped forward, bringing her legs up so that she would land in a seated position. At the same time, Hannah kicked her feet out behind her so that she would land on her stomach. Zoey rolled Hannah on to her back and went for the pin.

Hannah kicked out after two.

"Now what?" Hannah asked.

"Time to take it outside," Zoey said, knowing Hannah would understand what she meant. They had practiced this spot multiple times during a training session the previous weekend. Zoey wouldn't let Hannah quit until they could pull it off without messing up. "You got this."

"I know." Hannah nodded at Zoey to signal she was ready.

Hannah lunged at Zoey, tackling her to the mat. They rolled across the ring, fighting for the upper hand while throwing punches and pulling each other's hair.

Zoey let Hannah get the upper hand and throw some off-target punches. Hannah then grabbed Zoey by the hair, pulled her to her feet, and shoved her towards the ring ropes. Zoey fell into the ropes, the top one catching her in the upper chest. Behind Zoey, Hannah screamed like a mad woman. Over the noise of the audience, Zoey listened for Hannah's boots pounding on the boards. She waited until Hannah was almost on top of her before she squatted, pulling the top rope down with her. Hannah soared over the top rope and crash landed on the floor.

Please don't freak out and jump out of the way like you did in practice, Zoey thought as she climbed onto the top turnbuckle at the corner of the ring. She waited until Hannah clambered to her feet before leaping off the turnbuckle and crashing into her with a crossbody. They both went down hard.

"Zoey! Zoey! Zoey!" chanted the audience.

"One!" Terry shouted, beginning the ten count. "Two!"

Zoey rolled over, scrambled to her feet, and climbed back into the ring before Terry completed the ten count that would have forced him to declare the match a draw.

When Zoey turned back to face Hannah, the other woman was on her feet and had the pitchfork in her hands. Hannah bonked Zoey on the forehead with the wooden handle. Selling it, Zoey stumbled a few steps before falling over.

After getting back in the ring, Hannah threw punches, locked on a submission move that Zoey battled out of, and hit various moves—including her finishing move known as the Anabaptist Splash. Hannah also went for two pinfall attempts—both of which Zoey kicked out of before the three count. Whenever Zoey started to make a comeback, Hannah hit a move that put her back on the defensive.

"Time to bring it home, girls," Terry said. "Your time's almost up."

"Just like we planned it," Zoey said to Hannah.

Zoey made a big production out of struggling to her feet. She tried to look as worn out and beat down as possible. When Hannah reached for her, Zoey made a miraculous recovery that only happens in professional wrestling and Hollywood. Zoey kicked Hannah in the stomach, and, when she bent forward, Zoey wrapped her left arm around Hannah's neck. Hannah then draped her left arm over Zoey's neck. With their right hands, they grabbed each other's left hip—Hannah gripped the waistband of Zoey's leggings and Zoey gathered up a handful of Hannah's skirt and apron.

"Now!" Zoey whispered.

In unison, they crouched and then came up. Hannah jumped, and Zoey used the momentum to swing Hannah's legs upward. Zoey let Hannah hang upside down, making sure that her back faced where Leland was standing on the stage. When Zoey heard the audience start laughing, she knew that their prank had worked. Since none of them were certain what Amish women had on under their skirts, Leland insisted that Hannah wear a pair of ruffled, knee-length pantalettes. Hannah had swapped the unflattering pantalettes for a pair of hot pink shorts with "kiss my" written across the butt in sparkly black letters. Zoey held Hannah up long enough for Leland to get the message before she went over backwards, slamming both of their backs onto the mat.

Hannah writhed around in pain, overselling the move.

Zoey sprang to her feet and ran over to the closest corner of the ring. After climbing to the top rope, she glanced behind her to gauge where Hannah was before launching herself into a backflip. Zoey had been using the Moonsault as her finishing move since her first match.

After landing on top of Hannah, Zoey went for the pinfall.

"One!" Terry shouted as he dropped down and smacked his hand against the mat. "Two! . . . Three! . . . Ring the bell!"

FIVE

"Ladies and gentlemen . . ." Leland announced as he climbed between the ropes and entered the ring. "The winner of the match and your first ever Linville Association of Wrestling Women's Champion . . . Zoey 'The Wilde Woman' Wilde!"

Zoey grabbed the Women's Championship title out of Leland's hands, climbed the turnbuckle, and held the title above her head. The darn belt just kept getting uglier and uglier every time she looked at it. She had hoped that the monstrosity that Leland had originally shown her had been a joke belt that he had made to mess with her. But she knew Leland, and he would never waste money on a practical joke. No, the rhinestone studded pink title belt was for real.

"We will now take a brief fifteen-to-twenty-minute intermission," Leland announced. "Zoey and many of the wrestlers will be out to take photos and sign autographs."

Zoey's family escorted her through the crowd of people to her merchandise table where Justin was waiting. After a quick family photo with the title belt, Zoey greeted the line of fans that had gathered at her table. So many people wanted their picture with the Women's Champion that Zoey had to cut off selling merchandise and signing autographs. Instead, she just kept smiling for picture after picture even though she was sure she looked like a sweaty mess. Everyone from little girls who hero-worshiped her to older men who pinched her cheek and told her that she was a "cute gal" wanted their picture with the champion.

The intermission flew by, and Leland was soon back on stage to announce that all the wrestlers needed to make their way backstage.

"I'm going to make Devon pay for what he did to you," Justin whispered to Zoey.

"Don't do anything too reckless." Zoey pulled him in for a hug. "But if you can get in a shot below the belt . . . Do it for me."

"Already planning on it." Justin winked.

"You know he's going to do something asinine," Zack said once Justin was gone. Zack was the only one of her family members who remained at the merchandise table. The rest had gone back to their seats.

"It's Justin . . . I know he won't be able to stop himself from doing something stupid. That's why I told him not to do anything *too* reckless."

"Ladies and gentlemen . . . This match is a No Holds Barred, Falls Count Anywhere Match," Leland announced, drawing their attention to the stage. "Introducing first . . . He hails from Parts Unknown . . . Justin Wilde!"

Justin emerged through the smoke that filled the stage area, and Zoey gasped. Her little brother had changed outfits in the few seconds that had passed since he had gone backstage. Justin's typical outfit was worn-out jeans and a beat-up leather jacket. He had been wearing that during intermission. He now wore one of Zoey's Wilde Woman t-shirts and a pair of purple zebra-print leggings. Zoey had gotten him the matching pair months ago when they competed together in a mixed-gender tag team tournament. Justin had worn the pants, but Zoey didn't think he would ever forgive her for making him wear women's leggings.

Tears burned in Zoey's eyes. Justin's show of solidarity was not lost on her, and she was sure it wasn't lost on Leland, their family, or most of the fans. Justin had his faults—he could be self-centered, childish, and reckless—and he had let Zoey down more times than she could count, but tonight made up for all that.

"Zoey! . . . Zoey! . . ." Justin started the chant, and the audience joined in. Justin grabbed the microphone from a stunned Leland and said, "This one is for my sister!"

Zoey climbed up onto the merchandise table and saluted Justin. She also wanted Devon to see her when he came out. She wanted him to see her and know that this was her house. These were her fans. Zoey needed him to know that she wasn't afraid of him.

"And now . . . Making his long-awaited return to the area . . ." Leland said before Justin made it to the ring or his music cut off.

"You think anyone has really been waiting for Devon's return?" Zack asked Zoey.

"Aside from his mom?" Zoey asked. "No. Probably not. He never was that popular around here. Or anywhere else."

"You think his mom is here?" Zack stepped onto a chair and looked around the crowded room.

"I'm sure she is. Paula wouldn't miss her precious baby boy's return to the ring. Though I'm surprised she didn't come over here to give me a piece of her mind."

"Maybe she's finally forgiven you for 'ruining' her son's life."

Zoey rolled her eyes. "Fat chance of that happening."

Continuing, Leland said, "He's from just down the road in Peach Bottom . . . Give it up for Devon 'The Ice Man' Isler!"

Devon strutted onto the stage in a shiny white speedo that made him look like he was wearing a diaper. It was the same ring gear that he had worn years ago, and the all-white ensemble of speedo, kneepads, and boots still did not look good—though it had looked a lot better against his once-tanned and muscular body. Now Devon was pale and flabby. Zoey wasn't surprised that he hadn't bothered to come up with a new gimmick. Devon was just falling back on his old, dependable personae that had gotten him nowhere because it was boring.

"And here he told me that he was a brand-new man . . ."

Devon climbed into the ring and held out his hand to Justin. Zoey was shocked, and she was sure she wasn't the only one. She couldn't recall a time where Devon showed respect towards his opponent and assumed he was putting on a show. Or it could be a trick. Justin reached out as if he was going to shake Devon's hand, but then backhanded him across the face. Devon grabbed at his jaw as he stumbled back against the ropes.

"Oh, Justin," Zoey whispered as her little brother turned towards her and flashed her a smug grin. She knew he was proud of himself. "This match is going to be a disaster."

"What else did you expect?" Zack asked.

Chaos erupted in the banquet hall as Devon jumped on Justin's back. Terry, who was the referee for the match, wrenched Devon away from Justin. Leland sprinted to the ring, slipped between the ropes, and got between Justin and Devon before they could start exchanging blows. Zoey was too far away to hear what Leland was yelling, but she figured it had to be along the lines of telling them to calm down and get on with the match.

From her lofty perch, Zoey could see her family in the front row. Roxanne and Arielle were trying to prevent Vivian from climbing over the barricade that separated the fans from the action. Marlon—who had Paige in his arms—made it over the barricade, and he would have gotten into the ring had two volunteer security guards not gotten in his way. Paige's face was bright red as she screamed and reached for Arielle.

"Oh, come on, Dad," Zack shouted. "What are you doing with my daughter?"

Zoey had to hold Zack back and prevent him from joining the melee at ringside. Thankfully, a nearby fan plucked Paige out of Marlon's arms and handed her over to an irate Arielle. Meanwhile, a teenaged security guard restrained Vivian.

It took a couple minutes for Leland to get everyone calmed down, but whatever he said must have worked because Justin's and Devon's match got underway. From where she was standing, it was evident to Zoey that Justin was working stiff. He was using more force than necessary, and it didn't look like he was pulling his punches. He also wasn't selling any of Devon's moves. Instead, he mocked Devon for repeatedly messing up.

"This is bad," Zack said. "Not that I expected it to be any good. But Devon is terrible."

"Ring rust is a real thing," Zoey said. And Devon had a bad case of it—which was understandable considering he probably hadn't been in a wrestling ring since before going to prison. He was slow and sloppy, and he botched every third move. "Devon was never that good of a wrestler to begin with. But he looks a lot worse than I remember."

"Hey, you remember that blow-up doll I had to wrestle that time in Jersey?" Zack asked.

"How could I forget?"

"Let's face it, that blow-up doll had more talent and in-ring presence than Devon does."

Zoey laughed so hard that she cried.

The match continued with Justin and Devon going back and forth. Zoey watched with growing dread as Devon pulled the trash can full of weapons from under the ring. Devon picked up the metal trash can lid and whacked Justin over the head with it so hard that it split open Justin's forehead. Blood streamed from the wound.

"I can't watch this. I'm going outside. I need some fresh air."

"I'm coming with you."

"No. You stay here in case Justin needs you." Zoey threw her title belt on top of her box of remaining merchandise and headed for the side door. "I'm fine. I just need a couple minutes. I'll be back."

"Just go home."

"But I promised Uncle Leland that I would help with tear down," Zoey said. She used her butt to push open the door.

"Seriously? You don't owe Uncle Leland anything. Not after what he did to you."

"You're right. I don't owe him anything. I'll throw this stuff in my Jeep and then grab my bag out of the back. Hopefully, I can get out of here before this match ends and Devon goes backstage."

Before the door swung shut, Zoey caught a glimpse of Justin as he feigned hitting Devon over the head with the sledgehammer. She knew Justin had to be pretending to hit Devon, because, if he really hit Devon in the head with the sledgehammer, he'd probably kill him. No matter how rash Justin was, he was not dumb enough to bash in Devon's head in the middle of the ring. Or, at least, Zoey hoped her little brother wasn't that dumb.

So caught up in her thoughts, Zoey didn't realize that there was anything wrong with her Jeep until she was reaching for the handle to the rear hatch. The bumper, which usually sat at her mid-thigh, was now down to her knees. After opening the door and tossing the box of merchandise into the back, Zoey squatted for a closer look.

It didn't take her long to figure out why her Jeep was suddenly sitting lower to the ground. All four tires were flat. Someone had either slashed the tires or let the air out of them. And she had a pretty good idea of who had done it.

"Devon . . . If you damaged my wheels or my rotors . . ."

Letting the air out of her tires was just the type of nasty prank that Devon would play on someone. He had done it in the past to other wrestlers—Zoey had even witnessed him doing it once—and now he had done it to her. She could only hope that he had simply released the air and not slashed the tires with a knife. She knew what he was capable of when he was angry.

Zoey dug her phone out of the box of leftover merchandise and then used the built-in flashlight as she went around the car and took a closer look at her tires. Not only were all four valve stem caps missing, so were the metal pins that were supposed to be inside the valves. Zoey assumed that Devon had used a pair of pliers to remove the pins so that the air was quickly released from the tires.

"Now what am I going to do?" Zoey asked herself as she fought back tears. "Ugh! I am not going to cry over this. I'm not going to let Devon win with his stupid mind games."

She needed to breathe. She needed to calm down. She was not going to break down . . . not yet anyway. The night was not over yet, and she had sworn to herself that she would make it to tomorrow. Like Cinderella, at midnight Zoey could transform back to her old self. She wanted to go back to the woman that she was before her time with Devon. But she had no hopes of a fairy godmother making everything better.

With her nerves settled, Zoey took another lap around her car and checked it for additional damage. She didn't spot any new scratches or dings, but she did find the valve caps and pins stowed in the cupholder. Devon must have realized that Zoey had left her Jeep unlocked and tossed the tiny parts into the cupholder for her to find. At least he hadn't dropped them down the nearby drain. And Zoey could only hope that he hadn't done anything else to the interior of her car.

Zoey debated her next move. She could go inside, find Devon, and make a big deal about the vandalism to her car. But that's probably what he expected—and wanted—her to do. He'd deny it, of course. She could also call the police and report the vandalism—not that she thought the police could do much. There weren't any security cameras in the VFW parking lot to have caught Devon messing with her tires, and she doubted anyone had seen him do it. No, if someone had seen Devon messing with her distinctive Jeep, they would have told her—but it was possible that Devon had left fingerprints on her car. Since his fingerprints would still be in IAFIS—the Integrated Automated Fingerprint Identification System—thanks to his previous arrest, the Linville Police Department would be able to match fingerprints from the Jeep to Devon's fingerprints that were on file. Proving he messed with her car would help in getting a restraining order against him should he continue to harass her.

Zoey placed a quick call to 911 to report the vandalism to her car. Since deflated tires weren't a huge priority, she knew the on-duty officers would take their time getting to the VFW Hall. While she waited she decided to go in search of an air pump, and she knew just where to get one. Her dad always kept one in his truck in case of emergencies.

Zoey headed around to the far side of the VFW Hall. Marlon had mentioned to her earlier that he was parked in the overflow lot. It took her a few minutes to find his truck among the other vehicles. Once located, she flipped back the cover and then rummaged around in the bed until she finally found the air pump hidden under a pile of mismatched siding scraps and other jobsite debris. She also grabbed a pair of needle-nose pliers out of the toolbox. While searching for the air pump, Zoey overheard raised voices coming from nearby. It sounded like two people were arguing, but she could not make out any words. The argument lasted for about a minute, and then the people fell silent.

With the air pump and pliers in hand, she returned to her Jeep. The police had not yet arrived, and there didn't seem to be anyone else out in the parking lot.

"I better make sure Devon didn't mess with Justin's car," Zoey said as she set the air pump down next to her right rear tire. "Justin is worked up enough as it is. I don't want to know how he'd react to Devon messing with his car."

Heading around the driver's side of her Jeep, Zoey almost tripped over a gym bag. A few feet beyond the gym bag was Devon. He was face down on the pavement in the narrow space between her Jeep and Justin's. His head was almost touching Justin's right front tire, and his legs were tucked under his body with his knees pressed to his bare chest and his arms splayed out to either side.

"Devon . . . What the heck are you doing?"

Zoey kicked Devon's foot. When he failed to respond, she inched closer to him for a better look. In the dim light, she could see there was some kind of liquid on the ground around Devon's head. Using her phone's flashlight, she lit up the area. With the area better illuminated, Zoey noticed that there was something wrong with Devon's head. The right side of it appeared dented, and the pool of liquid was actually blood.

The sledgehammer lying under her Jeep gave Zoey an idea how that had happened.

"Oh my God . . . Devon . . ." Zoey's heart began to race and she could feel her anxiety swelling. Her chest felt tight and she couldn't draw in a deep breath. "Oh, crap. Oh no. No. No. No. This is not happening."

As she moved the flashlight beam around, the light reflected off something shiny that was lying by Justin's right rear tire. She picked up the object and recognized the leather bracelet as the one that Zack had worn every day since his daughter was born. Paige's name was etched on the metal plate that was part of the bracelet.

"How did this get out here?" Zoey dropped the bracelet through the open rear window of her Jeep and watched it land on the back seat. Zoey then spun around with the intention of heading into the VFW Hall to get help but instead crashed into another person who had crept up behind her. She was surprised to see Leland's wife in the parking lot considering the show was still going on. "Kim? What are you doing out here?"

"I could ask you the same thing." Kim pointed at Devon's prone body. "What did you do to Devon?"

SIX

"TELL ME IT WAS SELF-DEFENSE and not premeditated," Jim Coleman, Chief of the Linville Police, said as he joined Zoey in the cramped back seat of the police cruiser.

It had taken the police less than five minutes to arrive at the VFW Hall. Linville was one of the twenty or so boroughs in Lancaster County, Pennsylvania, and the total area covered about four square miles. On a typical Saturday night, the only criminal activities taking place would be speeders, drunk drivers, and teenagers breaking curfew so that they could party and maybe commit some minor acts of vandalism.

This was obviously not a typical Saturday night.

The responding officer had stuffed Zoey in the back seat of his cruiser before he went about securing the crime scene. It was her first time in the back of a police car, and she hoped it would be her last. At least, she wasn't in handcuffs or under arrest . . . yet.

Kim, who had used her cell phone to call 911, had also been placed in the back of a cruiser.

While stuck in the cruiser, Zoey had a front row seat as the officers processed the crime scene. From what she could see through the steel mesh screen that separated the back seat from the front, the officers had taken a lot of pictures of Devon's body and the surrounding area.

"No, Jim, I—"

Jim pressed his hand over Zoey's mouth, cutting her off.

"Shhh. It doesn't matter why you did it. You're going to say it was self-defense, and you're going to stick to that story. I can't imagine a jury would convict you after they find out what Devon did to you in the past." Jim leaned closer to Zoey and stared into her eyes. Zoey noticed that he had more crow's feet than the last time she had seen him. "Nod if you understand me."

Zoey nodded, and Jim removed his hand.

"Jim, I didn't kill him," Zoey said. "I just found his body."

"Seriously?"

"Yes, seriously."

Jim sighed. "I've known you since you were a teenager, and you've always been a horrible liar. Though you have a better poker face than either of my daughters. If you were lying about killing Devon, I would know it."

The Coleman family moved to Linville the summer before Zoey started eighth grade. They had relocated from northern New Jersey so that Jim could take over the job as police chief. Zoey met Jim's older daughter, Arielle, on the first day of eighth grade. They were in the same section and had all their classes together. Due to her punk-style clothes, pink highlights in her blonde hair, and the unfortunate distinction of being the 'new kid,' Arielle wasn't welcomed or readily accepted by their more conservative classmates. Thanks to her love of professional wrestling, Zoey had already been deemed a social outcast. Therefore, she was much more welcoming to the new girl. Zoey and Arielle had been best friends ever since.

"Zoey, the detective who will be leading the investigation needs to ask you some questions," Jim said as he helped her out of the cruiser. "His name is Tyler Gates, and he's new to the police department. He's only been here about a month."

The warm, humid air felt good after being confined in the air-conditioned cruiser. The officer had left the air conditioner on full blast, and the temperature inside the cruiser was comparable to an igloo.

Zoey followed Jim over to where a lone man stood under one of the overhead lights. She was expecting an older man, but Detective Gates looked like he was in his mid-thirties. The parking lot lights weren't very bright, and, while picking up the blonde highlights in his hair, the dim, flickering light cast shadows over most of his face.

"Chief Coleman, during my interview, I remember you telling me that nothing serious ever happens in Linville," Detective Gates said. He gestured over to where a police officer was taking close-up pictures of Devon's battered head. "This looks pretty serious."

"This is the first homicide in Linville since I took over as chief," Jim said. "We've had some accidental deaths and suicides over the years. And we've recently had a spike in overdoses. But we, thankfully, haven't had any homicides in a long time."

"Until tonight," Gates pointed out.

"Have you learned anything yet?" Jim asked the detective.

Detective Gates gave Zoey a look out of the corner of his eye before he responded. "I still have to question everyone who was backstage. But, from what I've gathered so far, the victim left through the back door following his match. Allegedly he caused a scene before he left, so things were chaotic afterwards. Hopefully, once I talk to all the wrestlers individually, I will have a better idea of what happened."

"You can start with questioning Zoey," Jim said as he grabbed her arm and tugged her forward a couple steps. "Zoey, this is Detective Tyler Gates. Ty, this is—"

"The Wilde Woman. I know who she is. Remember, Chief, I was at the show. The main event was almost over when you called about the body," Gates said, cutting Jim off. Having been at the show explained why Gates was wearing shorts and a t-shirt instead of a suit or a uniform. "First wrestling event I've been to in years. And it did not end the way I expected it to end."

"I didn't expect it to end this way either," Zoey said. Throughout her twelve-year career, she had witnessed some interesting incidents and had some bizarre encounters in the parking lot before and after shows, but this was her first time finding a dead body . . . and, hopefully, her last. "Have you been to a lot of wrestling events?"

"When I was a kid, yeah. My dad and uncle took me and my cousins almost every weekend. I started losing interest in wrestling when I was in high school. Aside from here and there, I really haven't watched in years. The only reason I came tonight was because two of the other officers were coming to the show, and they invited me along." Detective Gates held out his hand to Zoey. "You were pretty impressive, Miss Wilde. Congrats on winning the Women's Championship. Even if the title belt is an eyesore."

"Yeah, it is." Zoey tugged her hand away from Detective Gates. "I'd show you the belt, but it's in my Jeep. And, if the yellow tape is any indication, my Jeep is part of the crime scene."

"For the time being it is." Gates pulled a notebook out of his back pocket and flipped it open to a blank page. He jotted down a couple notes and said, "Tell me about what happened tonight, Miss Wilde. What were you doing in the parking lot?"

"I needed some fresh air. So, I came outside," Zoey said, keeping it simple. "I also wanted to put my remaining merchandise in my car."

"It was stifling in there," Gates said as he continued to write in the notebook. "Is that when you found the body."

"No . . ." It would be so much easier if that was what had happened. If only she had just stayed inside and watched until the end of the show . . . she still might have been the one to find Devon's body, but, at least, she would have been inside when he was murdered. "I came outside during Devon's match. I couldn't stomach to watch it."

"You couldn't stomach to watch your brother's match?" Gates asked as he glanced up at Zoey. "Justin Wilde is your brother, correct?"

Zoey nodded. "It wasn't my brother that I couldn't stomach to watch. It was Devon. He's my ex-boyfriend."

"That partially explains what the commotion was about." Detective Gates perked up. "How long ago did the relationship end? Was it recent?"

"Tonight is the first time I've seen Devon in almost seven years."

Zoey had done the math, and it had been six years, ten months, one week, and three days since Devon had tried to kill her.

"What was Devon doing here tonight?" Jim asked, earning a sharp look from Detective Gates for interrupting. "How long has he been back in the area?"

"A few days," Zoey said. "He apparently saw me wrestle at that show in Florida last weekend. He came back to PA sometime during the past week."

"You knew Devon was back?" Jim asked.

"No. I only found out he was back a few hours ago. When he showed up here."

Zoey didn't have an alibi. She was not serving up her motive on a silver platter . . . not that it would take Detective Gates long to figure out that she had a motive. She left out the part where Devon accosted her in the parking lot before the show. She also didn't mention that he threatened to ruin her life if she didn't get back together with him.

Zoey caught Gates giving her an intrigued look. It surprised her that, instead of asking about her relationship with Devon, he questioned her about what happened in the parking lot.

"Once I realized that my tires were flat, I called the police and then went to borrow the air pump that my dad keeps in his truck. Dad is parked on the other side of the building," Zoey said, answering Gates's question. "When I got back with the pump, I found Devon."

"Did you hear anything while you were in the other lot?" Gates asked. "See anything?"

"I definitely didn't see anything. I couldn't see around the back of the building from where I was," Zoey said. "And I don't know if I heard anything. I mean, I heard voices. It sounded like a couple people were yelling at each other. And I'm pretty sure I heard some kind of door slam shut. But I don't know if that was here or somewhere nearby."

"I wonder if there are security cameras in the parking lot," Detective Gates said as he looked around the area.

"There aren't," Zoey and Jim said in unison.

Gates huffed. "Did you touch anything, Miss Wilde? The victim? The sledgehammer? Anything besides your vehicle?"

"No. I didn't touch anything," Zoey said. "Well, I did touch the sledgehammer. But that was hours ago. Before the show started."

Zoey explained that the sledgehammer belonged to Justin. It was one of the tools he used in his job as a general contractor. Zoey had borrowed the sledgehammer from him earlier in the week. A local band had written a song about her, and then asked her to star in the music video. Zoey had used the sledgehammer to smash a pink, princess-style vanity and large mirror, as well as other girlie items in what the director had described as a "symbolic gesture of breaking the standard feminine mold."

"How did the sledgehammer wind up in the parking lot?" Gates asked.

Zoey shrugged. "When Uncle Leland asked us to find weapons for the street fight, I got the sledgehammer out of my Jeep and donated it to the cause. I figured Justin could get it back after the show. I didn't expect anyone to use it to kill someone."

"Allegedly," Jim said. "The coroner will have to determine if it was the murder weapon."

"I would appreciate it if you didn't tell anyone that the sledgehammer is the alleged murder weapon," Gates said to Zoey. "I am also going to need to get your fingerprints so that I can compare them to the ones that we might find on the sledgehammer."

"Zoey's fingerprints are already on file," Jim said. "The place she works at was broken into a couple years ago. Zoey was fingerprinted back then so we had something to compare to the prints we found on scene."

"Then you are free to go, Miss Wilde," Detective Gates said. He snapped his notebook closed and handed Zoey his business card. "I will need you to come into the police department to give an official statement within the next few days."

"Can do."

Detective Gates held out Zoey's cell phone. The responding officer had taken her phone before sticking her in his cruiser. Zoey snatched the phone out of the detective's hand and unlocked the screen. She had several messages and missed calls. Her family members and other wrestlers had been blowing up her phone over the past hour. She didn't know what they knew—if anything—about what was going on in the parking lot. But they had noticed that she was missing from the VFW Hall. Zoey opened her family's group message thread and typed in two words: "I'm okay."

"What about my car?" Zoey asked. An officer was photographing the right rear tire. "I live down the street above 3 Count Tattoos, so it's not like I can't walk home. But when can I have my car back?"

"I'll call you once we're done with it," Gates said. "It should only be a couple days."

A couple days? What did they have to do with her Jeep that would take them a couple of days? It's not like Zoey had run Devon over.

"I'll take you home." Jim put his arm around Zoey's shoulders and guided her away from the crime scene. "I don't care if it's just a few blocks. I am not letting you walk home when the killer might still be lurking around."

"Can I get the rest of my stuff out of the VFW before we go?" Zoey asked.

Jim and Detective Gates escorted Zoey through the back door of the VFW Hall. Inside, the wrestlers and referees were seated along both sides of the hallway. Justin—who had a bloodstained towel pressed to his forehead—was sitting between Hannah and Terry.

"Zoey!" Justin dropped the towel and jumped up. He ran towards his sister and crushed her in a massive hug. "Where have you been? Are you okay?"

"I'm fine. Are you okay?" Zoey pointed at the two butterfly bandages that held together the split skin along his hairline.

"It looks worse than it is."

"The ringside doctor doesn't think he has a concussion," Hannah said, referring to the doctor that Leland had hired to attend the show and treat any injuries. "It's just a flesh wound."

"What's going on outside?" Terry asked as he crowded in between Zoey and Justin.

"Yeah, word is that Devon is dead," Justin said.

"He is. Someone . . . someone killed him." Zoey leaned closer to Justin and whispered, "Did you . . . you know . . . kill him?"

"No. Did you?" Justin asked.

"No," Zoey said.

"Then who did?" Hannah asked.

"That's for me to figure out," Detective Gates said as he broke into their huddle. He sent Justin, Hannah, and Terry back to their seats. "Grab your things and get out of here, Miss Wilde. And please don't discuss what you saw with anyone. Especially the . . . you know what."

The sledgehammer. Also known as the alleged murder weapon.

Zoey grabbed her bag out of the women's bathroom and then followed Jim outside.

"I'm not going to lie to you, Zoey," Jim said as he pulled out of the VFW's parking lot. During the short, three block drive to her apartment, they would pass the Linville Manor Healthcare and Rehabilitation Center, two of the town's twelve pizza places, an accountant's office, an eye doctor, and a dozen houses. "I know you are not the only person with a motive to kill Devon. But you probably have the best motive. If you killed him—"

"I didn't kill him!"

"But your story about being over in the other parking lot looking for the air pump . . . It might be the truth, but it sounds like bull crap. Sure, I saw the air pump. But how do I know you didn't have it in your car? Or that you didn't go get it out of Marlon's truck after you killed Devon."

"Had I known someone was going to kill Devon, I would have stayed inside and made sure that I had an alibi." Zoey banged her head off the headrest. "That being said, I didn't do it!"

"I believe you. I'm just worried about whether Detective Gates will believe you. He doesn't know you like I do. He's going to find out that you absolutely had a motive to kill Devon. And then he might just focus his case on you."

"As the chief of police, isn't it your job to make sure he remains openminded?"

"I'll do my best . . ."

Jim turned off the main street and drove down the alley that ran alongside the two-story building housing 3 Count Tattoos and Zoey's apartment. Zoey's father had purchased the property seven years ago. The two-story Craftsman style house had been built in the early 1900s, and it had been sitting abandoned for years before Marlon bought it. The exterior of the house was rundown, and the inside needed updated—but it was fixable. Marlon's plan had been to fix up the house and flip it. Instead, Zack talked Marlon into remodeling the first floor into a tattoo shop and the second floor into an apartment for him and Arielle.

Zack and Arielle had lived in the apartment above the tattoo shop for a few years. Then, after her husband died, Vivian sold her house to Zack and Arielle. The plan had been for them to swap residences—Zack and Arielle would take Vivian's and Kazimir's house and Vivian would move into the apartment. At least, that was the plan until Zack realized it would be a mistake to let their eccentric nana move into the apartment. The last thing he needed was her hanging around the tattoo shop and getting in everyone's way.

It was Zoey who came up with a solution. Since moving back from Florida, she had lived with their parents. It hadn't been too bad since she had the entire second floor of their house to herself. But she was ready to be on her own—even if it meant having to do her own cooking, cleaning, and laundry. Zoey moved into the apartment, and Vivian moved in with Marlon and Roxanne.

"You probably shouldn't be alone right now," Jim said as he pulled into one of the parking spots behind the building. "Why don't you run inside and grab a change of clothes? I'll take you over to your parents' house."

"No, thanks. I'm fine."

"Are you sure? Because you don't look fine."

"Yeah, well . . . The past few hours have been a bit traumatizing. First, my ex-boyfriend unexpectedly shows up. And then, a few hours later, I find his dead body." No amount of Vivian's beloved true crime shows could have prepared Zoey for finding Devon's body. "I really just want to be alone right now. You know I won't get any peace at my parents' house."

"No, you won't. Not with Vivian badgering you for all the grisly details," Jim said.

"Exactly." It wasn't that Zoey couldn't use her family's support, but she needed some time to process everything that had happened. There was no way she would be able to do that while surrounded by her family. They would all be overreacting and demanding details. "I'll be all right, Jim. If I need someone, I'll call Arielle."

Zoey grabbed her gym bag and then headed up the exterior staircase to her second-floor apartment. The motion activated lights came on, lighting the way to the door.

Once inside, Zoey dropped the gym bag on the giraffe print rug and flipped on the lights. She walked through the small foyer area and into the combined kitchen and dining room. Glancing at the clock, she saw that it was after midnight.

"It's tomorrow."

A few hours ago, Zoey had promised herself that if she could hold on until tomorrow, she could give in to the breakdown that had been threatening her since Devon Isler returned. So much had happened in the few hours since he had accosted her.

Zoey's knees gave out and she sank to the floor. The old wood did little to cushion the fall. Curled up into the fetal position, she gave in to a breakdown. Tears streamed down her face, and intense sobs wracked her entire body.

"Why? Why? Why?" Zoey screamed as she pounded her fist against the floor. "Why did this happen to me?"

Zoey had believed she was better. Between the therapy and the progress of time, she thought she had mostly recovered from what happened with Devon. His reappearance showed that she hadn't come as far as she thought she had. The skin had healed, but there was still the wound festering underneath.

An indignant-sounding meow interrupted Zoey's breakdown.

Opening her tear-filled eyes, Zoey looked up at her cat. Lita, who Zoey had named after her favorite women's wrestler, was a green-eyed, orange-and-white American shorthair cat. Zoey found her not long after she moved into the apartment. One morning, while taking out the trash, Zoey had found a kitten trapped in the trash can. Zoey rescued the kitten from her predicament and adopted her. Lita continued to act like she's the one who did Zoey a favor . . .

"You're right. Devon is not worth it," Zoey said to her cat. "I will not waste any more time crying over him."

Even though Zoey knew Lita was meowing at her because she was hungry and demanding that her owner cater to her needs, she decided to interpret her meows as an order to pull herself together. Zoey sat up and then used the front of her t-shirt to wipe away the tears and the snot that were streaked across her face.

Zoey then scooped Lita up into her arms and clutched the cat to her chest. Lita squirmed, trying to escape the embrace, but Zoey refused to let her go.

While Zoey held Lita in her arms, she glanced around her apartment. It wasn't very large, but it was home. The L-shaped kitchen was small and cramped, but it was adequate for one person. Between the kitchen and the dining room was an archway into the living room.

Professional wrestling memorabilia was scattered everywhere throughout the apartment. In the living room, the entertainment center was packed full of action figures. A cardboard cutout of Shawn Michaels stood beside Zoey's desk in the office alcove next to the door. She'd had the cutout since she was a kid, and she had no intention of getting rid of it even though Shawn had been retired for years now. Framed pictures covered the walls. There were autographed pictures of some of Zoey's favorite wrestlers, pictures of her with some of the wrestlers that she had met throughout the years, and pictures of Zoey and her brothers—both in the ring and outside of it—ranging from childhood to adulthood.

"Let's get you something to eat," Zoey said to Lita.

Lita meowed in response.

Before tending to Lita's needs, Zoey peeled off her t-shirt and stuffed it into the trash can. No point in keeping this shirt that was stained with makeup, tears, and snot—not when she had boxes full of Wilde Woman t-shirts on hand.

After disposing of the shirt and getting a drink, Zoey turned her attention to Lita. She replenished the cat's food bowls with wet and dry food. She also topped off Lita's water dish.

Leaving Lita contentedly munching on canned salmon, Zoey grabbed her gym bag and headed around to the other side of the apartment where the bedroom, bathroom, and laundry room were located. The home's interior staircase came up through the middle of the apartment. Marlon had walled off the staircase and installed a door at the top. On either side, Marlon installed archways to form a foyer.

After dumping the gym bag in the laundry room, Zoey peeled off her clothes and then scuttled down the hallway to the bathroom.

Zoey glared at her reflection in the mirror hanging above the bathroom vanity. Her hair stuck out in all directions. Streaks of the black mascara ran from her eyes to her chin, and the purple eyeshadow and black eyeliner had smeared, reminding her of two black eyes. Zoey grabbed a makeup wipe out of the box on the counter.

"Girl, time to get yourself together."

After removing the makeup, Zoey stood in front of the full-length mirror and checked her body for any bruises that she might have sustained during her match. The more tattoos she got, the harder it was for her to see bruises. Aside from the sugar skull and the garter belt, she had numerous other tattoos—including a portrait of her cat that covered her left arm from shoulder to elbow.

After finding a large bruise on her left elbow and another on her right shin, Zoey got in the shower and let the hot water loosen up her sore muscles. Her entire body ached from her short match against Hannah, and she lamented not having a bathtub to soak in.

When the hot water ran out, Zoey toweled off and headed for the bedroom to grab pajamas. She had just stepped into the bedroom when the sound of a pot or pan clattering on the stove startled her. Zoey would have assumed it was her cat exploring the counters, but—having just been in the kitchen—she knew she hadn't left anything sitting out on the stove.

Someone was in the apartment.

Zoey tightened the towel and tiptoed down the hallway. She ducked between the two archways and pressed herself against the door. She could escape down the staircase if she had to.

Peeking around the wall, she caught a glimpse of gray hair and lime green feathers.

"Nana," Zoey hissed under her breath.

At least once a week over the past three years Zoey had asked herself why she thought giving Vivian a key was a good idea. Vivian had developed the bad habit of letting herself in whenever she felt like it; she felt like it on a frequent basis. In fact, this was not the first time Vivian had scared Zoey by letting herself into the apartment without warning.

Zoey crept across the room until she was only two or three feet away from Vivian. She then asked, "What are you doing?"

Vivian screamed and then whirled around to confront Zoey.

"You just about scared me to death!" Vivian whacked Zoey on the shoulder with a plastic spoon. "What were you thinking, sneaking up on an old lady like that?"

"I scared you? How do you think I feel? It's one o'clock in the morning, and I'm all worked up as it is after the absolutely horrible day I've had. And then I hear someone banging around in my kitchen." Zoey tightened the towel to prevent it from falling down. "Not to mention that I could have been walking around naked considering I thought I was alone."

"Oh, it's not like you have anything that I don't have. Given yours probably aren't as wrinkled or saggy as mine. My bosom migrated south for the winter and then never bothered to come back north." Vivian patted her ample chest. "Maybe I should get a boob job."

"Nana . . ."

"You're right, it's a bad idea. I've got enough geezers asking me out for the early bird special at the Linville Diner. I don't want to do something that'll attract even more of them."

"Yeah, I think your fan club is big enough," Zoey said. Not long after Kazimir died, various older men from around Linville began to show an interest in the new widow. In three years, Vivian had yet to take any of them up on their requests for a date. "Now . . . What are you doing here? Aside from being nosy."

"Me? Nosy? Well, I never . . ." Vivian turned back to the stove and dumped a box of elbow macaroni into a pot of boiling water. "Isn't it obvious what I'm doing? I'm making mac and cheese to feed my favorite granddaughter."

"I can see that you're making mac and cheese. I'm also your only granddaughter."

"And that automatically makes you my favorite," Vivian said. She stirred the pot of macaroni and then turned around to pat Zoey on the cheek. "You shouldn't be alone right now. Not after the day you've had. In fact, you should be thrilled that I'm here."

"Maybe I would be thrilled had you not freaked me out."

Zoey's heart rate was beginning to return to normal, but that didn't mean she wasn't miffed with Vivian for her unannounced visit.

"You should also be thankful that I'm the only one here. Your parents, your brothers, Arielle, Hannah, and Terry all wanted to see you. But I convinced them to go home."

"Thanks, I guess," Zoey said, imagining how much more startled she would have been had she come out of the bathroom and found her entire family crammed into the apartment.

Changing the subject, Vivian asked, "Did you really find Devon's body?"

"Yes."

"Did you kill him?"

"No!"

"Are you sure? You can trust me. I won't tell anyone."

"I. Did. Not. Kill. Devon," Zoey said, enunciating each word so that Vivian got the point. "And I don't know who did."

"All right. All right." Vivian harrumphed. "Tell me everything you do know. How did he die? Where did it happen? Was there a lot of blood? Start talking."

"Can I put on some clothes first?" Zoey spun around and headed towards the bedroom. "Plus, it's almost time for you to dump out the water and add the cheese."

In the bedroom, Zoey shucked the towel and put on an old t-shirt and a pair of shorts. She returned to the dining room and had a seat at the table.

"Start talking," Vivian said as she handed Zoey a bowl of macaroni and cheese.

"How about you tell me what happened inside while I eat." Zoey shoveled a forkful of steaming hot macaroni and cheese into her mouth and then gestured for Vivian to go ahead.

"Not much to tell. Especially since you know how the matches were supposed to end," Vivian said. "Terry helped your brother pull a fast one so that Justin could beat Devon. The biker dude won the triple threat match. The tag team titles changed hands. Pasqual retained the Heavyweight Championship. Leland was in the ring hyping up next month's show when Chief Coleman appeared out of nowhere and told us that we had to stick around for a while. After that, a couple officers went around getting everyone's information. They wanted our names and contact info. Then we sat around for a while longer until some nice-looking detective made another announcement."

"Detective Tyler Gates," Zoey mumbled around a mouthful of mac and cheese. "He questioned me about finding Devon's body."

"He's one handsome man," Vivian said. "Is he single?"

"How the heck would I know?"

"Was he wearing a wedding ring?"

"I don't know. I wasn't exactly thinking about the detective's relationship status while standing less than fifteen feet away from my ex-boyfriend's body," Zoey said as she rolled her eyes. "What did Detective Gates have to say?"

"He explained that there had been an incident in the parking lot and that's why we had to stick around for all that time. He then told us that we were free to go. I hightailed it out of there and came over here to see you." Vivian spooned more macaroni and cheese into the bowl. "Now, hurry up and finish eating. I want to know everything."

After eating most of the macaroni and cheese, Zoey obliged Vivian and gave her all the grisly details. Zoey even told her about the sledgehammer. Vivian was oddly jealous that Zoey had found Devon's body, and disappointed that she had not gotten to see the crime scene.

Around two in the morning, Zoey shut down Vivian's question and answer session.

Leaving Vivian in the living room, Zoey retreated to the bedroom. She debated grabbing one of her scrapbooks off the bottom shelf of the bookcase—particularly the scrapbook that covered the time period where she dated Devon. When she'd put the scrapbook together, Devon had featured prominently in the pictures. After the assault, Roxanne took it upon herself to redo the scrapbook. She removed all of the pictures that were just of Devon and she cropped him out of pictures that also featured Zoey. There were a few pictures where removing Devon was impossible, so Roxanne bought a bunch of various sized poop emoji stickers and used them to cover Devon's face. No, the scrapbook was no longer an accurate depiction of that time in Zoey's life, but she did still have her journals, and they had not been redacted despite her desire to rewrite that period of her life.

"You forced me on this trip down memory lane," Zoey said as she turned on her laptop. She wasn't quite sure why she felt compelled to do it—her therapist would probably have a field day trying to figure it out—but Zoey needed to relive that dark period of her life as part of her recovery process. Maybe now that Devon was truly gone from her life, the festering wound could finally heal. "I may as well finish the journey."

SEVEN

Sunday August 19, 2018

THE AGONIZING TRIP DOWN MEMORY LANE took the rest of the night. Even in her private journal, she had a mistaken belief that everything was okay between her and Devon. Although Zoey didn't write about the bad stuff at first, it didn't mean that she hadn't hinted at it or tried to make light of something nasty that Devon had done or said. It wasn't until the end of the relationship that Zoey began to express how unhappy and unsafe she felt.

In Florida, Zoey's wrestling career not only took a back seat to Devon's career, it was all the way back in the optional third row seating. Heck, her career was in the travel trailer attached to the back of the car. She wrestled at around two dozen events during the time they lived in Florida. The rest of the time, Zoey valeted for Devon—but only when he decided that her presence at ringside wouldn't distract the audience from him. He was worried that she might steal the spotlight away from him.

Zoey couldn't come up with many good memories outside of wrestling during that time either. Yes, there were the occasional good moments, but those moments never lasted long. Devon had to ruin everything with his callous remarks and childish complaints.

A grayish light was beginning to seep in through the curtains—casting an eerie glow over all the sugar skulls and Day of the Dead artwork that decorated the bedroom—when Zoey reached memory lane's dead end. She'd spent years in therapy trying to get over Devon, but, after seeing him again, she'd felt the need to relive the relationship. Her therapist had told her over and over that she needed to forgive herself before she could finally put the experience in the past. Now that he was dead, she finally felt like all of this was now behind her and she could forgive herself.

Giving up on getting any sleep, Zoey rolled off the bed and headed for the living room. She found Vivian sprawled on the sectional. The racket coming out of her nose and mouth was loud enough to drown out the audience at *WrestleMania*.

Next to the sectional, Lita crouched on the top perch of her multi-level cat tree. She was peeking over the edge to look down at Vivian. Zoey was surprised that Lita had yet to pounce on Vivian to wake her up. Or maybe that was a special treatment that Lita reserved solely for her owner when she was hungry or wanted to play.

"It's a surprising amount of noise for such a little, old lady," Zoey said to Lita.

Lita hissed at Zoey. She then scampered down the cat tree and raced into the kitchen.

"I don't blame you, baby. I'd run away and hide, too." Zoey knelt on the floor next to the sectional, leaned in close to Vivian's ear, and yelled, "Stop snoring!"

Vivian jerked awake in surprise. "I was not snoring. I have never snored in my life."

"Then how do you explain that loud noise you were making?"

"It's called breathing." Vivian slipped on her glasses with the orange frames. "You look like you were put through the wringer. How do you feel this morning, sweetie?"

"Scared. Upset. Exhausted," Zoey said, naming off a few of the emotions she was currently feeling. "Like I really need to punch someone or something."

"That's the spirit!" Vivian patted Zoey on the knee. "Why don't you go clean up and get dressed? I'll whip us up some breakfast."

"I like the sound of that."

Zoey got dressed and washed her face. By the time she had herself put together, Vivian had prepared French toast and was about to toss the bread into the skillet. She had bacon sizzling in another pan. Vivian's way of comforting people was to stuff them full of food. Zoey was not going to complain since she loved Vivian's cooking. Plus, French toast and bacon were much more appealing than the eggs or protein bar that she normally would have eaten.

"We better hurry up and get over to my parents' house. I'm sure they're anxious for me to show up so they can see that I really am okay," Zoey said after she and Vivian finished eating. "I also want to make sure I have enough time to tell them what I can about last night before the wrestlers start showing up for the open gym."

Every Sunday morning, Marlon hosted a training session for wrestlers in an old barn that he had converted into a gym. The barn sat towards the far side of the Wildes' property. Vivian's ancestors had owned the farmland since the mid-1700s, and it had passed through the Schmitt family for generations. Knowing that none of his children were interested in farming, Vivian's father split up the land and gave each of his children a section of acreage. Vivian had received the smallest section, but her inheritance included the old farmhouse and barn. Opting not to live in the farmhouse, Vivian and Kazimir had built a small home on the land. Years later, Marlon and Roxanne built a house next door. Marlon had to tear down the dilapidated farmhouse to make room for a new house, but he left the barn standing.

For years, Marlon used the barn for storage while Zoey and her brothers utilized it as a playhouse. Then, when Zoey and Zack were seven or eight, they were playing up on the second floor and some rotten boards gave way under their weight. Zack landed on the lawn mower and broke his ankle. In the aftermath, Roxanne demanded that Marlon tear down the barn.

Instead, Marlon restored the barn and converted it into a gym that Zoey and her brothers nicknamed the Wilde World of Pro Wrestling. It's where Marlon trained his three children—and several other people—to wrestle. For years, Marlon ran a pro wrestling training school out of the barn. He gave that up a few years ago to focus more on his home remodeling business. These days, Marlon rented the gym to other wrestlers to host their own schools and training camps. He also opened the gym up every Sunday morning so that local wrestlers could have practice sessions.

"I have a feeling that not much wrestling will get done this morning," Vivian said as she cleaned the dirty dishes at the sink.

"No, everyone is going to want to talk about Devon. Which is why I'm probably going to skip the open gym. Once word gets out that I found Devon's body, they'll all be bugging me for details. I am not in the mood to answer their questions. Or hear what they have to say."

"But that's why you need to go." Vivian slammed the skillet down on the stove and shuffled back over to the table. "We need to ask the other wrestlers what they saw backstage. We need to find out how the sledgehammer got outside. Did Devon take it outside with him? Or did he leave it inside? Because, if he left it inside, that means the killer must have grabbed it and followed Devon outside."

"If I had to bet on it, I would say that Devon did not have the sledgehammer with him," Zoey said as she considered both scenarios. "If he'd had it with him, the killer would have had to get it away from him. There would have been a scuffle, and I probably would have heard something. I mean, I did hear some shouting. But it didn't last long. And I wasn't paying attention, so I'm not sure what direction the shouting came from."

"But we need to know for sure," Vivian said. "And we need to get alibis and motives so that we can figure out who the killer is."

"Nana, this isn't one of your Hallmark Channel movies. In real life, great-grandmas don't go around solving crimes no matter how eccentric they are."

"This one does," Vivian said as she straightened her shoulders and puffed out her chest.

"And what makes you think you can figure out the killer before the police?"

"Well . . . I watch all those true crime shows. I'm almost an expert."

"Nana . . ."

"I'm not just being nosy, for once. This is to protect you. What if the killer finds out that you were in the parking lot while he was killing Devon? What's to stop him from coming after you? He might be worried that you saw or heard something that could identify him."

"Oh, crap. I didn't think of that," Zoey muttered as cold beads of sweat broke out along her hairline. Until Vivian opened her mouth, it hadn't crossed Zoey's mind that her close proximity to the murder might put her in danger. "Maybe asking some questions is a good idea."

Vivian's response was to toss Zoey her car keys. She must have thought that her granddaughter needed more comfort than her cooking provided.

Vivian never let anyone drive her pale pink 1959 Cadillac Coupe DeVille. The Cadillac was Vivian's pride and joy, and she called the car Bertha after her mother. Vivian had bought the car brand new using the money she made wrestling, and she had kept the car well maintained over the years. Someday Zoey would inherit Bertha, and that was the only reason Vivian let her granddaughter drive the car on occasion.

Instead of taking the side streets to her parents' house, Zoey drove down Market Street so that they passed the VFW Hall. The police were no longer collecting evidence, and the crime scene tape was gone. Zoey's purple Jeep was gone as well. She could only hope that the Linville police were taking good care of her car, and that they would return it to her soon.

After Vivian examined the pavement for bloodstains, they continued to Zoey's parents' house on the northwestern edge of Linville.

Zoey had barely brought the Cadillac to a stop in the garage before she was accosted by her parents, brothers, and sister-in-law. They had been lying in wait for her like guests at a surprise party.

While Roxanne crushed her in a hug, Zoey spotted Hannah and Terry lingering in the doorway. Terry shared a townhouse with Justin on the southwest side of Linville, and they would have driven over together, and, since Hannah's car was not parked in the driveway, Zoey assumed that her protégé had spent the night with Justin. Whatever their relationship was, it appeared to have just ascended to a new level.

Vivian's shrill whistle cut through the barrage of questions and just about burst one of Zoey's eardrums. Paige cried out in annoyance, and Zoey's parents' chocolate lab howled.

"Quit crowding the girl," Vivian commanded as she herded everyone through the door and into the rest of the house. "Zoey will tell you everything if you would stop flapping your gums and give her a chance to say something."

Within minutes, Zoey was sandwiched on the couch between Zack and Roxanne. Arielle squeezed in on the other side of Zack. Marlon and Vivian took the two recliners, leaving Justin, Hannah, and Terry to sit on the floor.

Zoey glanced at everyone gathered around her.

Roxanne—who Zoey resembled—was sitting so close to her daughter that Zoey could see the gray hairs mixed in with her shoulder-length dark brown hair. Roxanne was overdue for a dye job. She was also crushing Zoey's hand between both of hers.

On Roxanne's other side, Marlon was seated on the edge of the recliner. His white hair made him look older than he was, as did all the lines on his face. Marlon had had a hard life both inside and outside of the ring. Before starting his own home improvement company, he had worked construction for years.

Marlon wasn't the only one on the edge of his seat. In fact, Vivian was the only one sitting back in her chair. She had put up the recliner's leg rest and appeared relaxed. Of course, she had already heard what Zoey had to say.

André, the five-year-old chocolate lab, also looked unperturbed as he sprawled on the floor at Marlon's feet. Like all Wilde family pets, the dog was named after a professional wrestler. In this case it was André the Giant. Vivian's cat, a tuxedo named Classy Freddie Blassie, lounged on the back of the couch and kept batting at Zoey's ponytail.

"My dad told us that Devon is dead. And that you found his body," Arielle said as she tried to placate Paige, who was still upset over Vivian's attempt to deafen everyone. Arielle's blonde hair was pulled back in a messy bun, and her makeup-free face was pale. There were also purple bags under her blue eyes. "He couldn't really tell us more than that since it's an active investigation. What can you tell us?"

"Well, I didn't kill him," Zoey said. No one had asked her if she had killed Devon or not, but she assumed that they were all wondering. "But someone did."

"Yeah, someone bashed him over the head with a sledgehammer," Vivian said.

"Nana! You weren't supposed to tell anyone that."

"I didn't think the family counted. But I promise I won't tell anyone else." Vivian held up her hand and made a motion that she was zipping her mouth shut.

"That I doubt," Zoey said, knowing that Vivian loved to gossip.

"Hold on, did Nana just say that Devon was bashed over the head with a sledgehammer?" Zack asked as he clutched Zoey's wrist.

"Was it my sledgehammer?" Justin asked.

"Yes, to both questions," Zoey said. She pulled her arm away from

Zack. "Do any of you know what happened to the sledgehammer after the match?"

"Devon grabbed it and headed backstage," Roxanne said. "I don't know—"

Cutting Roxanne off, Hannah said, "Devon definitely had the sledgehammer backstage after the match."

"Yeah, Devon was waving it around while yelling at me to meet him out in the parking lot to finish the fight," Justin said. "Obviously, I didn't take him up on the challenge."

"Because I wouldn't let you," Hannah said. She poked Justin on the forehead next to the butterfly bandages that held the split skin together. "I had to sit on Justin to keep him backstage so that the doctor in attendance could patch him up. And a couple of other wrestlers crowded around us to make sure Justin didn't try to do something stupid. Big Daddy was one of them. And so were Pasqual and Jarvis."

"I was there, too," Terry said.

"You were?" Justin asked.

"Of course, I was," Terry said. "Where else would I have been?"

"I didn't see you hanging around us, Terry," Hannah said.

"I mean, at first I was with you guys. But then all the blood made me sick . . . So, I went in the bathroom to splash water on my face. I almost passed out while I was in there. You know I can't stand the sight of blood."

"Head wounds do bleed a lot," Vivian said.

"Sorry, man," Justin said to Terry. "I was just so ticked off. Aside from Hannah and the doc, I really have no idea who was there."

Vivian shushed everyone and gestured for Zoey to continue. It took a while to get through the story because everyone kept interrupting with their questions, comments, and observations. They all freaked out when Zoey told them when and where she found Devon's body.

"You were in the parking lot when it happened?" Marlon shouted. The blood drained from his sunburnt face, leaving his skin a faint pink color. "My God, what if you hadn't gone to look for my truck? Or if it hadn't taken you as long to find the air pump?"

"I'm trying not to think about what might have happened," Zoey said.

"Zoey, did you see the killer?" Terry asked.

"No, I didn't see the killer. I didn't see anything from where I was. Nor did I hear anything aside from some shouting and a door slamming. And, let me reiterate . . . I did not kill Devon."

"You might not have killed him. But I'm sure it's your fault he's dead."

"What . . .?" Zoey stuttered as she turned around to face the person yelling at her.

Leland, who had slipped inside through the front door and now lurked in the foyer, made a fashion statement in sandals and knee-high socks. His purple cotton shorts just barely came to his midthigh. Behind him, Kim cowered in the doorway. Cowering was difficult for her to pull off considering she was built like a heavyweight champion.

"How dare you accuse my daughter?" Marlon roared. "She didn't kill that bastard."

"I just said I know she didn't kill him. She doesn't have the guts to do something like that," Leland said as he walked farther into the living room. "I'm sure Justin or Zack is the one who killed him. They threatened to kill Devon multiple times yesterday."

"Yo, I was backstage the whole time," Justin said. "I didn't kill him."

"I didn't kill him either," Zack said.

"Uh huh," Leland said. "You all are unbelievable. That poor boy—"

"Don't you dare make Devon the victim. I mean, he *is* a murder victim but . . ." Marlon trailed off. "Speaking of unbelievable . . . You're the one who knew Devon was back in the area and didn't say anything to any of us. You're the one who hired Devon to wrestle last night. Zoey is the closest thing you have to a niece. Did you ever stop to think about how she would feel?"

"I needed another wrestler—"

"Stop it!" Marlon said, cutting Leland off. "I'm so sick of your pathetic excuses. For once, can you just own up to one of your mistakes?"

Leland sputtered. His face flushed a deep red, and his handlebar mustache quivered. "You're the ones who won't stop punishing Devon for a mistake that he made years ago."

"Devon's *mistake* almost cost me my life!" Zoey screamed.

"But you're still alive," Leland said. "And you're fine as far as I can tell."

"Trust me, I am nowhere near fine," Zoey said. Years of therapy had helped, but she still felt she had a ways to go. "Thanks to this, I'm probably going to need to go back to therapy."

"That's what's wrong with you millennials. You're weak," Leland said. He gestured not only to Zoey, but to Zack, Arielle, Justin, Hannah, and Terry. "You think you need therapy and safe spaces. But what you really need to do is toughen up. Life is hard. Deal with it."

"Get out of my house, Leland." Marlon walked over to the front door and yanked it open. "You're not welcome here anymore. Not after what you put my family through."

"I figured you, of all people, would understand that the show must go on. Over the years, you wrestled enough people that you hated," Leland said as he pushed past Marlon to get to the front door. "But I don't need you. I don't need any of you. Come on Kim, let's get out of here."

Marlon slammed the door shut behind Leland.

"I'm sorry," Kim said. She had stayed behind, lingering in the foyer after her husband's dramatic exit. She patted Zoey on the arm. "I had no idea what Leland was up to. If I had, I would have stopped him. But I didn't know that Devon was back in the area."

"It's all right, Kim," Zoey said. "You're not responsible for Leland's actions."

"Yeah, Mom, don't blame yourself," Terry added.

"You're obviously still welcome in our home, Kim," Roxanne said. "But it would be best if Leland stayed away for a while."

"A long while," Marlon grumbled.

After Justin befriended Terry in second grade, Roxanne and Kim formed a friendship. Zoey didn't think that Roxanne would let Leland's transgression come between her friendship with Kim. She did wonder if it would affect Kim's relationship with Leland.

Out in the driveway, Leland blasted the car horn.

"I better go talk to Leland." Kim moved towards the front door. "I just don't know what's gotten into him lately. He's been so moody. He's also been drinking more."

"Wait." Zoey grabbed Kim's arm and prevented her from leaving. "What were you doing in the parking lot last night?"

"Putting stuff in my car," Kim said. "I'd shut down the concession stand and was bringing the leftover snacks out to my car. I heard you . . . Well, I didn't know it was you at the time. But I heard a woman's voice and she sounded frantic. I looked around and that's when I found you standing over Devon's dead body."

Kim gave the Wildes an abrupt goodbye and stepped outside.

Everyone stood around in tense silence until Marlon slammed the door for a second time.

"Good riddance," Marlon muttered as he walked back into the living room.

"Marlon—"

"I don't want to talk about it." Marlon headed through the kitchen towards the French doors at the back of the house. "I'm going to open up the barn. Are any of you coming? Or would you prefer to stay in the house and gossip."

Everyone except for Roxanne, Arielle, and Paige followed Marlon outside. Even André tagged along.

They had just stepped out onto the back patio when they saw Carl Mease walking up the path that connected the house and the barn. Carl wrestled under the name Boris Pavlov, and he had a stereotypical Russian gimmick. He drove over an hour from Kutztown every Sunday for the open gym.

Jogging over to the patio, Carl asked, "What happened last night? I heard someone died in the parking lot after the show."

"It was during the show," Zoey said.

"And it was the guy that Uncle Leland hired to replace you," Justin said. "Why'd you cancel on him anyway?"

"I didn't," Carl said. "Leland cancelled on me. He called me up yesterday morning and told me that he didn't need me for the show."

"Then why the heck would Leland claim you cancelled on him?" Marlon asked.

"Something fishy is going on," Vivian said.

"So, what happened last night? Do any of you know the guy who died?" Carl asked. "His name sounds familiar, but I can't place it."

"Why don't you come help me open up the gym," Marlon said, gesturing for Carl to follow him over to the barn. "I'll give you the rundown."

Once Marlon and Carl had disappeared into the barn, Zoey turned to the group of her family and friends. "Do not—I repeat, do not—tell anyone about what we know happened last night. Do not tell anyone that we know the murder weapon was the sledgehammer. And do not let it slip that I was in the parking lot when Devon was killed. All we know is that Devon is dead."

"But do try to find out if Devon took the sledgehammer outside with him or not," Vivian said, drawing everyone else into her quest for information. "And try to subtly ask them where they were and if they saw anything last night."

"And when have you ever been subtle?" Zoey asked Vivian.

Zoey gestured to her nana's lime green mermaid leggings and the hot pink t-shirt proclaiming that she was a "Sexy Grandma." Zoey was beginning to have second thoughts about agreeing with Vivian's idea that they ask the other wrestlers about what they had seen backstage around the time that Devon exited the building.

"I can be subtle," Vivian said as she walked past the small building that housed Marlon's office and showroom and continued towards the barn. "When I want to be."

The old barn sat on the far side of the lot. It was two-stories tall and covered with weathered red siding. There were multiple doors on the ground level and windows around the second story. Marlon and Carl had opened all the doors and windows, and they had several large fans running to air out the large, stuffy room that reeked of stale sweat.

The wrestling ring took up most of the floor space in the front two-thirds of the barn. Marlon had converted the back part of the barn into two locker rooms. Above the locker rooms was a loft that served as a viewing platform for a bird's eye view of the ring.

Right around eight o'clock the other wrestlers began to arrive, and the turnout was more than usual. Between ten to fifteen wrestlers showed up for a typical open gym. Today, there were more than twenty-five wrestlers. Aside from Zoey, Justin, Hannah, and Terry, there were three other wrestlers in attendance who had been part of last night's event. Four of Justin's students who had attended the show were also there.

Vivian and Zoey were right—all of them were more concerned with gossiping about Devon than they were with training.

Thanks to Vivian, everyone soon knew that Zoey had been the one to find Devon's body in the parking lot, and everyone wanted to ask her about it. Speculation circulated about how Devon might have died—some thought he'd had a heart attack while others thought that Justin had done something to Devon during the match that resulted in him dying later. Vivian put all the speculation to rest when she announced that Devon had been murdered.

Despite not wanting to talk about Devon, Zoey was sucked into conversations about him. The wrestlers who knew of her history with Devon jokingly asked if she had killed him. The wrestlers who didn't know about the relationship peppered her with questions.

"Can I have a word with you, Zoey?" Pasqual Cipriani asked, approaching her while she was getting a drink at the upstairs water cooler. "I want to ask you some questions about last night. I've been hearing a lot of rumors, and I'd like to hear what you have to say."

Instead of telling Pasqual to leave her alone like she had done with the other wrestlers, Zoey agreed to talk to him. She knew he was asking for reasons that went beyond being curious. Wrestling was his hobby; criminal law was his day job. Pasqual was one of the best criminal defense attorneys that money could buy in the Philadelphia area. Over the years, he'd defended a few mobsters, a serial killer, and several other high-profile defendants. And he bragged about overcharging his clients so that he could afford his designer three-piece suits, sports cars, and his mansion in Chestnut Hills. Pasqual was close in age to Marlon, but he was in better shape. Zoey was surprised to see him at her dad's open gym. Pasqual very rarely drove out from Philadelphia to attend.

Since there were wrestlers scattered throughout the barn, and Zoey didn't want any of them to overhear what she had to say, she led Pasqual outside and over to the pool. Zoey opened one of the patio umbrellas to protect them from the light rain that was falling.

"Before we start, do you have any money on you?" Pasqual asked.

"Ummm . . ." Zoey dug around in her pockets and pulled out a crumpled dollar bill that looked like it had gone through the wash a few times. "This is all I've got on me."

"Consider it my retainer." Pasqual plucked the dollar out of Zoey's hand. "Before this is all over, there is a good chance you will need an attorney."

"But I didn't kill Devon!"

"That doesn't necessarily matter. But it would be a rare occurrence for me to defend someone who is actually innocent." Pasqual winked at Zoey, and she wasn't sure how to interpret it. "The police and the prosecution just need to prove that you were capable of killing the victim. Then they need to convince the jury."

"But, Pasqual, I didn't—"

"Let me explain." Pasqual said before giving Zoey a crash course on criminal law.

Zoey then gave Pasqual a detailed summary of the previous night's events. There was no point in denying that she had been the one to find Devon's body, but Pasqual was the only person who she told about being in close proximity to the murder.

When Zoey was done, Pasqual said, "Look, Zoey, I'm not saying that the police are going to try charging you with Devon's murder. For all we know, they've already arrested someone. I'm just asking you to give me a call if it starts to look like they suspect you."

"Last night, the detective told me that he'll need me to come in and give a statement."

"That's standard police procedure. It's fine to give a statement."

Changing the subject, Zoey said, "You were backstage last night. Did you see anything?"

"Like did I see anyone follow Devon out into the parking lot?" Pasqual asked, peering at Zoey over his designer sunglasses. "Sorry to break your heart, kid, but no, I didn't see anything. I was too busy keeping an eye on your brother and getting ready for my match."

"Did you see what happened to the sledgehammer after Devon brought it backstage?"

"He slammed it through the wall as Bubba and Tiny were shoving him out the back door. That much I saw."

Bubba and Tiny were a tag team with a hillbilly gimmick. Zoey wasn't sure how much of the gimmick was an act. They were either really good at staying in character all the time, or their characters were based on their true selves.

"Then there is no way I could have done it! I went outside before the match was over. How could I have gotten the sledgehammer if Devon left it inside?" Zoey paced along the edge of the pool. "The killer must have been backstage. All he had to do was grab the sledgehammer and follow Devon into the parking lot."

"It was dark backstage. And Devon had everyone in an uproar," Pasqual said. "But there were a lot of people backstage . . . The killer would have to be pretty cocky to think he could get away with following Devon outside without at least one person seeing him."

"Earth to Pasqual . . . How many wrestlers do you know who don't have massive egos?" Zoey asked, stopping in front of him. "And a bunch of the guys who wrestled last night knew Devon from before. I'm not the only person with a motive to kill him or a reason for wanting him dead. I need to talk to the guys."

"Zoey, no." Pasqual grabbed her arm and stopped her before she could rush back to the barn. "Word of advice . . . The police hate it when citizens stick their noses into investigations. And I know for a fact that Ty Gates won't appreciate it."

"You know Detective Gates?"

"Ty was a police officer down in Philly before he took the detective job out here. He was involved in investigations against a couple of my former clients. What I can tell you is that Ty's a good cop. Very thorough. I bet he is going to make a real good detective. I don't think you have to worry about him focusing solely on you. He will look for other options as well."

"What else do you know about him?" Zoey asked.

"Not too much aside from that his dad also worked for the Philly police. Retired as a captain a few years ago. And Ty was engaged to some drama queen divorce lawyer, but he broke that off not long before he moved out here. I've met the woman a handful of times, and, let me tell you, it was a smart move on his part to get out of that relationship." Standing, Pasqual said, "Whelp, I better get going. I have a case coming up that I need to finish getting ready for. But, remember, if you need me, call me."

"I just hope I won't have to. There's no way I can afford you."

"Don't worry, I'll give you the friends and family discount."

Pasqual gave Zoey a hug. He then drove off in his sporty little convertible.

Zoey had a seat by the pool and debated if she wanted to head back to the barn or not.

"Was Devon Isler really as bad as everyone is saying?"

"What the—" Zoey nearly fell out of the chair as she spun around to see who was speaking. Behind her was the shed where her dad stored the pool supplies. Peeking out of the crack between the two doors was Mortimer Cozma. "Holy crap, Mort! You scared me! Don't you know it's rude to eavesdrop on people!"

"I was in here before you and Pasqual came out," Mortimer said as he slipped between the doors. "I wasn't eavesdropping. I was overhearing."

"No, it still counts as eavesdropping. You should have let us know you were in there."

"But then I wouldn't have heard everything that you and Pasqual had to say."

Mortimer was the most bizarre person Zoey had ever met—and she had met some extremely weird people in her life. The nineteen-year-old was obsessed with death . . . though, that was probably because his parents owned a funeral home and he'd started helping prep the bodies when he was a kid.

"Mort . . . What were you doing in the shed?" Zoey asked.

"I needed some time to think. So, I crawled in the shed," Mortimer said. "You didn't answer my question. Was Devon Isler really as bad as everyone is saying?"

"Why should you care? Devon hasn't been around in years. You wouldn't have seen him wrestle when you were a kid since you weren't a fan yet."

Mortimer started hanging out at Marlon's open gym not long after he turned eighteen. He claimed he had only recently gotten into professional wrestling and wanted to learn more about it. Since he kept showing up every Sunday, Justin began training him.

"I want to know because . . . well, because . . . Because he's my birth father!"

"Devon Isler is your father?" Zoey slumped back against the hard, plastic chair in disbelief. If Mortimer was nineteen, and Devon was thirty-six . . . That meant Devon had only been seventeen when Mortimer was born. "No way. I spent a year-and-a-half with Devon, and he never even hinted at having a kid. Plus, you are the spitting image of your father."

"Adoptive father. And I look like him because he's actually my uncle. My birth mother is his younger sister." Mortimer collapsed into the chair next to Zoey. "I've always known I was adopted. And that my aunt Silviana is my birth mother."

"When did you find out Devon was your dad?"

"Right after I turned eighteen. Aunt Silviana told me about Devon and how he was a wrestler. She claims that Devon told her that, if she kept me, he wouldn't have anything to do with me. He wasn't going to let some kid come between him and his wrestling career."

"Now that sounds like something Devon would say," Zoey said.

In fact, he had said the same thing to her on the one occasion she had brought up having kids. He'd made it clear that he would leave Zoey if she got pregnant—never mind the fact that the only way she could have gotten pregnant was through his active participation. His mother, on the other hand, desperately wanted grandchildren and frequently chastised Zoey for not providing her with any.

"Devon is why I got into wrestling. I was hoping he was some famous wrestler and that he would be excited about meeting the kid that he gave up for adoption. But, when I looked him up, I found out that he was a crappy wrestler and that he was in jail for beating up his girlfriend. Despite that, I wanted to know more about him. So, I started hanging out at your dad's gym so that I could be around you. I was hoping you would talk about him, but you never did. Not that I blame you. I wouldn't have wanted to talk about him either."

"Mort, did you ever try to contact Devon? Or did you say anything to him last night?"

Mortimer shook his head. "I hadn't decided yet if I wanted to try contacting him or not. But then, when he showed up last night . . . I figured it was fate bringing us together. I told him who I was. And he said . . . he said he was glad he gave me up and that he was ashamed that he'd made such a pathetic freak like me. I was so mad . . ."

EIGHT

"Four hours, and only three people got in the ring," Marlon said as he accepted the sandwich that Roxanne handed him. He dumped a mound of potato chips onto his plate before sitting at the table. "And then, when I kicked them out, the bums had the nerve to complain about not getting any ring time. It's not my fault they spent the entire time running their mouths when they could have been doing something productive."

"What did you expect, Marlon?" Roxanne asked as she continued to hand out sandwiches to the rest of family. "They want to know what happened last night. We all do."

"Still . . ." Marlon took a bite out of his sandwich. He then mumbled something around the mouthful of bread, meat, and cheese. ". . . waste of time."

"It wasn't a total waste of time, son," Vivian said. She pushed her plate away to make room on the table for a notebook. Inside the notebook were pages of her nearly indecipherable scrawl. "I ferreted out some key information—"

"This morning was supposed to be about wrestling, Ma," Marlon snapped, spewing potato chip crumbs across the table. "It wasn't supposed to be a gossip session."

"Maybe not for you, but it was for me and Zoey," Vivian said, dragging her granddaughter into it. "She's most likely at the top of that handsome detective's suspect list. We were trying to gather some facts to help clear her."

"Vivi, you need to leave the investigating up to my dad and the rest of the police," Arielle said. "Dad will make sure Zoey is cleared."

"All I did was innocently ask some questions," Vivian said.

"From what I heard, you were hassling some of the wrestlers and asking if they killed Devon," Marlon said.

"I never said they weren't direct questions," Vivian said.

Before Marlon's and Vivian's conversation turned into a real argument, Zoey asked, "What did you learn, Nana? Because I heard Devon smashed the sledgehammer through the wall by the back door as he was being given the bum's rush."

Pasqual wasn't the only person who had informed Zoey of what Devon had done with the sledgehammer. Cove and Reef—a tag team with a surfer gimmick—told her the same thing, but neither of them said anything about Devon or anyone else removing the sledgehammer from the wall and taking it outside.

"Well . . . We know how it didn't get outside," Vivian said, backtracking. "I heard the same thing that you did, Zoey. Devon put the sledgehammer through the drywall as he left. That means that whoever took the sledgehammer outside must be the killer!"

"I'm not sure if that's a safe assumption or not, Ma," Marlon said. He leaned across the table and helped himself to the cookie platter. He grabbed one cookie for himself and another for Paige. "Devon could have stepped back inside and grabbed the sledgehammer."

"Which could be what happened," Terry said. He had been unusually quiet all day, but, considering who he was hanging out with, it would be hard for anyone to get a word in. The Wildes were chatterboxes.

Since there wasn't enough room at the table, Hannah, Justin, and Terry were standing at the kitchen island. Hannah had one of her arms wrapped possessively around Justin's waist. For someone who didn't like clingy women, Justin sure looked like he was enjoying it. In fact, Justin had his arm draped over Hannah's shoulders and was playing with her hair.

"Or someone could have removed the sledgehammer from the wall before it did any more damage," Arielle added. "That person could have tossed the sledgehammer out the back door."

"Who just throws a sledgehammer outside?" Roxanne asked.

Arielle shrugged. "I'm just saying."

"But I think we can all agree that the sledgehammer did not grow legs and walk outside on its own. It also did not bash Devon over the head by itself," Vivian said, pointing out the obvious. "We know that the sledgehammer was backstage. That means the killer must have been backstage for him or her to gain access to it. And that helps narrow down Zoey's and my suspect list to the twenty-five or so people who were backstage last night."

"What suspect list?" Zoey asked.

"The one we are about to come up with." Vivian flipped to a blank page in the notebook. "We know who was backstage last night. That means there's a good chance we know who the murderer is. And it's probably a wrestler."

"Or a valet," Zack said.

"Or a referee," Marlon added.

"It wasn't me," Terry said. "I was in the bathroom."

"Terry, we know," Zoey said. "And none of us think you did it."

"You know, a fan could have snuck backstage," Roxanne said as she began to gather up the dirty dishes. "I heard there were just over four hundred people there last night. Even omitting the children, that adds a whole lot of possible suspects to the list."

"And there were several fans who weren't happy that Devon was there," Marlon pointed out. "A dozen or so came up to me and said something about it. A couple guys wanted to run Devon out of town."

"There were also a few wrestlers—"

Cutting Zack off, Justin said, "Including four of my students. And Jarvis brought a couple of his students along, too."

"Plus, there were former wrestlers at the show last night." Zack swooped Paige out of her highchair and put her on the floor so that she could play with André. "They wouldn't have had any trouble getting backstage last night, and neither would I. It's not as if the guys Uncle Leland hires to stand by the stage doors are real security guards—"

Interrupting, Terry said, "All of those guys should be on your list, too, Vivi."

"They would be," Vivian said. "If I knew who they were."

"I'll get their names from my stepdad," Terry said.

Zack cleared his throat, "As I was saying . . . The so-called security guards wouldn't have thought twice about letting another wrestler backstage during the show."

"There were other wrestlers backstage during the show. All four of my students were backstage at some point. So were Jarvis's students," Justin said. He pulled away from Hannah so that he could grab a beer out of the refrigerator. "That's what really ticked me off. Uncle Leland claimed Devon was the only wrestler he could get."

Vivian cleared her throat and shot them an annoyed look. "All right. You've made your points. Our suspect list can't just be confined to the wrestlers, valets, referees, and volunteers who were part of the show. But we can go over the match card and narrow down a list of suspects from that."

"You're not going to drop this, are you, Vivi?" Roxanne asked.

"No, I am not. You may as well humor an old lady." Vivian held up a sheet of paper on which she had written down all the previous night's matches including the referees for each match. "Let's get started. The first match of the night was between Mort and the kid from West Virginia who claimed to be a descendent of the McCoy family. Or was he a Hatfield?"

"McCoy," Zoey and Zack said at the same time.

"No way was it the McCoy kid," Justin said. "First of all, he had no idea who Devon was. I know because he asked me what the big deal was about Devon. Second, what would his motive have been? That he saw Devon at a wrestling event when he was a kid, and Devon wouldn't sign an autograph for him? Yeah, right."

"He could be a serial killer," Vivian said.

"Not everyone is a serial killer or a homicidal maniac," Zoey said. And it was not the first time she'd had to point it out to her nana. "Don't you remember that true crime show you made me watch last week? The one with the detective that said around half of all murders are committed by a family member or someone who knew the victim? The chances are good that Devon knew his killer."

"Plus, the McCoy kid has an alibi," Justin said. "Reef and Cove claim he was with them and Mama while Bubba and Tiny threw Devon out the back door. The six of them then stood around talking for the rest of the show."

"Fine . . ." Vivian crossed some of the names off her list. "What about Mort?"

"Zoey, did you see any puncture wounds on Devon's neck? Maybe Mort got hungry and decided to kill Devon to feast on his blood," Zack joked.

"Oh, yeah, because that's plausible," Zoey said.

"You know, Mort was acting weird last night," Hannah said.

"Babe, in case you haven't noticed, Mort is weird." Justin chuckled. "Insanely weird."

"I mean, he was acting, like, weirder than usual," Hannah said.

"But was Mort acting like a murderer?" Vivian asked.

"And how exactly is a murderer supposed to act?" Zoey asked, prompting Vivian to lecture them on her extensive—though not entirely accurate—knowledge of murderers.

Zoey thought about how Mortimer had a motive to kill Devon. He admitted to her that being called a freak by his birthfather had devastated him. Could Mortimer have been so angry that he killed Devon? It was possible. Why hadn't Zoey asked him if he had an alibi for the brief timeframe during which Devon had been killed? Probably because she had been so shocked by Mortimer's disclosure that she couldn't think about anything else. To be honest, Zoey was still stunned that Devon was Mortimer's father. She opted to keep Mortimer's motive to herself since it wasn't up to her to share that Devon was Mortimer's birthfather. The only people who she would tell were Chief Coleman and Detective Gates. They needed to know.

"You may as well leave Mort on the suspect list for now," Zoey said. "At least until we can get an alibi for him."

Overall, there had been twenty-one wrestlers, two valets, and three referees who had taken part in last night's show. Not all of them could be considered suspects.

They had already discussed Mortimer and the McCoy kid. Clearly Devon had not killed himself. Zoey, Justin, and Hannah had not killed him either. Terry and the other two referees had alibis—Terry had been in the bathroom and the other two referees were either in the ring or backstage talking to wrestlers.

They were also able to eliminate the wrestlers who had competed in the final three matches of the night. The three wrestlers in the Triple Threat Match had most likely been in the ring when Devon was murdered; even if Devon was killed after their match, all three competitors were backstage and had been alibied by other wrestlers. One of the two valets was ringside for the Triple Threat match, which eliminated her from the suspect list as well. The four wrestlers who took part in the LAW Tag Team

Championship match could not have done it since they were all together prepping for their match or in the ring when Devon was killed. Pasqual and Jarvis had been getting ready for their main event match.

In the end, they narrowed down the suspect list to one wrestler.

"That just leaves Sasquatch," Vivian said. "And we know he had a motive to kill Devon. Not one of them came out and accused him of doing it. But a handful of the wrestlers said they wouldn't be surprised if he killed Devon."

"Squatch's motive is almost as good as mine," Zoey said.

Zoey didn't know the whole story—mainly because she had heard conflicting versions from the two people involved. But what she did know was that Sasquatch and Devon had been best friends growing up. After high school, they moved to Philadelphia to begin training as wrestlers. They then spent a few years working on the independent scene as a tag team. Zoey wasn't quite sure what prompted it, but, after a few years, Devon reported Sasquatch to the Philadelphia police after finding illegal drugs and steroids in the apartment that they shared. Sasquatch swore that the drugs were not his and accused Devon of planting them to get him in trouble. Regardless of what happened or who the drugs belonged to, Sasquatch was arrested for possession of illegal drugs. He spent some time in jail, and he would still occasionally claim that the criminal record had destroyed his life. Zoey knew Sasquatch remained angry about the incident, but had that led him to kill Devon?

"Was Squatch here today?" Zoey asked. "I didn't see him."

"No, Squatch didn't show up," Justin said.

"Which is surprising since Squatch always shows up. I don't think he's missed more than a half dozen open gyms in the past few years," Marlon said. He'd gotten up and was pacing in front of the French doors.

"Big Daddy told me that Squatch hurt his back last night during their match," Zack said. He was down on the floor trying to pry Paige's plastic pony out of André's mouth. It didn't look like André wanted to give up his new chew toy.

"That's what Squatch gets for letting a nearly four-hundred-pound man belly flop on top of him," Nana said.

"Squatch has always been known to exaggerate, but he texted Big Daddy that his back hurt so bad that he couldn't get out of bed this morning,"

Zack said.

"Yeah, he looked like he was in bad shape last night," Zoey said, recalling how she had run into Sasquatch as she was coming out of the women's bathroom. "I saw him as I was headed out for my match. He was limping and complaining about his back."

"Squatch was in the back with me, Devon, and a couple other wrestlers during intermission," Hannah said. Leaving Justin by the kitchen island, Hannah plopped down in the chair that Marlon had abandoned. "Devon and Squatch were arguing. I thought they were, like, going to start fighting each other and I was going to have to break them up. But Leland came back and yelled at them to knock it off. He then made Squatch go out and interact with the fans."

Since she played an Amish character—and the Amish refrained from getting their pictures taken because they believed photographs were graven images—Leland made Hannah stay in the back during the pre-show and at intermission.

"But what happened to Squatch after intermission?" Vivian asked. "No one I talked to today remembers seeing him backstage during the second half of the show."

Hannah shrugged. "He was there when Justin's match started. I didn't see him after that."

"Yeah, he wasn't backstage after the show when the cops had all of us sitting in the hallway. A bunch of us wondered where he was," Justin said.

"I figured he was out in the banquet hall," Terry said.

Vivian cleared her throat. "Maybe the reason no one saw Squatch during the second half of the show was because he was out in the parking lot waiting to confront Devon."

"But Squatch could barely walk," Hannah pointed out.

"Or so he claimed," Vivian said.

"If Squatch was outside, how would he have gotten the sledgehammer if Devon left it inside?" Zoey asked.

"I'll leave it up to the police to figure out how Squatch did it," Vivian said as she flipped her notebook closed.

"*If* he did it," Arielle said. "It doesn't mean Squatch killed Devon just because he has a motive and doesn't seem to have an alibi."

"Exactly! I have a motive and no alibi," Zoey said. "But I didn't kill him."

"Hey, what about the cameraman? JD or JT? It's J-something," Hannah said.

"You mean JT Perez?" Justin asked. He moved to stand behind Hannah's chair. "Chunky guy with a wispy beard? Part Hispanic, part Italian?"

"Yeah, him," Hannah confirmed. "It happened right after Squatch went off on Devon. After Leland hauled Squatch out, Devon went into the bathroom. I didn't see JT come backstage, but I heard him arguing with Devon in the bathroom. The McCoy kid and someone else went in and broke it up. They hauled JT out of the bathroom. Leland came backstage a second time, and he dragged JT back out in the banquet hall."

"Shoot . . . I forgot about JT," Marlon said. "He took a swing at Devon before the show. Zack and I pulled him outside to calm him down."

"JT said he wanted to kill Devon," Zack said.

"Yeah, but he was angry. He might not have meant it," Marlon said.

"If anyone aside from Zoey and Squatch had a solid motive, it's JT," Justin said. "If someone broke my neck doing something he had no business doing and then ruined my wrestling career, I'd want to kill him."

"JT's camera is stationary. I think all he does is make sure the focus is clear and that the camera doesn't shift. That way he can keep an eye on the monitor and watch what his cameraman is filming at ringside," Zack said. "JT could have left the camera unattended."

"I didn't see him backstage after Justin's match. But it's possible he cut through, grabbed the sledgehammer, and went after Devon," Hannah said.

"I'm adding him to my list of suspects along with Sasquatch," Vivian said as she scribbled something into her notebook. "We just have to figure out which one of them did it."

"No, we don't, Vivi," Roxanne said. She stood up and shoved her chair in. "I still don't get the purpose of this. Did we really accomplish anything this afternoon?"

"We came up with a list of suspects," Vivian said.

"But it's not a complete one," Zoey said.

"No, it's not," Marlon said. "You left Leland off of the list."

"That's because Leland never leaves the stage during the show," Vivian said.

"He did last night," Hannah said. "He came backstage and was yelling at Justin."

"Yeah, Uncle Leland told me that if I didn't calm down and start acting like a professional, he would never hire me for another LAW event. I told him . . ." Justin looked over towards where Paige was rolling around on the floor with André. "Well, let's just say Arielle would wash my mouth out with soap if I repeated it in front of my niece."

"Your mouth needs washed out with soap as it is," Arielle said.

Marlon smacked his hand down on the table a couple times to bring everyone's attention back to him. "Leland left the stage and didn't come back out until halfway through the tag match. Justin, was Leland yelling at you that whole time?"

"Nope. Once I told him . . . what I thought of him, he stomped off. I didn't pay attention to where he went," Justin said. "I was also a little distracted by the doc patching up my head."

"But what is Uncle Leland's motive?" Zoey asked. "He's the one who hired Devon."

"Maybe that's *why* he hired Devon. Leland lured Devon to the event so that he could later kill him," Vivian said as she added Leland's name to her list. "It makes perfect sense."

"No, it doesn't," Zoey mumbled.

Arielle stood up and said, "Vivi, leave it up to my dad and the police. It's their job to investigate and figure out who the killer is."

"Yeah, Nana. It's not your job." Zack gave Vivian a quick kiss on the cheek before he picked up Paige and headed for the front door. "Arielle and I need to get going. We've got some things to do this afternoon. And we promised Jim and Nancy that we'd come over for dinner this evening."

"We better get going, too. Hannah and I have some stuff we want to do," Justin announced. He motioned for Hannah and Terry to follow him.

Within a couple minutes, it was just Zoey, Vivian, Roxanne, and Marlon.

"I guess you'll be leaving soon, too," Roxanne said to Zoey.

"Nah, I got nowhere to be," Zoey said. Aside from work and wrestling events, Zoey rarely had anywhere she needed to be. "And even if I did, I have no way to get there since the police have my car. Plus . . . I need to ask you guys about something. Last night, Devon made a comment about how I never responded to any of the letters that he wrote. But I never got any letters from him—"

"I told you that you shouldn't have kept those a secret," Vivian said.

"Shhh, Vivi!" Roxanne snapped.

"I'm just saying—"

"Knock it off, Ma," Marlon shouted. "You know Roxanne and I had our reasons. You and Pops agreed with us at the time."

"So, Devon did send me letters . . ." Zoey leaned back in the chair and groaned. "And I'm guessing he sent them here since you guys got your hands on them."

During the years she had lived with her parents following her return from Florida, Zoey retrieved the mail from the mailbox countless times. How had she not come across any of Devon's letters?

"Yes, Devon mailed a few letters to our house," Marlon said.

"Four. He sent four," Roxanne said. "The first letter arrived not long after Devon went to prison. Zoey, you were finally starting to show some improvement, and we were worried that reading a letter—"

"Especially that first letter," Vivian interrupted. "Devon was ranting about being in prison and blaming you for it. He said some very nasty things."

"Isn't it a crime to tamper with other people's mail?" Zoey asked.

"We did it to protect you," Roxanne said.

"I understand," Zoey said. She probably would have done the same thing if she had been in their position. She had been in a precarious head-space for a while after the assault. Reading a letter from Devon might have pushed her over the edge. "What happened to the letters?"

"We kept them." Roxanne stood up. "I have them in a shoebox in my closet."

Zoey followed Roxanne down the short hallway to the master bedroom. Her parents had a good-sized suite with a walk-in closet and a bathroom. The walls were painted a unique shade of turquoise, and the wooden furniture had all been handcrafted by an Amish family that Marlon knew. Hanging on the walls were pictures of Marlon and Roxanne from throughout their thirty-three years of marriage.

Zoey and Vivian had a seat on the king-sized bed while Roxanne rummaged around in her walk-in closet. After a minute or two, she emerged with a battered shoebox. Zoey scooted backwards so that she was seated in the middle of the bed. She then knocked the top off the shoebox and pulled out four envelopes. The envelopes, which had all been torn open, bore the return address of the prison where Devon had been incarcerated.

Zoey pulled the first letter out of the torn envelope and scanned Devon's thick, messy handwriting. Every other word was a curse word or a derogatory name, and little of his ranting made sense. Vivian was right, if Zoey had read this letter years ago, it would have pushed her back towards the edge that she had painstakingly retreated from.

"Are you sure you want to read the letters?" Roxanne asked.

"Do I want to read them? No," Zoey said. She would prefer not to know that the letters existed. She also would have preferred that Devon not make a reappearance in her life. "Do I feel like I have to? Yes."

"I want to read them, too." Vivian tried to snatch the letter out of her granddaughter's hand, but Zoey held on to it. Vivian moved closer so that she could read over Zoey's shoulder. "It's been so long since I first read them I forgot what he wrote."

"Are all of the letters this nasty?" Zoey asked after she finished reading.

"The next two are," Roxanne said. She held up the final envelope. "In this one, Devon was apologetic. He took the blame for what happened. He also admitted he was a horrible boyfriend to you. He begged you to give him another chance after he got out of prison. His therapist at the prison included a note about how Devon was a changed man."

Zoey snorted. "Maybe those anger management classes he had to take while in prison really did work."

"This was the letter I was the most concerned about you reading. It arrived over a year after he almost killed you . . ." Roxanne paused to sniffle. "You were doing so much better. You'd finally gotten back in the ring. You were leaving the house to do something other than go to therapy. You were laughing again. Your dad and I were terrified that you would read this and decide to get back together with Devon."

"Trust me, that would not have happened," Zoey said. "But I do wonder why he stopped writing to me."

"He might not have," Roxanne said. "But I called the prison warden after we received the first letter and demanded he stop any more letters from being sent to our house. The warden promised to put a stop to it, but Devon had already mailed the next two letters—"

"Then how did the last letter get through?"

"Devon's therapist sent it."

Zoey pulled the remaining letters out of the envelopes and read over them. She wasn't sure if she should believe the apology letter or not. Devon had proven to her countless times that he was a liar and a master manipulator. The letter could have been just one more attempt at controlling her. Or maybe the therapy really had helped him—Zoey knew how much it had helped her. Either way, the apology would not have influenced her into getting back together with him.

"I'm glad you kept the first three letters from me. But I kinda wish you'd given me the last one. It might have helped me with moving on and closure and all that." Zoey rolled off the bed and stomped out of the room. "Now, if you'll excuse me, I need some time to myself."

Zoey made it all the way to the front door before she remembered that the police had seized her car. She could walk home, but it would take about an hour to walk the two-and-a-half miles. She wasn't feeling up to it—not after everything she had been through in the past day.

Backtracking, Zoey grabbed a set of car keys off the wall mounted key holder.

"I'm taking Bertha."

"Fine. But I'm coming with you," Vivian said. "You shouldn't be alone right now."

"Okay . . ." Zoey said through clenched teeth. She really did not want company at the moment. "But I do not want to hear one more word about Devon for the rest of the day."

NINE

Monday August 20, 2018

"YOU BETTER NOT BE WATCHING PORN AGAIN," Zoey said when she walked into the kitchen on Monday morning and found Vivian sitting at the table with her laptop.

"That was a one-time occurrence," Vivian said. "For research purposes."

"A likely excuse . . ."

While glancing around the room for her cat, Zoey noticed that the framed poster of Matt and Jeff Hardy that hung on the wall above the dining room table was missing. It had been replaced by a corkboard. Tacked to the corkboard were pictures of Sasquatch, JT Perez, Mortimer Cozma, and Leland Freeman. Next to each picture was a notecard.

Zoey pointed towards the corkboard and asked, "What is that supposed to be?"

"That's my suspect board," Vivian said. "It's a way to keep track of our suspects and their motives. As you can see—"

Interrupting, Zoey said, "Take it down, Nana. How many times do I need to tell you that it's not your job to find the killer? Leave it up to the professionals."

Vivian harrumphed in response.

As Zoey took down the corkboard and replaced the framed poster, she spotted her cell phone lying next to her laptop. Last night, before she went to bed, she had left her phone charging on the bedside table. This morning, her phone and the charger were gone. She wondered when

Vivian—her uninvited guest for the second night in a row—had snuck into the bedroom and snatched it. Despite taking a sleeping pill to help overcome her persistent insomnia, nightmares about Devon had kept her up. She dreamed about Devon alive. She dreamed about Devon dead. She also dreamed about Devon coming back to life in a zombie apocalypse scenario.

"Nana, what are you doing with my phone and my laptop?"

"I'm monitoring."

"Monitoring what? What's going on?"

"A lot."

"That's not a very informative answer."

"Last night, the local news did another segment on the murder," Vivian said. "This time they released Devon's identity."

"So word is out that Devon is dead . . ." Zoey grabbed a protein bar and a glass of orange juice, and then she sat across the table from Vivian. "Let me guess . . . My phone is blowing up and you're reading over my incoming texts and listening to voicemails?"

"People have been calling, messaging, and emailing you all night. So far, it's been other wrestlers mostly. And some of your friends. And a lot of fans. They've been making comments on your Facebook page, too." Vivian brought up the Wilde Woman Facebook page and scrolled down so that Zoey could see she had a long list of new comments. "You got almost a thousand page likes since last night. And over two thousand new followers on Instagram."

"I'm not sure if that's a good thing or a bad thing." Zoey yanked the laptop away from Vivian so that she could look under the settings. "Can we disable people from making comments? Or temporarily shut down the page?"

"They'll just find somewhere else to post." Vivian spun the laptop around. "A handful of reporters tried to contact you as well."

Vivian brought up the website for one of the local news stations. An article about Devon filled the screen. Vivian then showed Zoey other online articles about Devon. Between social media and the dirt sheets, the murder was big news within the professional wrestling community.

"How many of these articles mention me?" Zoey asked.

"I haven't been counting. But a lot of them mention that you are Devon's ex-girlfriend and that he spent a few years in prison for assaulting you."

Vivian scrolled down to the bottom of a local news article and showed Zoey where the reporter gave her name and mentioned that she was a local professional wrestling talent.

"Do any of them say that I found Devon's body?"

Vivian shook her head. "A couple of the dirt sheets have pointed out that you were at the same show. But no one is accusing you of killing Devon. Well, except for Reggie."

Reginald Drake was infamous for making snarky comments, spreading rumors, and making unsubstantiated claims about pro wrestlers on his blog, "Ringside with Reggie." He also put out a weekly podcast under the same name. For whatever reason, Reggie had always been one of Devon's staunchest supporters, and, years earlier, he published several vile posts defending Devon and accusing Zoey of hiring someone to beat her up so that she could frame Devon for assault and then capitalize off the ensuing notoriety.

"Why am I not surprised that Reggie is accusing me of killing Devon?" Zoey leaned forward and pounded her forehead against the table. "Ouch . . ."

"Reggie doesn't actually accuse you of anything in his post. He just made some insinuations." Vivian reached around the laptop and patted Zoey on the hand. "As for some of Devon's former fans . . . They have come out and accused you of killing Devon."

Zoey slumped back in the chair and groaned. Was she surprised people thought she had killed Devon? No, not really, but she didn't like that people were posting allegations all over the internet. Whoever had said that there was no such thing as bad publicity had probably never been falsely accused of murder . . . and they could not have predicted the impact that social media would have on mankind.

Zoey tried not to care what people thought of her. Being a pro wrestler put her in the public eye. A lot of people knew who she was—or thought they did. People either loved her, or they hated her. She was used to the rude and hateful comments. That didn't mean she enjoyed hearing some of the nastier things people said about her, but Zoey had learned to live with it.

Being falsely accused of murder was far worse than anything anyone had ever said to her. Okay, maybe it wasn't the most hurtful or degrading thing anyone had ever said about her, but it could be the most damaging.

"Please tell me you aren't responding to anyone," Zoey said to Vivian.

A couple years ago, Vivian had gotten Zoey in trouble when she replied to some unflattering comments made about her granddaughter on social media. Somehow Vivian had figured out Zoey's Facebook password, and she had made the responses while under Zoey's account instead of her own. Zoey changed her passwords after the incident.

"No, I haven't responded," Vivian said. "But I want to. Most people seem to be on your side, but Devon still has a few supporters out there. And they are trashing you all over Facebook. Same way they did back when he almost killed you."

"You mean the people who made idiotic comments about how I must have done something to deserve the beating?" Zoey asked. Disgusted, she shoved the laptop away. "And the others who asked what I expected considering I was dating a professional wrestler?"

"Yep. *Those* people," Vivian sneered. It had been in response to those people that Vivian had gotten Zoey in trouble for posting nasty comments. "Their ringleader created a new Facebook account just to send you a message. She accused you of killing her precious baby boy."

"Oh, Paula . . . She blamed me for everything else. Why wouldn't she blame me for Devon's death?"

Paula Isler had hated Zoey, and she made sure that Zoey knew it from day one. The woman hadn't even given her a chance. Zoey had not been the ideal woman that Paula would have chosen for Devon, and, therefore, she could not possibly be good enough for him. In fact, Zoey doubted Paula ever would have found a woman who she deemed worthy of her son.

In Paula's eyes, Devon could do no wrong. He was perfect—and on the rare occasion that he wasn't perfect, she made excuses for him.

Zoey really had tried to get along with Paula, but Paula had made it increasingly difficult. She was a judgmental, vindictive, and childish woman, and, as Vivian liked to say, Paula was nuttier than a fruitcake. There were times during the relationship where Zoey almost broke it off with Devon because she couldn't take any more of Paula's drama.

Even though it had been Devon's idea to move to Florida, Paula blamed Zoey for their relocation. Paula also blamed Zoey for the assault, and Devon's subsequent jail time. She had harassed Zoey so much after she moved home that Zoey had to file police reports and get a restraining order against her. Paula finally backed off after she was arrested for violating the restraining order. Zoey hadn't seen or heard from her in at least five years.

"I would read the message to you, but it's incoherent. And Paula uses language that a lady shouldn't even know," Vivian said.

"You use that type of language on a frequent basis, Nana."

"I also never claimed to be a lady."

"Neither is Paula."

"And, don't worry, I already sent Chief Coleman a screen shot of Paula's message," Vivian said. "If she keeps harassing you, the chief says you can probably get another restraining order against her."

Vivian pushed the laptop towards Zoey. On the screen was a message that started off with the words "YOU KILLED MY SON!!!!" Zoey skimmed the message, trying to make sense of Paula's run-on sentences and misspelled words. Various swear words and slurs against her made up most of the rambling email. In the end, Paula's main point was to accuse Zoey of murdering Devon. She didn't know how she had killed him. She just knew that Zoey had done it.

Finished with Paula's accusations, Zoey slammed the laptop shut.

"Paula can point the finger at me all she wants. I don't care what crazy theories she comes up with as long as the police don't take them seriously." A loud banging on the door startled Zoey. She glanced at the clock hanging on the wall above Vivian's head. It was seven-thirty. "Who would be knocking on my door this early in the morning?"

"I bet it's the Five-O!" Vivian whispered, using her favorite nickname for the police. She was a diehard Hawaii Five-O fan and had subjected Zoey to reruns at an early age. "They're probably here to arrest you for Devon's murder."

"Shhh! Don't say that."

Zoey tiptoed over to her office nook so that she could look out the window. She peeked around the curtain, terrified that there would be a horde of police officers armed with handcuffs and an arrest warrant gathered on the small deck. She breathed out a sigh of relief when she saw that the person persistently knocking on her door was Arielle. She had her blonde hair pulled back into a ponytail, and she wore yoga pants and a tank top.

Zoey yanked open the door and asked, "What are you doing here?"

"Good morning to you, too." Arielle stepped inside and gave Zoey a hug. "Don't you remember I said I'd pick you up on my way to the gym? My class starts in half-an-hour."

"Shoot! I did forget." Zoey glanced down at her pajamas. "Give me a minute to change."

Yesterday, Zoey and Arielle had talked about going to the gym where Arielle taught various fitness classes—including yoga, kick boxing, and cardio.

After Zoey changed into shorts and a tank top, the three women left for the gym. Zoey rode with Arielle while Vivian followed in her Cadillac. Vivian most likely wouldn't take part in the cardio class—she was in good shape for her age, but she wasn't quite fit enough to keep up with Arielle's high energy class—instead, Vivian would wander the gym and ogle the young men. Most of them were used to her and didn't mind having an elderly audience.

"You doing okay?" Arielle asked while she waited for a break in traffic so that she could pull out of the alley.

"I'm fine."

"I know you're not fine." Arielle gave Zoey a hard jab with her elbow as she pulled out onto South Market Street. "You can pretend with everyone else. But not me. You promised."

"I know, I know," Zoey sighed.

While Zack had been Zoey's closest confidant when they were kids, Arielle began to take his place not long after they became friends. Zoey still told Zack almost everything, but there were certain topics that she couldn't talk to her brother about. Her relationships had been one of them. Zoey had told Arielle everything about her relationship with her high school boyfriend, but she went silent when it came to Devon. Just like she had done with everyone else, she led Arielle to believe that everything was wonderful . . . that Devon was wonderful. Afterwards, when she was recovering in the hospital, she broke down and told Arielle the truth. Arielle then made Zoey promise not to keep secrets or pretend with her ever again.

"Devon came back. Now he's dead," Zoey said, breaking the silence as Arielle pulled into the parking lot at the gym. "I'm anxious. I'm stressed out. I'm glad it's over."

"Just because he's dead doesn't mean it's over," Arielle said.

Zoey didn't want to admit it, but the truth was that it would probably never be over. She may have moved on, but she would never forget what Devon had done to her.

Zoey and Arielle waited for Vivian to park, and then they went inside. The gym was housed in the old bowling alley that had gone out of business when Zoey was a kid. It wasn't as fancy as some of the franchise gyms, but it had the basic equipment and hosted numerous fitness classes throughout the day.

For a Monday morning, the gym was moderately full of people ranging from teenagers to octogenarians. Leaving Vivian chatting with the woman at the front desk, Zoey and Arielle walked towards the glass-walled fitness room at the far end of the gym. The room had once been the arcade, but the new owner had gotten rid of the pool tables and video games.

A Pilates class had just ended, and there were several people milling around the fitness room. Zoey and Arielle waited outside the door while the room emptied out. Had Zoey been paying attention, she would have spotted two of her former high school classmates. Instead, she had her back to the glass wall and didn't see them until it was too late.

Brittany Patterson and Michelle Harris had made Zoey's life a living hell from the first day of kindergarten all the way up through graduation. Even as children, they had had extremely high opinions of themselves, and they had bullied everyone who they thought were inferior to them. Since Zoey watched wrestling, declined to wear the trendy fashions, and refused to pretend that the entire school revolved around them, she was frequently the recipient of Brittany's and Michelle's harassment. Even though it had been twelve years since they had graduated, Brittany and Michelle continued to act like the exact same snobs.

"Zoey! Arielle!" Michelle squealed as she came through the door. She grabbed ahold of the other two women and pulled them in for an awkward hug. "It's been, like, forever."

"Didn't we talk to you just last week?" Arielle asked. "That's hardly forever."

Brittany came through the door after Michelle and latched onto Zoey's arm. Speaking loudly enough for almost everyone in the gym to hear, Brittany said, "Zoey, we heard about your boyfriend getting murdered."

"Ex-boyfriend," Zoey hissed.

"Ladies, we are not discussing this with you," Arielle said, coming to Zoey's defense like she had countless times since eighth grade. "It is an active police investigation."

"But everyone is talking about it." Michelle wedged herself further between Zoey and Arielle, forcing Arielle to take a couple steps backwards. "Zoey, I'm not being nosy or anything . . . but I have to ask, are you the one who killed him?"

"No," Zoey and Arielle said at the same time.

"Well, if you had, I wouldn't blame you. Not after what he did to you," Michelle said.

"Yeah, after he beat you up and almost killed you," Brittany added. "But I guess that's what you get for dating a pro wrestler—"

"What's that supposed to mean?" Zoey asked. Countless people had made the same comment to her over the years, but they never expounded on what they meant. Just once, she wished someone would elaborate.

Ignoring Zoey, Michelle turned to Brittany and said, "I bet Zoey's boyfriend getting murdered is the first time that something real has happened at a pro wrestling event."

Brittany giggled. "That's because pro wrestling is so totally fake. But we better not say that it's fake around Zoey. She might get offended. Or she'll argue with us about how it's real."

Rolling her eyes, Zoey said, "If anyone knows about being fake, it's you two."

"Excuse me?" Michelle took a step back and bumped into Arielle. "What is that supposed to mean exactly?"

"Well . . . the definition of fake is 'not genuine.' And you two are the least genuine people that I have ever met," Zoey said in a condescending voice. Brittany and Michelle always brought out the worst in her. "Plus, Michelle wouldn't be able to fill out her sports bras like that if not for help from a plastic surgeon and a large amount of silicone. Not to mention—"

"Zoey!" Arielle snapped, cutting her off and preventing her from commenting on Brittany's botched nose job or that fact that Michelle had been bleached, bronzed, and botoxed to the max. "Enough."

"How dare you?" Michelle crossed her arms over her silicone-filled breasts and scowled at Zoey. "You are so rude, and you always have been."

"If you want to talk about being rude . . ." Zoey said. "You're the ones airing my dirty laundry loudly enough for almost everyone in the entire place to hear."

"The two of you have been giving Zoey crap about watching wrestling for as long as I've known you," Arielle said. "But not once have you ever said what you have against it."

Brittany huffed in annoyance. "Michelle and I have told Zoey multiple times that we think pro wrestling is stupid. That's what we have against it."

"Oh, please, that's hardly a reason," Arielle said. "My daughter is eigh-teen-months-old, and she can make a better argument than that."

"But it *is* stupid," Michelle said. "Everyone knows that pro wrestling is the sport for delinquents. It's lowbrow entertainment. And only trashy people watch it."

"Have either of you ever watched wrestling?" When Brittany and Michelle confirmed that they had never watched it, Zoey continued, "Then how do you know you wouldn't like it?"

"I told you, because it's stupid," Brittany said.

"Look, I'll be the first to admit that wrestling can be ridiculous," Zoey said, speaking the truth. "I mean, what it all comes down to is a bunch of men and women wearing little more than their underwear pretending to beat each other up. But . . . Come on, give me more than that."

"Well, it's . . . it's lewd," Michelle said.

"I'll admit that pro wrestling has had some . . . shall we say . . . question-able moments," Zoey said. "But I've seen far worse things on cable than what I've seen on wrestling shows."

The majority of what took place during the WWE's Attitude Era could be described as lewd. Zoey had grown up during the Attitude Era that had covered the late-1990s and early-2000s, and it definitely had an impact on her, and it hadn't always been a positive impact.

"What else don't you like about wrestling?" Arielle asked.

"Well . . . uhh . . . the wrestlers use steroids and other drugs," Brittany said.

"Every sport has suffered from scandals involving steroids and other performance enhancing drugs. It's not a problem that's confined solely to wrestling. Even high school athletes have been known to use ste-roids," Zoey said. She decided not to acknowledge that she knew several wrestlers who used steroids despite the adverse effects it had on their bodies. "As for other drugs . . . Well, drugs are just a problem period. What else?"

"Wrestling . . . depicts violence," Michelle said.

"Well, of course, pro wrestling depicts violence," Zoey said. "Do I need to return to the point about how pro wrestling is basically a bunch of people pretending to beat each other up? Or do I need to reiterate the pretending part? We aren't purposely trying to hurt each other."

"Personally, I've seen more violence on some of the cartoons my daughter watches," Arielle said. "The cartoon characters survive trauma that would kill an actual person."

Brittany smirked. "If you're just going to stand here and argue with us, you may as well tell us what is so great about wrestling."

"Because it's about more than just the wrestling. It's about the wrestlers," Zoey said. "It provides multiple forms of entertainment for people of every age and gender."

"Are we arguing about wrestling?" Vivian asked as she elbowed her way into the group.

Continuing, Zoey said, "Like all good stories, wrestling has good guys and bad guys. Heroes and villains. We call them baby faces and heels. They all have backstories and unique appearances."

"And they are involved in different storylines," Vivian added.

"Sometimes the storylines are totally unbelievable, and you have to . . . suspend your belief," Arielle said. "It's like watching *Jurassic Park*. You know that the dinosaurs are fake, but you can enjoy the movie anyway."

"In wrestling there is action and drama," Zoey said. "Comedy and romance."

"Betrayal and rivalries," Vivian added.

"It's serious."

"And ridiculous."

"I already said it's ridiculous, Nana," Zoey said. "But wrestling can be heartbreaking."

"And heartwarming."

"It's the best thing since sliced bread."

"Actually . . . sliced bread was invented in 1928," Vivian said. "So, technically, sliced bread is the best thing since pro wrestling."

"Pro wrestling tells a story. It's like theater or a live action movie. An athletic soap opera where the wrestlers do all their own stunts. And they only have one chance to get it right."

"Not to mention that there's a whole lot of hot, sweaty men in speedos," Vivian said.

Michelle and Brittany exchanged a look before they both burst out laughing.

"It still sounds totally stupid," Michelle said.

Zoey opened her mouth to respond, but Arielle cut her off with a sharp pinch on the arm.

"Ladies, we won't argue with you any longer," Arielle said as she dragged Zoey into the fitness room. "Talking to the two of you is about as productive as beating a dead horse."

Pitching in to help Arielle get the fitness room ready for class, Zoey said, "Thanks for getting me out of that. I would have argued with them all morning."

"I know you would have." Arielle gestured over her shoulder to the floor-to-ceiling windows. On the other side of the glass, Vivian continued lecturing Michelle and Brittany. "And it looks like Vivi plans to keep at it."

It was a relief when Arielle got the class started. It was the first time since her match on Saturday night where her every thought wasn't about Devon and what happened to him. For a brief period, she didn't think about his death at all.

After class, Zoey said goodbye to Arielle and left her at the juice bar to rehydrate.

Since Vivian was no longer arguing with Michelle and Brittany, Zoey took a lap around the gym to look for her. She found her nana taking a leisurely stroll on a treadmill while chatting with a college-aged girl. They both appeared to be eyeing up a muscular young man who was using a pulldown machine to work out his arms and the muscles in his upper body.

"Stop ogling that guy and let's get out of here," Zoey said as she leaned against the front part of the treadmill. "I'm hungry, and I need a shower."

"Yes, you do need a shower," Vivian said as she waved her hand around in front of her nose. "And I'm only pretending to look at the stud muffin."

"Sure . . ." Zoey winked at Vivian.

"All right . . . Maybe I was admiring the view." Vivian returned Zoey's wink. "But look who's on the other side of him. That's who I'm really looking at."

Zoey leaned to the side so that she could see around the pulldown machine. At the far end of the gym was the free weight area. Several people were using the weights and bench press equipment. Zoey recognized a couple of the people—including a man who had an overabundance of thick, dark hair covering his body from head to foot. She watched as Sasquatch leaned down and grasped a barbell that had two one-hundred-pound weights on each end. Sasquatch then lifted the barbell straight up towards his waist in a deadlift.

"And . . .?" Zoey wasn't quite sure why Vivian was suddenly so interested in Sasquatch. "We see Squatch at the gym all the time. Is there a reason you're checking him out today?"

"Use your brain." Vivian flicked Zoey's temple. "Yesterday, Squatch's back hurt so badly that he couldn't get out of bed to come to the open gym . . . Today he's in the gym deadlifting four-hundred pounds . . . That can't be good for his alleged back injury."

"Maybe he recovered fast," Zoey said, giving Sasquatch the benefit of the doubt. "Or he was being a drama queen yesterday morning. Wouldn't be the first time."

"Uh huh." Behind her thick glasses, Vivian rolled her eyes. "I think we need to mosey on over there and say hello. Find out how Squatch's back is and see what he has to say about Saturday night. Maybe he'll tell us where he disappeared to after intermission."

"Yeah, and maybe he'll confess to murdering Devon," Zoey said sarcastically.

"Exactly!" Vivian grinned. "Come on, let's go talk to him."

"Absolutely not." Zoey grasped Vivian's upper arm and tried to pull her towards the exit. Vivian swatted her granddaughter's hand away. "We are not interrogating Squatch. Just because you suspect him doesn't give you the right to question him. Let the police handle it."

"I just want to hear what Squatch has to say."

Knowing Vivian wouldn't drop it, Zoey decided to just go along with what her nana wanted to do. What was the worst that could happen? Sasquatch might get mad at them?

"Just let me do all of the talking," Zoey said to Vivian as they made their way to the other side of the gym. "I'm much more subtle than you. Plus, Squatch doesn't like you."

"Why doesn't he like me?" Vivian asked, sounding offended.

"Oh, I don't know . . . Maybe because you constantly harass him about his body hair."

Vivian claimed that Sasquatch's excessive body hair disgusted her. For years, she had been pestering him about doing something to get rid of it. Her latest suggestion was to remove the hair permanently through laser treatments.

Zoey wasn't a big fan of Sasquatch either. He was arrogant and condescending to just about everyone. And his body hair grossed her out as well. She was used to male wrestlers—like Devon and both of her brothers—who shaved or waxed their body hair.

Sasquatch also hadn't exactly been the most sympathetic person after Zoey moved back from Florida. She didn't quite know how to define their friendship—or if "friendship" was even the right word—but there was no doubt that it had been built on a solid foundation of their mutual hatred of Devon Isler.

"Hey, Squatch," Zoey said as she walked up to him. He grunted in response. "So . . . Saturday night was pretty crazy, right? Can you believe that someone killed Devon?"

Sasquatch shrugged his hairy shoulders. "Can't say he didn't deserve it."

"That's not nice, Squatch."

"I'm not a nice guy." Sasquatch grimaced. "The way I see it, we both have someone to thank for killing Devon. Unless the rumors are true, and you're the one who killed him. Then I guess I have you to thank."

"I didn't kill him," Zoey hissed.

"All right . . . Just saying I wouldn't blame you if you had." Sasquatch bent down and lifted the barbell again. After setting it back down, he said, "But, if you didn't kill him . . . who did?"

"I don't know. All I know is that I didn't do it," Zoey said. She decided not to tell Sasquatch that she was the person who found Devon's body. If he hadn't heard about that yet, he would hear about it soon enough. "But I'm not the only person who the blabbermouths are starting rumors about. Some people think you killed Devon."

"Yeah, I saw what people are saying about me online. Heck, I'd suspect me, too. I mean, the weasel planted drugs on me and then called the cops. He ruined my life. Seems like a pretty good motive to kill him."

"Why would Devon plant drugs on you?" Zoey asked. "You were his best friend."

Zoey had heard Sasquatch claim countless times that the drugs had not been his. She had always wondered why he hadn't been able to prove it, but Sasquatch had never offered up an explanation. Maybe he didn't have one.

"I thought Devon was my best friend." Sasquatch grabbed Zoey by the shoulders and gave her a violent shake. "The same way you thought he was your loving boyfriend. Out of everybody, you should know what a backstabbing, egotistical jerk he was. Devon only cared about himself, and he would take anyone down to get what he wanted."

"I can't argue with you there," Zoey said. Devon had no idea what loyalty meant. "That still doesn't explain why he did it."

"Because he was jealous. We were at a show and a WWE scout approached me. He thought I showed potential. Devon overheard the conversation and tried to butt in. The scout basically told Devon he didn't have a chance of making it past the indies. Devon was furious. Afterwards, he went off on me. Claimed I was holding him back and making him look bad. He said if he wasn't so busy carrying the team and making me look good, he would have been noticed by the scout. I told him he was being delusional. A few days later, the cops came knocking on our door."

"But if the drugs weren't yours . . . how come you couldn't prove it?" Zoey asked.

"They never found any drugs in my system," Sasquatch continued. "No steroids. No painkillers. Not even a trace of marijuana. Clearly, I wasn't using any of the drugs. But Devon got his little minions to back his lies about how I was selling the drugs to other wrestlers. If anyone was dealing drugs, it was him. I know, for a fact, that he was using the steroids."

"Before Saturday night, when was the last time you saw Devon?" Vivian asked.

"Years ago. When he sat on the stand in court and lied about the drugs. I went to prison. He moved to Florida. I was still in prison when he moved back after his dad died. By the time I got out, he'd moved back to Florida. And dragged you along," Sasquatch said to Zoey. "Now, if you'll excuse me, ladies, I want to get back to my workout that you two so rudely interrupted."

"One more thing." Vivian stepped between Sasquatch and the barbell. "We heard you had an altercation with Devon during intermission."

"So what?" Sasquatch harshly laughed. "It's not like I was the only one. I just told Devon what I thought of him. And took a swing at him. Leland broke it up before it turned into a real fight. He ripped me a new one for being immature and dwelling on the past. Leland also told me that if I didn't calm down and learn how to play nice, he'd never hire me again. I told Leland to go to hell. And then I left."

"You left?" Zoey asked. "Before the show was over?"

"Yeah. I took my stuff and went home," Sasquatch said.

That would explain why no one saw Sasquatch backstage after intermission.

"Can anyone confirm that you went home?" Vivian asked. "Roommate? Neighbor?"

"What? Are you serious? Is this some kind of interrogation?" Sasquatch asked.

"We're just wondering if you have an alibi for the time of death," Vivian said.

"You two are nuts." Sasquatch crossed his arms over his chest and glared at Vivian. "I didn't kill Devon. But I do want to personally thank whoever did."

"That doesn't answer my question," Vivian said. "Do you have an alibi or not?"

"Yes. I have an alibi," Sasquatch said. "On my way home, I got pulled over by a State Trooper for having a busted taillight. I don't know what the exact time was, but it wasn't any more than twenty minutes after I left. Anything else you need to ask me about?"

"Yeah. How come you missed yesterday's open gym?" Zoey asked.

"What? I'm not allowed to miss on occasion. Did I lose my perfect attendance award for the year?" Sasquatch asked. "Maybe my back hurt from being slammed through a table the night before, so I decided to take the day off."

"Seems a little strange you decided to take off the day after Devon was murdered. Even if you were injured," Vivian said. She jabbed Sasquatch in the chest. "I figured you would have shown up to gossip with everyone else."

"Like I said . . . Maybe I just needed a day off." Sasquatch winked at Zoey. "I also had some . . . uh . . . female companionship yesterday morning."

"I did not need to know that," Zoey said.

Sasquatch grabbed his towel and his water bottle. Without any parting words, he headed towards the men's locker room. Vivian took a few steps after him, but Zoey grabbed her and hauled her in the other direction.

As Zoey guided Vivian outside and into her car, she reminded her nana that they were not the police and that it was not their job to question suspects or investigate what happened in the VFW Hall's parking lot on Saturday night.

"I'm just worried about you. What if that handsome detective comes after you?" Vivian pulled out of the gym's parking lot and headed towards the tattoo shop. Changing the subject, she asked, "What are your plans for the rest of the day?"

"Laundry and cleaning." The tattoo shop was closed on Mondays, so Zoey used the day off to catch up on mundane chores.

"Bah! Why don't you come to the historical society with me?" Vivian asked. "Now that she's eighty and halfway to senile, the board finally decided they're going to force Philomena Lyster to step down as the president at the end of the year. They're electing her replacement today. I need to go rub it in the old coot's face—"

"Nana, Philomena is only a year older than you. And, no, I will not tag along just to join you in terrorizing your nemesis."

"That's not my only reason for going to historical society meetings. I also go for the wine and the snacks," Vivian said. Her rivalry with Philomena dated back to when they went to school together. Vivian renewed her membership at the historical society every year just so she could attend all of the meetings and hassle Philomena. "Or I could skip the meeting, and we can go track down our other two suspects. Maybe Leland or JT will be more willing to talk."

"They're not our suspects. And it's not our job to question them. I just explained that."

"Oh, you're no fun!"

Vivian pulled into the tattoo shop's parking lot and parked her Cadillac between Zack's Jeep and a dark gray SUV. Zoey wasn't surprised that Zack was there. Just because the shop was closed on Sundays and Mondays didn't stop him from coming in to work. He frequently scheduled appointments on his off days or used them to catch up on sketches.

Zoey gave Vivian one last warning about leaving the investigation up to the police, and then sent her on her way. She could only hope her nana would go to the historical society in the afternoon instead of tracking down "suspects."

Zoey walked over to the side porch and let herself in through the French doors that opened into the shop's breakroom. A hallway ran through the house to the front door, and the walls had been painted a dark red. Between the dark paint and the old wood flooring, the hallway always seemed much darker than it really was.

On the one side of the hallway, three doors led to private rooms. When Zack started out tattooing, he had worked at a shop where all the artists shared one big, open room. He hated the lack of privacy—for himself and for his clients. When Marlon started remodeling the old house to turn it into a tattoo shop, Zack had him put up walls for four private rooms. The fourth room was on the opposite side of the hallway between the breakroom and the staircase.

Zoey headed down the hallway. As she passed the extra-large mirror that hung on the wall, she caught sight of her reflection. Thanks to the intense workout, Zoey was a flushed, sweaty mess with frizzy hair.

Zoey was about to push open the door to Zack's room when she heard her brother say, "My sister did not kill Devon. Zoey isn't capable of doing something like that."

TEN

WHO ARE YOU TALKING TO? Zoey wondered as she peeked between the door and the doorframe. There was enough space for her to see a sliver of the room.

Zack sat at the desk tucked into the far corner of the room. Between Zoey and Zack—seated on the edge of the client chair—was Detective Tyler Gates. Today he wore a blue dress shirt and gray pants that made him look a lot more professional than he had at the crime scene in his shorts and t-shirt.

After taking a good look at him, Zoey understood why Vivian kept referring to him as the "handsome detective." At the crime scene, it had not escaped Zoey's notice that the detective was a good-looking man. Thanks, however, to the parking lot's hazy overhead lights, she hadn't been able to get a good look at him. She had also been distracted by her ex-boyfriend's dead body.

Like Devon, Detective Gates was attractive in a clean-cut, All-American way. They both looked like they could have once been the blue-eyed, blonde-haired heartthrob lead singer of a teeny bopper boy band. While he was in good shape, Detective Gates was nowhere near as muscular as Devon had been. Zoey also got the feeling that the detective was not as arrogant as Devon and didn't flaunt his good looks.

What was the detective doing at the tattoo shop? Zoey couldn't imagine that he was there to get a tattoo—especially when he appeared to be on the clock. Had Detective Gates come by to talk to Zoey, but, since she wasn't home, had to settle for Zack? Was Detective Gates here to arrest Zoey for murdering Devon? She hoped not—especially since she knew she hadn't killed him. Or was Zack the person that Detective Gates wanted to talk to? It wasn't implausible that the detective would want to question her brother.

"I attended the victim's autopsy earlier this morning," Detective Gates said to Zack. "Devon Isler died because of blunt force trauma to the head. Part of his skull was crushed. The coroner believes that the victim was attacked from behind while kneeling to tamper with your brother's tires."

"Yeah. And?" Zack asked, sounding confrontational. "What makes you think Zoey killed Devon just for messing with her Jeep or trying to do something to Justin's tires?"

"I'm not saying your sister murdered the victim because she caught him tampering with your brother's car," Detective Gates said. "But, as far as I can tell, she did have plenty of other reasons for wanting Devon Isler dead. Maybe the vandalism to her car was the last straw."

"So what if Zoey had a motive?" Zack asked. Zoey heard a clacking noise as Zack slammed something—most likely a pencil—against the top of his desk. "She'll be the first person to admit she had a motive. That doesn't mean she killed Devon. I'm telling you, there is no way Zoey would have or could have done it."

"Correct me if I'm wrong, Mr. Wilde, but your sister appears to be stronger than the average woman," Detective Gates said. "I saw her wrestle on Saturday night, and she didn't seem to have much trouble throwing around the faux-Amish girl. Your sister appears to be physically capable of bashing in a man's head. Especially Devon Isler's head."

"I keep telling you . . ." Zack said. "Just because Zoey *could* have bashed in Devon's head with the sledgehammer doesn't mean she did it."

Zoey watched as Detective Gates slid off the edge of the chair and leaned over Zack. "How do you know the murder weapon is a sledgehammer?"

"Duh," Zack said. "Zoey told me."

Shut up, Zack! Zoey thought.

"Of course, your sister told you . . . After I specifically asked her not to tell anyone. Just don't tell anyone else." Detective Gates sighed and sat back down on the client chair. "I read the police report, and I saw the pictures that were taken when your sister was admitted to the hospital. I know what the victim did to her."

"No. You have no idea what that bastard did to my sister," Zack said. He shoved his chair back and stood up. Zoey couldn't see Zack, but she could hear his flip flops slapping against the wood floor as he paced the small room. "The pictures might show the physical damage, but they don't show the emotional or mental trauma Devon caused. And the pictures don't show how much Zoey's changed as a person. How she used to be this confident, fearless, kick-ass woman until Devon's verbal abuse and manipulations wore her down to an anxious, introverted hot mess."

Detective Gates cleared his throat. "You're right, the pictures only show the physical outcome of the assault. I have no idea what your sister's relationship with the victim had been like. Nor do I know what your sister has gone through since then."

"Exactly," Zack said. Zoey watched as her brother stopped pacing and collapsed into his chair. "For the six months they lived in Florida, Devon isolated Zoey from us. We didn't see her, and none of us talked to her that much. Yeah, we texted. But we hardly ever talked on the phone. That should have been the first indication that something was wrong. But we all thought she was busy spreading her wings. None of us really thought that anything was seriously wrong. Nonetheless, I should have known something was up with Zoey. We've always had a sixth sense about each other. You know, the 'Twin Thing' that people talk about. It's real. And Zoey and I have it. I can't read her mind or anything. But I know when something is wrong. But . . . but she was so far away. And I had just gotten married, so I was caught up in starting out my married life with Arielle. Plus Quincy and I were opening our tattoo shop. If I had only paid attention to my gut—"

"You can't blame yourself for what happened." Detective Gates shook his head. "If Zoey didn't open up to you—"

"Yes, I can blame myself. And I still do." Zack kicked the plastic trash can next to his desk and slammed it into the wall. "Do you have any idea what it's like to get a call telling you that your twin sister is in intensive care because her boyfriend beat the crap out of her?"

"No. Thankfully, I have never received one of those calls. But I have made that call more times than I care to remember." Detective Gates spoke softly, and Zoey got the feeling that informing family members that their loved ones were in the hospital or dead had taken an emotional toll on him. "But I do have a sister. We aren't twins. Nor are we as close as you and Zoey seem to be. But I would be devastated if something happened to her."

"To this day, it makes me sick thinking about it," Zack said. "It was right after five in the morning on a Sunday when the police called my parents to tell them what happened. Justin was fresh out of high school and still living at home. He was the one who called me. By the time I got to my parents' house, Mom was hysterical and Dad had a broken hand. I still don't know what he punched, but it did more damage to him than he did to it. Pop-Pop had to force Dad to go to the hospital to get his hand taken care of. Meanwhile, Mom, Nana, and Arielle managed to get on a direct flight from Harrisburg to Orlando. Chief Coleman . . . he's my father-in-law . . . drove them to the airport in one of the Linville cruisers so that they could make the flight."

"Why didn't you go down on the flight with your mom?" Detective Gates asked.

"Believe me, I wanted to. Mom and Nana were going. Dad would have been with them had he not broken his hand. I wanted to take his place, but Arielle insisted that she should be the one to go. We had a huge fight about it. I still regret the things I said. But Arielle was right, Zoey needed her more than she needed me."

Of course, Zoey had wanted Arielle. Arielle had been the only sane one in the bunch. Roxanne and Vivian had tried to coddle Zoey, and everyone had treated her like a fragile bauble that was on the verge of breaking. She was already broken. How much more broken did they think she could get? Yes, Zoey had been in a delicate place at the time. Being handled with kid gloves had only made her feel worse, and the combined rage of Zack, Justin, Marlon, and Kazimir had only made her mad at them. They had wanted to rush to her rescue and fight her battles for her, but it was too late for that. Her war was over. It didn't matter if she had won or lost. All that mattered was that she had survived.

Arielle—while probably not as calm and collected as she had portrayed herself—had treated Zoey the same way that she always had. Arielle was the only one who could see what Zoey needed in those first days after the assault. It wasn't a shoulder to cry on or a knight in shining armor. It was a friend who would hold her hand and help her rebuild herself. Arielle was the one who reached down into the abyss and pulled Zoey out of a spiraling state of depression.

"How long did it take you to get to Orlando?" Detective Gates asked Zack.

"Too long," Zack said. "Justin and I didn't get to Orlando until late afternoon. But that was for the best. I'm sure you read about it in the report, but Devon took off after the neighbors broke into the apartment to save Zoey. The police didn't catch him until early afternoon. My brother and I had this crazy idea that we were going to find Devon before the police could. But they caught him while we were in the air."

"What would you two have done if you found him?" Detective Gates asked.

"Probably killed him," Zack said.

"I understand the sentiment, but killing Devon wouldn't have helped your sister."

"I know, I know. It's just that Justin and I were so scared and angry. We felt helpless. Talking about finding and killing Devon was the only thing that kept us sane," Zack said. His voice sounded heavy and strained. "It took years of therapy to build Zoey back up to where she is today. For a couple weeks after she moved home, she was having anxiety attacks almost every day. One second, she would be fine, the next she would be curled up in the fetal position. She didn't leave my parents' house for three months except to go to therapy. And she gave up wrestling for over a year. Zoey couldn't bear to get back into the ring because getting physical with another person would trigger an anxiety attack."

Prior to moving to Florida, Zoey had never experienced an anxiety attack. Sure, she had anxious moments. But the anxiety had never overwhelmed her. The longer she was with Devon—and away from her family—the worse her anxiety got. It controlled her life worse than Devon had. The anxiety attacks had been sporadic at first. Then, as her anxiety mounted, the attacks came more frequently. By the time she decided to leave Devon, she was having at least one anxiety attack a day. She was on the edge, and anything could nudge her over. Devon, of course, had ridiculed her for the attacks.

Zoey tuned back into the conversation she was eavesdropping on when she heard Detective Gates say, "I saw your sister on Saturday night. She looks like she's doing okay now. And had I known what she was going through with her abusive ex-boyfriend showing up out of the blue, I wouldn't have been able to tell she was upset."

"What you saw on Saturday night was an act. That was Zoey the Wrestler. It's her alter ego. It's totally fake. But it's also the closest she ever gets to being like her old self."

"People change over time," Detective Gates pointed out.

"Yeah, I know." Zack drew in a deep breath and sighed. "But it's like Zoey hit a wall during her healing process. She got to a point where she was comfortable and then she quit trying. She's been stuck treading water since then. Her therapist tried to help her. We all tried to help her. But Zoey . . . Well, it's like she didn't want to help herself. I know everyone puts up a wall to protect themselves. Zoey built an entire armed fortress to keep people out. Maybe now that Devon is dead, she can get closer to being the woman that she was before he broke her."

"Hopefully, she does." Changing the subject, Detective Gates said, "Mr. Wilde, did you talk to the victim on Saturday night?"

"Heck no. I avoided Devon. I was afraid of what I might do to him if I got near him."

"Does that mean you still haven't gotten over the urge to kill Devon Isler?" Detective Gates asked. Zoey stepped back from the door as the detective slid off the edge of the client chair and stood up. "I have to ask, but where were you following the victim's match?"

"Inside the banquet hall. Watching the rest of the show," Zack said.

Before Detective Gates could ask Zack another question, Zoey knocked on the door and then walked into the room.

Detective Gates spun around to face Zoey. "Miss Wilde, just the person I was looking for. I need you to come to the police department with me."

"HOW DID YOU AND YOUR BROTHERS get into wrestling?"

Zoey glanced at Detective Gates out of the corner of her eye. He hadn't even fired the engine of his police-issued SUV and already he was grilling her. Zoey took it as a good sign that he let her sit in the passenger seat opposed to sticking her in the back seat.

Detective Gates had stopped by the apartment while Zoey was at the gym with Arielle. After determining that Zoey was not home, he had been about to return to the police department when Zack showed up. Zack, who had come in to get some sketching done, invited the detective to wait until Zoey got back from the gym.

"My dad was a wrestler. And so were his parents," Zoey said, answering the detective's question. "My brothers and I pretty much grew up in the ring. We spent almost every other weekend of our childhood traveling around the Mid-Atlantic states to watch our dad wrestle."

By the time Zoey and Zack were born, Marlon had cut back on how many wrestling events he took part in every year. In the early part of his career, Marlon had been on the road at least two-hundred days of the year. Still, two or three weekends a month, Marlon wrestled at an event somewhere within driving distance of their home.

"How did you get into wrestling?" Zoey asked.

"My dad and my uncle used to take me and my cousins to wrestling events in the Philly area when we were kids," Detective Gates said as he turned the key and started the ignition. "Maybe I saw your dad wrestle. What was his ring name?"

"He was half of the tag team Wilde and Free."

"I remember them!" Detective Gates said. He looked over at Zoey and flashed her a toothy smile. "Wilde and Free were one of my favorite tag teams when I was a kid. I know I've got pictures with them somewhere. What a small world."

"Microscopic."

"What are Wilde and Free up to these days? I assume that they're both retired by now."

"Yeah, Dad retired about eight years ago. He's gotten into the ring a couple times since then, and he still occasionally runs training camps," Zoey said. After being a tag team for all those years, Leland had felt betrayed when Marlon hung up his boots. "Uncle Leland finally gave up wrestling last year when he started up the Linville Association of Wrestling."

"Hold on, Leland Freeman is the other half of Wilde and Free? I interviewed him Saturday night. He never said a word about it. Of course, I only asked Leland about the victim. I didn't really ask him anything about wrestling that wasn't related to Saturday night," Detective Gates said as he drove a block down Market Street. "But that's really cool that you're a third-generation wrestler."

Zoey could make an argument that she was a fifth-generation wrestler.

After immigrating to the United States from Russia in the late-eighteen-hundreds, her freakishly strong great-great-grandfather Vladimir Vilde was recruited to be a strongman at Coney Island. At first, Vladimir was merely a strongman who showed off his abnormal strength. A few years later—after leaving Coney Island and joining a traveling circus—he began wrestling other strongmen. These were real matches, and the wrestling was viewed as a legitimate sport. The matches could sometimes last for hours without much action taking place. While these lengthy matches might sound boring compared to the current level of entertainment provided by professional wrestling, they were top quality entertainment back in the day.

While he was part of the traveling carnival, Vladimir married one of his fellow carnies. Great-great-grandmother Zoje—who Zoey was named after—was the tattooed lady in the freak show. According to family lore, she grew tired of being gawked at and decided to join her husband in the wrestling ring. Zoje wrestled some of the other women who were part of the circus troupe. She also wrestled men—including her own husband. By the time Zoje got in the ring, wrestling was transitioning from a real sport to fixed sports entertainment. Since people gambled large amounts of money on the legitimate wrestling matches, the carnies decided to stage the outcome of the matches. That way they could swindle the customers out of large sums of money.

During their time with the carnival, Vladimir and Zoje had a few children. Their oldest son, Maksym Vilde, left the carnival as a young man. After changing his name to Max Wilde, Zoey's great-grandfather took what he had learned during his childhood with the carnival and got involved in booking and promoting pro wrestling events. He also managed Zoey's grandfather, Kazimir "The Wilde Man" Wilde, during the first half of his career.

"Here we are," Detective Gates said as he pulled into the police department's lot.

The Linville Police Department and borough offices were housed in a relatively new two-story brick building. It had been constructed fifteen or so years earlier to replace the older, smaller police department. The tattoo shop was only a few blocks away.

Zoey reluctantly followed Detective Gates inside to the lobby. On the left side of the lobby were the borough offices, and on the right was the police department. Chief Jim Coleman was in the front office with the receptionists. He spotted Zoey through the bulletproof window and rushed out into the lobby.

After saying hello to Zoey, Jim turned to Gates and asked, "What is she doing here?"

"Ms. Wilde needs to give her formal statement about Saturday night," Detective Gates said as he brushed past his chief and headed back the hallway towards the offices. He gestured for Zoey to come with him. "I also need to ask her some more questions about her past relationship with the victim. Just standard procedure stuff."

"You don't have to answer any questions that you don't feel comfortable answering," Jim whispered to Zoey. "In fact, you don't have to answer any questions without a lawyer present."

"It's okay, Jim," Zoey said.

Belatedly, Zoey remembered Pasqual Cipriani had told her not to talk to Detective Gates again unless he was present. She thought about calling him, but decided not to. She hadn't killed Devon. She had nothing to hide. Besides, Pasqual knew she had to give a statement, and he hadn't said anything about wanting to be there when she did that.

"All right, Zoey. But you can come get me at any time if you need me. You know where my office is," Jim said as he led her past his office to the one that was next door.

Detective Gates's office was spartan. The desk, an office chair, and two uncomfortable looking guest chairs took up most of the floor space. There were no personal items sitting around on the desk, nor was there anything hanging on any of the walls. Zoey reminded herself that Detective Gates was new to the Linville Police Department.

"I know you're the one who's supposed to be asking the questions," Zoey said. She had a seat in one of the chairs. It turned out to be even more uncomfortable than it looked. "But would it be okay if I asked you a question? For my peace of mind?"

"You can ask," Detective Gate said. He had a seat behind his desk. "And

I'll answer if I can. You understand I might not be able to answer considering this is an active investigation."

"I know Devon was living somewhere in Florida since he was released from prison. But when exactly did he get back to Lancaster County?"

"Mr. Isler left Florida sometime on Sunday. He was driving, and he spent Sunday night in North Carolina. He arrived at his mother's house early Monday evening. According to his mother, this is the first time he's been back since getting out of prison."

"So he was back for about five days before we crossed paths on Saturday." A bubble of anxiety swelled in Zoey's gut, and she had to fight to hold it back. "How could he do that? After what he did to me? Shouldn't he have had to stay away from me?"

"The way the law sees it . . . Mr. Isler paid his debt to society. He served his sentence and was a free man. You didn't have a restraining order against him. There was nothing preventing him from contacting you or approaching you—"

"That's so unfair to victims." Zoey leaned back in the chair and ran her hands through her damp hair. Detective Gates had given her a few minutes to jump in the shower and change. She appreciated the gesture, but she figured he did it more for his benefit than her own. After sweating profusely during Arielle's class, she smelled almost as bad as a locker room following a wrestling event. "Devon came back to Pennsylvania because of me. He saw me at a show down in Florida last Saturday. I wrestled for a promotion that put on a show in Kissimmee. Devon told me that he saw me pictured on an advertisement. He went to the show and apparently got his picture taken with me. I checked my Wilde Woman Facebook page, but I have so many fans who post pictures of themselves with me . . . But how did I not recognize him at the time?"

Detective Gates cleared his throat. "I found the victim's cell phone in his gym bag and was able to go through his photo gallery . . ."

Gates flipped open a folder and shuffled through some paperwork. He then held up an 8x10 photograph of Zoey and a man. She was dressed in her typical purple animal print leggings and Wilde Woman tank top. The man had his arm wrapped around Zoey's shoulders and was holding her tightly against his side. The stiff, fake smile on her face showed how uncomfortable she was with the encounter.

Zoey leaned forward and snatched the picture out of Detective Gates's hand so that she could get a better look at it. The man next to her had hidden his eyes behind mirrored aviator sunglasses. He also had shaggy brown hair and a wispy beard. Aside from being a similar height and weight to Devon, the man in the picture only vaguely resembled him. Even when he'd had long hair, he always kept it styled. He also shaved daily. Devon hated having anything more than a five o'clock shadow—and that he had only just barely tolerated.

But it was no wonder Zoey hadn't recognized him at the time. She tried to give all fans a few seconds of her time, but she brushed off the single men who hit on her. She would just sign her autograph and smile for the picture before sending the man on his way.

"Is that him?" Detective Gates asked.

"That's Devon." Zoey tossed the picture onto the desk. She couldn't stand looking at it any longer. "What was Devon up to for the five days he was back? Where was he living?"

"I shouldn't tell you this," Detective Gates said. "But . . . he'd been living with his mother. And, from what I can tell, he'd been spending the majority of his time stalking you. About a month ago, he made up social media accounts under fake names so that he could follow you on Facebook, Instagram, and every other social media platform you use."

"He must have done that after he saw my picture on the advertisement." Zoey pulled her phone out of her purse and opened her Facebook account. "What name was he using?"

"That I can't tell you," Detective Gates said. "But he posted numerous pictures from the Kissimmee show on your Facebook page. And tagged you on Instagram. Including the picture he had taken with you. You'll be able to find him very easily."

Zoey scanned through the pictures that fans had posted on her Wilde Woman Facebook page. She always encouraged fans to share pictures of her. Over the years, she had gotten some good in-ring photos of herself that way. Within seconds, she found the one of her and Devon. He'd used the name Mike Snyder to create the account. She checked and saw that he had been quite active on her page in the past few weeks. She had even interacted with him.

"Did Devon limit his stalking to online?" Zoey asked. "Or was he . . ."

"Stalking you in person? Yes, he was."

Detective Gates pulled a short stack of pictures from the folder and spread them out across his desk. There were pictures of Zoey at two wrestling events—at the Kissimmee show the previous Saturday and in Scranton on Friday night. There were also pictures of her sitting on the small deck at her apartment, outside the tattoo shop, and at her parents' house. There were ones of her in the grocery store, the gym, and walking down the street in Linville.

The bubble of anxiety burst, flooding Zoey with a nauseous feeling. Her heart rate increased, and a cold sweat broke out along her hairline.

"How many other times did he approach me before Saturday?"

"At least once." Detective Gates laid down one more picture. It was of Zoey behind her desk at the tattoo shop. "It was taken this past Friday. Do you remember who came in that day?"

Zoey grabbed the picture and held it close to her face as she searched for clues. She had only worked until two on Friday because she had wrestled in Scranton that night. She remembered a prospective client coming in not long before Terry came to pick her up. The man had insisted on seeing Zack. Because Zack had been in the middle of a tattoo, she hadn't wanted to interrupt. Instead, one of the other tattoo artists talked to the man.

The picture slipped out of Zoey's quivering fingers as she slumped back in the chair. Black dots swam before her eyes, and a buzzing sound obscured her hearing. She weakly grabbed the arms of the chair to keep from toppling forward.

ELEVEN

"**M**ISS WILDE!" DETECTIVE GATES RUSHED around the side of his desk. He grabbed Zoey by the upper arms before she tumbled out of the chair. "Are you all right?"

The office door crashed open and Chief Jim Coleman—who must have been lingering in the hallway—rushed into the room. "I heard shouting. What's going on?"

"Miss Wilde fainted."

"That's ridiculous," Zoey mumbled. The buzzing in her ears faded and she blinked away the black dots that swarmed in front of her eyes. "I've never fainted in my life."

"It sure looked like you fainted," Detective Gates said.

Zoey shook her head. "Anxiety attack."

Jim took a step closer to Gates and demanded, "What the heck did you say to her?"

Detective Gates snatched one of the photos off his desk and handed it to his chief. "I informed her that the victim had been stalking her for the past few days."

Jim mumbled a curse. "No wonder you fainted—"

"I had an anxiety attack."

"Either way, you've had enough for today." Jim gripped Zoey by the upper arm and pulled her out of the chair. "I'll take you home."

"I'm not done talking to Miss Wilde," Detective Gates said. He stepped in front of Jim and blocked the doorway. "And she still needs to give her statement."

"Some other time." Jim pushed Gates aside. "You've upset Zoey enough for one day."

"I'm fine." Zoey pulled away from Jim and sat back down. She was so sick and tired of being coddled by everyone. "I just want to get this over with."

"You're sure?" Jim asked.

"Positive."

Jim huffed a few times before he stalked out of the office, taking Detective Gates with him. Through the closed door, Zoey could hear Jim reading Gates the riot act for upsetting her. Jim also explained to Gates that Zoey had had stalkers in the past. One sent her thousands of text messages from burner phones. Another had blown up her personal email. A third consistently sent her love letters, flowers, and other gifts for a year-long period. Despite Jim's tireless investigating, the identity of her stalkers had never been determined. Luckily for Zoey, the stalkers went away on their own and she had not heard from any of them in a long time. The stalking had caused Zoey countless sleepless nights, and she'd been hyper-vigilant whenever leaving her apartment. She remained on high alert, but it clearly had not paid off considering she hadn't noticed Devon lurking around last week.

Pushing aside thoughts of her previous stalkers, Zoey tried to recall the two known interactions that she'd had with Devon in the past week and a half. She had a feeling he said something to her at the wrestling event in Kissimmee—something that she hadn't really paid attention to. Knowing Devon, he probably hinted at his real identity and then spent the rest of the night laughing because she hadn't recognized him.

Zoey had just remembered something that Devon said to her on Friday afternoon at the tattoo shop when Detective Gates returned to the office and interrupted her train of thought. He carried two bottles of water and a pastry box bearing the logo of a local donut shop.

"I thought cops and donuts were a cliché."

"Depends on the cop." Detective Gates handed Zoey one of the water bottles. He then set the pastry box on his desk and opened it to reveal two donuts. One was glazed and the other was coated in chocolate and filled with some type of cream. "And the donuts are for you."

Zoey eyed up the high calorie treats, and her mouth began to water. She hadn't eaten a donut in at least five years. Zoey wasn't exactly on a diet, but, because she had to remain in shape for her physically demanding career, she no longer ate certain foods. Donuts—which were loaded in sugar and trans-fats—were one thing that she had cut from her diet. She'd also eliminated several other sweets and unhealthy foods.

"Thanks. But no thanks. I don't eat donuts."

"One donut won't hurt. In fact, getting some sugar in your system will probably make you feel better." Detective Gates held the box out to Zoey. "The one is filled with peanut butter."

The detective was right. One donut wouldn't do any serious harm . . . and she hadn't eaten anything since the protein bar that she'd had for breakfast—plus, peanut butter was her weakness. Zoey plucked the chocolate coated donut out of the box. She bit into the donut, and the sugar stung her teeth as the peanut butter and chocolate rolled over her tongue. She'd forgotten how sinfully good donuts could be. She could feel the sugar rushing through her body, restoring her spent energy.

When Zoey finished eating, she held up the picture of her and Devon from the Kissimmee show and asked, "Can I have this? I know I can just print one off from my Facebook page, but . . ."

"Is there a reason you want it?"

"To show this to my family and the other two tattoo artists. Maybe they will remember seeing Devon lurking around."

"I shouldn't since it's technically evidence. But, you're right, there is nothing stopping you from printing out a copy when you get home." Detective Gates flipped through his file and pulled out another picture. This one was a selfie of Devon. "This goes against everything I've been taught and believe in, but . . . you can have this one, too. But on one condition. If you learn anything, you pass along the info to me."

"No problem." Zoey glanced over the picture. Knowing Devon, he had taken a dozen selfies before settling on this one. "Though, if I'm agreeing to pass along any info, I should tell you about what happened yesterday morning."

After explaining that Marlon hosted an open gym every Sunday morning, she told Detective Gates about everything she had learned from the wrestlers who had attended yesterday. Zoey left out the part that her nana was determined to conduct her own amateur investigation, but she did give him the names and possible motives of the people that Vivian had on her suspect list. Zoey also told Gates about her encounter with Sasquatch while at the gym.

"I have not yet interviewed Sasquatch—I mean, Eugene Ackerman. But I will contact the State Police to confirm his alibi," Detective Gates said. Zoey had almost forgotten that Squatch had a real name. "But I did speak to Mr. Cozma. And he failed to mention that the victim was his biological father. In fact, he told me . . . Well, what he told me isn't really any of your business."

"Does Mort have an alibi?" Zoey asked.

Gates stared at Zoey for a few seconds and then said, "He claims to. I will have to verify it. Now, unless you have anything else you need to inform me of, I'd like to ask you a few questions and then proceed with your statement."

"I can't think of anything else," Zoey said. "But, if I do, I will let you know."

Detective Gates grabbed a notebook and flipped it open to a blank page. "I've heard a little bit about your relationship with Mr. Isler from your brother, Chief Coleman, and from the victim's mother—"

"You can disregard whatever Paula told you. That woman lives in her own reality."

Zoey pulled her phone back out of her purse and brought up the email that Paula had sent. She then handed the phone to Detective Gates so that he could read it.

"As you can see, Paula Isler hates me," Zoey said. "I'm sure she told you all sorts of lies to make me look bad. And I'd bet my life savings that she told you Devon was perfect and never did anything wrong in his entire life. And that she blamed me for everything."

Detective Gates cracked a smile. "Your life savings is safe. Now, why don't you tell me about your relationship with the victim."

Aside from leaving out some personal details, Zoey told Detective Gates almost the same story that she had told Hannah on Saturday night. Gates interrupted a few times to ask Zoey to clarify certain things, but, for the most part, he let her talk uninterrupted.

"What prompted you to finally leave him?" Detective Gates asked.

"I knew I wasn't happy. And that I hadn't been for a long time." Unable to make eye contact with the detective, Zoey looked down at her clenched fists. "My parents' marriage isn't perfect. And neither was my grandparents'. They had their ups and downs and disagreements. But they loved each other. They supported each other. I never heard them put each other down. The longer I was with Devon, the more I realized how messed up and one-sided our relationship was. By the time we moved to Florida, I was the only one who was making an effort. It wasn't a relationship of equals. We weren't partners. Honestly, I think he was trying to use the Wilde name to advance his career. I was nothing more than a stepping stone for him."

"He couldn't have always been horrible."

"No. In the beginning, he was charming. He not only had me fooled, but my parents, my grandparents, and my brothers. Even Arielle. Everyone thought he was great. Once we were in Florida and away from my family, he didn't have to pretend anymore. Looking back, I know I should have left him not long after we moved to Florida. But he was the only person I really knew in Orlando. Plus, he'd slowly chipped away at my self-esteem. And I was starting to have anxiety attacks. Between Devon's putdowns and the anxiety, I felt helpless."

"What prompted you to finally leave him?"

"A talent scout with the WWE called and invited me to a tryout. He said he'd seen me wrestle at a few shows and was really impressed. He also hinted that I should ditch the mediocre wrestler that I was valeting for and focus on my own career." Zoey didn't know it at the time, but the industry was in the process of increasing the focus on women's wrestling. AJ Lee was shaking things up on the WWE's main roster. Paige had just been signed to a developmental contract, and it wouldn't be long before the main players in the Women's Revolution—Charlotte Flair, Sasha Banks, Bayley, and Becky Lynch—would also sign developmental contracts. These were all women that Zoey knew. She'd also wrestled against most of them. "Hearing that from the talent scout was the kick in the butt that I desperately needed. I was so excited to be offered the tryout. I figured Devon would be happy for me, too. Instead, he was jealous. He totally flipped out when I told him. He accused me of messing up his chances and stealing his dream. He said it wasn't fair that I was offered a tryout and he wasn't. At one point, he tried to tell me that he wasn't going to allow me to tryout. It was insane. That's when I realized how out of touch he was with reality. I knew I had to leave Devon after that. And, since you've read the police report and seen the pictures of me taken at the hospital, you know how well that worked out."

Detective Gates didn't make Zoey talk about the assault or the aftermath. Instead, he asked her about Saturday night. After Zoey had written out her official statement, Gates explained that fingerprints belonging to seven people had been found on the sledgehammer.

"Some of those fingerprints belong to you, Miss Wilde."

"That's because I touched it before the show started."

"I am aware of that." Detective Gates drummed his fingers on the edge of the desk. "As for the other fingerprints . . . One print we have not been able to identify. The victim's fingerprints are all over the handle. As are Leland Freeman's and Terrance Gibbs's. Your brothers—"

"Obviously you found Justin's fingerprints. For the same reason that you found Devon's and Terry's."

"I know how Justin's fingerprints got on the sledgehammer," Gates said. "But the lab also found Zack's fingerprints."

"Zack?" Zoey was stunned. Why would Zack's fingerprints be on the sledgehammer? He'd had no reason to touch it. Then she remembered. "Zack handled it before the show. He was helping Justin put the trash can full of weapons under the ring."

"Yes, I heard about that," Gates said. "I also heard that Zack made some comments about how he wanted to use the sledgehammer to bash in Mr. Isler's head."

"Zack was just running his mouth. He didn't mean anything by it."

"That may be true. But it's suspicious that your brother stated he wanted to bash in Mr. Isler's skull and then, a few hours later, someone used the same sledgehammer to do just that."

"It's a coincidence," Zoey insisted.

"I don't believe in coincidences."

Zoey knocked her chair over as she jumped up. "You think Zack killed Devon."

"You can't deny that your brother had a motive." Detective Gates stood up and leaned across the desk so that he was at eye level with Zoey. "He also had means and opportunity—"

"This conversation is over." Zoey grabbed her purse. "And, just so you know, my brother was inside the VFW Hall when Devon was killed."

"So you say."

Zoey faltered for a few seconds before a blinding rage carried her down the hallway to the lobby. She whipped open the police department's front door and was about to step outside when Gates stopped her.

"I have nothing else to say to you," Zoey said. "And, as far as I know, I'm free to go."

"Yes, you are," Detective Gates said. "But I figured, while you're here, I may as well give you your car back."

"Where's my Jeep?" Zoey asked as she pulled her keys out of her purse.

"It's in the sally port. If you'll follow me . . ." Detective Gates gestured for Zoey to follow him back the hallway towards the far end of the police department. "I put air in your tires."

"Thanks."

Zoey yanked open the driver's side door and climbed inside. She was about to start the engine when she looked over and saw Zack's bracelet lying on the dashboard.

"I found that on the back seat," Detective Gates said as he leaned in through the open window. "Is it yours?"

"It's Zack's," Zoey said. She'd forgotten that she'd found it on the ground near Devon's body. "His daughter's name is Paige."

Zoey stuffed the bracelet into her purse and then fired the ignition. Without another word, she backed out of the sally port and rushed back to the tattoo shop.

"Zoey!" Quincy Durand said as she hurried into the breakroom. Stopping her, he gathered her into his arms and squeezed her against his chest. "I've been so worried about you. Are you okay? Why didn't you return any of my calls or texts?"

"I've been a little busy," Zoey said as she struggled to escape Quincy's embrace.

Quincy Durand was Zack's best friend and partner in the tattoo shop. He was also Zoey's high school sweetheart.

Zoey and Zack had met Quincy in the cafeteria on their first day of middle school. As one of the only other kids wearing a pro wrestling t-shirt, the twins had gravitated to him. Zoey and Quincy started dating when she was sixteen and he was seventeen. They were together for almost four years before Zoey ended the relationship. Back then, Quincy had been immature and uncertain about his future. He seemed content to live in his parents' basement, work as a dishwasher at a local restaurant, and spend most of his spare time playing video games. While Zoey hadn't quite been ready for a serious commitment, she was ready for something more serious than Quincy was willing to give her.

Not long after the breakup, Quincy hooked up with a woman named Elena. A year later, the two were married and about to have a child. A couple years after the birth of their second child, Quincy's and Elena's marriage soured. They tried to make things work for their kids' sake, but called it quits a couple years ago.

Quincy had been trying to get back together with Zoey ever since his divorce was finalized. Over the past few months, Zoey had gone out to dinner with him a handful of times, but she hadn't made any sort of commitment . . . and she wasn't sure she wanted to. Yes, she loved Quincy—and always would—but only as a friend. Any romantic feelings she'd had for him had died a long time ago. She was also turned off by the unruly beard he had grown following the premature loss of his hair. Zoey had nothing against facial hair, but the beard did not help Quincy's looks .

"Hey, Zoey, you're back," Zack said as he walked into the breakroom. "How'd it go?"

"Not good." Zoey held up Zack's bracelet. "What is this?"

"I think you know what it is." Zack plucked the bracelet out of her hand. "When and where did you find it."

"I found it Saturday night. It was on the ground next to my Jeep. And just a few feet away from Devon's dead body." Zoey snatched the bracelet back and waved it around in front of Zack's face. "Did you kill Devon."

"Are you kidding me?" Zack smacked Zoey's hand away. She lost her grip on the bracelet, and it flew into the sink. "No, I didn't kill him. I lost the bracelet before the show even started. Don't you remember? You were running low on medium t-shirts and you sent me out to your car to get more. I must have lost the bracelet then. With everything that was going on, I didn't realize it was missing until later."

"I totally forgot about that." Zoey collapsed into one of the breakroom's plastic chairs. "But please tell me you have an alibi."

"Not exactly." Zack sat down next to Zoey. "I stepped outside for a few minutes after Justin's and Devon's match. Like you, I needed to get out of there."

"What? Seriously, Zack? Why didn't you say anything yesterday?"

"Duh . . . Because I didn't want anyone to know I was out in the parking lot with Devon right before he was killed."

"Did he have the sledgehammer with him?"

"Not that I saw," Zack said.

"This isn't good," Zoey groaned. "What if someone saw you go outside?"

"I'm not worried about it."

"Well, I am." Zoey reached into her purse and pulled out the two pictures of Devon. She slapped the pictures down on the scarred Formica tabletop. "Have either of you seen this guy hanging around?"

Zack leaned over her shoulder and looked at the two pictures. "No. Who is he?"

"It's Devon," Zoey said. "Before he cleaned himself up for Saturday night."

"No way." Zack picked up the selfie of Devon. "Okay, now I see it. But, aside from the eyes, it really doesn't look like him. Prison had a negative effect on his appearance."

"Devon came into the shop on Friday." Zoey grabbed the picture away from Zack and then handed it to Quincy. "You talked to him."

"Yeah, I know," Quincy said.

"You know you talked to this guy?" Zoey asked. "Or you know this guy was Devon."

Quincy groaned. "I knew it was Devon. It took me a couple minutes—"

Zoey stood up and smacked her hand on Quincy's chest. "You knew Devon was back and you didn't say anything to me."

"Or me," Zack said.

"I didn't want to upset you." Quincy rubbed at the tender spot on his chest. "I told Devon to go away and leave you the hell alone. And, if he didn't, he'd have me to deal with."

"SORRY, I'M LATE."

Bernadette Sullivan hustled down the steps into the tattoo shop's basement. The middle-aged Black woman's violet pantsuit hugged her generous curves, and her six-inch, hot pink stiletto heels pounded on the wooden steps as she made her way downstairs. Zoey—who hardly ever wore high heels—couldn't help but wonder how the woman didn't twist an ankle . . . or fall and break her neck. Between the heels and the beehive of coiled braids, Bernadette appeared an entire foot taller than her five feet—and, thanks to her flawless, wrinkle-free skin, she looked about ten years younger than she really was.

When she reached the bottom of the stairs, Bernadette pulled the local section of that day's Lancaster County newspaper out of her purse and waved it around in Zoey's face. On the front page was an article about Devon's murder alongside an old picture of him. Unfortunately, the local reporter had mentioned Zoey in the article.

"Tell me you didn't kill him," Bernadette said.

"I didn't kill him." Zoey snatched the newspaper out of Bernadette's hands and shoved it into the trash can. "But I did find his body."

"Girl . . . Did you know he was back in the area?"

"Nope." Since she had left the two pictures of Devon upstairs, Zoey opened her Facebook page and brought up the picture of her and Devon from the July show. She handed her phone to Bernadette. "He was at the show in Florida. That prompted him to come back to PA last Monday. Then he was stalking me for a few days before he was killed."

"And you didn't recognize him? For real?" Bernadette asked as she zoomed in on Devon's face. "Well, I guess that's understandable. He doesn't look like a Greek God anymore."

"No, he does not." Zoey walked over to the basement's tiny kitchenette and began filling the coffee pot with water. Every Monday night for the past four years, Zoey and her former therapist had hosted meetings for a victim's support group in the basement of the tattoo shop. "I feel like an idiot."

"Oh no, Zoey, you are not getting back on the Blame Train." Bernadette joined Zoey at the kitchenette and opened up a box of pastries. "Not after I spent all that time getting you to see that none of what Devon did to you was your fault."

"I know. It's just that he was right there." Zoey gestured towards the empty spot beside her. "He talked to me. He touched me. And I had no idea it was him."

"That means you weren't living in fear and looking over your shoulder like you were back when we first met." Bernadette pulled Zoey in for a crushing hug. "How are you doing?"

"Are you asking as my friend? Or as my therapist?"

"Either. Or both. Whichever you need," Bernadette said. She smiled, her hot pink lips parting to reveal the small gap between her upper front teeth. Bernadette's lipstick perfectly matched her heels. "And, if you need to book some sessions, I will make time for you."

Not long after moving home from Florida, Zoey started going to therapy. She'd been hesitant at first—talking about her problems and secrets with a stranger had been awkward. But Bernadette was persistent, and she'd finally gotten Zoey to open up.

"Right now, I don't know what I need," Zoey said. "But I've got a top-notch criminal defense lawyer lined up in case I'm arrested for Devon's murder."

"Let's hope that doesn't happen." Bernadette clucked her tongue. "Tell me how you feel."

"I feel . . ." Zoey tipped her head back and exhaled. "I feel weightless."

"Is that a good or bad feeling?"

"It's a good . . . No, make that a great feeling." Zoey turned back to the counter and set out a stack of Styrofoam cups and a basket of sugar packets. "It's like this huge weight has been lifted off my shoulders. I feel free."

"Devon was a burden on you. You've known that for years now."

"Yes, and the longer I was with him, the heavier that burden got," Zoey said. By the end, the weight had nearly crushed her. She'd thought that the weight had lifted when the relationship ended, but it turned out that Devon had still been weighing her down all these years later. "I'm not saying I'm happy that Devon is dead. I mean . . . He was murdered. It would be wrong if I was happy about that, right?"

"Just a little bit. But . . . After what he put you through, I don't think it would be wrong for you to be relieved he's dead."

"Well, I definitely am relieved that I don't have to keep looking over my shoulder for him any longer. Not that my hypervigilance was worthwhile considering I didn't even recognize him. I'm just saying that . . . I don't know . . . The spell is broken, I guess. Or the curse has been lifted. Devon is gone for good. There is no way that he can hurt me anymore." Zoey ran her hands through her hair. "I know it sounds cheesy and cliché, but today is . . . well, it's kinda like the first day of the rest of my life."

"And, in a way, it is."

The sound of a door slamming upstairs warned them that one or more of the people who attended the victim's support group had arrived.

"We can talk more later," Bernadette said.

A few seconds later, a young, heavyset woman clomped down the stairs. Her hair had been poorly dyed a vibrant shade of purplish-red. Zoey couldn't recall her having attended any previous support group meetings, but there was something familiar about the woman.

"A newbie." Bernadette clapped her hands and stepped forward to welcome the woman. "Hello, I'm Bernadette. And this is Zoey. What's your name."

"It's . . . uh . . ." The woman glanced at Zoey over Bernadette's shoulder. "It's Kelsey. I saw an ad for the support group online and decided to stop by. I hope that's okay."

"Of course it is," Bernadette said as she guided Kelsey over to the kitchenette and poured her a cup of coffee. "We're happy to have you join us."

Not long after Kelsey arrived, six other women and a lone man joined them in the basement. Once everyone was seated, Bernadette made an announcement that, yes, the murdered professional wrestler mentioned in the newspaper and on the news was Zoey's abusive ex-boyfriend. Bernadette also asked that they respect Zoey's privacy and not ask her about it until she was ready to talk. She then introduced Kelsey and asked her to tell the group a little bit about herself.

With a bit more encouragement from the others, Kelsey launched into a story about how she had spent several years with a man who had taken advantage of her and abused the relationship. She had moved to another state to be with him, drained her bank account to support him, and took care of just about everything for him. And, after all that, he wound up leaving her for another woman.

Zoey zoned out of the meeting not long after Kelsey started talking. She was so lost in her own thoughts that she didn't realize it was nine o'clock and the meeting was over until everyone began to stand up.

"I know I said we could talk afterwards, but one of my patients has called me seven times in the past two hours. This might be an emergency,"

Bernadette said. She grabbed her purse and headed upstairs along with the others. "Sorry, girl. I'll call you tomorrow."

"I can help you clean up," Kelsey said. She lingered over the coffee pot as everyone else rushed out. "I mean, if you need help."

"I appreciate it."

Zoey handed the coffee pot to Kelsey and gestured for her to rinse it out in the sink. Zoey then yanked a disinfectant wipe out of the plastic container and cleaned up the spilled coffee and pastry crumbs from the counter.

"You know it's your fault Devon's dead."

TWELVE

"WHAT DID YOU SAY?" Zoey spun around and came face-to-face with the business end of a handgun. She looked past the gun to Kelsey's rage-contorted, flushed face. The other woman's pupils were dilated, and her nostrils flared as she sucked in short, shallow breaths.

"I said it's your fault Devon is dead," Kelsey said, enunciating each word.

The cleaning wipe slipped out of Zoey's hand and splatted on the floor. She'd been in some scary situations before, but she'd never had a gun pointed at her prior to this. Zoey had thought her encounter with Devon in the VFW Hall parking lot had been bad. This was much worse. Devon could have been dangerous, but Kelsey's gun was deadly—especially at such close range. If Kelsey pulled the trigger now, the bullet would strike Zoey in the head. Fear ripped through her as she backed up against the low counter.

"Who . . . Who are you?" Zoey stammered. "What do you want from me?"

"I want you to admit that it's your fault Devon is dead."

"But I didn't kill Devon," Zoey insisted. "I only found his body."

"I know you didn't kill him." Kelsey spoke in a singsong voice that adults sometimes used when speaking with children. "But you're the reason he's dead."

"Who are you?" Zoey asked again.

"You didn't recognize Devon. You don't recognize me." Kelsey giggled hysterically. She lowered the gun until the barrel was pointed at Zoey's midsection. "But, unlike Devon, I didn't want you to recognize me."

"He didn't exactly look the same."

"And neither do I. Take a closer look, Zoey. You know who I am."

Shifting her focus from the gun to the woman holding it, Zoey looked Kelsey over and searched for something familiar. She finally recognized the woman's hazel eyes beneath the thick eyeliner and dark eyeshadow.

"Chelsea . . ." Zoey whispered as recognition dawned on her. "You're right, you don't look the same."

The woman took her left hand away from the gun so that she could run her fingers through her short tresses. "I've changed my hair."

And put on a hundred pounds, Zoey thought. She then said, "I should have known you'd show up sooner or later. You always were Devon's shadow. Wherever he went, you were one step behind him. I guess I figured you would have gotten over your obsession with him while he was in prison."

"No, Zoey. I'm not like you. Devon was the center of my world. Unlike you, there was no getting over him for me."

Chelsea Neville had been a thorn in Zoey's side throughout her entire relationship with Devon. Along with Devon's mother, Chelsea had been an annoying and unwanted third wheel. If Zoey's and Devon's relationship had been a grocery cart, Paula and Chelsea would have been the wonky wheels that wobbled, locked up, and prevented the cart from steering straight.

Back before she'd started dating Devon, Zoey had assumed that Chelsea was his girlfriend. She had seen Chelsea alongside Devon at every show. She worked Devon's merchandise table, ran his fan club, managed his social media pages, and did everything humanly possible to help him or make his life easier. The woman had even done his laundry and cleaned his apartment. When Devon first asked Zoey out on a date, he'd had to explain that Chelsea was nothing more than a fan-turned-friend before Zoey would agree to go out with him. Devon had sworn that there was not—and had never been—anything romantic between them though it was obvious that Chelsea had desperately wanted there to be. She was in love with him, and she allowed him to manipulate and take advantage of her hoping that he would one day return her feelings. Zoey had gotten in the way of Chelsea's plan. She tried to run Zoey off, but Zoey had been too stubborn. The more Chelsea pushed, the harder Zoey pushed back.

While trying to run Zoey off, Chelsea had done everything she could to make her rival look bad. She would post unflattering pictures of Zoey on Devon's social media pages—or she would crop Zoey out of pictures altogether. Chelsea would even mess with Zoey's personal belongings. She had "accidentally" destroyed a pair of Zoey's brand-new custom-made wrestling boots, spritzed bleach on her ring gear, and played countless mean-spirited pranks. While somewhat intimidated by her, Zoey had also felt bad for Chelsea because her obsession with Devon had seemed so pathetic and childish.

Almost from the beginning, Zoey had begged Devon to stop associating with Chelsea, but he had refused. He also refused to take any of Zoey's complaints or concerns about Chelsea seriously. Instead, Devon had tried to convince Zoey that she was paranoid and jealous. He insisted that she get along with Chelsea. He also claimed that he needed Chelsea to handle "public relations" for him. Truthfully, he was just too lazy to run his social media accounts and didn't want to be bothered with keeping track of his merchandise sales. Chelsea would also drive Devon to and from events. When Devon moved to Florida the first time, Chelsea followed on his heels. When he came back to Pennsylvania after his dad died, she was right behind him.

Zoey had hoped she'd seen the last of Chelsea when she and Devon moved to Florida, but, a few weeks later, Chelsea moved into their apartment complex. She had uprooted her life in Pennsylvania for a second time to follow Devon to the Sunshine State.

The last time Zoey had seen Chelsea was a few days after the assault. A distraught Chelsea had snuck into the hospital room and begged Zoey to drop the charges against Devon. When Zoey refused, Chelsea tried to attack her. Luckily, hospital security was nearby, and they responded to Zoey's cries for help. Chelsea was charged with harassment, but she'd only been forced to pay a fine and promised to leave Zoey alone. Zoey had only heard from her once since then, and that was the day Devon was sentenced to five years in prison. Chelsea had sent Zoey a message through Facebook to ask if she was happy with herself now that Devon was behind bars and then accused her of ruining his life. Zoey blocked Chelsea's account, and had not heard anything from her since then.

"How did you find me?" Zoey asked.

"It's not like you made it difficult considering you moved back to your hometown."

"Okay, I guess you're right about that. But how did you find out about this support group?"

"If you don't want people to know about your personal life, you shouldn't advertise it all over Facebook."

Zoey's hands curled into fists. She tried to be careful about what she posted on social media concerning her personal life for just this reason. All her Facebook privacy settings had been set to "friends only," and she was selective about who she accepted friend requests from. The only way Chelsea would have been able to see any posts Zoey had made would be if they were friends on Facebook—and Zoey could guarantee that they were not. It was possible Bernadette or one of the other group members had made a public post about the meetings and tagged Zoey in it. Chelsea could have also befriended someone that Zoey was friends with on Facebook and used their account to stalk her.

Zoey debated tackling Chelsea while the gun was pointed away from her, but she was afraid to risk it. She was also terrified that, if she failed to get ahold of the gun or disarm her, Chelsea would shoot her. Zoey didn't know what to do other than to keep Chelsea talking.

"Did Devon put you up to this?" Zoey asked. "Were you helping him stalk me?"

Chelsea shook her head. "Saturday night was the first time I've been able to really talk to Devon since he took off last Sunday. After everything I'd done for him . . . That's how he thanked me. You know, I went to see him once a week, every week while he was stuck in that hellhole."

"That was him you were talking about earlier, wasn't it?" Zoey asked. "The guy you claimed took advantage of you?"

"He did take advantage of me." Chelsea used her sleeve to wipe away the tears streaming down her cheeks. "It kills me to admit you were right . . . but you were. All those times you told me Devon was just using me and taking advantage of me . . . I refused to believe it. I refused to see it. I was just so blinded by love for him. For years, I hoped that if I sacrificed and took care of everything for him, he would eventually fall in love with me. But he never did. Maybe if you hadn't gotten in the way—"

"Chelsea, that wasn't my fault. We both know that Devon never really loved me. He was just trying to use my family's name to advance his own career. He was using me the same way he used you. We were both manipulated by him. And we both suffered. I almost lost my life—"

"Now he lost his. And it's all your fault."

"I didn't kill him, Chelsea."

"I know you didn't kill him. But, if it wasn't for you, he wouldn't be dead. He'd still be in Florida with me. And everything would be perfect."

"You two were together? Like in a relationship?"

Chelsea nodded. "He had to attend therapy sessions while in prison. Once he got over hating you, he finally saw me. He realized I was the only woman for him. I always supported him. I was there for him while he was in prison. He promised me that once he got out, we'd start a life together. He swore he was done with wrestling. And done with you. Things were good for a year. No, it wasn't perfect. But it was good. We were good until you somehow came back into the picture—"

"Devon saw an advertisement for a show in Kissimmee. I was booked on the card. That's what started all this."

"I didn't know that at the time. I just knew something was up with him. Something had changed."

"How did you not know he went to the show?"

"I worked that night. When I got home, Devon was packing up a suitcase. He told me he was going to drive back to Pennsylvania to see his mother. I thought it was a bit weird since he hadn't bothered to go see her since getting out of prison." Keeping the gun trained on Zoey, Chelsea paced a few steps in each direction. "But it wasn't until he stopped responding to my texts and answering my calls that I knew something was going on. I logged onto his tablet and checked his browser history. That's how I figured out he'd gone to that show to see you. I figured you were the real reason he came back here. He swore to me that he was over you. But I should have known that Devon was never going to let you go."

"The same way you refuse to let him go? You're obsessed with him—"

"No, I'm in love with him!" Chelsea screamed.

Zoey shook her head in disbelief. "After all the mean things Devon did to you. How poorly he treated you. The way he took advantage of you. And you're defending him?"

"You're supposed to stand by your man."

"Devon wasn't *your* man," Zoey said. "He was *my* man. At least he was back then."

"But he was my man now."

Zoey sighed. "What do you want from me, Chelsea?"

"The same thing I've always wanted. I want Devon. But now he's dead because of you. You took him away from me, and now he's dead. Don't you realize that I can't live without him? I won't live without him." Chelsea raised the gun and pointed it at Zoey's head. "And since it's your fault he's dead, you shouldn't get to live either. I'm here to do what I should have done years ago. I'm going to—"

Footsteps on the basement stairs drew their attention to the far side of the room. Zoey recognized the hot pink high heels as they came into view.

"Zoey, is everything all right? I heard shouting and—" Bernadette stopped two-thirds of the way down the stairs. Her eyes widened as she surveyed the scene in front of her. "What is going on? You put that gun down right now, you hear me!"

Taking advantage of the distraction, Zoey grabbed a steel chair that one of the support group attendees had left leaning against the wall. Holding the chair by the legs, Zoey swung it at Chelsea and struck the other woman as hard as she could. The chair connected with Chelsea's right hand, knocking her arm sideways as she pulled the trigger. The discharged bullet harmlessly struck the wall, but the loud *bang!* echoed in the small room.

Swinging the chair up and around, Zoey brought it down on Chelsea's head with a resounding thud. Stunned, Chelsea slumped to the floor. Dropping the chair, Zoey threw herself on top of Chelsea and wrestled the other woman's hands behind her back. Despite having her bell rung, Chelsea had some fight left in her, and she struggled to buck Zoey off her.

"Get something to tie her up with," Zoey shouted at Bernadette as she tightened her grip on Chelsea's flailing arms and dug her knees into her back. Zoey used her chin to gesture towards the area of the basement that her brother used as an art studio. "Zack should have something over there that'll work."

When Marlon had finished the basement it was so that Zack could use it as an art studio. Since becoming a father, Zack didn't have as much time to work on his art, and he'd tucked his easels and art supplies off to the side and strung a curtain across the far end of the basement.

Bernadette grabbed ahold of the old sheet and yanked it aside to reveal Zack's art studio. A half-finished painting of Paige sat on an easel. Bernadette rummaged around the table and the packed, disorganized shelves until she found a tangled-up ball of twine. She then hustled to Zoey's side and helped her wrap the twine around Chelsea's wrists.

After securing Chelsea's wrists and ankles, Zoey scrambled across the floor until she collided with the wall. Between the ringing in her ears and the pounding of her heart, she couldn't hear what Chelsea was screaming at her.

"Are you okay?" Bernadette asked as she laid a hand on Zoey's shoulder. Zoey flinched away from her. "It's all right, girl. Everything is going to be all right. You work on taking some deep breaths while I call the police."

Zoey closed her eyes and leaned her head against the wall. As her therapist instructed, Zoey focused on breathing while she fought to keep it together. *In the nose and out the mouth*, she thought as she forced air into her lungs. She could feel her heart rate begin to slow as the adrenaline faded. The anxiety attack was subsiding.

Within minutes, the basement was teeming with police officers and EMTs. Bernadette took charge and explained to the police what had happened since she had walked into the basement. Having spent hours discussing Chelsea in past sessions, Bernadette knew who the trussed-up woman really was and gave the police some basic information about her identity.

"Where's Zoey?" Zack asked as he ran down the stairs. After summoning the police, Bernadette had called Zoey's brother and told him to get over to the tattoo shop. Zack hurried to Zoey's side and wrapped his arms around her shoulders. "What the heck happened here?"

"She was going to kill me," Zoey mumbled.

"Devon's dead because of you!" Spit flew out of Chelsea's mouth. "You deserve to die."

"Chelsea?" Zack asked.

"Get this woman out of here," Detective Gates commanded as he hauled Chelsea to her feet. Zoey hadn't realized the detective was in the basement until he spoke. After handing Chelsea off to one of the other officers, Detective Gates knelt on the floor. His light blue eyes bore into Zoey as he looked her over. "Are you injured, Miss Wilde? Do you want one of the EMTs to check you out?"

Zoey shook her head. "I'm okay. It's just an anxiety attack."

Bernadette snorted. "*Just* an anxiety attack."

"I'll be fine." Zoey stood up and forced her wobbly knees to cooperate as she made her way to the stairs. She had to get out of the claustrophobic basement. "I just need a minute."

Zack took Zoey by the elbow and guided her up the staircase to the first floor. He then led the way down the hallway and up the second set of steps to Zoey's apartment. After getting Zoey settled on the couch with Lita in her lap, Zack and the detective stepped into the kitchen. Over the sound of Lita's purring, Zoey could hear her brother and the detective talking but she couldn't make out the words.

A few minutes passed and then Zack walked back into the living room and handed Zoey a glass of orange juice. "Drink this."

Zoey gulped down half the contents of the glass. Orange juice—and the sugar it contained—had been her saving grace back when she had been suffering one or more anxiety attacks every day for months on end.

"You sure you're okay?" Zack asked. After Zoey nodded, he said, "I'd stay over to keep you company. But Paige has an ear infection and is screaming bloody murder. I need to get back home to help Arielle. I'd take you with me, but—"

"I love my niece. But listening to her scream all night will drive me up the wall," Zoey said. She patted Zack on the arm. "Don't worry about me. I don't need a babysitter."

"No, but I'd feel better if you weren't alone. And so would the rest of the family. That's why I called Justin. He should be here in about ten or fifteen minutes. You know how long it takes him to get moving. The detective is going to sit with you until Justin gets here."

Zack gave his sister a hug and kissed her on the forehead. He then went downstairs to see if the police were done in the basement.

"Your brother told me enough about this Chelsea person for me to understand who she is and what she has to do with the victim," Detective Gates said as he had a seat on the couch next to Zoey. "How 'bout you tell me what happened tonight."

Zoey summed up the encounter as quickly as possible.

"Chelsea kept accusing me of being responsible for Devon's death. But she also said she knows I didn't kill him," Zoey said. "She told me she was at the VFW Hall on Saturday night. Maybe she followed Devon outside after his match and saw who killed him. Or maybe *she's* the one who killed him."

"Do you really think she could have killed him?" the detective asked.

Zoey shrugged. "Chelsea said she and Devon were in a relationship this past year. She couldn't handle that he took off and came rushing back here to find me. Maybe, once she caught up to him, she snapped. I mean, she always seemed at least somewhat mentally unstable to me."

"I'll give Miss Neville the night to calm down in one of the holding cells at the police department, and then I'll question her in the morning." Standing, Detective Gates looked at the oversized collage frames that hung on the living room walls. The collage he focused on included pictures of Zoey in front of landmarks and tourist attractions throughout North America and the rest of the world. "Looks like you travel when you're not wrestling."

"It's because of wrestling that I've been able to travel the world," Zoey said. "I've wrestled in thirty-three states and four Canadian provinces. I've also wrestled on every continent except Antarctica."

Detective Gates whistled. "I'd like to hear some of your wrestling stories. Maybe I can buy you a drink sometime . . ."

Had Detective Gates just asked her out on a date? Zoey wasn't quite sure. She was used to getting asked out on a regular basis by her fans and other wrestlers. She always said no. After her disastrous relationship with Devon, she still wasn't ready for another relationship. She was fine by herself . . . but there was something about Gates that made her want to accept his offer.

Before she had a chance to give him an answer, the exterior door swung open and Terry Gibbs raced into the apartment. Justin strolled in after his friend.

"Zoey!" Terry rushed to her side and grasped her upper arms. "Zack said Chelsea had a gun and tried to kill you."

Zoey nodded. "Chelsea kept blaming me for Devon getting killed."

"You ask me, whoever killed Devon did you a favor," Terry said. "You should be grateful to that person for removing Devon from your life for good."

"Devon was *murdered*. That's not something to celebrate." Zoey pushed Terry backwards a couple steps so that he was no longer hovering over her. "Besides, all the killer has done is cause more drama in my life."

"But you don't have to worry about Devon bothering you ever again," Terry insisted.

"You want to talk about it?" Justin asked as he walked into the living room after showing Detective Gates out and locking the door.

"Not at the moment, no."

"Hey, what's this?" Justin asked as he picked up the two pictures of Devon that Zoey had left lying on her coffee table. "Or who is it?"

"It's Devon."

"No way . . ."

Terry yanked one of the pictures out of Justin's hand. "He approached you? When?"

"Last Saturday in Kissimmee. He came back to Pennsylvania a couple days after that. And, no, I don't want to talk about that either." Zoey stood up and walked out of the living room. She gave her brother a hug as she passed him. "Right now, all I want to do is go to bed."

After a quick shower, Zoey slipped down the hall to her bedroom. She had only taken two or three steps into the room when she stubbed her foot against something soft and squishy. Losing her balance, Zoey fell forward and crash landed on an air mattress. The mattress was occupied by her brother.

"Ouch! Watch it," Justin snapped as Zoey's knee collided with his shoulder. "I'm trying to sleep down here."

Zoey rolled off her brother and bumped into her dresser. Justin had tucked the air mattress into the narrow space between her bed and the dresser.

"Thanks for almost giving me a heart attack." Reaching behind her, Zoey flicked on the lights. "What do you think you're doing anyway?"

"Keeping you company." Justin sat up and brushed his long hair out of his eyes. "You remember when I was a kid and you let me sleep in your bed when I was scared?"

"Hard to forget. You'd sleep just fine, and I'd end up with bruises from you hitting and kicking me because you'd flop around all night," Zoey said. Between the ages of two and seven, whenever Justin had a nightmare or got scared by a thunderstorm, he would creep down the hall to Zoey's room because Zack, who he shared a room with, played the tough older brother role and would make fun of him for being scared. Justin was then too afraid to go downstairs to their parents' bedroom, so he'd go to his soft-hearted sister for comfort. "But that doesn't explain why you're sleeping in here and not out in the living room?"

"I know you're not going to admit it, but I can tell you're freaked out by everything that's happened the past couple of days. You know, Devon showing up and then getting murdered. And now this craziness with Chelsea. I figured I'd sleep in here to keep you company. You know, to make up for all those times you made me feel better when I was a kid."

"Who are you? And what have you done with the real Justin?"

"What's that supposed to mean?"

"Just that my little brother is normally pretty selfish." Zoey turned off the lights and then stepped over Justin to get to her bed. Lita curled up on the pillow and wrapped herself around Zoey's head. "And I appreciate the gesture."

"See . . . I care about people other than myself."

Zoey lay on her back and stared up at the ceiling. Light from the streetlamps filtered in through the cracks in the blinds and cast shadows throughout the room. She tried to think about anything other than Devon and Chelsea, but it was nearly impossible to do. Her mind was racing, and she couldn't get it to focus on anything else.

"Justin . . ."

"Yo . . ."

"What's up between you and Hannah?" Zoey asked. "Because if you're planning to treat her like you've treated some of your ex-girlfriends—"

"I'm not . . . Look, I can't make any promises. Other than that I won't intentionally hurt her," Justin said. "But I like Hannah. We've got something good. Will it work out? I don't know. But Hannah and I have talked about it, and we want to give it a shot and see what happens."

"Seriously . . . Who are you and when did you suddenly decide to grow up?"

THIRTEEN

Tuesday August 21, 2018

"Girl, I am still worked up from last night," Bernadette said as she hugged Zoey. "I darn near had a heart attack when I walked downstairs and saw that woman had a gun pointed at you."

"*You* almost had a heart attack?" Zoey asked as she pulled away from Bernadette. "How do you think *I* felt?"

"Tell me about it," Bernadette said as she gestured for Zoey to have a seat in one of the many chairs in her spacious office. "These past few days must have been stressful for you."

"Not at all," Zoey said sarcastically.

After a long night, Zoey had finally fallen asleep around the time that Justin and Terry headed off to work. They both worked for Marlon, and they were scheduled to demolish a kitchen by removing the cabinets and flooring. Zoey had still been in bed when Bernadette called to let her know that her eleven o'clock appointment had cancelled, and that Zoey needed to get her butt over to the office for an emergency therapy session.

Zoey had mixed feelings about the session. She did not want to talk to Bernadette—mainly because Bernadette would pick her brain and force her to talk about how she was feeling regarding Devon's unexpected reappearance and subsequent murder. Bernadette would also want to talk about Chelsea.

What Zoey wanted to do was stay in bed—to pull the covers up over her head and pretend that the past few days had never happened. She wanted to believe that it was a bad dream, and she would wake up from it at any moment . . . but that was what she'd done years ago. Instead of facing her problems head on, Zoey had pushed them to the side and tried to forget about them. In the short term, her plan somewhat worked. In the long term, she caused herself far more harm than good. She couldn't do that to herself a second time. After all the effort she had made to move forward, she couldn't risk falling back. She owed herself to keep her life on track.

Zoey sucked in a deep breath. "I'm really not in the mood to talk about Devon or Chelsea. I can't stop thinking about them—"

"That is precisely why we need to talk about them, Zoey. You can't—"

"I'm not. I won't. I just don't want to talk about it today," Zoey said. She was barely keeping it together as it was. If she talked about it, she knew she would have a breakdown.

Bernadette leaned back in her chair and studied Zoey. "Do you remember your first therapy session with me?"

"Vaguely."

"The first thing you said to me was that you didn't want to talk about any of it," Bernadette said. "You said that nothing good could come of talking about it and that you just wanted to move on."

"Yeah, well, I was wrong," Zoey admitted. "I couldn't move on until after I talked about it and got my feelings sorted out."

"Yes. But for weeks you fought me," Bernadette reminded her. "Back then, you were coming to see me three times a week. And what did we talk about during all those sessions? We talked about professional wrestling."

"It's a good subject." Zoey tightened her abdomen so that she could sit up. "You want to hear about how I won the LAW Women's Championship on Saturday night?"

"Not at the moment, no." Bernadette scrunched up her nose and gave Zoey a stern look. "I didn't ask you to come down here to talk about wrestling. You might think it is a perfectly good topic for discussion. And it is. But not with me. Not today. Years ago, I was more than willing to discuss wrestling with you. To be honest, I was thrilled that you were willing to talk about anything at all. But we got past that a long time ago—"

"Are you trying to make some sort of point?"

Bernadette sighed. "The point I'm trying to make is that professional wrestling is your security blanket. You can't keep hiding behind it."

"According to Zack, I'm hiding behind an armed fortress that I built around myself."

"What?" Bernadette moved over to sit on the chaise lounge by Zoey's feet. "Your brother said that? Why? What did he mean?"

Zoey shrugged. "I overheard him talking to . . . to someone. He was talking about how I'm a different person than I was years ago. You know, before Devon."

"Everyone changes over time, Zoey," Bernadette reassured her. "Especially someone who has gone through a traumatic experience. Zack can't expect you to be the same person you were ten years ago. I'm sure he isn't. You've both grown up. You've matured."

"I know that." Zoey leaned back and stared up at the ceiling. Bernadette had painted her office walls and ceiling a pale, calming blue. "I think what Zack meant was that I put up this armed fortress to keep people out. And to keep myself locked in."

"I'd say it's more of a labyrinth," Bernadette said. "And you're sitting at the middle of the maze. You make people work to get to you."

"You found your way through it," Zoey pointed out.

"Yes, but it was also my job to do so. And I just bulldozed my way through the walls."

"You got that right." Zoey laughed. "You were persistent."

"I didn't know you before you were with Devon. I didn't know you while you were with him. I only know what you were like afterwards."

"Yeah, a hot mess."

"Yes, you were a hot mess. But, deep down, you wanted to get better. You just had to haul yourself out of that pit of misery first. Once you did that, you started to make progress almost immediately. And you worked hard to make that progress."

"Yeah, I did," Zoey said. Bernadette was the only person who understood how hard Zoey had worked in her quest to heal. "Zack said I hit a wall in my healing process. Something about how I was getting better and making progress. But then I just quit."

"Well . . . Zack is not wrong."

"Seriously?" Zoey lifted her head to look at Bernadette. "What's that supposed to mean?"

"It means . . . it means that once you were willing to open up about your relationship with Devon and confront your demons, you made significant progress in a short amount of time." Bernadette patted Zoey on the knee. "Then it's like you got to where you were comfortable and you stopped . . . Yes, you've made some progress since then. You just stopped putting as much effort into healing yourself and shifted that energy and focus elsewhere."

"Oh yeah? And where did I shift it to?" Zoey asked as she sat up. "When did I hit this supposed wall?"

"About the same time that you got back in the ring." Bernadette stood up so that she could pace the room. "Like I said earlier, you use professional wrestling as a security blanket. For that year or so when you weren't wrestling, you lost that security blanket. Well, not entirely. You were still watching wrestling on television. But, once you got back in the ring, Zoey the Wrestler came back to life. Your focus shifted from the real Zoey to the wrestler Zoey."

Zoey slumped backwards and closed her eyes. It was hard to admit, but Bernadette was right. As soon as she stepped back into the ring, she had thrown all her focus and energy into her career. Zoey the Wrestler had flourished while Zoey the Woman languished.

"Zack said I've been treading water since then."

"That's a good way to put it. When it comes to wrestling, you dive in headfirst. I have seen you do some crazy and questionable things in the ring. It would be more understandable if you worked for WWE and were on television every week—"

"But I wrestle in firehalls in front of a couple hundred people," Zoey said. "I know the risk isn't worth it. But I do it anyway because I love it."

"You're right, the risk isn't worth it. But I'm not going to waste my breath lecturing you about it." Bernadette smiled. They had discussed Zoey's inclination for risky spots on countless occasions. "What I will lecture you about is your unwillingness or inability to take risks in your personal life—"

"Are you saying I should start jumping out of airplanes?"

"Well . . . I wouldn't suggest that. Unless that's something you really want to do," Bernadette said. "What you should do is start off with baby steps. To make another water analogy . . . When we first met, you—as in Zoey the Woman—were hanging out in life's baby pool. I got you into the roped off shallow end. And that's where you've been stuck. Occasionally you have dipped your toe into deeper water, but you haven't really ventured in. And it's time you took that risk. In fact, you should have taken that risk a few years ago. Meanwhile, Zoey the Wrestler is doing backflips off the high dive."

Before Zoey could respond, a high-pitched beeping signaled the end of the session.

"It's my lunchbreak," Bernadette said. "My next client doesn't come in until one o'clock. You can stick around and talk some more if you want to."

"Nah, I need to get to work." Zoey swung her legs off the chaise lounge and stood up. "But next time you get a cancellation, give me a call."

"Or you can give me a call when you're ready to talk about it."

"One of these days I'll be ready," Zoey said. "Just not today."

Zoey skipped down the steps and out to the street. Bernadette's office was a half-mile up the street from 3 Count Tattoos. It was on the second floor above a toy store that sold both new and used collectible toys.

Taking her time, Zoey strolled down South Market Street away from the center of town. Two blocks down the street from Bernadette's office—and on the opposite side of the street—was the VFW Hall. Zoey gawked as she walked past the building. A handful of people were gathered alongside the Linville Community Park office building near where Devon had been killed. From a distance, Zoey couldn't tell who the people were—if they were park staff, law enforcement officers, members of the local media, or ghoulish people who were drawn to the murder scene.

After getting her curiosity under control, Zoey continued back to the tattoo shop. As she walked, she thought about when she would be up for another therapy session. She didn't want to put it off for too long. But she knew she wouldn't be ready to talk about it for another few days. Hopefully, by the time she was ready to talk, the killer would have been arrested.

Zoey was walking up the porch steps at the shop when she heard Zack's voice drifting out of an open window. Zoey peered through the slats in the blinds and into the front office. The room was Zoey's domain, but, today, she found it being intruded upon by Zack, Quincy, and Santino Cruz. Zack was slumped on one of the two leather couches, and Quincy and Santino were behind Zoey's desk.

Santino started working at 3 Count Tattoos about two years earlier. He'd been working at a shop in Lancaster City, but it was not an ideal situation due to animosity with another artist. After meeting Santino at a local tattoo convention, Zack invited him to come work for him. Santino specialized in the traditional tattoo style, and he was an asset to the shop despite being the most disorganized person that Zoey had ever met.

"Where the hell is she?" Zack asked. "I've been calling and texting Zoey since I got here. And that was over half-an-hour ago. She's still not answering."

Zoey pulled her phone out of her purse and saw that she had several missed calls from Zack. He had also sent her a dozen text messages. She'd turned off her phone during the therapy session and hadn't bothered to check it since leaving Bernadette's office.

"I'm sure she's fine," Santino said.

"Then where is she? Zoey's never not here. And when something occasionally does come up, she either texts me or leaves a note. Plus where would she have gone without taking her car?"

Zoey would have left a note, but she'd forgotten. She'd still been in bed when Bernadette called about the unplanned therapy session. She barely had enough time to eat breakfast and get dressed before she had to rush up the street.

"You don't think she's been arrested for Devon's murder, do you?" Quincy asked.

"God, I hope not," Zack said. "But maybe the detective took her down to the police department to make a statement about almost getting shot last night."

Zoey watched as Zack grabbed his phone. Seconds later, her phone vibrated.

Knowing she couldn't keep Zack—or Quincy and Santino—waiting any longer, Zoey pushed open the door and stepped inside. Jangling bells announced her arrival.

"Where the heck have you been?" Zack asked as he jumped off the couch and pulled Zoey in for a hug. "I was scared you were dead or something."

"Maybe dead tired. But not dead. I walked up the street to see Bernadette."

"Next time could you let one of us know that? That way I don't have to force Santino to go upstairs and check for your corpse." Letting go of his sister, Zack stepped around her and entered his private tattooing room. "I've got a client coming in any minute. I need to get myself calmed down so I'm ready for him."

Turning to Santino, Zoey asked, "Did he really make you check my apartment?"

Santino nodded. "He couldn't bring himself to do it."

"He also made me call Justin to make sure you weren't with him," Quincy added. "Seriously, next time you need to let us know what's going on. Zack told us about Chelsea attacking you last night. He was worried she escaped police custody and had killed you."

"Or kidnapped you," Santino said. He tried to straighten out some of the mess he had made on her desk. Somehow, he wound up making it worse. "But, *Chica*, what I'm finding hard to believe is that you was once in a relationship. I've known you guys for what . . . Almost two years now. And not once have I seen you actually date anyone. I was beginning to think you ain't interested in relationships. If I'd known about this—"

"You didn't need to know," Zoey said. She was surprised that neither Zack nor Quincy had mentioned anything to Santino about her disastrous relationship with Devon. "And I have, too, dated in the past two years—"

"Yeah, you went on some dates." Santino frowned at Zoey, drawing his bushy black eyebrows into a unibrow. "But how many of those guys did you actually have a relationship with?"

"Umm . . . None of them," Zoey said.

After Devon, Zoey swore to never ignore another red flag. But, if she was being honest, she went into those handful of dates looking for red flags. Heck, even a glimpse of a pale pink flag was enough for Zoey to end the date early and decline a second one.

"Tino, don't you remember me telling you that Zoey and I dated for almost four years starting back when we were in high school?" Quincy asked. He possessively draped his arm around Zoey's shoulders. "And we've been dating again for the past month or so."

"We are not dating." Zoey shoved Quincy's arm away from her. After turning on the neon "open" sign, she ducked around to the other side of her desk. "Just because we went out to dinner a few times does not mean we are dating."

Quincy looked crestfallen. "I thought it might lead to something. You know I want to get back together and—"

Interrupting, Zoey said, "And I have made it clear that I don't want to. I don't feel that way about you. Not anymore."

"Can't we just give it a try?" Quincy asked.

"She said no, man. Leave it alone," Santino said as he took up a stance next to Zoey and crossed his arms over his chest. Santino's left arm was covered in tattoos from his shoulder down to his wrist. His right arm was bare. "You ain't her type anyway, Quincy."

"You must know me better than I do, Tino," Zoey said. "I wasn't aware I had a type."

"Well . . . Okay, maybe I don't know what your type is. But I do know what it ain't. And it ain't clingy guys who are gonna hang all over you. A strong, independent woman like you needs her space. A clingy man like Quincy would smother you." Santino nodded at Zoey. He then turned to Quincy and said, "Besides, don't you know that getting back with your ex is like reheating fast-food French fries?"

"What's wrong with that? I do it all the time," Quincy said.

Santino sighed. "You would, man. You would."

Quincy—who looked bewildered—glanced between Zoey and Santino. "But, seriously, what's wrong with reheating French fries?"

"They're never as good the second time around," Santino said. "Let me put it another way . . . Getting back with your ex is like taking a shower and putting your dirty boxers back on."

Quincy gave Santino a blank look. "And that's wrong because . . ."

"Man, you are hopeless."

Zoey chuckled. "This is coming from the guy who gets back together with his ex-girlfriend every other month."

"I never said I was a good example. Besides, every time I get back together with Gabriella, I know it's going to be a disaster." Santino pushed past Quincy and walked out of the office. "Now, if you'll excuse me, I've got a client coming in at one."

"So do I." Quincy waved his hands at Zoey's desk. "Sorry about the mess. And you might want to listen to the voicemails. It looks like the machine is full."

"Yeah, okay."

Zoey had a seat and then hit the play button on the shop's answering machine. The first of the twelve voicemails was from a prospective client calling to set up a consult. The other eleven voicemails were from reporters with the local newspaper and news stations asking her for a comment concerning Devon's murder. A reporter for one of the online wrestling dirt sheets had also called.

After deleting the voicemails, Zoey turned her attention to the tattoo shop's email account. There were forty-one emails—which was about thirty more than usual. Only one in every six emails pertained to tattoos. The rest were about Devon. Same with the messages sent through the tattoo shop's Facebook page. Zoey skimmed over the messages, and one popped out at her.

"YOU KILLED MY SON!!!!"

Devon's mother had sent the same message to the tattoo shop that she had sent to Zoey through her Wilde Woman page. Zoey took a screen shot of the message and sent it to Chief Coleman so that he would know Paula was still harassing her.

Switching accounts, Zoey checked her personal email and Facebook. She hadn't been brave enough to check either of them since Vivian had showed them to her yesterday morning. As Zoey suspected, both were full of emails and messages about Devon.

The office phone rang, distracting Zoey from a new—and even nastier and incoherent—message from Paula.

"Thanks for calling 3 Count Tattoos. How can I help you?"

"Is this Zoey Wilde?"

"Yes . . ."

"Zoey, this is Rachel with the ABC News affiliate in Harrisburg. I was wondering—"

"No comment!" Zoey snapped before slamming down the phone.

"DAD SENT ME AND TERRY OVER TO FIX THE DRYWALL," Justin announced as he sauntered into Zoey's office after four-thirty. "Hey . . . Are you all right? You look like you're ready to either cry or kill someone."

"If I start crying now, I won't stop," Zoey said as she slumped lower in her chair. "And since Devon is already dead . . . Though, if Devon were still alive, I wouldn't be having any of these problems. I'd probably be having other complications . . . Like trying to get a restraining order."

"Hold on. What problems are you having? What's going on?"

Before Zoey could answer, the office phone rang. Fighting back the urge to scream—because it wouldn't do to have the clients hear her shrieking like a mad woman—Zoey plastered on a fake smile and slipped into what she called her customer service voice.

Answering, Zoey said, "Thank you for—"

"You killed my son!"

"Stop calling me!" Muttering a string of curse words, Zoey slammed the phone into its base station. "Gahhhh!"

"Who was that?"

"Paula." Zoey glanced down at the notepad on which she had been keeping a running tally of how many times Paula had called the tattoo shop that day. "That makes an even dozen calls since noon."

Justin braced his elbows on the counter and leaned over the desk. "If you know it's Paula, why do you keep answering? Why not just let it go to voicemail?"

"Because I don't know it's Paula. She keeps calling from different phones. Each time it is a different name and number on the caller ID."

"Did you let Jim know?"

"Of course. I also called Pasqual to see if there's anything he could do. He's in court and hasn't gotten back to me yet." Zoey held up her cell phone and then gestured at the laptop and office phone. "But it's been all day. They're calling, texting, and emailing—"

"Who is? Aside from Paula?"

"Everyone," Zoey said as she flung her arms to the side in an expansive gesture. "Mostly other wrestlers and fans. But newscasters are calling from the local stations. And a reporter from the newspaper. Plus people from the dirt sheets—"

"The dirt sheets have been calling me, too," Justin said. "And so have a bunch of the wrestling podcasts."

"I know. I saw the interviews you gave," Zoey said as she shot her brother an icy glare. Since news of Devon's murder had first leaked, her name had appeared alongside some of the top wrestlers in the business. She had ignored anyone who had contacted her from the dirt sheets and podcasts about giving an interview or a statement. Now, thanks to Justin, her name and image—as well as some wild rumors—were being spread over the internet. At least Justin hadn't talked to Reggie Drake, but Paula had. Less than an hour earlier, Reggie posted the interview with Paula on his blog. Not only had Paula accused Zoey of killing Devon, she made other salacious statements concerning Zoey and the rest of the Wildes. "Thanks . . . Ever since you started giving interviews, they've tripled the pressure on me. They all want to know what I have to say about Devon."

Justin shrugged and gave his sister a sheepish smile. "Well . . . if you've been reading the dirt sheets and checking social media—"

"I'm trying to avoid social media until all this blows over," Zoey said. She'd turned off the notifications on her phone because it seemed to be almost constantly alerting her to a new follower, comment, like, or message. "I'm not even checking my email. And I'm only reading texts or listening to voicemails from people I know."

"You better start checking. And responding. Especially to all the promoters and bookers who I know are contacting you. If they're trying to book me for their shows, I have no doubt they're trying to book you, too." After coming around the desk, Justin put his arm around Zoey's shoulders and hugged her. "Devon getting killed is the best thing that has ever happened to your career. You're the hottest thing on the independent scene right now, sis. And I'm the second hottest—"

"We might be the hottest thing right now. But, come tomorrow, we could be nobodies again. The only reason anyone cares about us right now is because I'm Devon's ex-girlfriend—"

Justin interrupted to say, "And because you found his body."

"Thank you for reminding me. I almost forgot that Devon was killed right next to our cars and that I found his body. Would you also like to remind me that Devon almost killed me years ago?" Zoey asked as she thumped her brother in the ribs. "I hate to burst your bubble, but the only reason you're the second hottest thing is because you wrestled Devon just before he died. And because the police think you were somehow involved in Devon winding up dead. That's the real reason anyone is calling. They think one of us might be the killer."

"Who cares why they're calling?" Justin asked. "All that matters is that they are calling. Heck, I got a call from a promotion in Japan. And another in Mexico. This could be our big break. We need to take advantage—"

Zoey pushed away from Justin. "Who said I'm going to take advantage of it? I don't want my big break to be because my ex-boyfriend was murdered."

"Come on, sis. Just jump on and ride it for as long and as far as you can," Justin said. "If you don't take advantage of it, you're nuts."

"Well then I guess I'm nuts."

"Fine . . . Be that way." Justin exhaled in a huff of exasperation. "I gotta tell you something. But you have to promise that you won't get mad—"

"When you start out by telling me not to be mad, the chances are probably pretty good that I'm going to get mad."

"You know how I'm wrestling in Harrisburg tomorrow night? Well, earlier today, the promoter called and asked if you'd come, too. He wants to put us in an intergender tag match against these wrestlers who go by Kenny and Barbara Jean. I told him you'd do it."

"Justin . . ."

"Before you say no . . . It's a charity event. All the money goes to a pit bull rescue."

"All right. I'll do it for the dogs." Zoey was a sucker for animals. Changing the subject, she said, "Since you're here . . . Do you mind taking some pictures of me with the LAW title belt? I haven't posted anything on social media since Saturday afternoon. Maybe if I post pictures from my match and of me with the title belt it'll give them something else to talk about aside from Devon."

"I don't know, Zoey," Justin said. "I mean, that title belt is ugly. But I don't know if it's ugly enough to distract people from Devon's murder."

Zoey rolled her eyes. "It's worth a shot, right?"

While Justin joined Terry in the basement, Zoey headed upstairs to her apartment. After fixing her hair, she swiped on some gray eyeshadow and black eyeliner. She also applied a coat of hot pink lipstick to match the title belt.

Zoey then changed into a pair of light gray skinny jeans and a black Wilde Woman t-shirt. So her fans didn't think she had lost the will to live—and because she didn't feel like herself without wearing at least a small amount of animal print—she grabbed the pair of zebra print stilettos that she had worn for Zack's and Arielle's wedding.

Carrying the title belt, her camera, and the heels, Zoey made her way downstairs. Her bare feet moved silently across the old wood floor.

She descended one or two steps when she overheard a conversation that brought her to a halt.

"You'd think Zoey would be happy that Devon is dead," Quincy said. His voice drifted upstairs from the basement. "Instead, she seems depressed."

"Of course, she's depressed," Justin said. "She's also stressed out and traumatized. I can't begin to imagine how traumatic it was for her to see Devon again. And, if seeing him again wasn't bad enough, can you imagine finding his dead body? And then finding out that Devon was stalking her for the past few days? That would traumatize anyone. Personally, I think Zoey is keeping it together pretty well considering everything."

Zoey tilted her head back and looked up at the sloped ceiling. She agreed with Justin—she was traumatized. And she was also keeping it together. For the most part, at least. Aside from her brief breakdown on Saturday night and the couple of anxiety attacks, she was doing all right. A few years ago, she would have crawled into bed and stayed there.

Tuning back into the conversation, Zoey heard Terry say, "I just don't understand why Zoey isn't grateful to the killer for taking care of her problem. When I mentioned it last night, she told me that we shouldn't be happy that Devon got murdered."

"It is kinda cold hearted," Justin said.

"Are you telling us you're not happy about what happened to Devon?" Quincy asked.

Justin laughed. "Between the three of us . . . I'm thrilled. You ask me, Devon got what he deserved. But Zoey isn't the kind of person to wish death on someone."

"Not even Devon after what he did to her?" Terry asked.

"No. Not even Devon," Justin said. "Now, the two of you better leave Zoey alone about all this Devon crap. It's only making her feel worse than she already does."

Deciding that she had heard enough—and that her brother was a bit of a hypocrite since he had just been giving her a hard time about how they needed to take advantage of the increased interest in them that was in response to Devon's death—Zoey slipped on her high heels and clomped down the wooden steps.

FOURTEEN

Wednesday August 22, 2018

"Hey Arielle," Zoey said as she tucked the cell phone between her ear and her shoulder. She then leaned over to tie the laces of her neon purple sneakers. "I didn't forget about the gym this time. As soon as I finish tying my shoes, I'll be on my way over."

"What? No . . ." Arielle trailed off. Over the phone, Zoey heard her inhale and then exhale. It took a lot to rattle Arielle's composure, and it sounded like she had been rocked to her core. In the background, Zoey could hear Paige screeching—which could explain why Arielle sounded so frazzled. "Zoey, it's Zack. They took him. The police . . . That new detective . . . They came to the house and they took Zack . . ."

Leaving her shoe half-tied, Zoey sat up. "What do you mean they took Zack?"

"I mean they took him. To the police department."

"For what? Is he under arrest?"

"I don't know. They didn't put handcuffs on him or anything," Arielle said. "The detective said . . . Well, I don't remember exactly what he said. But then my dad said something else. And, obviously, I'm going to believe my dad . . . and . . . and . . ."

"Arielle, you have got to calm down and explain what's going on."

"I don't know what's going on," Arielle screamed, losing what little composure she had left. "My husband just got hauled out of here by the police."

"Okay, I get that," Zoey said as she tried to remain calm. "What did your dad say?"

"That it looks bad and to get a lawyer."

"What?" Zoey stood up so that she could pace across her living room. Lita scampered around her feet, batting at the untied shoelaces. "So Zack is under arrest?"

"Maybe. I don't know." Arielle yelled something at Paige and then said, "I don't even know what my dad meant when he said it looks bad but—"

Interrupting, Zoey said, "On Monday, the detective told me that the lab found Zack's fingerprints on the handle of the sledgehammer. He must think Zack killed Devon."

"What are we going to do?"

"I'm going to do what your dad suggested and call a lawyer." Without saying goodbye, Zoey hung up on Arielle. She then called Pasqual Cipriani. While waiting for him to answer, Zoey kept saying, "Please pick up. Don't be in court or with a client . . . Please pick up."

Just when Zoey thought she was going to be sent to voicemail, Pasqual answered. Skipping the formalities, Pasqual asked, "Did Detective Gates arrest you?"

"No. But he might have just arrested Zack." Zoey gave Pasqual a quick summary of what all had happened since she had last seen him on Sunday morning—including Monday's chat with Detective Gates and the confrontation with Chelsea. Pasqual had encountered Chelsea numerous times in the past, and he was aware of her obsession with Devon. "Arielle isn't sure if Zack's under arrest or not. But her dad is the Chief of the Linville Police, and he told her it doesn't look good and to get a lawyer."

Pasqual sighed. "Let me call the police and find out what's going on. Hang tight. I'll let you know what I find out."

While Zoey waited for Pasqual to call her back, she finished tying her shoelaces. Knowing she wouldn't make it to the gym today, Zoey settled for an impromptu at-home workout. She ran up and down the stairs a few times before cycling through various calisthenics. She was in the middle of a set of squats when her phone rang.

Answering, Zoey said, "Please tell me Zack's not under arrest."

"He's not," Pasqual said. "At least not yet."

"What's that supposed to mean?"

"Detective Gates brought Zack in for questioning," Pasqual explained. "That being said . . . Arielle's dad is not exaggerating. I spoke to Chief Coleman, and he told me what he could about the situation. He's being partially kept out of the loop since Zack is his son-in-law, but—"

"There is no way Zack killed Devon."

"But the evidence is saying differently. We both know that Zack has motive. His fingerprints are also on the murder weapon—"

"That's because he touched the sledgehammer before the show."

"I'm aware of that," Pasqual said. "But there is security camera footage of him leaving the VFW Hall right after Devon's match. And an eyewitness also claims to have seen Zack confront Devon in the parking lot not long before you found Devon's body."

"Someone saw Zack hit Devon with the sledgehammer?" Zoey sat down on the edge of the coffee table. "No way. Didn't happen. I bet Chelsea is this so called 'eyewitness' and she's making up lies about Zack to get back at me."

"Let's hope that's all this is," Pasqual said. In the background, Zoey heard a car door slam shut. "I'm about to head your way. It'll probably take me two hours, but Zack knows not to answer any questions until I'm there. You can count on me to get this straightened out."

"I'm going to hold you to that promise." Zoey stood up and walked towards the door. "What do you need me to do?"

"Right now, there really isn't anything you can do beside hold down the fort," Pasqual said before he hung up.

Zoey returned to the living room and collapsed on the couch. She was an active person. She did not excel at twiddling her thumbs. Her anxiety was mounting, and she needed something to do to keep herself occupied. She debated going over to her brother's house, but she knew she would probably get Arielle even more worked up than she already was.

"There is one thing I can do." Zoey sprang off the couch and dashed towards the door. On her way, she grabbed her purse and the keys to the Jeep. "I have a statement to make."

Within minutes of leaving her apartment, Zoey was seated across from Arielle's father. Jim had been the Chief of the Linville Police for going on twenty years and his lengthy presence showed. The walls were covered in commendations and framed photos.

"Can I talk to Zack?" Zoey asked.

Jim shook his head. "No can do. I can't even talk to him other than when I told him that his lawyer is on the way. I'm not sure what exactly is going on. I know Zack's fingerprints are on the sledgehammer. And that he has a motive. But now Detective Gates is saying that a witness can place Zack in the parking lot with Devon right around the time that he was killed. I just . . . I don't know what to think."

"Don't tell me that you actually think Zack did it?"

"I don't *want* to think he did it," Jim said. He held up his hand and motioned for Zoey not to interrupt. "We both know Zack could have killed Devon if it was to protect you. The same way we both know he could kill if it was to protect Arielle or Paige. If Zack thought Devon was going to hurt you—"

"But Devon was attacked from behind while he was kneeling to mess with Justin's tires," Zoey said. She propped her elbows on her knees. "Yes, Zack could have killed Devon. But not from behind like that. He's not that kind of person. Plus, how would he have gotten the sledgehammer? Devon took it backstage and put it through a wall."

"There are conflicting stories concerning what happened to the sledgehammer. Everyone who was backstage and saw what happened agree that Devon smashed it through the drywall near the door. Some people say he left it there. Others say he pulled it out of the wall and took it outside with him."

"Isn't there a security camera above the back door?"

Jim nodded. "The footage was grainy and it doesn't have the best angle. The sledgehammer doesn't appear in the couple seconds that it took Devon to move out of frame. But that doesn't mean he wasn't holding it in a way that his body blocked it from the camera."

A knock at the door startled Zoey and Jim.

"Chief, I . . ." Detective Gates said as he swung open the door and stepped into the office. He looked from Jim to Zoey. "What are you doing here, Miss Wilde?"

"I came in to give my statement," Zoey said. "You remember two nights ago when Chelsea tried to kill me? I assume she's the one who allegedly witnessed Zack confront Devon in the parking lot not long before Devon was killed."

Detective Gates shook his head. "No, Miss Neville is not the eyewitness. I have been unable to speak with her—"

Interrupting, Zoey asked, "What's that supposed to mean?"

"Miss Neville was admitted to the hospital—"

"Seriously?" Zoey asked. "I mean, yeah, I hit her over the head with the chair. But I didn't hit her that hard."

"Miss Neville has been three-oh-twoed."

"What does that mean?" Zoey turned away from the detective and faced Jim. "What is he talking about?"

"Early Tuesday morning, Chelsea was involuntarily committed into a mental health institute for a psychiatric evaluation," Jim said. "While the EMTs were checking her for signs of a concussion, she made multiple comments about how she was going to harm herself."

Zoey turned back to Detective Gates. "How soon can you talk to her?"

"The hospital can keep her for up to five days—"

"Five days?" Zoey scoffed. "But if Chelsea isn't the eyewitness, who is?"

"That I cannot tell you," Detective Gates said. "But between the eyewitness' statement and the evidence against your brother—"

"The eyewitness is lying," Zoey said. "And I don't care what your evidence says. Zack didn't kill Devon. I'll prove it."

"Miss Wilde, please refrain from getting involved in police business," Detective Gates said. He stepped out into the hallway and pulled the door shut behind him.

"He's right, Zoey," Jim said. "Nothing good can come from you sticking your nose in a police investigation."

"Where's Zack?"

"What?" Startled, Zoey shot to her feet and sent her office chair careening into the wall. She'd been so lost in thought that she didn't hear Quincy come into the tattoo shop. "Jeez, Quincy, don't sneak up on me like that."

"I wasn't sneaking. But sorry if I startled you," Quincy said as he walked farther into the front office. He wrapped his arms around Zoey and pulled her into a suffocating embrace. "I was just wondering where Zack is. Usually, he's the first one here."

"Zack is at the police department," Zoey said. Quincy's beard tickled her forehead and nose. She despised the sensation, so she pushed away from him. "The detective in charge of the case thinks Zack killed Devon."

"No way." Quincy sat down on the leather couch that was across from Zoey's desk. "I can't believe it . . . Actually, I *can* believe it—"

Zoey smacked Quincy on the arm. "Way to have faith in your best friend."

"I'm not saying I think Zack actually killed Devon," Quincy said. "I'm just saying it's a believable scenario. I mean, if some dude beat up one of my sisters, I'd probably kill him. So, yeah, I can believe Zack could have killed Devon."

"Yeah, I know." Zoey flopped down onto the couch next to Quincy. "Ugh . . . I don't know what to do. I've never been this nervous in my life. Okay, I have. But this is . . . it's . . . I want to scream. I want to cry. I want to rush back over to the police department—"

"What do you mean by back over? When were you at the police department?"

"Earlier today. When I found out Zack was there, I went over to find out what I could. I also gave my statement about Chelsea trying to kill me on Monday night." Zoey's knee bounced, jackhammering her heel against the floor. "I'm just so worried about my brother. I know he didn't kill Devon. But I'm terrified that the detective will arrest him."

"Everything will be fine. You'll see." Quincy put his arm around Zoey's shoulders and squeezed her against his side. "The detective will talk to Zack and realize there's no way he killed Devon."

"I hope so," Zoey said as she squirmed away from Quincy. "But until Zack gets here, I'll keep freaking out."

"I don't have much of anything on the schedule until two-thirty," Quincy said. He gestured in the direction of his private room at the end of the hall. "I'll go grab my sketchbook and sit up here to keep you company."

"No." The word came out much harsher sounding than Zoey meant it to, but she couldn't stand the thought of being stifled by Quincy's attention for the next couple of hours. Hadn't Quincy heard a word that Santino said yesterday? Clingy men were not her type, and Quincy was clingier than a wrestler hanging on to the top rope to prevent being disqualified from a Battle Royal match. "I mean, I appreciate the offer. But Zack has someone coming in at twelve-thirty. It's a small tattoo. Nothing special. Can you cover for him?"

"Yeah, I got it," Quincy said before he got up and shuffled out of the office.

Sitting down at her desk, Zoey started weeding out the non-tattoo related emails and Facebook messages. A few minutes later, the front door swung inward.

"Welcome to 3 Count Tattoos," Zoey said, calling out the greeting.

Because the wall obstructed her view of the front door and foyer, she stood up and headed around her desk. She was halfway to the arched doorway when her steps faltered. What if the person who had just entered the building wasn't one of the two people who were scheduled to get tattooed at twelve-thirty? What if it was Chelsea? It wasn't implausible to think that Chelsea could have checked out or escaped from the hospital and come back to the tattoo shop to finish the job. It could also be Devon's mom. Or it could be any one of the people who had posted nasty comments about Zoey online since Monday morning.

Fighting back a surge of paranoia, Zoey stepped out into the foyer and said, "How can we help—Mort? What are you doing here?"

"Hi, Zoey." Mortimer Cozma smiled, flashing his vampire incisors. "Is Zack here?"

Zoey shook her head. "Zack's . . . not here right now. What did you need to see him for?"

"He drew up a tattoo for me." Mortimer glanced around the foyer and then took a couple of steps closer to the staircase. He ran his fingers along the velvet rope that cordoned off the staircase. "He said I should stop by some time to look at it. But if he's not here—"

"I'm sure I can find it." Zoey herded Mortimer into Zack's room. "What's the tattoo of?"

"A vampire."

Why did I even ask? Zoey thought as she rummaged through the sketches that littered the top of Zack's desk. She found a sketch of a cartoonish-looking vampire and assumed that had to be it. She handed the paper to Mortimer.

Mortimer looked over the drawing, tilting his head from side to side as he did so. Finally, he nodded. "Tell Zack I approve."

"You may as well make an appointment while you're here."

Zoey led the way back across the foyer to the office. She had a seat behind her desk and scrolled through the electronic calendar. Zack was booked solid for the next month, but he had some openings towards the beginning of October. After getting Mortimer scheduled, Zoey decided to take advantage of the opportunity and ask a few questions. Jim, Pasqual, and Detective Gates had all warned her not to get involved in the investigation, but she couldn't stop herself—not while Zack was at the top of the suspect list.

"I didn't think to ask you on Sunday . . ." Zoey said. She picked up a pen and tapped the capped end against the desktop. "But did you see anything suspicious backstage following Justin's and Devon's match?"

"Nope. But I also wasn't backstage." Mortimer had a seat on the arm of the couch. "I was out in the banquet room watching the second half of the show. I wanted to see Devon wrestle. He really isn't that good, is he?"

"No, he's not," Zoey confirmed. "I mean, he used to be pretty good years ago. But he was never as excellent as he thought he was."

Mortimer chuckled. "After Devon's match, I stayed out there to watch the rest of the show. And to learn stuff. Watching live wrestling is a lot different than watching it on the TV."

"You don't need to tell me that." Zoey looked past Mortimer and stared out the window. Across the street, two of the neighbor's kids were using colored chalk to decorate the sidewalk. "Can anyone vouch for you?"

Mortimer's head snapped up. "Why does that matter?"

"Because . . . Well, because Zack is currently at the top of the detective's suspect list," Zoey said. "I know he didn't kill Devon. So . . ."

"So you're going to accuse me? I bet you're the person who told the detective that Devon is my birth father—"

"You should have told—"

"I knew it! You're the only other person I've told."

"Not telling the detective makes it look like you were trying to hide the relationship."

"Maybe I *was* trying to hide it. But thanks for blabbing my business and getting me hauled into the police department a second time." Mortimer jumped to his feet and leaned over the desk. Zoey might have been intimidated, but Mortimer wasn't all that menacing. "Look, I'll admit I have a

. . . a motive for wanting to kill Devon. He had no reason to be such a jerk when I told him who I was. But just because he made me mad doesn't mean I killed him."

Zoey felt a twinge of remorse for accusing Mortimer. "Do you have an alibi or not?"

"It just so happens that I do. I just don't know his name. But one of the guys that Leland hires for security was standing with me the whole second half of the show."

FIFTEEN

"I'M BACK," ZACK ANNOUNCED AS HE STRODE into the office around three-thirty. He spun on his heel and headed back into the hallway. "And I don't want to talk about it."

"But Zack . . ."

Zoey dropped the notebook in which she was keeping track of inventory and stepped out of the small closet that was behind her desk. She hustled after her brother, but he slammed shut the door to his private room before she caught up to him. Zoey reached for the doorknob, but someone grabbed her wrist and prevented her from opening the door.

"Give him a minute," Pasqual Cipriani said as he pulled Zoey away from the door. He wore gray pants and a yellow dress shirt. It was the first time Zoey had seen Pasqual dressed in something other than ring gear or athletic clothes. "He's had a rough day."

"What happened? Tell me everything," Zoey said as she allowed Pasqual to escort her back into her office. "Is Zack under arrest?"

"If he was under arrest, he wouldn't be here," Pasqual said. He had a seat on the couch and gestured for Zoey to sit next to him. "But it doesn't look good for him. Zack's fingerprints are all over the murder weapon. He has a motive for wanting Devon dead. And on Monday he apparently told Detective Gates that he wanted to kill Devon—"

"Yeah, but he was talking about the day Devon almost killed me," Zoey said.

"Zack still shouldn't have said that." Pasqual leaned forward and ran his hands over his closely cropped salt-and-pepper hair. "Your brother needs to learn how to keep his mouth shut. He's too honest and forthcoming for his own good. I sincerely hope that Gates finds a better suspect and doesn't arrest your brother. I'd hate to have to put Zack on the stand to defend himself. He'd probably wind up undoing all my work and make himself look guilty."

"Did Detective Gates tell you who the eyewitness is?"

Pasqual glanced over at Zoey. "Yeah, it's Leland."

"Uncle Leland?" Zoey scrambled to her feet and paced the short distance between the couch and her desk. She stopped in front of Pasqual and planted her hands on her hips. "What is Uncle Leland claiming he saw?"

"Well, he didn't actually *see* anything. He's more of an earwitness." Pasqual patted the cushion next to him and waited until Zoey sat down. "After ripping Justin a new one, Leland went into the storage room to cool down. He cracked one of the windows so that he could smoke. That's how he heard Zack and Devon arguing a few minutes after the match ended."

"If Uncle Leland only heard them, how can he be sure it was Zack?"

"Because of what they said. According to Leland, they used each other's names. And they talked about you. Zack told Devon that if he didn't leave you alone, he'd kill him."

"Oh, Zack . . ." Zoey buried her face in her hands and fought back the urge to scream. "This really does look bad."

"And not just for Zack." Pasqual patted Zoey on the back. "Gates thinks you, Zack, and Justin might be in on it together."

"What?" Zoey's hands slipped away from her face and she stared at Pasqual in horror.

"Gates's theory is that Justin told Devon you'd be waiting outside for him after the match. You lured Devon to the back of the parking lot. And Zack bashed Devon over the head while you had him distracted."

"That's crazy. I was over in the other parking lot. I had nothing to do with Devon winding up dead," Zoey said. And she refused to believe that either of her brothers was involved. The fact that Zack confronted Devon in the parking lot mere minutes before he was killed was just a coincidence. "What can we do to prove our innocence?"

"There is nothing you really can do." Pasqual leaned closer to Zoey and forced her to look him in the eye. "For now, you lay low. Gates assured me that the three of you are not his only suspects. He wouldn't tell me who else is on his suspect list, but there are other people he is looking in to. Let Gates do his job. He'll find the person or people who killed Devon. Everything will turn out all right. And if it doesn't . . . Well, rest assured that you've got a darn good lawyer."

Zoey walked Pasqual out to his car. She then went back inside and forced her way into Zack's room. She found him putting various colored inks into little plastic cups. He had an appointment scheduled for four-thirty. It was the person's second session on a piece that covered her arm from shoulder to elbow. Zack had done all the linework during the first session and would begin shading today.

"I told you I don't want to talk about it."

"Well, you're going to have to because we're suspects." Zoey grabbed the bottle of baby blue ink out of Zack's hand and slammed it down on top of his desk. "Did you really confront Devon in the parking lot after his match."

Zack tipped his head back and groaned. "Yeah, I did. I didn't say anything because I didn't think anyone saw me. Or heard me. But I can guarantee Devon was alive when I went back inside. And the only reason I went back inside was because I thought you had left. Had I known you were still in the parking lot, I would have followed Devon to make sure he left you alone. I've been sick to my stomach since Saturday night worrying about what Devon might have done to you had he run into you in the parking lot. Terry's right, you know. Whoever killed Devon did you a favor. He or she might have even saved your life."

"Yeah . . . I know."

Before Zoey could say anything else, the front door opened. Zack's client had arrived. Leaving Zack to his work, Zoey went back to her office and resumed taking inventory. She was finding it hard to concentrate and kept making mistakes while counting bottles of different colored inks. She didn't dare place an order for supplies while she was in this foggy headspace.

Even though she had been told by multiple people to stay out of it, Zoey was determined to prove Zack's innocence—as well as hers and Justin's.

She grabbed her cell phone and sent Justin a lengthy text summing up everything that had happened today and how they were officially suspects.

Justin texted back with instructions to meet him at Schmitt's Restaurant and Brewhouse after she got off from work.

SCHMITT'S WAS THE MOST POPULAR and second longest established restaurant in Linville. Vivian's brother, Elwood, had opened the restaurant nearly fifty years earlier. After Elwood retired about fifteen years ago, his son, Dave, took over management. It was Dave that added the brewery.

The interior of the restaurant was bedecked with a conglomeration of taxidermy, cardboard cutouts of celebrities, vintage arcade games, and whatever else tickled Elwood's and Dave's fancy—including a six-foot-tall alien statue that stood inside the front door. Elwood and Dave picked up most of the décor at flea markets and antique shops. There was no rhyme or reason to how they placed the décor, and the regulars enjoyed making new discoveries with each visit.

Zoey arrived at Schmitt's at eight-thirty. Dave was working the hostess stand alongside the fiberglass alien. After giving Zoey a hug and mumbling something that he probably thought sounded comforting, Dave informed Zoey that Vivian, Justin, and Terry were waiting for her out on the pirate ship.

Cutting through, two of the three dining rooms, Zoey made her way to the outdoor area. Just before retiring, her great-uncle Elwood had expanded the deck to add additional seating. The deck was the only part of the restaurant that had a theme—not that it was a totally cohesive theme. A half-scale replica of the Cape Hatteras lighthouse towered over the enormous tiki bar. Fiberglass pirates, fisherman, mermaids, and manatees were scattered about the deck. There were also a few smaller sized versions of Easter Island heads lined up near the bar. A flock of plastic flamingos lorded over the mini man-made lagoon. Faux fish and sharks hung from the ceiling of the covered portion of the deck, and there were ships' wheels, buoys, life rings, and anchors mounted on the exterior walls.

At the very back of the deck was a replica pirate ship. There was enough room on the deck for four tables, and they were the most popular seats in the house.

Zoey walked up the gangplank and boarded the ship. She found Vivian, Justin, and Terry seated at the table next to the ship's wheel. They had ordered the appetizer sampler platter and were making significant headway into devouring it. The onion rings and chicken wings were long gone—not that Zoey would have eaten any of them. There was a cheeseburger slider and two soft pretzel logs left. And the others had left her a pittance of Schmitt's famous fries. The fries were smothered in melted cheddar cheese, ranch dressing, and bacon bits. As she sat down, Zoey grabbed the appetizer platter and pulled it closer to her.

"What are you doing here, Nana?" Zoey picked up one of the pretzel logs and took a bite.

"I'm the Watson to your Sherlock." Vivian plunked her purse down on the wooden table and pulled out a notebook. "Justin told me that the handsome detective suspects the three of you worked together to take out Devon. I told you that would happen. Well, I didn't know he'd suspect you did it together, but—"

"I know. I know." Zoey finished eating the soft pretzel. "But Detective Gates has got a lot of nerve. He went from asking me out on a date—"

Terry slammed his glass of beer onto the table. "He did what?"

"Well, I don't know if he was asking me out on an official date or not. But he offered to buy me a drink." Zoey jabbed at the air with the second pretzel log. "But, as I was saying, it takes a lot of nerve to ask me out and then, less than twelve hours later, accuse me of murder."

"I hope you turned him down," Justin said.

Zoey shook her head. "I didn't get a chance to say yes or no. Right after he asked, you and Terry showed up at my place."

"But you were going to turn him down, right?" Terry asked.

"I don't know. But now that he thinks I helped kill Devon, I'm definitely going to say no if he asks again."

"I think you should take the detective up on the offer," Vivian said. "He's cute. If I was thirty years younger—"

Justin snickered. "More like fifty—"

"Watch your mouth, Justin Hogan Wilde," Vivian warned. She held up her notebook and waved it around. "Now, let's get down to business. We've got a murder to solve."

"Any ideas on how to clear our names?" Zoey asked.

"Interrogate the other suspects," Vivian said. "Torture them into confessing."

"I like the way you think, Nana. But torturing people seems a little extreme," Justin said. He reached across the table and snagged a cheese-covered French fry. "I talked to JT Perez earlier. Told him that the detective suspects us of killing Devon. He's filming a football scrimmage somewhere in Harrisburg tonight. When he's done with that, he's going to meet us at Zoey's apartment. I don't know if watching the footage from Saturday night will help us—"

"But it certainly can't hurt," Vivian said. "And it will be the perfect opportunity to interrogate JT."

"Question, Nana," Zoey said, correcting Vivian's word choice. "We're going to question JT. And we're going to wait until we're done watching the footage before we start accusing him of anything."

Inside the restaurant, a gong sounded the hour. Seconds later, the deck of the pirate ship rattled as the replica cannons shot out puffs of white smoke. "Shiver me timbers!" blasted out of the speaker mounted above the fiberglass pirate captain.

"Who else is on the suspect list?" Justin asked as he waved the acrid smoke away from his face. "I remember us talking about Squatch and Mort on Sunday. Are they still on the list?"

"Zoey and I talked to Squatch. He claims he left the VFW and went home right after your match started. Allegedly he got pulled over by a State Trooper on his way home," Vivian said. "As for Mort—"

"He also has an alibi," Zoey said around a mouthful of cheeseburger slider. She chewed and then swallowed. "He told me he was out in the banquet hall watching the second half of the show with one of Leland's security guards."

Vivian turned to Terry and asked, "Did you ever get a list of names from Leland?"

"Mom got it for me," Terry said. He pulled a folded-up piece of paper out of his pocket. "I doubt any of them are suspects since they're mostly in their late teens and early twenties. They probably didn't even know who Devon was."

"They might not be suspects. But they could be witnesses." Vivian plucked the paper out of Terry's hand and read over the list. "What about Leland? Did you get to talk to him?"

Terry shook his head. "Mom kicked Leland out of the house on Sunday. She told him to go spend a few days at a hotel and think about what he did to Zoey. She's really upset with him. And he's only making it worse by not answering his phone. Mom has no idea where he is, and she's been trying to get ahold of him since last night."

"You don't think something happened to him, do you?" Zoey asked.

"No. We know he's alive," Terry said. "Or that he was this morning. While Mom was at work, Leland went by their house. He left his dirty clothes in the laundry room with a note asking her to wash them. He also took clean clothes with him. That's why Mom started calling him. That stunt only made her madder than she already is. Instead of washing his dirty clothes, she stuffed them in a trash bag and hauled them out with the rest of the garbage."

"Good for Kim," Vivian said.

"Well, I don't know where Uncle Leland is right now. But I know where he was on Saturday night." Zoey shoved the empty platter away from her and then explained what she had learned from Pasqual. "We're going to have to track down Uncle Leland and question him about what he claims he overheard Zack and Devon say."

"You think he's lying?" Terry asked.

"I don't know." Zoey turned to Vivian and said, "Keep Uncle Leland on the suspect list for now. And be sure to add Chelsea. The way she was acting on Monday night . . . She might be crazy enough to have killed Devon in a fit of rage."

"Already added her," Vivian said. She held up the notebook so that Zoey could see the list of names. "Did the handsome detective ever question her?"

Zoey shook her head. "I forgot to tell you . . . Chelsea was threatening to harm herself so the police had her involuntarily committed to the psych ward at Hershey Medical Center. As far as I know, she's still there."

Vivian harrumphed. "Who else should we add?"

Zoey, Vivian, Justin, and Terry all looked around at each other.

"Well, maybe we'll come up with more suspects once we watch JT's footage," Zoey said. "We might even be able to eliminate some people. When did JT say he would be done filming the scrimmage?"

"The game probably won't be over until ten-ish. Until then . . ." Justin propped his elbows on the edge of the table and leaned towards his sister.

"There has been a change of plan for tomorrow. The promoter called me a little while ago. He wants us to get to the arena in the early afternoon. The event blew up after he added you to the card."

"What does that mean?" Zoey asked.

"The show was supposed to be in the sale arena at the Farm Show Complex," Justin said. "But, after the show sold out less than two hours after he announced you would be there, he got the event moved into the equine arena. He said the current advanced ticket sales is just over a thousand. And you know there will be people trying to buy tickets at the door. It's possible we could sell out."

"For real?" Zoey asked. She had been to the Farm Show many times over the years. She knew that the equine arena had over 1,500 stadium seats. They could also put a couple hundred chairs on the floor around the ring. "I'll believe it when I see a butt in every seat."

SIXTEEN

Thursday August 23, 2018

T HE HIGH SCHOOL FOOTBALL SCRIMMAGE ran late, and JT Perez didn't get to Zoey's apartment until just after midnight. To keep themselves occupied while they waited, Zoey, Vivian, Justin, and Terry caught up on WWE's *Raw* from Monday night.

When JT showed up, he set to work hooking up his laptop to Zoey's television. Since breaking his neck, JT had stopped going to the gym and let himself go. He had once been in excellent shape and had a physique rivaling that of professional body builders. In the years since the career-ending injury, JT's muscle mass had decreased and turned to fat. If asked, JT would lovingly blame his weight gain on his mother's countless Italian pasta dishes and cannoli.

"I don't know what youse guys are hoping to learn from watching the footage from Saturday night. But I'll do whatever I can to help prove youse didn't kill Devon," JT said. He finished hooking up the laptop and his desktop screen popped up on the TV. "I had three cameras going during the show. Which one do youse want to watch first?"

"Three cameras? I thought you only use two," Justin said as he walked into the living room with a bowl of popcorn. He had a seat on the sectional between his sister and their nana.

"Until this past show, yeah." JT turned around and faced the couch. "I've got the stationary camera up on a scaffold. That's my main camera. And my brother Rocco works the ringside camera. He's quicker on his feet than I am."

Rocco was also five years younger than his brother, and seventy-five pounds lighter. Like JT, Rocco had briefly trained as a pro wrestler. After attending one of Marlon's intense weeklong training camps, Rocco decided he didn't have what it takes and gave up on pursuing a career as a wrestler. Not long after that, he went to work for his brother's video production company as a camera operator.

Continuing, JT said, "This weekend I decided to try out my crane. I spent a lot of money on it, and I don't get to use it all that much. Darn thing is a pain in the butt to operate."

"Is it the same crane you used last week to film that music video I starred in?" Zoey asked. At her recommendation, the band had hired JT and Rocco to film the video. "You didn't seem to have any problems operating it then."

"It's easy to use when I know exactly what I'm filming and can plan out my shots," JT said. "It's a little different filming a live event. Sure, I can sometimes anticipate what youse guys are going to do in the ring. But it's not easy trying to follow the action with the crane."

"Did you get any good shots?" Terry asked.

JT shrugged. "A few. Not enough to make using it worthwhile. I did get a great shot of Zoey hitting the moonsault. But that was probably the best of the night. I'll send youse a clip of it, Zoey. And Vito got some good pictures, too."

Vito Costanzo was JT's cousin. He handled the still photography. JT and Vito made extra money by selling video clips and photos to the wrestlers. Because of the longstanding friendship, JT passed along videos and photos to Zoey and Justin at a discount.

"Sounds like operating the crane kept you busy during the show," Vivian said to JT.

"And it's a good thing it did. It got me off that detective's suspect list. I was too busy working the crane to follow Devon outside and kill him."

"Unless you had someone else work the crane while you went outside after Devon."

Zoey leaned around Justin and shot Vivian an evil look. The plan had been to wait until they were done watching the footage before they accused JT of anything. They couldn't risk upsetting JT and having him leave before they had a chance to watch the footage from Saturday.

"That detective said the same thing when I talked to him yesterday afternoon," JT said. He moved his laptop from the floor to the coffee table. He then had a seat next to Terry at the far end of the sectional. "But between the stationary camera and Rocco's ringside camera, there are enough shots of me working the crane to prove that there's no way I could have snuck outside long enough to kill Devon."

There went one of their suspects. Zoey felt twin pangs of relief and frustration. She hadn't wanted JT to be the killer and she was glad that he had an alibi. But determining that JT had a solid alibi narrowed down their already short suspect list by one person.

Out of the corner of her eye, Zoey watched Vivian draw a line across her notebook. She assumed that her nana had just crossed JT's name off the suspect list.

"Which camera angle do you guys want to watch?" JT asked.

Zoey, Vivian, Justin, and Terry all exchanged looks. It had been Justin's idea to watch the footage from Saturday night, but he didn't have a particular reason as to why he thought watching it was necessary. Personally, Zoey didn't think they'd learn much of anything from the footage—but it was worth a shot.

Anything was worth a shot when it came to proving their innocence.

"Which camera would you suggest?" Zoey asked JT.

"Your best bet is the stationary camera. Watching it won't make youse guys carsick like the ringside camera and the crane will. Plus, it not only shows the ring but some of the banquet hall." JT clicked around on his laptop and brought up a video. The image was out of focus, but the blurry shape that predominated the screen was clearly a wrestling ring. "What exactly is it youse guys are looking for?"

"We have no idea," Zoey said.

"But we'll know it when we see it," Vivian added.

"You'll probably have more luck spotting something useful or suspicious than that detective will," JT said.

"You gave Detective Gates a copy of your footage?" Zoey asked.

"Had to. He had a warrant," JT said. He clicked around on his laptop. "So, do youse guys want to watch the whole show? Or just Justin's and Devon's match?"

"When did you start filming?" Zoey asked. "At the beginning of the show?"

"That's what I normally do. But, because I was using the crane, I turned on the stationary camera around the same time that Leland opened the doors." A deep flush crept up JT's neck and spread across his face. "Not my smartest move since I got footage of me punching Devon."

"Devon's dead," Justin pointed out. "It's not like he's going to press assault charges from beyond the grave."

"Yeah, but at the time, I didn't know Devon would wind up dead by the end of the night." JT leaned across the coffee table and grabbed a handful of popcorn. "But punching Devon was not as satisfying as I thought it would be."

"It was for me," Justin said.

"Yeah, but Devon remembered who you was." JT smacked his hand down on top of the coffee table. "When I confronted him, he didn't remember me. Yeah, I don't look the same as back then. But he didn't even remember me when I told him my name. I had to remind him that he broke my neck. And you know what he did? He laughed and said breaking my neck was more my fault than his. He's the one who messed up the move and dropped me!"

Zoey decided not to point out that Devon had blamed JT for the incident since the day it happened. Devon had refused to take any responsibility.

"Is that why you punched him?" Justin asked.

"Well, that's *when* I hit him." JT pounded his fists against his thighs. "No way I wasn't going to hit him. Not after I waited almost ten years to do it. You know, Devon never once tried to contact me or apologize afterwards. I'm going to be honest with youse guys, I think Devon got what he deserved on Saturday night. I'd like to thank the person who killed him."

"I told Zoey she should be thanking the person, too," Terry said.

"And I told you we shouldn't be happy that Devon was murdered," Zoey said. She shifted, leaning forward so that she could see around Justin and Vivian. After locking eyes with Terry, she said, "No one had more reason than me to hate Devon. But even I didn't want him dead. Only a cold, soulless person would wish death on someone."

"Then call me soulless," JT said. "During those six months I was stuck in that cervical halo, the only thing that kept me going was promising myself that once I was out of the darn thing, I would beat the crap out of Devon. But he moved to Florida while I was recovering."

"Why did you go backstage during intermission?" Justin asked.

JT chuckled and his face flushed a deeper shade of pink. "I did that because . . . well, because I wasn't done giving Devon a piece of my mind. Before the show, Rocco, Vito, Zack, and Marlon hauled me away from Devon after I punched him. I wanted to finish telling Devon that he was a piece of crap human being. So, I went backstage during intermission. Not that it really accomplished anything. At least Devon died knowing my name."

After a few seconds of awkward silence, Zoey cleared her throat and said, "We may as well watch the footage from before the show started. Maybe someone approached Devon . . ."

"Yeah, okay." JT jabbed at a key on his laptop and started the footage. "Just yell if youse see something."

The stationary camera had been focused on the ring, leaving the foreground and background slightly blurred. JT had used a wide angle so that the area surrounding the ring was also included in the shot. Zoey was relieved that hers and Justin's merchandise table was to the side of the ring. They were out of focus in the background, but it was obviously them. As long as JT hadn't messed with the camera's angle or zoomed in on the ring, Zoey would be able to keep an eye on herself and Zack during Justin's match against Devon.

Speaking of Devon, Zoey spotted him right away. He had taken up a stance about twenty feet in front of her merchandise table. Several fans got in the way and blocked him at times, but Devon never strayed far from the spot, and it was easy to keep an eye on him.

"Who's the hussy?" Vivian asked as she flapped her hand towards the TV.

"You need to get your eyes checked, Nana. That's Beverly Hill," Zoey said when she recognized the blonde hanging on Devon's arm. They conversed for a minute or two, and then Beverly walked off. "She's not much older than Hannah. She would have been just a kid when Devon and I moved to Florida. There's no way she would have known him."

"Yeah, but Beverly will hit on anyone who looks semi-decent in a speedo," Justin said. "She was hitting on me and most of the other guys at the July show. If Beverly killed every guy who turned her down, she'd be leaving piles of bodies in her wake. Mine included."

"Me, too," JT said.

Terry raised his hand.

A few minutes—and a few "hussies"—later, Zoey spotted a plump woman with unnaturally red hair enter the frame. "There's Chelsea. And she's making a beeline for Devon."

"Where?" Vivian asked. "I don't see her."

"There." Zoey grabbed Lita's laser pointer toy off the coffee table and directed the beam at the TV. She had enough time to focus the beam on Chelsea before having to point the beam at the floor. As soon as she saw the red dot, Lita leaped off Zoey's lap and went in pursuit. "Devon doesn't seem happy to see her."

"No, he don't," Justin said. "I wish we could hear what they were saying."

From what they could see, Chelsea appeared to do most of the talking . . . and, if the angry look on her face was any indication, Chelsea was not happy with Devon. After a minute of arguing, Devon turned his back on Chelsea and went back to the simpering female fans.

Meanwhile, Chelsea stalked off in the opposite direction and bumped into Sasquatch. They exchanged a few words and then walked out of frame. Zoey had Vivian make a note to question Sasquatch about Chelsea. She recalled hearing that—back before Chelsea became obsessed with Devon—she briefly dated Sasquatch. Zoey didn't know the whole story, but she was interested to find out more. She also wanted to know why Sasquatch hadn't mentioned Chelsea was in the area when they had talked at the gym on Monday morning.

Aside from the scuffle between JT and Devon, the rest of the pre-show footage was uneventful.

Leland had just called for all the wrestlers to head to the back so that they could start the show when Vivian tossed her notebook aside and jumped off the couch.

"Rewind the tape! Rewind the tape."

JT snorted. "Vivi, it's digital. No one uses videotapes anymore."

Vivian grabbed a handful of popcorn and flung it at JT. "Just back it up."

"Who or what did you see, Nana?" Zoey asked.

"I'll let you know." Vivian walked over to the TV and adjusted her glasses. The footage crept across the screen in slow motion. Suddenly, Vivian jabbed her finger against the screen and yelled, "There! Stop! Is that who I think it is?"

"Hard to tell with you blocking the TV." Zoey got up and went to stand beside her nana. "Hey, that guy looks like Quincy."

"That's what I thought," Vivian said.

Zoey looked over the slightly blurred person. A baseball hat blocked the top part of his face—but the bushy beard was the right length and color—and the dark blotches covering his left arm resembled Quincy's dragon tattoo.

"What was Quincy doing at the show? He had an appointment scheduled from six to ten," Zoey said. She knew about the appointment because she was the one who had booked it. Quincy was working on a tattoo that covered a customer's entire back. They had monthly sessions scheduled in advance.

JT restarted the footage, and the five of them watched Quincy confront Devon. They exchanged a few words. Quincy shoved Devon and then walked out of frame.

"Did Quincy just make the list?" Vivian asked.

"Oh, yeah. He made the list," Zoey said.

"Who's this Quincy guy?" JT asked. "What's his motive?"

"He's my ex-boyfriend," Zoey said. "I dated him before Devon."

"Is he still trying to get back together with you?" Justin asked.

"Yeah, he is," Zoey said.

"Do you want to get back together with Quincy?" Terry asked.

"If I had to choose between Devon and Quincy, I would choose Quincy in a heartbeat. But, no, I do not want to get back together with him," Zoey said. "But he can't seem to accept that. Plus . . . He knew Devon was back in the area. Devon came into the shop on Friday afternoon. I didn't recognize him, but Quincy did. He warned Devon to leave me alone."

Zoey was a bit concerned. Quincy hadn't said anything to her about coming to the show. Was it because he had only popped in for a few minutes to say something to Devon? Or had Quincy stayed for the entire show? And what about his appointment? Zoey would have to ask Quincy. First she would talk to Santino. He also had an appointment booked for Saturday night. Santino would be able to tell her if Quincy was at the shop or not.

After JT took a screenshot of Quincy and Devon, they watched the final couple minutes from the pre-show. Because she had been hiding in the bathroom, Zoey had not seen Devon or heard what he had to say at the start of the show. After seeing the video, she was glad that she hadn't witnessed it in person. Devon had not received a warm welcome—which wasn't all that surprising. He hadn't made things any better for himself by talking trash to the fans.

After wasting a few minutes to watch Zoey's and Hannah's match, JT jumped forward in the footage to Justin's and Devon's match.

"I'll keep an eye on me and Zack," Zoey said. She used the laser pointer to pinpoint herself and Zack on the screen. "That way we can see when we both went outside. And when Zack came back in. JT, does your camera have a time code setting?"

"Of course, it does." JT hit a button and the time code popped up in the lower left corner of the screen. "And, don't worry, it's accurate."

"Good." Zoey moved the laser pointer's beam over to the upper right corner. "There's Mort and the security guard. You keep an eye on him, JT. And Nana, Justin, and Terry can just . . . just watch the audience, I guess. Keep an eye out for Chelsea. And Quincy."

JT hit play and the footage resumed. Zoey reached across Justin and grabbed Vivian's notebook. She jotted down that Leland started the second half of the show right after eight-thirty. Justin's and Devon's match didn't officially get started for another seven minutes. She then kept an eye on herself until she walked out the door at eight forty-four. The match ended five minutes later. Zack left the banquet hall a minute after that. Leland went backstage at about the same time.

"Now what, Zoey?" JT asked. "Should I keep playing the footage?"

"Keep playing until Zack comes back inside," Zoey said.

Zoey tried not to blink as she kept her eyes focused on the exterior door. With each minute that passed, the knot of dread in her stomach grew. The longer Zack was outside, the worse it looked.

"There's Zack," Vivian said.

"Where? I didn't see him come in," Zoey said. She'd been laser focused on the door that was behind her merchandise table. Yes, she had blinked a couple times, but there was no way she would have missed seeing Zack come back inside.

"Right there." Vivian used the laser pointer to pinpoint where Zack was now seated in the front row alongside the rest of the family. "He must have come in through the front door."

Zoey checked the timecode and saw that it was five after nine when Zack returned to his seat. After jotting down the time, Zoey slumped back against the couch cushions.

JT paused the video. "What's wrong, Zoey?"

"Zack was outside for over ten minutes," Zoey said.

"That's plenty of time to have argued with Devon and then bashed him over the head," Justin said. "Not that I think Zack did it."

"How would Zack have gotten the sledgehammer? He went out through the side door. And isn't the general consensus that Devon left the sledgehammer backstage?" Vivian asked. She then leaned around Justin to address Zoey. "What time did you find Devon?"

"How should I know?" Zoey asked. "It's not like I stopped to check the time."

"You called 911, right?" Justin asked. "Won't there be a record in your phone?"

"No. Kim called 911."

"I'll ask her to check her call log," Terry said as he tapped out the message on his phone.

While they waited for Kim to respond, Zoey checked the call log on her phone. "I called the police to report my flat tires at eight fifty-two. It was right after I called that I walked over to the other parking lot to get the pump out of Dad's truck. It took me at least ten minutes to find Dad's truck, get the stuff I needed, and then get back over to my Jeep."

"Mom says she called 911 at ten after nine," Terry said.

"That leaves us with a pretty narrow timeframe," Vivian said.

Zoey groaned. "We know Devon was killed sometime after I called the police at eight-fifty-two and before Kim called the police at nine-ten. That means Devon had to be dead by . . . let's say . . . five after nine . . . That's roughly ten minutes between Devon getting tossed outside and getting bashed over the head. That leaves plenty of time for someone to have gone after Devon."

"And Zack was outside during most of that time," Vivian said.

"Well I don't think it's Mort," JT said. "He hasn't moved."

"But Chelsea has," Vivian said. "JT, rewind a minute or two. You can see her walk through the lower left corner. I can't tell if she went outside, but . . ."

"But it's possible," Zoey said.

After reviewing the footage a second time, they confirmed that Chelsea got up from her seat and walked out of frame at eight fifty-three. While keeping an eye on the audience to see if Chelsea came back to her seat, Zoey spotted a familiar baseball hat and beard. Quincy was back. Perhaps he had never left. Less than a minute after Chelsea walked off, Quincy got up and walked out of frame. Neither Chelsea nor Quincy came back into frame throughout the rest of the footage.

Leland came back onto the stage at a ten after nine—leaving him plenty of time to have followed Devon out into the parking lot and bashed him over the head.

It was almost three in the morning when they finished watching the different camera angles. JT had been right, the footage from the crane and ringside camera were enough to cause carsickness. And neither had been all that helpful other than to prove that neither Rocco or Vito had gone after Devon in revenge for what he did to JT years earlier. After making Zoey a copy of the footage, JT packed up his laptop and left. Justin and Terry left a few minutes after him.

"What do we do next?" Vivian asked.

"Aside for get some sleep?" Zoey yawned. "I have no idea . . ."

SEVENTEEN

"I SEE YOUR SUSPECT BOARD IS BACK," Zoey said when she walked into her kitchen on Thursday morning and found her nana seated at the table. "And that you updated it."

"It gave me something to do while I waited for your lazy butt to get up," Vivian said.

Zoey stuck her tongue out at Vivian and then turned to examine the corkboard.

Pinned to the middle of the board were the two pictures of Devon that Detective Gates gave Zoey. To the left of Devon's pictures was a timeline of events from Saturday night. There was also a picture of a sledgehammer along with a list of whose fingerprints had been found on the murder weapon. Down the right side of the board—under a notecard that had 'SUSPECTS' written across it—were pictures of various people.

"Is there a reason Zack, Justin, and I are at the top of your suspect list?"

"Would you prefer to be at the bottom?" Vivian asked.

"I'd prefer not to be on it at all," Zoey said.

"But that's the whole point of this." Vivian waved her hands over the corkboard. "To prove to that handsome detective that you and your brothers are innocent."

"We know Mort, Squatch, and JT couldn't possibly have done it. But you left their pictures on the suspect list." Zoey jabbed at the three pictures. "Shouldn't you remove them since they're no longer suspects?"

"I was getting to that." Vivian picked up a red marker and drew big X's over the pictures of Mortimer, Sasquatch, and JT. She also drew a slash across Justin. "We know Justin couldn't have killed Devon. He has an alibi."

"Shouldn't you cross me and Zack off since you know we didn't do it?"

"Both of you *claim* you didn't do it," Vivian said. "But the handsome detective isn't going to take your word for it. And neither am I. We need to prove it."

"Thanks for the vote of confidence, Nana."

Vivian's remaining list of suspects included Chelsea, Leland, and Quincy. A picture of an oversized question mark represented suspects unknown. Tacked next to each picture was a notecard on which Vivian had jotted down motives, alibis, and other comments. Leland's motive had been left blank. Quincy's motive was listed as "wants to be Zoey's knight in shining armor." Vivian had also made notes of known interactions between Devon and the suspects on Saturday night.

"Which one of the three do you think did it?" Vivian asked.

"We don't know if any of them did it. I'm sure there are other people who had motive to kill Devon. There is a good chance that the question mark is the murderer."

"But of those three . . . Which one do you think did it?"

After grabbing a glass of orange juice and a couple breakfast bars, Zoey had a seat across from Vivian. "If I had to guess . . . Chelsea. She has the best motive—"

"And she's nuts."

"More like batshit crazy." Zoey broke off a piece of the breakfast bar and popped it in her mouth. "Devon took advantage of Chelsea for years. Maybe coming back to Pennsylvania after me was Chelsea's breaking point. But I have no idea how she would have gotten her hands on the sledgehammer considering Devon left it inside the VFW Hall as he was being given the bum's rush."

"Same with Quincy," Vivian said. "He wouldn't have been able to get backstage to grab the sledgehammer either."

"Quincy also doesn't have much of a motive."

"Aside from still being in love with you after all these years?"

"Yeah, well . . ."

"Are you still in love with him?"

"No. And I don't want to talk about it," Zoey said before Vivian could ask any more personal questions. "As for Uncle Leland . . . He doesn't have a motive."

"That we know about."

"True . . ." Zoey tapped her finger against her chin as she considered possible motives for Leland. She couldn't come up with anything plausible. "You know what didn't make any sense on Saturday? Uncle Leland seemed excited to see Devon. And he was acting all buddy-buddy with him. But, back before Devon and I moved to Florida, Uncle Leland could barely stand him. And he thought Devon was a crappy wrestler. The sudden change of heart is a little weird."

Vivian shrugged. "It's Leland. I've known him for over thirty years, and almost nothing he does ever makes much sense to me. Like marrying Kim. I still can't figure that out. Leland has a type. And Kim is not it."

Ignoring Vivian's comments about Leland and Kim, Zoey said, "Uncle Leland might not have a motive, but, out of your three suspects, he did have the best access to the sledgehammer. Plus he doesn't have much of an alibi. He claims he was in the storage room smoking. But, as far as I know, no one actually saw him in there."

Vivian clapped her hands together and asked, "Which one of our suspects should we interrogate first?"

"Interrogating the suspects is Detective Gates's job."

"Then which one of our suspects should we question?"

"Nana . . ." Zoey groaned as she ran her hands over her face and back through her hair. "I've been thinking . . . Maybe we shouldn't try conducting our own investigation. We aren't the police. All we're going to do is get in the way and mess up the actual investigation."

Vivian crossed her arms over her chest and scowled at her granddaughter. "If you won't help clear your name, I'll just have to do it myself."

"Fine . . ." Zoey stood up and carried her empty glass to the sink. "But we can't talk to Chelsea if she's still at the hospital."

"Not unless one of us gets committed or checks in to the nuthouse."

"Considering the stupidity of what you want to do, we probably should be committed to a nuthouse. Normal people don't go around sticking their noses in police investigations."

"Since when have we been normal?"

Zoey sighed. Her nana made a good point. Neither of them—nor any other members of the Wilde family—could be considered "normal."

"There's no way for us to talk to Chelsea," Zoey said. "We don't know if she is still at the hospital or not. She could have been released already. And, if she was, we have no idea where to find her. Not that I want to find her. After she pulled a gun on me the other night, I really do not want to see her again."

"Understandable," Vivian said. "How 'bout we talk to Quincy. I just know that boy is hiding something."

"I don't know about that. But I do want to know what he was doing at the show. He had an appointment scheduled that night." Zoey glanced at the clock and saw that it was nine-thirty. "But Quincy will be here in a few hours. What's the point of tracking him down when he'll be coming to us soon enough?"

"That just leaves Leland," Vivian said. "But he's missing in action."

"Still?"

"Kim called your mom earlier this morning. She's getting really worried. Leland isn't answering his phone and she has no idea where he is," Vivian said as she scowled. "I told her that Leland's a grown man and can take care of himself—"

Zoey cleared her throat. "If we don't know where Leland is, we can't talk to him."

"Then who should we talk to?"

"I know who we should talk to," Zoey said. "But she's someone I had hoped to never speak to again."

Vivian gasped. "Have you lost your mind?"

"Possibly. But we need to talk to Devon's mother." Zoey nodded confidently even as her stomach churned with unease. She then turned around and headed for her bedroom. "Give me a few minutes to clean up. Then we can go."

When Zoey returned to the kitchen fifteen minutes later, she found Justin and Terry seated at the table along with Vivian.

"Aren't you two supposed to be at work?" Zoey asked.

"Not much else we can do in the kitchen until after the flooring is installed," Terry said.

"So Dad sent us over here to keep an eye on you and Nana while you're . . . in his words . . . 'doing asinine stuff.'"

"I told Marlon we don't need a babysitter," Vivian grumbled.

"More like bodyguards," Terry said as he held out a sheet of paper to Zoey. "I found this tucked under one of your windshield wipers when we got here."

Zoey plucked the paper out of Terry's hand. Scrawled in black marker was the message: "*I did you a favor. Now do me a favor and stop trying to figure out who I am.*"

"Is this supposed to be some kind of threat?" Zoey asked.

"I wouldn't exactly call it threatening," Justin said. "But it's not a love note either."

"I think you should take it seriously," Terry said.

"If the killer is sending us threatening notes, that means we must be closing in on him or her." Vivian grabbed the note. She then crumpled up the paper and tossed it towards the trash can. The paper ball fell short of the mark, and Lita shot out from under the table and pounced on it. "A vaguely threatening note is not going to stop me."

"I JUST LOVE WHAT PAULA'S DONE to the place," Vivian said.

"It always was a dump." Zoey pulled to the side of the road and parked in the gravel lot that was across the street from Paula's house. "But Paula's really let it go since the last time I was here."

"The toilet bowl in the flower bed is a nice touch." Vivian slipped out of the passenger seat and then walked around the Jeep. Turning her back to the eyesore of a house, she faced the river. A line of oak trees along the bank partially obscured the view. "She's got some beautiful scenery though."

Paula Isler lived in Peach Bottom. The small, unincorporated village was along the Susquehanna River—the longest river on the East Coast. Her house was in the middle of a row of homes that sat on a low ridge overlooking the river.

During the first year of her relationship with Devon, Zoey had spent an excessive amount of time at Paula's house. After her husband died, Paula had become increasingly dependent on her son and expected him to cater to her every whim. Habitually, she would come up with some reason for him to spend time at her house. More often than not, she caused the problem herself and then demanded that Devon come fix it. If Devon ever tried to refuse, Paula would remind him that she was a widow and manipulate him into doing whatever she wanted. Unfortunately for Zoey, Devon had always dragged her along with him. And not once had Paula made her feel welcome.

"Let's get this over with," Zoey said as she mounted the lopsided metal staircase that provided access from the road up the ridge to the house. Halfway up the staircase, Zoey stopped. Turning around, she faced Vivian, Justin, and Terry. "Maybe you three should wait out here. I can't imagine that Paula is going to be happy to see us. And she's going to be difficult enough to talk to. And that's even if she will talk to me. We probably shouldn't overwhelm her with a small horde of people."

"Yeah, all right," Justin said. He retreated down the steps, forcing Terry along with him. "We'll wait out here."

"I'm not waiting outside." Vivian pushed past Zoey and continued up the staircase. "I've got a few things I'd like to say to Paula . . ."

"Can you try to be civil?" Zoey asked as she followed her nana.

"She was hardly civil to you during the time you dated Devon." Vivian yanked open the storm door, slamming the aluminum against the railing. "Why should I be civil to her now?"

"Because her only son was just murdered." Zoey stepped through the doorway and into the screened-in porch. All the window screens had holes in them, and one was missing entirely. The porch was piled high with junk including a freezer, a rusty bicycle, and a dilapidated set of wicker chairs among other junk. "Just because we didn't like Devon doesn't mean we can't feel some compassion for Paula."

Vivian crossed her arms over her chest and harrumphed.

Zoey was about to knock when the door swung open and a young woman with bleached blonde hair stepped out onto the deck.

"I see you finally got your purple Jeep, Zoey."

"Hi, Danielle," Zoey said, greeting Devon's younger sister. She leaned against an old dresser with a broken drawer. "Don't tell me you're still living here with Paula."

"Heck no." Danielle had a seat on a beat-up plastic lawn chair. She stuck a cigarette between her red lips and used a match to light it. "I live in Baltimore now. I'm just home for the week to help Mom take care of Devon's funeral. It's not like she's got anyone else to help her."

When she started dating Devon, Zoey tried to befriend Danielle. They were the same age and had similar interests. They probably would have been friends had Devon not interfered. He had purposely caused animosity between his girlfriend and his sister to keep them from forming a friendship. It didn't help that Danielle didn't like her only sibling and spent as little time as possible in his company.

The last time Zoey had seen Danielle was a few weeks after she moved home from Florida. Paula had showed up at Marlon's and Roxanne's house to confront Zoey, and Danielle had tagged along with her. After Paula had finished screaming at Zoey, Danielle rubbed it in Zoey's face that she had long ago warned her about Devon's true nature and mocked her for not taking those warnings seriously.

"Did you know Devon was back in the area?" Zoey asked Danielle.

"Nope. Not until Sunday morning when Mom called to tell me he was dead." Danielle used the end of her cigarette to light up a second one. "Had I known he was back, I would have looked you up and sent you a message. It's the least I could have done. But, by the time I found out he was back, he was already dead. Wouldn't have done you much good."

"No, it wouldn't have."

"So . . ." Danielle ground out the second cigarette in a terracotta pot that housed a dead plant. "Did you kill him?"

Zoey had been waiting for that question. "No, I didn't."

"Wouldn't really blame you if you did." Danielle stood up and turned towards the door. "I guess you're here to see Mom."

"Is she home?"

"Yeah, she's here," Danielle said as she pushed open the door. The hinges squealed in protest. "And she's not going to be happy to see you."

"That'll be nothing new. Your mother always hated me."

"She hates you even more now."

Zoey followed Danielle into the house and almost tripped over a bulging trash bag. The interior of Paula's house—which had never been all that neat—was now a hoarders' paradise. There was junk piled up on the floor and on every available flat surface. Even one end of the couch was buried under a pile of flattened cardboard boxes.

Stepping around a plastic tub full of squashed soda cans, Zoey crept into the living room. As Vivian turned to shut the door, her oversized purse brushed against a pile of junk that was stacked on top of a table. A small avalanche of mail slipped to the floor, and it carried a framed picture of Devon along with it. The glass shattered when it hit the floor.

"What are you breaking now, you useless girl?" An overweight woman in a stained "Ice Man" tank top stomped into the living room. Her beady eyes locked on Zoey. "You!"

"Hi, Paula."

Paula's face turned as red as her faded leggings as she screamed in rage. She reached behind her into the kitchen and grabbed a knife that had a long blade and a serrated edge. Clutching the knife in her fist, Paula charged towards Zoey. With the agility of an Olympic athlete, Paula hurdled over a stack of old Tupperware containers. Zoey was about to take a diving leap over the couch when Vivian stuck out her leg and tripped Paula.

Dropping the knife, Paula held out her arms to break her fall as she slammed face-first onto the coffee table. Two of the table's short legs snapped off, and the table collapsed beneath Paula's weight. The knife clattered on the floor near Zoey's feet. She booted it under the couch.

"Really, Mom?" Danielle asked. "Is that any way to greet our guests?"

Rolling off the coffee table, Paula pressed her face to the worn-out carpet and howled.

"Everything okay?" Justin asked as he and Terry slipped inside. "We heard screaming."

"Does everything look okay to you?" Vivian asked as she gestured towards Paula.

While Danielle tried to get Paula calmed down, Zoey took the opportunity to look around the living room. There were framed pictures of Devon everywhere. Almost every square inch of wall space was covered in frames, and there were more frames sitting on every flat—and nearly flat—surface. The pictures ranged from Devon's infancy to around the time of his incarceration. Paula even had Devon's mugshot hanging on the wall.

"I know you killed my son," Paula shouted as Justin and Terry helped her up from the floor and guided her over to an old recliner. She blew her nose and then focused her bloodshot eyes on Zoey. "And I told that detective—"

"I did not kill Devon."

"Liar! I know you killed him!" Paula tossed the crumpled tissue at Zoey's face. "Back when I first met you, I knew you were trouble. I told Devon to stay away from you. But you put a spell on him and—"

"Oh, so now I'm a witch?"

"You'd have to be. Bewitching him is the only way a trashy woman like you would be able to get a good man like my son." Paula shifted forward to the edge of her seat. Her plump fingers clenched around the arms of the chair. "You were never good enough for Devon. He was a wonderful man. He was perfect—"

"Lady, you got it backwards." Terry leaned over Paula and caused her to shrink back against the stained cushions. His entire body vibrated with rage, and the veins in his neck bulged as he shouted in Paula's face. "It was Devon who was nowhere near good enough for Zoey. She's an amazing, beautiful woman. And your maggot of a son treated her like a doormat. Devon wasn't even worthy of breathing the same air as Zoey. After what he did to her . . . After he almost killed her . . . On Saturday night, Devon finally got what he deserved—"

"Cool it." Justin placed his hand on Terry's shoulder and drew him away from Paula. "Maybe we should go back outside."

Danielle escorted Justin and Terry to the door. She then came back into the living room and said, "That guy is right, Mom. Devon was an awful human being. He got the worst parts of you and Dad. He was a conceited, abusive piece of sh—"

Paula slapped her daughter across her face. "Shut up! I won't listen to your lies about your father and your brother. They were perfect. And they were both taken from me too soon. I wish it had been you who died instead of Devon."

As Danielle staggered backwards, Zoey reached out and grabbed her arm to prevent her from tripping over what was left of the coffee table.

"After everything I've done for you . . ." Danielle pulled away from Zoey and took a couple steps closer to Paula. "You are delusional. Dad drank and smoked himself into an early grave. And Devon was a spoiled mama's boy. But that's your fault. You coddled him. You never held him responsible for anything he did. You put him on a pedestal and worshipped him. You turned him into a horrible human being—"

"Devon was my son. He was my pride and joy. Unlike you," Paula said to her only daughter. "I did my best to raise Devon right. To raise both of you right."

Vivian snorted. "Wolves would have done a better job raising your kids."

Paula snarled at Vivian. She then turned to Zoey and said, "You ruined my son's life. Meeting you was the worst thing that ever happened to him."

"Worst thing that ever happened to me, too," Zoey said.

"No, meeting him was the best thing that ever happened to you. Without him, you'd be nothing. A nobody. My son gave you your fifteen minutes of fame."

"By almost killing me!"

"If you hadn't tried to leave him, he wouldn't have done that. You provoked him. And then you left him to rot in that jail cell." Sweat streamed down Paula's wrinkled forehead, and she was almost frothing at the mouth. "You ruined his life and his career. Devon was going places. He could have been someone. Then you came along and held him back. If you hadn't been so determined to ride his coattails—"

"Ride *his* coattails? Oh, please." Zoey clenched her teeth. "Devon never would have made it. None of the top pro wrestling organizations in the US showed any interest in him. And none of the second-tier companies that hired him ever brought him back for another show because he was so difficult to work with. But they all invited me back—on the condition that I promise not to bring Devon along. I'm the one who could have been someone—"

"Then why aren't you?" Paula asked. "I watch wrestling on TV every week. I've never seen you on any of the shows."

Zoey decided that it wasn't worth getting into. That's not why she and Vivian were here. Changing the subject, Zoey said, "I know Devon was staying with you for a few days before he died. What was he up to? Who else knew he was here?"

"I don't have to answer your questions. You're not the police." Paula pushed herself to her feet and then flapped her hands towards the front door. "I want you out of my house."

Zoey stood up. "Come on, Nana. This was useless."

"Uh . . . Before you go . . ." Danielle stepped between Zoey and the door. "There's something I want to show you."

Leaving Vivian in the living room with Paula, Zoey followed Danielle up the narrow staircase to Devon's former attic bedroom. The air upstairs was stifling, and Zoey had to stand hunched over to keep from whacking her head against the ceiling.

"I figured you should see this."

Danielle stepped to the side and then gestured at the sloped ceiling. There were pictures of Zoey tacked up everywhere. Most of the pictures were old, but Zoey spotted some that had been taken recently. Paula had turned her living room into a shrine for her son. Devon had done the same thing in his bedroom—except his shrine was for Zoey.

"This is really creepy."

"The police found this when they came to interview Mom and search Devon's stuff for evidence. I wasn't here for that." Danielle flopped down onto the twin mattress and kicked at an old, faded rug that covered part of the floor. "I wonder if the police found Devon's secret spot."

"What secret spot?" Zoey asked.

"There's a loose floorboard that Devon used to hide stuff under. Mostly weed and girly magazines. He didn't know that I knew about it." Danielle flung back the rug and began poking at the uneven floorboards. One popped up. "Ah, here it is."

Zoey knelt next to Danielle and peered into the shallow space. Danielle turned on her phone's flashlight and illuminated the cobwebs and mouse droppings that filled the hole. There was also a crisp white envelope.

Using one of Devon's socks to cover her hand, Zoey reached into the nasty cavity and pulled out the envelope. She then turned the envelope upside down and six pictures slipped out. Danielle spread out the pictures on the mattress.

At first glance, the pictures appeared to be terrible selfies. Devon's ear and part of his face featured prominently in the foreground of each picture. Judging by the shadowy, slightly blurry background, the pictures had been taken in a dimly-lit dive bar.

"Why would Devon bother hiding these?" Danielle asked as they studied the pictures. "I mean, why even keep them? It's not like they're good pictures of him."

"I think Devon kept them because of who's in the background."

Zoey looked past Devon's ear to the two shadowy figures who were seated at a table behind him. One of the people had a familiar looking handlebar mustache. The first two pictures were innocent enough. Leland Freeman was seated in the back corner of the bar with Beverly Hill. In the third picture, Beverly was sitting a little too close to Leland. In the fourth, he had his arm around her. And in the last two pictures, they were sharing a passionate embrace.

"Who are they?" Danielle asked.

"That's my uncle Leland. He's the promoter of the Linville Association of Wrestling. He hired Devon to wrestle on Saturday night." Zoey jabbed at the blonde woman next to Leland. "And the woman he's kissing . . . Well, she's not his wife."

"Blackmail?" Danielle asked.

"I think so."

EIGHTEEN

"What did you say to Paula while Danielle and I were upstairs?" Zoey asked as she and Vivian emerged from the house. "I've never seen her so contrite."

"I told her exactly what I thought of her. And her good-for-nothing son." Vivian smirked. "She didn't enjoy hearing it. But she couldn't deny any of it either."

Zoey laughed. For years, she had listened to Vivian's rants against Devon and Paula. While she didn't know exactly what her nana had said, she had a fairly good idea . . . and no, Paula would not have appreciated it. She could never tolerate anyone speaking badly about her son.

"You all right, Terry?" Zoey asked as she and Vivian made their way down the shoddy exterior staircase. Terry was seated on the bottom step alongside Justin.

"Yeah, I'm all right." Terry rubbed his hands over his face and back through his hair. "I don't know what came over me. I just couldn't stand listening to her insult you."

Zoey patted him on the shoulder. "Paula didn't say anything today that she hasn't said on numerous other occasions. I don't take it personally."

"How'd it go after we came outside?" Justin asked. "Did you learn anything?"

"I got Paula to admit that she knew Devon was stalking Zoey. And that Chelsea was the only other person who knew Devon was staying here,"

Vivian said as she walked across the overgrown lawn to Zoey's Jeep. "Other than that, it was a waste of time."

"I wouldn't say it was a complete waste," Zoey said as she climbed in behind the wheel. She waited until Vivian, Justin, and Terry were inside the car before pulling the pictures out of her purse. "I figured out Uncle Leland's motive."

"What have you got there? Let me see." Vivian snatched the pictures away from Zoey and spread them out on her lap. She picked up one of the pictures at random and held it in front of her face. "What am I looking at? Aside from someone's ear?"

"Look at the upper left corner," Zoey said.

"Oh." Vivian moved the pictures a little closer to her face and adjusted her glasses that had hot pink frames. Her eyes widened in shock and she slammed the picture facedown onto the dashboard. "Oh! That dirty, rotten scoundrel."

"What is it? I want to see." Justin reached between the seats and snagged one of the pictures. "Oooohhhhh. Not good."

"Son of a bitch!" Terry shouted as he ripped the picture out of Justin's hand. He then flung the picture aside as he scrambled to pull his cell phone out of the side pocket of his cargo shorts. "I have to tell my mom."

"No!" Zoey turned around and grabbed Terry's cell phone out of his hands. "You can't tell her. At least not yet."

"Why not?" Terry asked. He reached for his phone, but Zoey held it out of reach. "My mom needs to know that Leland has been cheating on her."

"And we'll tell her," Zoey said. "But not until *after* we talk to him. If you tell your mom, she'll call Leland. That'll ruin our element of surprise. And it'll give Uncle Leland time to think up excuses and lies."

Terry groaned. "Yeah, all right. But how are we supposed to talk to him? Mom has no idea where he's been the past few days. And he won't return any of her calls. Last night and again this morning Mom drove past all the rental properties Leland owns to see if he's staying in an empty unit. But she didn't see his truck at any of the apartment buildings or houses. And she drove by the hotel, the motel, and both bed and breakfasts in Linville. She didn't see his truck in any of their lots either."

"He's probably shacked up with Beverly." Justin snickered. "Too bad we don't know where she lives."

"Enough, Justin," Zoey said. She held Terry's phone out to him. "Maybe Leland will answer if you call him. Just don't mention that we know about Beverly."

Terry called Leland but was sent to voicemail. He left a message about how Kim was worried about him and asked him to call as soon as possible.

"You know, this could explain some things," Vivian said as she flipped through the pictures. "On Saturday, Leland said that Carl Mease cancelled and that's why he had to hire Devon to wrestle Justin. But on Sunday, Carl claimed it was the other way around. Leland cancelled on him. If Devon was using these pictures to blackmail Leland—"

"That's what I'm assuming," Zoey said.

"Leland obviously wouldn't want Mom to know he was cheating on her," Terry said. He had his forehead pressed to the back of the passenger seat. "Before they got married, Mom made Leland sign a prenup. It was mainly to protect her since she owns the house and everything. But she also had her lawyer include an infidelity clause. If Leland cheats on her and she can prove it . . . Well, Leland is shit out of luck."

It wasn't until a few years ago that Zoey learned about what really happened to Terry's birth father. All Kim had ever said was that he'd left when Terry was six and they'd had no contact with him since. The truth was not that simple. Terry's father was a few years older than Kim. They had met while he was attending college, and she was a senior in high school. About the time she graduated from high school, Kim realized that she was pregnant. Terry's father dropped out of college, married Kim, and settled down to family life. But being a family man did not suit him. Kim claimed that the abuse had started off as verbal and later escalated to physical. Despite the abuse, she stayed with her husband for Terry's sake—until she caught him striking their son. That was Kim's last straw. She divorced her husband and got sole custody of Terry. She then moved to Linville to start over just in time for Terry to begin second grade.

"I wonder when and where the pictures were taken," Vivian said.

"Had to be sometime between Monday night and Friday night of last week," Zoey said.

"Should I add Beverly to the list?" Vivian asked.

"Definitely," Zoey said. "Beverly was at the show on Saturday. And, thanks to JT, we have proof that she talked to Devon. It's possible Devon was blackmailing her as well. For all we know, she might have a husband or a boyfriend—"

Interrupting, Justin said, "I doubt it considering the way she was hitting on me and the rest of the guys in the locker room back at the July LAW show. I don't know about the other guys, but I didn't take her up on her offer to have a 'sleepover.' That was around the time that I started seriously talking to Hannah. Not that I would have gone to Beverly's if I hadn't been talking to Hannah. Beverly sends nudes, and that is a major turnoff for me."

"I hope you deleted those messages before Hannah gets the wrong idea," Zoey said.

"Hannah's already seen them," Justin said. "She was with me when Beverly sent them."

"I'm sure that went over well . . ." Zoey said. She was surprised Hannah hadn't flipped out and gone after Beverly. "Regardless of her motive, Beverly could have followed Devon outside and bashed him over the head so he couldn't tell anyone about the affair she was having with Leland. If they even are having an affair. All these pictures prove is that they kissed each other."

"Kissing another woman is cheating," Terry mumbled.

"I don't know what Beverly would want with Leland," Vivian said. "He's not ugly but he's not all that good looking either. And he's old enough to be her father. Heck, he's almost old enough to be her grandfather."

"Sugar daddy?" Zoey asked.

"Leland doesn't have enough money to be a sugar daddy," Terry said. "He was in debt when Mom married him. And his credit score is still really bad."

"What do we know about Beverly Hill?" Vivian asked. She pulled her notebook out of her purse and flipped to a blank page. "What's her real name? Where does she live?"

Zoey opened the Facebook app on her phone and brought up the other woman's profile. "Her real name is Beverly Hillegas. She's twenty-two. She lives in Hershey, and her relationship status is listed as 'it's complicated.' And, according to this, she is a dancer at one of the strip clubs up in Harrisburg."

"Which one?" Justin asked.

"The Velvet Lounge," Zoey said.

"Ugh." Justin made a gagging sound. "That place is a dump."

Zoey adjusted the rearview mirror so that she could see her brother's face. "And you know it's a dump how?"

"Don't ask questions unless you really want to know the answer," Justin said. In the mirror, Zoey watched Justin nudge Terry in the side and wink. "The club isn't too far from the Farm Show Complex. After the show, we could stop by and see if Beverly's working."

Vivian jotted down notes. "We could interrogate Beverly about Saturday night."

"And interrogate her about what she's doing with Leland," Terry added.

"Question. We are *questioning* people. Not that we should be." Zoey glanced at the dashboard and saw that it was going on eleven-thirty. "We better get back to Linville. I need to put in a couple hours at the tattoo shop before we head up to Harrisburg for the show."

"Actually . . ." Justin said, drawing out the word. "We need to get to the Farm Show Complex by three at the latest. The guys from Gutbuster are driving out from Philly to interview us for their podcast."

"Justin . . ."

"What? I told you we need to take advantage of this, Zoey."

A LITTLE OVER AN HOUR AFTER LEAVING Paula's house, Zoey pulled into the parking lot at the Linville Police Department.

"What are we doing here?" Vivian asked.

"Turning over evidence." Zoey parked her Jeep in front of the building. She then leaned over the center console and plucked the incriminating pictures of Leland and Beverly Hill out of Vivian's purse. "Why else do you think I stopped at CVS to make copies of the pictures?"

"So we each had our own set."

"And because you want my mom to have a copy," Terry said.

"Well, yeah, I want your mom to have a copy," Zoey said. "But you can't give them to her until—"

"Until after we talk to Leland," Terry said. "I know, I know."

Vivian tried to snatch the pictures from Zoey. "But that's our evidence."

Holding the pictures out of Vivian's reach, Zoey said, "And we are not the police."

"Why do you want to help the handsome detective?" Vivian asked. "He thinks you and your brothers are murderers."

"Hey," Justin said as he leaned forward and stuck his head between the front seats. "I didn't kill Devon. I have an alibi. At least four people—"

Interrupting, Vivian said, "We know you didn't kill Devon. But the detective still thinks you might have been involved in his death."

"But I wasn't."

"And neither was I. Or Zack. And that's why I want to give the detective more suspects . . . So he has someone else to look at other than us." Zoey opened the driver's side door and stepped down to the pavement. "Are any of you coming with me?"

Vivian crossed her arms over her chest and turned to face the passenger side window.

Terry shook his head and then went back to staring dejectedly at his phone.

"Police departments give me hives," Justin said.

"Fine. Be that way."

Zoey tossed the car keys onto the front seat and then slammed the door.

After a brief discussion with one of the police department's receptionists, Zoey found herself seated across the desk from Detective Gates. Zoey noticed that he had hung a couple framed diplomas on the wall since she had last been there.

"You have evidence pertaining to the case?"

Zoey slapped the pictures onto the desktop. "Chances are you already have them. But just in case Devon deleted them from his phone, I figured I better share these with you."

After examining them, Gates looked up at Zoey and asked, "Where did you get these?"

"I know you told me to stay out of it. But we . . . uh . . ."

"Who's we?"

"Me, my nana, Justin, and Terry," Zoey said. "We paid a condolence call on Devon's mom this morning. His sister found these hidden in Devon's room and gave them to me."

"Uh huh. We'll pretend it was a condolence call instead of you snooping. And I won't waste my breath lecturing you. But, yes, I have seen these pictures. I did not know they were important until now. I recognize Leland Freeman." Detective Gates held up one of the pictures and pointed at Beverly. "Do you know who this woman is?"

"Her name is Beverly Hillegas. She wrestles under the name Beverly Hill. She was at the show on Saturday night."

"Thank you for passing along this information, Miss Wilde. I appreciate it," Gates said. "Do you have any other information to share with me?"

"JT Perez told me that he gave you a copy of the footage from Saturday night—"

"Is it safe to assume he gave you a copy as well?"

Zoey nodded. "Did you see Chelsea Neville confront Devon before the show?"

"Yes, I did. And I plan to ask her about it whenever I get to interview her." Zoey took that to mean that Chelsea was still being held at the hospital.

"Did you also see Chelsea get up and walk out of frame right after Devon's match?"

"No, I did not." Detective Gates sat down behind his desk and clicked around on his laptop. He then turned the laptop around to face Zoey. "Show me."

Zoey moved through the footage until just after Justin's and Devon's match ended. She then hit play and pointed out Chelsea as she briefly appeared in the frame.

"I don't know where Chelsea's headed," Zoey said. "But she never reenters the frame."

"Thank you for showing me this." Gates backed up the footage and took a screen shot. "What about the pictures of the victim that I gave to you? Did you show them to anyone?"

Zoey nodded. "I showed the pictures of Devon to my family and the guys at the tattoo shop. The artist who talked to Devon on Friday . . . his name is Quincy Durand. He knew Devon from before. And he recognized him."

"But Mr. Durand didn't say anything to you?" Detective Gates asked. After Zoey shook her head, he continued. "I'll have to swing by the shop later today to speak to Mr. Durand—"

"Quincy was also at the show on Saturday night," Zoey said. She hated throwing Quincy under the proverbial bus. But she had to do whatever she

could to save Zack. And if that meant serving Quincy up as a possible suspect, then she had to do it. "He confronted Devon before the show. He also
stuck around to watch the show. You can see him walk out of frame right
after Zack comes back inside. I don't know if he left the building or—"

"You didn't ask him?"

"No . . . I haven't talked to him since I watched the footage last night."

"And I would prefer if you did not speak with him until after I do,"
Detective Gates said. "It's unfortunate that you are a person of interest—"

"You mean suspect?"

"Otherwise, I could use your help. In an unofficial role, of course. I'm
sure you could help me identify some of the other people in the footage.
As it is . . ." Detective Gates stood up and gestured towards the door. "I
know you want to clear your name as well as both of your brothers. But,
going forward, please refrain from interfering with my investigation,
Miss Wilde."

"GOOD, HE'S HERE." VIVIAN CLAPPED HER HANDS and cackled as Zoey
pulled around to the back of 3 Count Tattoos and parked next to Quincy's
motorcycle. "Time to interrogate Quincy."

"Question, Nana. We are *questioning* people. Not interrogating them,"
Zoey said, correcting her nana's word choice for what felt like the tenth
or twelfth time that day. "And we are not going to say anything to Quincy
until after the detective has a chance to talk to him."

"What does the detective want to talk to Quincy about?"

"For starters . . . About how Devon came into the shop last week and
what they talked about," Zoey said. She also wanted to know what Quincy
and Devon had said to each other. On Monday, she had been too angry to
ask for the details of the conversation. Since then, she had been too distracted or worried about other things to bring it up. "I also told Detective
Gates that Quincy was at the show on Saturday night."

"I thought you were only giving him the pictures of Leland and that
hussy."

"Which I did," Zoey said. "After I gave him the pictures, he asked me if
I had learned anything else. So I told him that both Quincy and Chelsea
were at the show—"

"Why are you sharing all our leads?"

"Because Gates is the one investigating Devon's murder. We're just being nosy."

"She makes a good point, Nana," Justin said.

Vivian harrumphed. "If the detective can't find the clues himself—"

"I'm going to point them out to him."

"I don't see why we can't ask Quincy a few questions—"

"I told you . . . I made a promise to Detective Gates," Zoey said. "I also promised to stop sticking my nose where it doesn't belong."

"That's no fun."

"I hardly consider any of this to be fun."

"But I do."

"You're also not a 'person of interest', Nana."

Vivian glared at Zoey before she climbed out of the Jeep and slammed the door shut.

Zoey mumbled a few words under her breath before she turned to face Justin and Terry in the backseat. "Are you two ready to go?"

"When is Justin prepared for anything?" Terry grumbled.

"Nah," Justin said as he elbowed Terry in the ribs. "We need to go back to our townhouse so I can get my gear and merch. We'll be back in . . . I don't know . . . An hour, I guess."

"Is Hannah coming tonight?"

"Nope," Justin said. "She has to work."

"Okay. I'll see you two in an hour." Zoey slid out of the driver's seat and jogged after her nana, "Are you coming to the show tonight?"

"Of course, I'm coming to the show. It's the perfect opportunity to talk to people about Devon," Vivian said as she slung her massive purse over her shoulder. "Unlike you, I didn't make any promises to the handsome detective."

"Nana . . ." Zoey ran her hands over her face and back through her long hair. "We need to back off. The killer already left one threatening note—"

"That note was hardly threatening," Vivian said. "And for all you know, it could have been someone playing a prank."

"Or it was the killer."

"Did you tell the detective about the note?"

"No . . ."

"Why not? Sounds like you told him about everything else."

Zoey bit down on her lower lip to keep from snapping back at her nana. The reason she hadn't mentioned the note to Detective Gates was because she had forgotten about it.

"What's wrong with you?" Vivian asked as she spun on the heels of her orthopedic sneakers and made her way over to the side porch. "Last night you were ready to charge in full bore to prove Zack's innocence."

"I told you this morning . . . I did some thinking overnight," Zoey said. "I've come to my senses since then."

"Come to your senses about what, *Chica*?" Santino called out as Zoey and Vivian walked up the short set of steps. He sat slumped in a plastic chair on the small porch. "What were you two up to?"

"We were on a fool's mission." Zoey grabbed a chair and pulled it closer to Santino. Vivian leaned against the back of the chair. "Can I ask you something, Tino?"

"You can ask me whatever you want." Santino glanced down at his phone. "Just make it fast. My client asked for a break so she could go to the bathroom. I need to get back to her in a few minutes."

"It's about Saturday night," Zoey said. She might have promised Detective Gates that she would not talk to Quincy. But that didn't mean she couldn't ask Santino a few questions. "You were here all night, right?"

"Well, not *all* night." Santino held a pen-sized metallic vape to his mouth and inhaled. He then exhaled a citrusy-smelling cloud of smoke. "I finished up with my client around eight-thirty. By the time I was done cleaning my room and got the place locked up, it was nine-ish."

"What about Quincy?" Zoey asked. "Was he here on Saturday night?"

"At first he was." Santino leaned back in the chair and closed his brown eyes. "Quincy left . . . I wanna say it was around six-thirty. He wasn't gone too long. Twenty minutes. Maybe thirty. Probably got dinner. Then he left again about an hour later and didn't come back."

"What about his appointment?"

Santino shrugged. "You'd have to ask him what happened to that. Is there a reason you're asking me about Quincy?"

"Nope. No reason."

"Sure . . ." Santino winked at her. "Just remember, Zoey, he's not your type. And you deserve fresh-from-the-fryer French fries. Not reheated ones."

"You are so bizarre, Tino."

"But I make a good point."

Zoey stood up and headed inside. Vivian and Santino followed. After passing through the breakroom, Santino veered off into his private room. He had the room that was tucked in between the breakroom and front office. It was the smallest of the four rooms, but Santino preferred it because the window overlooked the parking area and allowed him to keep an eye on his beloved muscle car.

Forcefully guiding Vivian past Quincy's room, Zoey led the way to the office. She was surprised to find someone seated behind her desk.

"What are you doing here?"

Arielle glanced up from Zoey's laptop. Her blonde hair was pulled back in a messy ponytail, and she had bags under her eyes. The last time Zoey had seen Arielle looking this worn out was right after she had given birth to Paige.

"I wasn't teaching any classes today, so Zack asked if I could manage the office since Vivi told him you weren't going to be around."

"We had things to do," Vivian said.

Zoey had a seat on the couch. "How are you holding up?"

"I'm not." Arielle moved over to the couch and sat next to Zoey. Vivian sat down on the other side of her. "I'm freaking out. I'm so scared that Zack's going to be arrested for something I know he didn't do. I can't eat. I can't sleep. I can't even be around my daughter. Everything Paige does drives me nuts. She dropped her cup of milk on the floor at breakfast. It was only a small mess, but I broke down in tears. Zack told me I need to pull myself together, but . . . but . . . ."

"But it's hard to do when you're constantly on the verge of an anxiety attack." Zoey wrapped her arms around Arielle and hugged her. "I know. I've been there."

"Is it safe to assume Zack is being his usual self?" Vivian asked.

"Pretending it doesn't bother him while it eats him up inside? Yeah, the usual," Arielle said. "I tried to talk to him last night, but Zack refused to talk about it."

"That's because there's no point in talking about something that isn't going to happen," Zack said as he strode into the room. He leaned against the desk and crossed his arms over his chest. "Are you two done playing Nancy Drew and Miss Marple for today?"

"You can knock off the attitude," Zoey said.

"And you can knock off this amateur detective idiocy. You're smart enough to know that sticking your nose in police business is a good way to get yourself in trouble," Zack said. His tone of voice implied that he was currently questioning Zoey's intelligence. She had always been the smartest of the three Wilde children. Zack was the most creative, and Justin was the most athletic. "Besides, I need you here. Doing the job that I pay you to do."

"You don't pay me—"

"No, but I let you live upstairs rent free."

"Give Zoey and Vivi a break," Arielle said. "They're trying to clear your name."

"Plus mine and Justin's." Zoey stood up and moved closer to her twin brother. Zack was a couple inches taller than her, but they were at eye level while Zack remained in the slouched position. "Unless we can prove we had nothing to do with Devon getting killed, you might not be here much longer. And neither will I. I don't know about you, but I don't want to go to jail for something I didn't do."

Zack rolled his eyes. "Have the two of you somehow managed to prove our innocence?"

"Not yet," Vivian said.

"But we did figure out Uncle Leland's motive," Zoey said. "He's been cheating on Kim. And Devon had proof. He was using it to blackmail Uncle Leland."

"What a jerk!" Arielle jumped to her feet and came to stand next to Zoey. "You know, Leland hit on me a few times over the years."

"He did *what*?" Zack shouted.

Vivian clucked her tongue. "I always said that man was no good."

"Seriously, Arielle? Uncle Leland hit on you?" Zack pushed away from the desk. His arms slipped to his sides, and his hands curled into fists. "Why didn't you ever say anything?"

"I did," Arielle said. "To Leland. I told him to knock it off. I didn't say anything to you or anyone else because I didn't want to cause any issues between Leland and your family."

"You should have told me . . . But we can talk about it later. In private." Turning to Zoey, Zack asked, "How old—or should I say young—is the woman?"

"It's Beverly Hill."

Zack screwed up his face in disgust. "The older he gets, the younger the women get."

NINETEEN

"A ND NOW, THE MAIN EVENT MATCH that you've all been waiting for ..." The ring announcer's voice echoed in the indoor arena. "The following intergender tag team match is scheduled for one fall and has a fifteen-minute time limit ..."

"Let's do this," Justin said to their opponents.

"Whoo!" Kenny bounced up and down a couple times. "My first main event match. This is so awesome."

Kenny—who had the musculature of a scrawny teenage boy—was dressed in a pair of oversized khakis. He also had a pale blue sweater draped around his shoulders that had been unevenly spray tanned. His girlfriend, Barbara Jean, wore a hot pink romper with white knee high, fur-lined boots and a matching faux fur coat. Tucked under her arm was a knock-off designer purse and a stuffed chihuahua.

Neither Zoey nor Justin had wrestled Kenny or Barbara Jean before. They had never even crossed paths at other events. After speaking with the two, they learned that Kenny had been wrestling for about two years. His skill set was limited, and it didn't appear that he had a very bright future ahead of him. As for Barbara Jean ... She was not a wrestler. She was a valet. Yes, she'd been trained in a few of the basic moves and knew how to take a bump. She'd also interfered in several of Kenny's matches in the past, but she'd never wrestled in an actual match, or even a practice match.

Zoey and Justin had hoped to get in the ring against Kenny and Barbara Jean prior to the doors being opened. But their opponents arrived late, and there hadn't been a chance to practice. They had talked about the match and preplanned most of it. Barbara Jean seemed more interested in doing her makeup and playing with her phone than she did with paying attention to the conversation. Barbara Jean also hadn't said more than a handful of words to either Zoey or Justin since the two teams met. Zoey expected the tag match would be a disaster.

After generic elevator music began blasting out of the arena's speakers, the announcer said, "Introducing first . . . They hail from the Hamptons where they indulge in the lifestyle of the rich and the famous . . . Kenny and Barbara Jean!"

Zoey and Justin watched as their opponents pushed through the curtains and stepped out onto the stage that was set up at one end of the arena. Kenny and Barbara Jean were met with boos and jeers from the crowd.

Rows of chairs packed the floor around the ring, and the stands were full of people. The promotor was right—they had filled the equine arena to capacity. Disappointed fans had to be turned away at the door.

Zoey was glad that Justin insisted she bring along extra merchandise since they had both sold out of their t-shirts and pictures. The siblings had also done something that they'd sworn they would never do—they charged fans for their autographs and to get their pictures taken with them. It had been the promotor's idea, and he hadn't given Zoey or Justin much choice in the matter. Zoey—who felt guilty over charging the fans for something that she had always done for free—donated the money to the pit bull rescue. Knowing that the dogs would benefit helped make her feel less guilty. She also didn't feel too guilty about charging the ghouls who only wanted to meet her and Justin so they could ask about Devon. They'd been able to dismiss most of them by saying either "no comment" or "I can't talk about an active police investigation." The only person who got upset by the lack of answers was Reggie Drake. He'd driven down from New York City to attend the show and harass Zoey. Two security guards had to haul him away from Zoey and Justin, and the promoter had Reggie kicked out of the building. The brief encounter had rattled Zoey and she couldn't wait for the night to be over.

"I still can't believe they gave us the main event," Zoey said.

"And I can't believe you talked me into wearing these stupid pants again," Justin said as he gestured to the matching purple and black zebra print leggings that they both wore. "But why are you surprised they put us in the main event?"

"Because we don't deserve it," Zoey said. The two wrestlers scheduled for the main event had not been happy to get bumped down to a lower spot on the card. "I mean, yeah, the two of us are worthy of being in main event matches. We've both earned the spot. But Kenny and Barbara Jean certainly haven't earned it. They're nobodies."

"I told you, sis, we are the hottest thing on the independent scene right now," Justin said. "Tonight we were a bigger draw than a WWE Hall of Famer."

"We might be the hottest thing, but it's only because Devon was murdered. And people think we're the killers."

"Yeah, well . . . I still think we should take advantage of it."

Before Zoey could respond, their "Wilde Ones" entrance music began to play. Stepping through the curtain, Zoey and Justin were showered with unfurling rolls of purple and black streamers. Camera phones flashed while the fans cheered and waved around homemade signs.

"And their opponents . . . Hailing from Parts Unknown . . . Zoey and Justin Wilde . . ."

The fans continued to throw streamers as Zoey and Justin made their way down the ramp and climbed into the ring. While three young men gathered the streamers and cleared the ring, the two tag teams went toe-to-toe in the middle of the ring.

"Remember, Barbara Jean . . . Just like we planned it," Zoey said as the referee pushed the two women apart. "Follow my lead and I'll get us through the early part of the match."

The referee sent Justin and Kenny to opposite corners and then signaled for the announcer to ring the bell to start the match.

Zoey lunged forward and attempted to pull Barbara Jean into the Collar and Elbow Tie-Up. Her left hand had just brushed the back of Barbara Jean's neck when the other woman shrieked. Dropping to her knees, Barbara Jean wrapped her arms around her head and cowered.

Zoey stumbled backwards. Barbara Jean's terrified reaction was not part of the plan. Either she was having a genuine meltdown or she was improvising. It wouldn't be the first time one of Zoey's opponents froze or forgot what they were supposed to do. It didn't happen very often, but there were times when Zoey got distracted and messed up. But Barbara Jean's meltdown—whether real or fake—threw Zoey off her game.

Glancing across the ring at Kenny, Zoey hoped he would be able to provide an answer. Kenny shrugged, causing the sweater to slip from his shoulders.

"She's not a wrestler," Kenny mouthed.

She's not going to be much of anything if she doesn't get it together, Zoey thought.

Zoey grabbed Barbara Jean by her bleached blonde tresses and yanked her over. Still shrieking, Barbara Jean stared up at Zoey through wide, unblinking eyes.

"Work with me, Barbara Jean. We need to save this match." Thinking on the fly, Zoey said, "Roll out of the ring. I'll chase you around."

Zoey had to give Barbara Jean a few nudging kicks, but she got the other woman to roll across the ring. When she reached the edge, Barbara Jean fell over the side and landed on the floor. Zoey stepped between the bottom and middle rope and then jumped to the floor.

"Run," Zoey instructed Barbara Jean.

Barbara Jean took off up the ramp. Zoey had to sprint to catch up. She grabbed Barbara Jean by the back of her romper just before the other woman disappeared through the curtains.

"Please . . . Don't kill me like you killed your ex-boyfriend."

"What?" Zoey stopped halfway down the ramp and looked at Barbara Jean. It was the first full sentence Barbara Jean had spoken to her all evening. "I didn't kill Devon."

"But . . . but . . . it's all over the internet."

"Not everything on the internet is true." Zoey resumed dragging Barbara Jean down the ramp and shoved her back into the ring. "Now get it together and . . . and . . . act like you're stomping on me. And then gloat to rile up the crowd. You're the heel in this match. You need to act like one."

As Zoey slid under the bottom rope and reentered the ring, Barbara Jean kicked her in the side.

"I said stomp," Zoey hissed as the toe of Barbara Jean's boot dug into the soft flesh just below her ribcage. "Not kick."

Barbara Jean tramped on Zoey's back and shoulders. She put a little too much force behind the kicks, driving Zoey's chest and stomach into the mat.

"One more," Zoey instructed. "Then prance around gloating."

Barbara Jean's final kick caught Zoey on the back of the neck. Zoey hadn't been expecting it, and therefore was not able to brace herself. Her head snapped forward and her face smacked into the mat—flattening her nose and bringing tears to her eyes. Zoey's front teeth were driven into her lips, and the metallic taste of blood filled her mouth. She hadn't been in a good mood to begin with, and Barbara Jean's botched move sent her over the edge.

"Enough of this," Zoey muttered as she sprang to her feet.

Unable to control her temper, Zoey grabbed Barbara Jean by the arm and spun her around. She then drew her arm back and swung. Zoey didn't bother holding back on the punch or switching to an openhand slap. Her fist caught Barbara Jean on the jaw and snapped the other woman's head back.

"What . . ." Barbara Jean stammered as she pressed a hand to her jaw. "Why . . ."

"It's called a receipt," Zoey said before she tackled Barbara Jean to the mat. She straddled the other woman and rained blows on her head and shoulders. "If you don't know what one is, you better learn before you ever step foot in a ring again."

In the wrestling business, a receipt was a legitimate hit or assault that was dealt out by one wrestler in exchange for a stiff hit, move, or submission hold that their opponent had previously landed. Zoey had been on the receiving end of a receipt a few times early in her career. She'd also given countless receipts over the years.

"Hey, that's enough," Kenny yelled as he climbed between the top and middle ropes. His interference was part of the plan, but he seemed to be sincerely concerned about his partner. "Get off her, Zoey. She doesn't know what she's doing."

"Then get her some training," Zoey said as she stood up and got in Kenny's face. "If either of you want to learn how to really wrestle, sign up for one of my dad's wrestling camps. Let us teach you how it's supposed to be done."

Wanting out of the ring, Zoey jumped forward a few moves. Stepping up behind Barbara Jean, she stuck her head under the other woman's right arm. She then wrapped both arms around Barbara Jean's waist and picked her up. Falling over backwards, Zoey slammed Barbara Jean's back onto the mat. Without letting go, Zoey arched her back and forced Barbara Jean into a pinning position. Not knowing if Barbara Jean would remember to kick out, Zoey broke the hold at the two count.

Leaving Barbara Jean in the middle of the ring, Zoey rolled to her corner and tagged in Justin.

"That looked ugly."

"It felt ugly," Zoey said. "Try to get us back on track."

Zoey slid under the bottom rope and dropped to the floor. Sitting next to the ring steps, she poked at her tender nose. It didn't feel broken, but Zoey knew she had to get some ice on it immediately after the match. She was also worried about her lower lip swelling up.

Above her, Zoey could hear Justin and Kenny battling back and forth. They were going to handle the middle section of the match. Zoey had roughly three minutes until she would need to get back into the ring. After wasting a couple minutes on the floor, Zoey climbed back onto the ring apron. She was just in time to witness Barbara Jean's attempt to distract Justin by blowing kisses.

Zoey watched as Justin stepped away from Kenny and pretended to be overcome by Barbara Jean's charms. While Justin made a big production out of flirting with Barbara Jean, Kenny took the opportunity to recover. Back on his feet, Kenny snuck up behind Justin and pulled him over into a schoolboy pinning position. The referee dropped down to make the three count. As planned, Justin kicked out after two.

Justin made a quick comeback and laid out Kenny. Instead of pinning Kenny, Justin turned to Zoey and tagged her into the match.

"End this."

"Gladly," Zoey said as she tagged into the match.

Stepping between the bottom and middle ropes, Zoey entered the ring just as Kenny staggered to his feet. Seeing that Zoey was now in the ring with him, Kenny laughed and mockingly offered his cheek for her to slap. This was all part of what they had mapped out for the match, but the original plan no longer made much sense considering Zoey had delivered a right hook to Barbara Jean mere minutes earlier. It was just silly to have Kenny invite Zoey to slap him after she decked his partner.

Instead of slapping Kenny, Zoey leaned to her left and raised her right leg in a side kick. Her combat boot caught Kenny on his pointed chin. Overselling the move, Kenny flung himself over backwards. He then flopped around like a stereotypical fish on dry land.

Ignoring Kenny's theatrics, Zoey climbed up onto the turnbuckle and stood on the top rope with her back to the ring. She glanced back to judge how far away Kenny was from the corner before she arched her back into a moonsault. After flipping backwards through the air, Zoey landed directly on top of Kenny's midsection. She then hooked her arm around one of his legs and pressed his shoulders to the mat.

The ref dropped to the mat and began the count. "One . . . two . . . three . . . Ring the bell."

"JEEZ, JUSTIN. YOU WEREN'T KIDDING WHEN you said this place was a dump," Zoey said as she looked around the dim interior of the Velvet Lounge. The strip club's main room was long and narrow. A stage took up one end of the room, and there was a horseshoe shaped bar at the other. Tables and chairs were scattered between the stage and the bar. "I'm pretty sure everything in here is held together by duct tape."

"Including some of the dancers," Vivian said.

Strips of duct tape covered some of the seams in the linoleum floor. The assortment of plastic tables and chairs that served as furniture were held together by duct tape. Even the tops of the two stripper poles were affixed to the ceiling by duct tape. The place should have been called the Duct Tape Lounge—especially since Zoey didn't see anything that even remotely resembled velvet anywhere in the main room.

"Let's find out if Beverly is working," Zoey said as she jumped away from an intoxicated elderly man who seemed to think she was one of the dancers. "I do not want to hang out here any longer than we have to."

"I don't see Beverly in the main room. She could be in the back," Justin said.

"Maybe the bartenders will tell us if she's working," Terry said. "Or one of the dancers."

"Let's try the bartenders." Zoey took a few steps towards the bar and then stopped when she realized one of their group was missing. "Where's Nana? She was right here a second ago."

"She must have wandered off like she always does." Justin grabbed an empty chair and stepped up onto the seat so that he could look around the room. "Unless there is another crazy old lady wearing giraffe print pants, she's over by the stage."

"Of course, she is." Dodging tables, chairs, and customers, Zoey made her way to where Vivian had taken up a stance in front of the stage. "Come on, Nana. We're not here to watch."

Vivian pointed at the woman who had wrapped her legs around the pole and was hanging upside down as she swung around in slow circles. "I bet I could do that."

"Not with your bad hips and knees," Zoey said as she continued to drag Vivian away from the stage. "And even if you could, who do you think would want to see it?"

"Hey! I'm still pretty sexy for my age."

Zoey was about to make a sarcastic comment when someone shouted over the thumping techno music. The shout startled not only Zoey and Vivian, but everyone else in the club. The dancer lost her balance and fell from the pole while the handful of customers looked for the cause of the commotion.

"What's going on?" Vivian asked.

"How should I know?"

Zoey stood on her tiptoes to see around the customers. She caught sight of Terry just as he crashed into a scantily-clad woman who was carrying a tray of drinks. The drinks went flying, and the woman fell sideways and landed in a customer's lap. Terry didn't break stride as he continued sprinting towards the other end of the club.

"What the heck . . ." Zoey mumbled as she scanned the far side of the room to see what had Terry so worked up. She spotted Leland sitting at the bar just before Terry knocked him off the stool with a flying tackle. "Oh, crap . . ."

"I guess we've figured out where Leland has been the past few days," Vivian muttered.

Zoey charged across the room and pushed her way through the crowd of dancers and customers who had gathered around the bar to watch the fight. Wading into the fray, she tried to help Justin break up the scuffle. Terry was throwing punches and screaming at Leland. Going on the defensive, Leland covered his face with his arms and was trying to get out from under his stepson. Zoey and Justin attempted to grab Terry's arms, but he shoved them aside. Vivian—who had caught up to Zoey—bounced around on the edges and whacked at Terry with her purse.

Two of the club's bouncers had to step in and break up the fight. Without a word, they each grabbed Terry by an arm and hauled him to the exit. Justin and Zoey then pulled a stunned Leland off the floor, handed him a bunch of cocktail napkins to staunch his bloody nose, and then helped him limp out to the parking lot. Lowering the tailgate of Leland's truck, Justin gestured for the older man to have a seat.

"Mom has been worried sick about you," Terry said as he stomped across the parking lot to join them. "And here you were hanging out at a strip club."

"If Kim is so worried about me, maybe she shouldn't have kicked me out," Leland said around the wad of bloody napkins. "How did you figure out I was here, anyway?"

"We didn't know you were here," Zoey said. "We came here looking for Beverly Hill."

"Beverly? What does she have to do with anything?" Leland asked.

"I don't know, Leland," Terry said as he held up one of the pictures of Leland and Beverly. "How about you tell us?"

Leland snatched the picture away from Terry and groaned. "How did you get this?"

"How we got it doesn't matter," Zoey said. "But we know Devon is the one who took it. And that he was using it to blackmail you."

Leland sighed. "Can we keep this between the five of us?"

"No way," Terry said. "You cheated on my mom."

"But if Kim finds out about this, she'll divorce me," Leland said.

"Good," Terry said. "She never should have married you in the first place. I tried to tell her you were no good, but she wouldn't listen."

"That's enough, Terry," Zoey said as she pushed him away from Leland. "You want to explain yourself, Uncle Leland. And, for once, no lame excuses."

Leland sucked in a deep breath and exhaled. "I'm human. I made a mistake. It's not that I don't love Kim. I really do. But I have a weakness for younger women. Beverly started flirting with me last month at the show. And she sent me pictures—"

"She sends *everyone* pictures," Justin said. "Terry and I got them, too. And they were probably the exact same pictures."

Leland glared at Justin. "Then you understand why I couldn't help myself."

"Yes, you could have," Vivian said. "You chose not to."

"How many other times have you cheated on my mom?" Terry asked.

"This was the only time. I swear," Leland said.

Zoey didn't know about the others, but she didn't believe Leland. She'd grown up watching Leland cycle through girlfriends. Before Kim, he'd never had a relationship that lasted longer than a year. Zoey was almost positive that Leland had cheated on Kim before. After all, she'd seen him flirt with other women on countless occasions since the wedding.

"When did this happen?" Zoey asked as she flicked the picture that Leland still held.

"That was last Thursday night," Leland said. " I was here to see Beverly. I always scope the place out for people Kim and I know. I didn't want to be caught out with her . . . For obvious reasons. I didn't see Devon at the bar. He didn't look the same anymore. He must have taken the pictures during one of Bev's breaks. She'd come over and sit with me when she wasn't working."

"Devon approached me at least twice before Saturday. I didn't recognize him either," Zoey said. "But I'm guessing Devon used these pictures to blackmail you."

Leland nodded. "Devon came up to me when Beverly was dancing. He showed me the pictures he had taken and threatened to tell Kim. He must have Facebook stalked me and saw that I was married . . . I'm such an idiot."

"I've known that since I met you," Vivian said.

Leland glared at Vivian. "Devon said he'd pass the pictures on to Kim if I didn't put him on the card for Saturday's show. He insisted on wrestling Justin. I didn't want to do it, but I had to. If I didn't play nice, Devon would have ruined my marriage."

"You already ruined it." Terry pounded his fists on the tailgate. "I hope your sorry attempt to get away with cheating was worth upsetting Zoey.

Did you really think giving Devon the match against Justin would be the end of it? That he'd stop blackmailing you?"

"I hoped he'd stop," Leland said. "But he kept pushing the issue and asking for more. It was his idea to cancel the women's title reveal so that he could make a speech. And it was Devon's idea to make his match with Justin a street fight. He had me by the short hairs, and I couldn't say no. Whoever killed him did me a favor."

"Not really," Vivian said. "We found the pictures of you and Beverly, and we have every intention of telling Kim about your shenanigans."

Leland leaned forward and pressed his forehead against his palms. "My life is ruined."

Zoey nudged Leland's head and forced him to look up at her. "What I don't understand is why you didn't say anything to me about Devon being back in the area."

"Like I told you on Saturday night, it wasn't any of my business to get involved," Leland said. "Yeah, I always thought Devon was a crappy wrestler. But I never had anything against him as a person. Not until he started blackmailing me."

"You're despicable. And one of the most selfish human beings I have ever met. I can't say you're the most selfish because you're not quite as bad as Devon." Zoey crossed her arms over her chest and scowled at Leland. "It's bad enough what you did to me. When Devon approached you last week, you should have told me. And you know it. But I can almost forgive that. What I can't forgive is you blabbing to the police about Zack. Thanks to you, my brothers and I are at the top of Detective Gates's suspect list."

"Not cool, man," Justin said.

"What was I supposed to do? Withhold evidence in a murder investigation?" Leland asked. "I overheard Zack and Devon arguing in the parking lot. Zack threatened to kill him. Minutes later, Devon was dead."

"But it makes Zack look guilty," Zoey said.

"Maybe he *is* guilty," Leland insisted. "Like I said, I heard him threaten to kill Devon if he ever came near you again. Since Devon was killed next to your car—"

"What exactly did Zack say?" Zoey asked.

"He said . . . I can't remember exactly—"

Vivian snorted. "You'll make a great witness."

"I don't remember *exactly* what was said," Leland said. "But it was something along the lines of 'Come near my sister again and they'll never find your body.'"

"Except I found Devon's body," Zoey said.

"Maybe Zack was going to get rid of the body but then he heard you coming back to your car. He got spooked and ran away," Leland said.

"No way." Zoey paced. "There is no way Zack would have done that."

Vivian leaned closer to Leland and asked, "How do we know you didn't kill Devon?"

"Because I didn't," Leland said.

"Can you prove it?" Vivian asked.

"What? No. Why should I have to?" Leland asked. He looked between the four of them. "You don't think I did it, do you?"

"You have a motive," Terry pointed out. "Devon was blackmailing you, and you didn't want my mom to find out that you were cheating on her."

"And your fingerprints are on the murder weapon," Zoey added. "Explain that."

"I'm the one who pulled the sledgehammer out of the wall after Tiny and Bubba threw Devon out the back door."

"Then what did you do?" Vivian badgered. "Did you follow Devon outside—"

"No!" Leland shouted. "After I yelled at Justin for being unprofessional, I pulled the sledgehammer out of the wall and laid it on the floor—"

"I didn't see it on the floor when I went in the bathroom," Terry said.

"Well that's where I left it. Then I went into the storage room to smoke a cigarette. Whatever happened to the sledgehammer after that had nothing to do with me," Leland said. "While I was in the storage room, I opened one of the windows. That's how I overheard Zack and Devon arguing. I don't know how long I was in the room, but I know I missed the entire triple threat match and part of the tag match."

"We watched the footage from Saturday night," Zoey said. "You returned to the stage at ten after nine. That's about the same time Kim called the police to report Devon's body was in the parking lot."

"I don't think you went into the storage room at all," Vivian said. "I bet you took the sledgehammer and followed Devon outside. You killed him to stop the blackmail."

"I always knew you Wilde women were crazy. But this is crazier than normal." After sliding off the tailgate and slamming it shut, Leland walked around to the driver's side. "Now, if you'll excuse me, I have to go break my wife's heart before one of you does it for me."

Terry tossed Justin his car keys and then rushed to the passenger door. "I'm coming with you to make sure you tell Mom the truth."

"Is Uncle Leland still a suspect?" Justin asked as they watched Leland and Terry drive out of the parking lot.

"Yes," Zoey and Vivian said simultaneously. Continuing, Vivian said, "He has a good motive. And no one can confirm his alibi. I think he did it."

"But we have no proof he did it," Zoey said. "And I still want to talk to Beverly Hill and see what she has to say for herself."

"Good luck getting back inside." Justin pointed towards the front entrance of the Velvet Lounge. The two bouncers standing outside the door had been watching them for the past few minutes. "I think Terry earned us a lifetime ban."

"There has to be a back entrance," Vivian said as she walked across the parking lot and slipped into the alley that separated the strip club from a Vietnamese restaurant. "Follow me."

"I'll stay out here and keep an eye on the bouncers," Justin said.

Following Vivian, Zoey picked her way through the alley until she reached the back of the building. They found a young, Hispanic woman dressed in thigh-high boots and skimpy shorts smoking a cigarette while she flirted with one of the restaurant's cooks.

"We don't have much use for old ladies around here," the dancer said to Vivian. She then gave Zoey the once over. "As for you . . . You here looking for a job? Because you don't look like one of them church ladies that come around to preach at us."

"Neither," Zoey said. "I'm looking for Beverly Hill."

"What you want with her? Did she steal your man or something?" the dancer asked. "Hold on . . . I saw you inside. You were with that guy who beat up Beverly's boyfriend. Is that old man your dad?"

"No, he's my uncle."

"And he's married," Vivian added.

"No shit . . ." The dancer dropped her cigarette and ground it out beneath her shoe. She then turned to the door. "Does Beverly know you two?"

"Just tell her the Wilde Women need to talk to her."

The dancer slipped inside. Less than two minutes later, the door swung open and Beverly trudged out. Her makeup was smeared, and her puffy eyes proved that she had been crying. An oversized t-shirt hung to her knees.

"What the heck was that all about?" Beverly asked as she shoved Zoey. "I'm in the back giving a lap dance, and one of the girls rushes in to tell me that someone is beating up my boyfriend—"

Interrupting, Zoey said, "You do realize that your boyfriend is married, right?"

Beverly huffed. "Leland told me he was going to leave Kim."

"And you believed him?" Vivian asked. "What do you want with an ugly old man like Leland anyway? Did he tell you he's rich? Because he was lying."

"Leland offered to be my manager," Beverly said. She gathered up her waist-length blonde hair and pulled it back into a ponytail. "He said I have potential, and he's going to help me make a name for myself as a wrestler."

Zoey snorted. "I hate to break it to you, Beverly, but, if I couldn't make it, what makes you think you could? You're not even half the wrestler that I am."

"You're also old and washed up." Beverly stuck out her tongue at Zoey. "I'm young. I still have a chance."

Zoey rolled her eyes. "First off, thirty is not old. Second—"

"Second, what did you really think Leland could do to advance your career?" Vivian asked. "He runs a crappy monthly promotion out of a small-town VFW Hall."

"He told me he has connections . . ."

"I bet Uncle Leland told you all sorts of lies," Zoey said. She held up one of Devon's pictures from the club and asked, "Did you know about these?"

Beverly nodded. "Leland told me that Devon blackmailed him to get a spot at the show. I guess Devon told Leland that he would get rid of the pictures if he gave him a match against Justin. Leland made me flirt with the guy to find out if he'd done that or not."

"Since I found these, it's pretty obvious that Devon did not destroy them," Zoey said.

"No, Devon told me he wasn't done blackmailing Leland," Beverly said. "I told Leland, and he said something about how he should kill Devon to shut him up . . ."

TWENTY

Friday August 24, 2018

"H EY, SQUATCH," ZOEY SAID AS SHE COLLIDED with the man as he exited the gym.

"Not you two again." Sasquatch glanced between Zoey and Vivian. "I told you I didn't kill Devon. You've got no reason to interrogate me again."

"But I do have a question for you." Zoey stepped in front of Sasquatch to keep him from brushing past her. "Did you hear that Chelsea threatened me with a gun on Monday night?"

"Yeah, I heard about that," Sasquatch said as he moved away from the doors to allow a group of middle-aged women to exit the gym. "Crazy bitch stole my gun—"

"It was your gun?" Zoey shouted, drawing the attention of the women. She'd wondered where Chelsea had acquired the firearm, but Chief Coleman wouldn't tell her. Now she had an answer. Lowering her voice, she asked, "When and how did she steal it from you?"

"She came by my house on Saturday night," Sasquatch said. "I don't know how she even knows where I live. I talked to her for a few minutes before the show, but I definitely did not give her my address and invite her over to reconnect."

"What did you talk about before the show?" Zoey asked.

"I don't remember exactly." Sasquatch ran a hand through his sweaty hair. "I didn't even recognize her at first. Once I realized who she was, I said something about Devon. I figured she would have gotten over her obsession with him while he was locked up. I was wrong. She told me they were living together down in Florida but that he took off a few days earlier to come find you. I told her she needed to move on from Devon. Then I walked away."

Vivian yanked a notebook out of her purse. "What time did Chelsea show up at your place?"

Sasquatch shrugged his hairy shoulders. "I don't know. It's not like I looked at a clock. When I got home, I turned on my hot tub and waited for the water to heat up. I hadn't been in the hot tub all that long when Chelsea showed up. She was freaking out about how someone had smashed in Devon's head with a sledgehammer—"

"Whoa, whoa, whoa," Zoey said as she held up her hands and gestured for Sasquatch to stop talking. "If Chelsea knew Devon was dead and that he had been hit over the head with the sledgehammer, that means she either witnessed the murder or she saw Devon on the ground not long after he was killed—"

Interrupting, Vivian said, "Or she killed him herself."

"Or that," Zoey said. "What I'm saying is that there's no way Chelsea would have been able to get close enough to see Devon's body once the police were on site and the crime scene tape was up. Not without an officer noticing she was there."

"At first, I figured she was telling another one of her crazy stories," Sasquatch said. "You remember how she was, Zoey. Always telling some far-out story that she had convinced herself was true. I figured Justin made it look like he hit Devon over the head with the sledgehammer during the match and she convinced herself that it had killed him. It wasn't until the morning . . . You know, when I checked my phone and saw all these messages about Devon being dead that I realized Chelsea was telling the truth."

"Chelsea didn't say anything about what she saw?" Zoey asked.

"She was so incoherent I couldn't understand half of what she was saying. I really didn't want her at my place, but I didn't want her to leave either. Not in the condition she was in. So I let her stay the night. In the morning, after I found out that Devon really was dead, I tried asking her some questions. By then she didn't have much to say. She was practically comatose. It's like whatever shaky grip she had on reality snapped when Devon died.

All she would say was that Devon was dead and that it was your fault," Sasquatch said as he gestured towards Zoey. "She never accused you of killing him. Just kept saying it was your fault. To be honest, I wondered if maybe she had killed him."

"The woman always was five-and-a-half beers short of a six pack," Vivian said. "Is it safe to assume that Chelsea was your 'female companionship' on Sunday morning?"

Sasquatch nodded. "Not that I got any 'companionship' from her. Or even wanted any. That ship sailed about the same time Chelsea became obsessed with Devon."

"How long were you two dating before she turned her attention to Devon?" Zoey asked.

"Honestly, I think she was after him all along and was just using me to get close to him," Sasquatch said. "Devon and I met Chelsea not long after we moved to Philly when we were eighteen. She hung out at the gym where we were training. I started talking to her and we went on some dates. Then her attention shifted to Devon. He didn't return her feelings, but that didn't stop her from fawning over him. Devon took advantage of the situation. And of her. Eighteen years later, and it was pretty clear that nothing had changed. That woman wasted half of her life on that deadbeat."

Vivian cleared her throat. "You still haven't told us when Chelsea stole your gun. And why you didn't report it stolen."

"That's because I didn't realize she'd stolen it until Justin called me on Tuesday morning and told me about what had happened the night before. And the reason I didn't report it stolen is because it's not registered. And I, obviously, don't have a concealed carry permit. I also shouldn't have the gun since I'm an ex-con—"

"Squatch . . ."

"I know, Zoey. I know. I don't need a lecture. I also don't need you telling the police that it was my gun."

"I could have been killed!"

"But you weren't." Squatch put his arm around Zoey and hugged her. "And that's what's important. You weren't killed. Or even injured."

Zoey wanted to punch him, and it took all her willpower to control herself. "The least you could have done was warn me she was back in the area. And lock up your gun."

"First of all, I figured you knew Chelsea was back. She always was closer to Devon than his shadow," Sasquatch said. "Second, I thought I had locked up my gun when I got home from the show. It's what I always do. This time I forgot and left it in my bag. She must have gone through my stuff while I was at work on Sunday night. She wasn't at my place when I got home Monday morning. I was so glad she was gone that I didn't think—"

"Right there is your problem." Vivian smacked Sasquatch upside the head with her notebook. "You don't think."

"We talked to you on Monday morning. How did it not cross your mind to mention Chelsea was staying at your place?" Zoey asked.

"I don't know. Maybe because you were accusing me of killing Devon," Sasquatch said. "Look, Zoey, I'm sorry. I should have said something to you about Chelsea being around. I never should have left her alone at my house. And I definitely should have made sure my gun was locked up. I screwed up, I know. If Chelsea had shot you, I never would have forgiven myself."

"At least Chelsea is finally getting the help she needs at the psychiatric ward," Zoey said.

Vivian leaned down and stuck her face close to Sasquatch's. "What did you and Chelsea talk about before the show?"

"What . . . Or who do you think we talked about?" Sasquatch asked. "We talked about Devon. Chelsea told me about everything she did for him over the past few years and how he didn't appreciate any of it. She was livid."

"You think she was mad enough to kill Devon?" Zoey asked.

"Mad enough? Maybe. Crazy enough? Oh, yeah." Sasquatch shrugged. "There's not much else I can tell you. Other than to say I'm sorry again."

Zoey waved Sasquatch away. She didn't have anything else to say to him. And she did not want to be in his presence any longer. Chelsea's actions were not Sasquatch's fault. He had no control over her. But he did have control over the gun—which he wasn't even supposed to have. Due to Sasquatch's irresponsibility, Chelsea had gotten her hands on the gun and used it to threaten Zoey. Had Bernadette not come downstairs when she had, the outcome could have been far different. Chelsea could have shot Zoey. Or Chelsea could have shot herself.

"Are you okay?" Vivian asked after Sasquatch walked off. "Do you want to go home?"

"No. I'm done hiding at home. I'm done sitting around feeling sorry for myself," Zoey said. Wrenching open one of the doors, she was hit with a blast of sweaty smelling, stale air. "We're here. We may as well workout."

Zoey and Vivian parted ways inside the door. Vivian headed for the treadmills while Zoey joined Arielle's cardio kickboxing class that was underway. Zoey threw herself into the high energy workout and used it as a release for the adrenaline and anger that surged in her veins. As she went through the motions, she pretended it was Devon that she was punching and kicking. A right hook to the nose followed by multiple kicks below the belt.

After class, Zoey left Arielle to set up for a yoga class and went in search of Vivian. After a lap around the gym, Zoey found her nana seated at the juice bar. Vivian had a smoothie in each hand, and she was encouraging a pair of young men to flex their muscles.

"I can't take you anywhere without you causing trouble, can I?" Zoey asked as she pushed her way in between the young men. "Come on, Nana . . . These two should get back to their workout, and we need to go home."

Vivian bid goodbye to the young men. She then asked, "Are you okay?"

"I will be." Zoey grabbed the orange creamsicle smoothie that Vivian had ordered for her and took a sip. The tangy, citrusy concoction fizzed over her tongue. "Let's go home."

Out in the parking lot, Zoey was so wrapped up in her thoughts that she didn't notice the sheet of paper tucked under her windshield wiper until she had climbed behind the wheel.

"What the heck is that?" Zoey asked as she peered over the steering wheel at the underside of the paper. Scrawled in black marker was the warning "*Back off. Haven't you heard the saying 'don't look a gift horse in the mouth?' And stop sticking your nose where it don't belong.*" Zoey banged her forehead against the steering wheel and accidentally honked the horn. "You have got to be kidding me."

"What does it say?" Vivian asked as she leaned across the center console for a closer look. "Oh, that's hardly original. And their grammar is atrocious. It should be 'where it *doesn't* belong.' How are we supposed to take this person seriously when—"

"Someone leaves a threatening note, and the only thing you're worried about is their grammar?"

"It's hardly threatening . . ."

Zoey glared at Vivian. "I was stupid not to take yesterday's note seriously. I'm not making that mistake again."

"Do you think Squatch might have left the note?"

"Why would he? He has an alibi. There is no way he killed Devon. So why would he want to scare me out of investigating?"

"Maybe he's trying to protect you. Sticking your nose into a murder investigation . . . I can't say it's the dumbest thing you've ever done. But—"

"Sticking *our* noses in the investigation was *your* idea." Zoey used her cell phone to take pictures of the note. "What I do know is that whoever left these two notes knows too much about me. He or she knows where I live and what kind of car I drive—"

"It is the only purple Jeep in town," Vivian pointed out. "And the 'Wilde Woman' decals are also a dead giveaway."

Ignoring Vivian, Zoey said, "Whoever is doing this knows which gym I use. And what time I usually go to the gym every day. This is getting freaky. Well, freakier than it already was. I'm calling Jim."

Zoey turned off the camera and then called the chief of the Linville Police.

"Hey, Zoey," Jim Coleman said as he answered the phone. "I was meaning to call you. Chelsea is out of the psych ward. She was released this morning, and we have her in custody. Detective Gates is interrogating her as we speak."

"Tell him to lock her up and throw away the key." Zoey exhaled. She had nothing to worry about. Chelsea could not get to her for the time being. "I also need you to send a police officer over to the gym—"

"What's wrong? Is Arielle okay?"

"Arielle's fine. But someone left a threatening note on my car. I figure it has something to do with Devon's murder so . . ."

"Hang tight. I'll send an officer right over," Jim said before he hung up.

Zoey and Vivian sat in the Jeep and sipped their smoothies while they waited. Less than ten minutes after Zoey called Jim, a SUV pulled up next to the Jeep. Detective Tyler Gates climbed out from behind the wheel. The sunlight brought out the blonde highlights in his hair.

"Too bad the detective thinks you killed Devon," Vivian whispered. "He's really cute."

"Knock it off, Nana."

"What? Don't you think he's cute?'

"Yes. He's cute. Now shhhhh . . ."

Zoey rolled down the driver's side window and smiled at the detective.

"Hey, Miss Wilde." Detective Gates leaned against the driver's side door. "Heard someone left you a love note."

Zoey pointed at the piece of paper stuck under the windshield wiper. "And I heard you were interrogating Chelsea. Shouldn't you still be doing that?"

"I spent the morning listening to her blame you for Mr. Isler's death. I needed a break."

"Is she claiming I killed him?"

"Nope. Just keeps saying it's your fault he's dead." Gates motioned for Zoey to get out of her Jeep. He then slid into the driver's seat and examined the note. "Not very original. And the writer clearly didn't pay attention during grammar class."

"That's what I said," Vivian stated.

"Do you know if the gym has any security cameras in the parking lot?"

Zoey shook her head. "Only at the doors. There aren't any in the parking lot. Last year, someone broke into my sister-in-law's car and stole my niece's stroller. Arielle's been complaining about the lack of security cameras since then. Unfortunately, the owner of the gym is too cheap to install cameras in the parking lot."

"I wonder if any of the nearby places have cameras," Gates said as he got out of the Jeep. Turning in a circle, he looked around the area.

The gym was on a side street behind a shopping center. Zoey thought it was possible there were security cameras located along the back of the shopping center—especially at the doors and loading docks—but she doubted they would be able to get a clear shot of the gym's parking lot. Next to the gym was a home and garden store. Rows of trees and shrubs blocked the gym's parking lot from the neighboring building.

"I'll send the note to the State Police lab. If there are fingerprints on the paper, the lab might be able to match the prints to someone in the system," Gates said as he photographed the note. He then removed it from under the windshield wiper and tucked it into a clear evidence bag. "It seems you have the killer's attention."

"Or it's just someone playing a prank."

Detective Gates slid his sunglasses down his nose and peered at Zoey over the frames. "Either way, the person makes a good point. I told you yesterday to stay out of my investigation—"

"And I have."

"But you haven't stopped running your mouth," Detective Gates said. "I listened to the podcast you were on yesterday afternoon."

"If you listened to it, then you should know Justin was the one who ran his mouth," Zoey said. "I kept trying to steer the conversation away from Devon and his murder."

"I noticed." Gates stuck the evidence bag in his car and slammed the door. "But you still brought attention to yourself by going on the podcast. And I refuse to believe that neither you nor your brother discussed the murder with any of the wrestlers at last night's show."

Zoey tried not to talk about Devon at all, but it was difficult when everyone wanted to know more about his reappearance and subsequent murder. Zoey had known some of the other wrestlers for years, and a few of them also knew Devon. Not only were these other wrestlers her colleagues, they were also her friends. She considered some of them as family.

Jarvis Brooks was the only wrestler who she had pulled aside to discuss Saturday night. He'd been preparing for his main event match when Devon was escorted out of the building by the Hillbilly tag team. Like Pasqual, Jarvis hadn't seen anyone grab the discarded sledgehammer and follow Devon outside into the parking lot.

"I was there last night, too," Vivian said. "And so was Terry."

"Did the two of you talk to anyone about Mr. Isler's murder?" Gates asked.

"I don't know about Terry, but I talked to everyone I could. I wouldn't be much of an investigator if I didn't try tracking down new leads."

"Mrs. Wilde, need I remind you that you are not a detective?" Gates asked. "Please leave the investigating up to me. If you keep at it, next time the killer might do more than just leave a threatening note under your granddaughter's windshield wiper."

Vivian harrumphed. "This isn't even the first note—"

"How many other threatening notes have you received?"

"One," Zoey said as she held up a finger. "Terry found it stuck under my windshield wiper yesterday morning. I didn't take it seriously at the time."

"Where is the note now?" Gates asked.

"At my apartment."

"Let's go get it," Detective Gates said as he held open Zoey's car door. "I'll follow you."

During the five minutes it took to drive to the apartment, Zoey grilled Vivian on who all she'd talked to and what she'd said to them about Devon. Vivian spent the short drive either ignoring the questions or giving vague answers.

"We will discuss this more later," Zoey said to Vivian as she parked her Jeep behind the tattoo shop and climbed out from behind the wheel. "And I want answers."

"Where was your Jeep parked when yesterday's note was discovered?" Detective Gates asked as he followed Zoey up the exterior staircase and into the apartment. "Was it here or . . ."

"It was here. Parked in my usual spot," Zoey said as she unlocked the door and let them into the apartment. "Now . . . What happened to that note?"

"You didn't put it somewhere safe?" Gates asked. "Or hang it on the fridge?"

"Nana didn't take it seriously—"

"So I crumpled it up and threw it out—"

"Except you missed the trash can and my cat ran off with it."

As if on cue, Lita sauntered out of the living room and rubbed against Zoey's legs.

"What did you do with it, Lita?" Zoey asked. Lita meowed in response and then scampered out of the room. Calling after the cat, she said, "Thanks. You're super helpful."

"Is this it?" Detective Gates pulled a chair away from the table and scooped up a paper ball from the floor. He unfolded the paper and said, "Oops . . . Never mind. It's a receipt."

Not finding the note in the kitchen, Zoey moved into the living room and checked Lita's multilevel cat tower. The tower featured scratching posts, ramps, platforms, a hammock, and two kitty condos. Lita hoarded most of her toys in the two condos. Zoey shifted through the catnip mice and crinkle balls. She didn't find the note, but she did find a couple of her hair ties, a sock, and another one of Paige's pacifiers. Zoey finally found the note entombed under the couch along with more cat toys, a hairball, and a small army of dust bunnies.

"Here it is," Zoey said as she smoothed out the note. Lita's toenails and teeth had left countless gouges and holes. She handed the note to Detective Gates and said, "Sorry . . . Like I said, we didn't take it seriously. I hope we didn't destroy any evidence."

"It's possible the lab technicians can still get fingerprints." Detective Gates looked over the tattered piece of paper. "I can see why you didn't take it seriously. It's not much of a threat . . . '*I did you a favor. Now do me a favor and stop trying to figure out who I am.*' Hmmm . . . 'I did you a favor' . . . Is the murderer saying they killed Devon for you?"

Zoey shrugged. "I can't think of anyone who would kill for me."

"Aside from your brothers?" Detective Gates asked as he slid the note into a clear evidence bag.

"Aside from them," Zoey admitted. "And my dad. But they didn't do it."

"I'd kill for you," Vivian said. "Your mom and Arielle would, too."

"I know you would, Nana. But you, Mom, and Arielle all have alibis," Zoey said. "I can't think of anyone—"

"You did have those three stalkers," Vivian said. "Maybe one of them killed Devon."

"But I haven't heard from any of them in over a year," Zoey said. "And, for all we know, it was just one person using different tactics to contact me."

"It's still worth looking into," Gates said. He pulled a notebook out of his back pocket and jotted down some notes. "Chief Coleman told me about your stalkers—"

"Then he also should have told you that we never figured out who they were."

"True. Damn it." Gates slapped the notebook against his thigh. "Do you have any other fans that are a little too infatuated with you that you know were at the show on Saturday night? Maybe the killer is an obsessed fan."

Zoey rattled off the names of a few of her more exuberant fans.

Vivian snapped her fingers. "We forgot about Quincy. He would probably kill for you."

"Yeah . . . Quincy might," Zoey said. "And leaving a lame, threatening note to scare me out of investigating—"

"Which you shouldn't be doing," Detective Gates said.

"I know. I know. But what I'm saying is that these threatening notes fit Quincy's style. It's something he would definitely do," Zoey said. She still had a shoebox full of insipid love notes that Quincy gave her back when they'd dated. She also had some lackluster text messages that he'd sent her over the past few months while trying to convince her to give him a second chance. Quincy might be an exceptional artist, but he did not have a way with words. "Quincy has made a bunch of comments about how I should be glad that Devon is dead and be grateful to the person who killed him. Maybe if I—"

"Maybe nothing, Miss Wilde. I will continue looking into Mr. Durand. You need to stay out of it," Detective Gates said as he tucked the notebook back in his pocket. "Now, I better get back to the police department."

"Before you go, we should compare notes," Vivian said.

"What notes?" Detective Gates asked.

"Investigation notes." Vivian walked into the kitchen and glared at the wall above the table. Once again, Zoey had taken down the corkboard and replaced it with the framed poster. "What happened to my suspect board."

"It's behind Shawn."

Vivian moved the cardboard cutout of Shawn Michaels to the side and grabbed the corkboard that Zoey had leaned against the side of the desk. She then laid the corkboard on the cluttered desktop. Before Zoey had taken the corkboard down, Vivian had added Beverly Hillegas to the list of suspects. She joined Quincy, Leland, and Chelsea as the remaining suspects. Vivian had also filled in Leland's motive on his notecard.

"This is quite thorough, Mrs. Wilde," Detective Gates said as he examined the contents of the corkboard. "I'm impressed."

"Are Zoey and I on the right track?"

Detective Gates grabbed a red marker and used it to draw an X over Beverly's picture.

"Thank you for your time, ladies," Detective Gates said as he strode towards the door. "If you receive any more threatening notes or learn anything else, please let me know."

"That's it?" Vivian asked. "You're not going to share anything else?"

"That's not how this works, ma'am." Detective Gates held up the threatening note and said, "You clearly have the killer's attention, ladies. You both need to stop poking around before I wind up having to investigate your murders."

TWENTY-ONE

"You know, Zoey, sometimes you are absolutely unbelievable."
Zoey pulled the door shut behind her and double checked to make sure that it was locked. She then descended the staircase to the tattoo shop. Quincy glared up at her.

"What's up with you?" Zoey asked as she tried to push past Quincy to unlock the front door. It was almost noon, and she had to open the shop for the day.

Quincy grabbed Zoey by the arm and guided her down the hallway to his private room. "You told the detective that I was at the show on Saturday night. And that I confronted Devon."

"Yeah . . . And?"

"Now I'm a suspect in Devon's murder!"

"What were you doing at the show? You were supposed to be here working on that guy's back piece. But, yesterday, Tino said—"

"Tino needs to mind his own business."

"Quincy . . ." Zoey hissed through her clenched teeth.

Ignoring Zoey, Quincy walked over to the rolling tool chest that he used to store his tattooing equipment and supplies. He scooped up one of his tattoo guns out of the bottom drawer.

"You want to know what happened on Saturday night?" Quincy asked. He spun around to face Zoey. "When Zack told me that Devon was at the VFW Hall for the event, I freaked out. The day before . . .

Please don't get mad at me—"

"You mean madder than I already am?" Zoey asked. She was mad at him for not telling her about Devon, and she knew she would remain mad at him for some time.

Breaking eye contact with Zoey, Quincy focused his gaze over her shoulder. "Like I told you the other day, it took me a couple minutes to recognize Devon on Friday."

"How did you recognize him?" Zoey asked. "I dated him for a year-and-a-half, and I didn't recognize him."

"It was the tattoo." Quincy tapped the left side of his chest. "When I asked what kind of tattoo he was looking to get, he told me he already had a tattoo but that he wanted to get it redone because it wasn't the best quality. I asked to see the tattoo so I knew what I had to work with. He took his shirt off to show me. I said something about how our office manager is also named Zoey, and that you spell your name the same way. Devon said something like, 'I know. Do you think she will like it?' That's when I realized who he was."

"What I don't understand is why you didn't tell me Devon was back in the area?"

"I didn't tell you because I didn't want to upset you. I was trying to protect you. I know what Devon did to you before. I saw how he broke you. And I watched you put yourself back together afterwards. I didn't want to watch him break you again. So I told him to leave you alone, or he'd have me to deal with."

"I know you meant well. But you should have warned me Devon was back."

"I know that now."

"And you can't honestly believe that Devon would have left me alone just because you told him to," Zoey said. On Monday, she had been so upset when Quincy admitted that he'd recognized Devon that she hadn't asked what they had spoken about. "What did Devon say after you threatened him?"

"Devon made a comment about how I was the first person who recognized him. He claimed he'd spoken to you a couple times in the past few days, but you had yet to realize it was him. He thought it was hilarious. He also insinuated that he bumped into your parents somewhere and they didn't recognize him either." Quincy moved closer to Zoey and had a seat on the edge of his desk. "If I'd known Devon was going to be at the event on Saturday night, I would have warned you that he was back. I know it was stupid of me not to say anything the day before. And you have every right to be mad at me. But I was just trying to protect you—"

"I'm not some damsel in distress. I don't need you to protect me. So stop trying to be my knight in shining armor."

"I can't do anything right, can I?" Quincy threw up his arms and turned his back to Zoey. "I know I messed up on Friday. I should have told you Devon was back. And I was an idiot for thinking he'd leave you alone just because I told him to."

"You still haven't told me why you cancelled on your client and came to the show."

"I didn't cancel on my client. He cancelled on me," Quincy said. "And I went to the show to confront Devon. But also to support you. I didn't tell you I was there because . . . Well, because every time I try to support you, you get mad at me. All I want is to be there for you. But you just get annoyed and push me away."

"That's because you're so clingy," Zoey said, reminding Quincy of what Santino had said on Tuesday. "You're not my boyfriend anymore—"

"But I want to be your boyfriend," Quincy said as he leaned over her. "I want to get back together and try again—"

"Stop it, Quincy. Just stop it." Zoey stood up, forcing Quincy to take a couple steps backwards. "I've told you multiple times that I am not interested in getting back together. I don't feel that way about you anymore. You need to stop living in the past and move on—"

Quincy snorted. "So do you. Until you get over Devon, you'll never be in a healthy relationship. Heck, you won't be in any type of relationship. It's been how many years? Are you just going to remain single forever because—"

"Why I've remained single for the past few years is none of your business. I am not discussing my love life with you. What I want to talk about is what you said to Devon on Saturday night."

"I reminded him about what I said to him the day before. That if he didn't leave you alone, he would have me to deal with," Quincy said. "Devon said you owed him—"

"Owed him for what?"

"For him being stuck in prison and ruining his life. He told me that if you didn't get back together with him, he was going to ruin your life. Then he taunted me and asked what I was going to do to him if he didn't leave you alone."

"Did you do anything?"

"Like what? Kill him?" Quincy's eyes widened. He grasped Zoey's upper arms, and his nails dug into her flesh. "Oh my God . . . Is that why you're asking me all these questions? Do you seriously think I'm the one who killed Devon?"

"Did you?" Zoey tried to pull away from Quincy, but he tightened his grip. She worried that he would leave bruises. "Did you kill him?"

"No!" Quincy released his grip on Zoey. "I only confronted him before the show. I never saw him again after that."

"There is footage of you walking towards the banquet hall's front door not long after Devon's match ended. Where did you go?"

"Seriously? I came back here to get my bike. Then I went home."

"You didn't go around to the back of the VFW Hall to confront Devon?"

"Of course not!"

Before Zoey could ask if Quincy could prove any of this, there was a knock at the door.

Quincy stepped around Zoey and yanked open the door. "What do you want?"

"I want to know what's going on in here?" Zack said as he shouldered past Quincy and forced his way into the room. "Are you okay, Zoey?"

"I'm fine."

Zack shot her a look of disbelief. He then turned to Quincy and said, "Your client is also here. Are you ready for me to send her in?"

"Give me five minutes," Quincy mumbled.

"Will do." Zack guided Zoey out into the hallway and then slammed the door shut behind them. "What was that all about? And what happened to your arms?"

Zoey examined the red marks on her upper arms. "Quincy grabbed me."

"Let me guess . . . He was begging you to get back together with him."

"No, he was trying to convince me that he didn't kill Devon. But why can't he just take no for an answer when I tell him I do not want to get back together? He's driving me nuts."

Zack muttered something under his breath and then said, "I'll talk to Quincy and tell him to knock it off."

"I GUESS YOU'RE OVER BEING MAD AT ME."

Zoey joined Mortimer on the front porch of the Cozma Funeral Home in Quarryville. It was the first of the three Cozma Funeral Homes in Lancaster County, and had been opened by Mortimer's grandfather Serghei when he first moved to Quarryville over fifty years earlier. The funeral home in Linville—which was managed by Mortimer's adoptive parents—came next. The Cozma Funeral Home in Columbia was opened about fifteen years ago when Serghei purchased a funeral home that was going out of business. Mortimer's birth mother, Silviana, and her husband were the current owners of the Quarryville funeral home.

Zack had not been happy with her when she'd told him she needed to abandon her post at the tattoo shop. And he'd been downright furious when she had told him why. Zack couldn't wrap his head around why Zoey wanted to see Devon one last time at the funeral home. Zoey didn't quite understand it herself, but she thought it might help with closure.

"Well, I'm still kinda mad you shared my secret with the detective," Mortimer said as he opened the door and ushered Zoey inside the funeral home. "He accused me of killing Devon."

"At least you have a solid alibi," Zoey said. "The detective still thinks my brothers and I are involved in Devon's murder."

"Are you?"

"No."

As Zoey's feet sank into the plush dark blue carpet, she glanced around the funeral home's spacious foyer. Hideous, bold wallpaper covered the walls. Thin dark blue vertical stripes alternated with thick cream stripes. There was a repeating pattern of pink roses down each cream stripe. Scattered about the foyer were antique chairs and sofas with dark pink upholstery. Zoey thought the décor was too chaotic and colorful for a funeral home.

"Where is Devon at?"

"Uncle Grigore has him set up in the Magnolia Room," Mortimer said as he walked down a hallway and opened the second door on the left. "We've got less than an hour until the memorial service, so we need to be quick."

"We could have done this after the service," Zoey said. "Or tomorrow morning."

Mortimer shook his head. "Uncle Grigore plans to start the cremation process as soon as the service is over. This is your only chance."

Zoey followed Mortimer into the Magnolia Room. The room—which wasn't much larger than a walk-in closet—was decorated in shades of pale green and ivory. It was much more subdued and peaceful than the foyer.

Crossing the room, Zoey approached the ice white casket. A spray of white roses and calla lilies lay across the closed lid, and there was a poster-sized image of Devon displayed on an easel. The picture was an old one—Devon's hair was still long and dyed a golden blonde. Aside from his cold, expressionless eyes, Devon had been gorgeous. It was those good looks that Zoey had initially fallen for.

Tapping the casket's closed lid, Zoey asked, "Can we look inside?"

"Yeah, we can."

Mortimer moved the flowers to the floor. He then unhooked the latches and flipped open the casket's head panel.

"Wow," Zoey said as she leaned down to get a better look at Devon. Despite being dead, he looked good. "You'd never know he was bashed over the head with a sledgehammer."

"Is that what it was?" Mortimer asked. "The coroner would only tell Uncle Grigore that Devon had died from blunt force trauma. He wouldn't say what type of weapon was used. We had some guesses but . . . But was it the sledgehammer Devon and Justin used in their match?"

Zoey nodded. "Somehow it wound up in the parking lot after the match. I don't know if Devon took it outside with him or if the killer grabbed it from backstage . . . Just don't tell anyone that I told you what the murder weapon was."

"I gotta tell Uncle Grigore. But he won't tell anyone else."

"How does your . . ." Zoey almost said "mother" but caught herself. She had met Silviana and Mortimer's adoptive parents a few times. She would keep their secret that Silviana was Mortimer's birth mother, but it was strange knowing the truth. "How does your aunt feel about preparing Devon's body and having the service here considering—"

"Considering when I was sixteen Devon pressured me into having sex and then abandoned me after I got pregnant?" Silviana asked as she emerged from behind an ivory curtain. The petite woman had the same brown eyes and unruly black hair as Mortimer. "Honestly . . . He's just another body. I spent a lot of years . . . Too many years . . . Hating Devon. I let the hatred consume me. I didn't realize how much it was weighing me down and holding me back until I finally let go of it."

"How do you let go of it?" Zoey asked.

"You just do. You decide you're not going to let it control your life anymore. And then you let it go," Silviana said. She placed her hand on Zoey's shoulder and gave her a sad smile. "But, more importantly, you have to forgive yourself. You'll never fully heal until you stop blaming yourself."

"But if I hadn't—"

"You can't change the past. All you can do is let it go, forgive yourself, and allow yourself to heal." Silviana gave Zoey's shoulder a hard squeeze. "Come on, Mort. Let Zoey have a moment alone with Devon so she can say goodbye."

Zoey waited until Mortimer and Silviana left the room before she looked back down at Devon. As she stared at the face that was so familiar yet so different, she realized that Silviana was right . . . and so were Zack, Quincy, and Bernadette. For years, the three of them—as well as others— had encouraged Zoey to let it go—to let Devon go. Any love that she had once had for him was long dead, but the hatred and anger had festered inside her. She routinely fed it—keeping it alive so that it could control and consume her, and that anger and hatred would remain alive until she let it go. She would remain stuck treading water in the roped off shallow end until then. Only after she released the anger and hatred from her could she venture out into the deeper water.

She wanted to say something else to Devon, but she didn't have any more words left. Over the years, she had cried them out. She had screamed them out. She had even whispered. Now, there was nothing left to say except goodbye.

"Goodbye, Devon."

Zoey grabbed the head panel of the casket and slammed it shut, securing the latches with a definitive click.

"What do you think you're doing? Get away from my son!"

Zoey turned and came face-to-face with a seething Paula. The older woman wore an unadorned, frumpy black dress. A short black veil failed to conceal her red-rimmed, swollen eyes. Danielle hovered behind Paula.

"I'm just here to say goodbye."

"More like admiring your handiwork." Paula reached out and jabbed Zoey in the chest. "I know you killed Devon. Ruining his life wasn't enough for you—"

"I didn't kill Devon." Zoey swatted Paula's hand away and then strode towards the doorway. "He ruined his own life. And part of mine, too. But not anymore."

TWENTY-TWO

Saturday August 25, 2018

BECAUSE OF ALL THE YEARS SHE HAD SPENT watching professional wrestling, Zoey would always associate the sound of glass shattering with Stone Cold Steve Austin.

When the sound interrupted the recurring nightmare of her senior prom—an event she hadn't attended because she'd wrestled at an event in Delaware—she assumed Steve Austin was about to stride under the balloon archway and hit someone with a Stunner. She had a long list of people who she wouldn't mind seeing him go after. At the top of the list was Devon. For whatever reason, he also made an appearance and was twirling her around the dance floor just before the breaking glass brought the prom to a stop.

The breaking glass was followed by a succession of high-pitched but muffled beeps. With each beep, Zoey was pulled farther and farther out of her dream and into the foggy area where she was no longer asleep but wasn't quite awake either.

There were also several sharp pinpricks to her scalp, neck, and upper back. Swatting at whatever was stabbing her, her hand connected with something small and furry. Lita yowled in Zoey's ear.

With her heart thumping in her chest, Zoey sat up and looked around her darkened bedroom. The persistent beeping was not part of the nightmare. Now that she was awake, Zoey recognized it as the alarm system. Because the sound was muffled, she assumed it was the alarm for the tattoo shop and not the one for her apartment.

"Breathe. Just breathe," Zoey commanded herself. Her heart raced, her hands shook violently, and cold sweat beaded her forehead. She had to get her anxiety attack under control before it overwhelmed her and left her useless. Something was going on, and she needed to keep it together until she figured things out. "You've got this."

In the dark, she blindly reached for her bedroom door and slammed it shut. She then grabbed the nightstand and dragged it in front of the door. Her alarm clock—which informed her that it was just after two in the morning—crashed to the floor.

On top of the nightstand, Zoey's cell phone vibrated and flashed a notification that she had an incoming call.

"This is Jill with the security—"

"I think someone is trying to break into my apartment. The police—"

"Have already been notified," Jill said in a calm, reassuring voice. "I will also let them know that you are on the premises."

"Tell them I'm on the second floor."

In the distance, sirens wailed.

Pressing her ear against the wall that separated her bedroom from the interior staircase, Zoey strained to hear any telltale sounds that would prove that someone was downstairs and might be trying to come upstairs. The door at the top of the stairs was locked. There was also a deadbolt and a chain. She knew it would take considerable force for anyone to get through the door, but that didn't stop her from panicking.

When she didn't hear anything, Zoey raced across the room to the windows. Ripping aside the curtains and blinds, she peered outside just as a police cruiser came to a halt in the street.

Shoving open the window, Zoey greeted the responding officer.

"Are you all right, ma'am?"

"I'm fine," Zoey said. It was a bit of an understatement. She would be okay though. Once she calmed down. "But I think someone tried to break in."

"The window in the room below you is broken," the officer said. "Can you shut off the alarm from up there?"

"Yes," Zoey shouted. "I can shut it off using my phone."

"Stay where you are while I take a lap around the building," the officer commanded as he walked towards the porch. "Is there an exterior entrance to your apartment?"

"It's around back."

"I'll meet you there in a few minutes."

After assuring the woman with the security company that everything was under control, Zoey logged into the security system app and shut off the alarm. She then answered Zack's call. It was actually his fourth or fifth call, but she had been unable to answer before now.

"What the heck is going on over there?" Zack asked. "I got an alert that the shop's alarm system was set off and that police are on site. Are you okay?"

"Everything is okay. I'm okay."

"Good." Zack sighed and the phone amplified the noise. In the background, Zoey could hear Arielle talking. "What happened?"

"Someone tried to break in," Zoey said. "The police officer said the front window is shattered."

"I'm on my way," Zack said before he hung up.

A pounding on the door caused Zoey to jump.

"Coming," Zoey shouted. "I'm coming."

Leaving Lita penned up in the bedroom, Zoey made her way down the hallway and over to the exterior door. She removed the chain and then unlocked the deadbolt and lock.

"Everything is clear, ma'am," the officer said as he stepped through the doorway. He was a tall, thin man with a babyface. Zoey didn't think he looked old enough to be a police officer. "I'd appreciate it if you came downstairs and looked at the damage."

"Yeah, I can do that," Zoey said as she took a step towards the interior staircase. "We can get downstairs this way."

"You'll want to put on a pair of shoes, ma'am. There will be glass all over the floor."

Zoey grabbed the pair of slip-on sneakers that she kept by the door. With her feet protected, she unlocked the interior door and then followed the officer down the stairs. At the officer's request, she unlocked the front door to let in an older policeman.

"Careful where you step, ma'am," the officer said as he guided Zoey to the office's arched doorway. "We have to document the damage before we can disturb anything."

While the second officer got to work photographing the office, Zoey's eyes darted around the room as she took in the destruction. Two side-by-side double hung windows overlooked the porch. One of the windows was intact. The other had a shattered bottom sash and there was a hole the size of a ring bell in the pane. Lying on the floor in front of her desk was a rock the size of her fist. Wrapped around the rock was a piece of paper that had been secured with a rubber band.

"Do you think it was an attempted robbery?" Zoey asked. "Most of the clients pay in cash—"

Interrupting, the officer asked, "Where do you keep the money?"

"In a safe that's hidden in the breakroom. But, aside from the people who work here, no one would know that. A few years ago, someone broke in through the French doors. We didn't have the alarm system back then."

"I'd say it was probably an attempted robbery then," the younger officer said.

"I don't think so." The older officer had finished photographing the rock and shattered glass that littered the wood floor. He had picked up the rock and removed the piece of paper. He held the paper out to Zoey. "I think you were specifically targeted, ma'am."

Zoey took a couple steps into the room, crushing shards of glass beneath her feet. She snatched the paper out of the officer's hand and read over the short note.

Do I have your attention now? Knock off your amateur investigation and just be thankful that I got rid of Devon for you.

"You . . . Call Detective Gates," Zoey stammered as she backed out of the room and collapsed on the bottom step leading up to her apartment. "It's . . . the murder. The murderer."

Zoey pressed her forehead to her knees and made one last valiant attempt at holding back the anxiety attack. But her defenses had been breached, and the anxiety oozed its way into her system. Her thoughts swirled into a chaotic jumble as black dots flashed in front of her eyes. Her clammy skin felt like both fire and ice, and the adrenaline coursing through her veins left her shaking. Over the roaring buzz that filled her ears, Zoey heard one of the officers ask if she was okay. She could also feel his hand gripping her wrist as he monitored her pulse.

Fighting to get her breathing under control, Zoey latched onto one of the countless thoughts ricocheting around her brain and held on as she slipped into the darkness. *Stupid.* She had been so stupid to think that she could somehow figure out who killed Devon. Instead, all she did was interfere in the police investigation and put a target on her back. Whoever killed Devon was coming after her.

The first warning note had hardly been threatening and she failed to take it seriously. The second note had been alarming—especially since whoever left it must have followed her to the gym. Tonight's note was terrifying. The implied threat was bad enough. What made it worse was that the murderer had broken the tattoo shop's front window to leave the threat. Next time, it might be her apartment . . . and the murderer could be coming to do more than just leave a note.

Zoey wasn't sure how long the anxiety attack lasted, but, when she drifted out of the darkness, Zack was seated on the step next to her.

"I'm good now." Zoey shook her head to clear the last of the cobwebs. She was so emotionally and physically drained that she could barely speak above a whisper. "It's over."

"Are you sure?" Zack asked. He wrapped his arm around Zoey's shoulders and pulled her in for a hug. "I haven't seen you have an anxiety attack that bad in years."

"That's because I haven't." Zoey held up her trembling hands. It sickened her to be so weak and uneasy. "I just lost it. It's been too much. This past week has been too much."

Until this week, Zoey hadn't blacked out during an anxiety attack in at least five years. Towards the end of her relationship with Devon—when she'd been having at least one anxiety attack a day—she suffered from chest pain, heart palpitations, and full body shakes. She also cried a lot and felt detached. It wasn't until after the assault that she began to have blackouts. It only happened a handful of times, but it terrified her. She'd been relieved when the blackouts stopped after a few months, and she was able to get her anxiety under control.

"Miss Wilde?" Detective Gates strode out of the office and knelt on the floor. Zoey didn't miss the antagonistic scowl that Zack exchanged with the detective. "Are you all right? Do you need to be checked out by a medic?"

"I'll be okay."

Detective Gates stood up. He then held out his hands and helped Zoey to her feet. "How about we step into the other room and you can tell me about what happened tonight."

"I need to go upstairs. My cat . . ." Zoey pulled her hands away from the detective and pointed towards the ceiling. "That's her yowling because I've got her penned up in my bedroom. I need to let her out."

"That explains the noise." Detective Gates made a sweeping gesture towards the stairs and said, "Let's go rescue your cat."

After freeing an irritated Lita, Zoey grabbed a glass of orange juice and then joined Detective Gates at the dinner table.

"It looks like you could use something a little stronger than orange juice," Gates said. "My offer for a drink still stands . . ."

"I guess my answer depends on who you arrest," Zoey said as she glanced around for Zack. Her brother had come upstairs along with them. Now he was nowhere to be found. "Where did Zack go?"

"I sent him back downstairs. I would like to speak with you in private," Gates said as he flipped open his notebook. "Your dad is also on his way with a replacement window. Once the officers are done documenting the evidence, your dad and brother can pop in the new window."

"Of course, Dad would have a window lying around that's the right size."

Marlon had three storage units packed full of odds and ends that had been left over from jobs over the years. He hated to throw anything away because he might be able to use it someday. Every couple of years, Roxanne forced him to purge the storage units.

Zoey gave the detective a quick summary—after all, there wasn't all that much to tell. She'd woken up, realized someone was attempting to break into the tattoo shop.

"Now, Miss Wilde—"

"Zoey. Call me Zoey."

"All right . . . Zoey." Detective Gates cleared his throat. "When I was here yesterday morning, I explicitly told you and your grandmother to stop interfering with my investigation—"

"And I have," Zoey protested. "I can't say the same for Nana. But I haven't done anything or talked to anyone. Well, aside from Quincy. But he confronted me."

"Do you still believe Mr. Durand could be behind the notes?"

Zoey spun the glass in her hands and watched the orange juice swirl. "I don't know. Maybe. I didn't say anything to him about the notes. But, if it is him, at least I know he won't physically harm me. I hope."

"You would be surprised at what some people are capable of doing when their back is against the wall. Is there anyone else you spoke to? Anyone at all?"

"Well . . . I went to the Cozma Funeral Home in Quarryville this afternoon. Mort let me in before the service so that I could see Devon one more time."

"The memorial service was just about to start when I got to the funeral home. I must have just missed you," Detective Gates said. "But why did you want to see the victim again?"

"To . . . I don't know . . . Say goodbye and get some closure. And . . . Well, because the last time I saw him, he was lying in a pool of blood. I wanted to replace that image," Zoey said. "Paula came in as I was about to leave. She wasn't happy to see me. She accused me of killing Devon."

Detective Gates flipped his notebook closed. "One more question, Zoey . . . Are you or either of your brothers behind the notes—"

"Are you kidding me?" Zoey shoved back the chair and jumped up. "No, we are not behind the notes. I don't know how many times I have to tell you this, but my brothers and I did not kill Devon."

"I had to ask." Detective Gates stood up and walked towards the interior staircase. "I will have an officer keep an eye on the building in case this person comes back. I also urge you to take precautions and stop sticking your nose into my investigation."

"Then stop assuming that my brothers and I were involved and go find the actual killer."

"THE WINNER OF THE MATCH . . . And your new Steel City Pro Wrestling Women's Champion . . . The Wilde Woman, Zoey Wilde!"

Stepping over Mama as she rolled out of the ring, Zoey grabbed the title belt out of the referee's hands. While unattractive, the Steel City Women's title belt at least looked professional—unlike the LAW Women's title that reminded her of a bedazzled children's toy.

The Steel City belt had a dark gold leather strap, and the metallic plates were black and white.

This would be Zoey's third reign as the Steel City Women's Champion. She had dropped the title to Mama two months ago at the June show. Tonight was Zoey's rematch—a match that she had originally been scheduled to lose. Putting the title back on Zoey was a last-minute decision that the promoter made just prior to sending the women out to the ring. Zoey and Mama were forced to rework their match on the fly to accommodate the revised ending.

Zoey soaked in the standing ovation as she dodged the rolls of purple and black streamers that the fans flung at the ring. She had wrestled for Steel City Pro Wrestling two dozen times since the promotion's first show three-and-a-half years ago. Up until tonight, Zoey had played the role of a heel. The plan was for her to continue with her heel personae, but the fans had a different idea. As soon as the doors opened an hour before showtime, almost two-thirds of the estimated five hundred fans flocked to Zoey's merchandise table for pictures and autographs. Terry, who'd driven Zoey to the show and handled her merchandise sales, struggled to keep up with the fans' demands. Zoey sold out of t-shirts before the show started, and she sold the last of her photos during intermission.

Leaving the referee and a couple teenagers to clean up the streamers, Zoey headed up the aisle to the makeshift entranceway that was set up at one end of the indoor soccer arena. Waiting for her on the other side of the curtain was Mama. Her teased-out hair had escaped the lopsided pigtails, and the makeup she'd used to dirty up her appearance had smeared. There also appeared to be a few new rips in her jeans and tank top.

Crowded around Mama were Bubba, Tiny, and the rest of their "kin" from the hollers of West Virginia. Zoey recognized the McCoy kid from last weekend. It appeared he'd been admitted into the ever-expanding Hillbilly family stable.

Zoey clasped the title belt so hard that her knuckles turned white. She'd known Mama, Bubba, and Tiny for at least ten years. They were roughly the same age as Zoey and her brothers, and their paths had crossed numerous times over the years. Zoey had always gotten along with Mama, and she counted the woman as a friend. She worried that the decade-long friendship had come to an abrupt end.

"Another great match," Mama said as she cracked a smile. She slung her arm around Zoey's shoulders and hauled her close for a hug. "Maybe even one of our best."

"Nothing will ever top that six-person intergender tables match we had down in Virginia Beach," Zoey said as she returned the hug.

"Tell Zack to come out of retirement, and we can have another one." Mama kept her arm around Zoey's shoulders. Leaning closer, she said, "Now you know I normally don't mind droppin' a title to you. But tonight . . . Well, Mama ain't too happy 'bout it. You do know the only reason you got the title is 'cause of your ex-old man gettin' himself killed."

"Yeah, I know." Zoey sighed as she pulled away from Mama. "But you said that you don't think I'm the one who killed Devon."

"Nah. Never even crossed my mind," Mama said. "I know you just ain't got it in you to murder someone. Even if he did deserve it. Now me on the other hand—"

"Shhh . . . Mama, Zoey don't need to know 'bout them bodies we got buried out back of the moonshine still," Bubba said. He winked at Zoey and then grinned, revealing the gap where his two upper front teeth should be. Bubba was barely five-and-a-half feet tall, and he weighed in at over two hundred pounds. Despite his size, Bubba could move quickly when he had to. Zoey knew this firsthand as she had been in the ring with Bubba multiple times.

Stepping closer to Bubba, Zoey asked, "Are you and Tiny sure you didn't see anything suspicious after you tossed Devon out the back door?"

"We already told you what we saw," Bubba said.

"And we ain't thought of nothing new since we talked earlier," Tiny added. Tiny's nickname was contradictory to his stature as he was nearly seven-feet tall and almost as skinny as the ring posts. "Bubba and me grabbed Devon's stuff and tossed him out the door after his match. Told him to get out and stay out."

"He smashed that sledgehammer through the wall as we was hauling him out," Bubba said. "I saw Leland pull the hammer out of the drywall, but that's it."

"Last I saw, it was layin' on the ground where Leland left it." Mama gestured past Zoey and said, "Your boy toy is comin'."

Zoey glanced over her shoulder, worried that Reggie Drake had managed to make his way backstage. Like in Harrisburg, Reggie had confronted her during the preshow and demanded she answer his questions about Devon. Bubba and Tiny dragged him away from Zoey, but the promoter had not kicked Reggie out of the building. Zoey knew he was lurking around somewhere. But, instead of Reggie, it was Terry that was making his way towards her through the crowd of wrestlers. "Terry is not my boy toy. He's just a friend."

"Terry might not be your boy toy, but he wants to be," Tiny said. "Seems pretty obvious to us that he wants out of the friend zone."

Zoey shot Tiny an annoyed scowl as Terry sidled up beside her. "What's up?"

"Zack called while you were in the ring," Terry said as he scuffed the toe of his sneaker along the floor. "Quincy crashed his motorcycle."

"What?" Releasing her grip on the title belt, Zoey let the strap slide off her shoulder. It landed next to her feet. She hated Quincy's motorcycle, and had hated it since the day he bought it not long before she broke up with him. In fact, the motorcycle played a deciding factor in the breakup. Over the years, she'd warned him at least a million times to be careful while riding the motorcycle. Tonight, he finally crashed it. "What happened? Is he . . ."

"Oh, no. He's alive," Terry said it as if Quincy's condition was an afterthought. "But Zack said Quincy is hurt pretty bad. He's on the way to the hospital."

"We need to go." Fighting back tears, Zoey scooped up the title belt and handed it to Mama. She then turned to Terry and said, "Let's grab my stuff and get out of here."

"I already got your stuff out of the women's locker room. It's in my car," Terry said. "And I got your pay from the promoter. He said—"

"I don't care what he said. Stop lollygagging and let's get out of here." Zoey grabbed Terry by the arm and hauled him towards the back door. Outside, she hustled across the parking lot to Terry's SUV. "We need to get home."

There was no going anywhere fast in downtown Pittsburgh on a Saturday night. Traffic crawled as Terry made his way to the turnpike that would carry them east towards Linville. As Terry navigated between the stop lights and around the other cars, Zoey repeatedly called Zack.

"Answer your phone, damn it," Zoey shouted when she was sent to Zack's voicemail for the fourth time.

"For claiming you don't have feelings for the guy, you're sure acting like you do."

"Just because I'm not in love with Quincy anymore doesn't mean I don't care about him," Zoey said as she gave up calling Zack. "Quincy is still my friend."

"But earlier you said you're annoyed with him."

"And I am." Zoey whacked her phone against the dashboard when her mother failed to answer. *Where is everyone? And why are they too busy to answer my calls?* "Quincy has been badgering me for months to get back together. And he just won't take no for an answer. He's gotten on my last nerve. Not to mention I'm furious with him for not telling me that Devon was back in the area."

"Yeah, that was a real asshole move."

"You're telling me. Had he said something, maybe Devon wouldn't have wound up dead. And I wouldn't be this anxious mess."

"I still think you should be grateful to the person who killed Devon. That guy . . . or girl . . . did you a huge favor."

"And I told you before, I can't be happy that Devon is dead despite what he did to me. I do not wish death on another person. Even Devon." Zoey almost screamed when she got her dad's voicemail. "Plus Nana and I have a theory that Quincy killed Devon in some kind of misguided 'knight in shining armor' moment. If Quincy—God forbid—dies, we may never know if he killed Devon or not."

"I don't know what's so misguided about it," Terry muttered. "Whoever killed Devon did you a favor."

"Finally," Zoey said when one of her calls was answered. "Nana, what happened?"

"That's what I'm trying to figure out. I only just got home from the theater with the girls," Vivian said. Even though she almost always tagged along to Zoey's wrestling events, Vivian skipped the show in Pittsburgh to go to a show with some of her friends. She'd told everyone they were going to see a dance performance. What she had failed to mention to everyone but Zoey was that the dancers were all male. And would be shirtless throughout most of the act. "All I know for sure is that Quincy wrecked his bike after leaving the tattoo shop. According to Zack, he went right through the red light by the VFW Hall and laid down his bike to avoid hitting a car. Zack said Quincy is pretty beat up. Whatever that means. But he's alive. The EMTs took Quincy to Hershey Med. And Zack is on his way there, too."

Zoey glanced down at the LCD screen set into Terry's dashboard. "It'll be over three hours until we get back to Linville. Keep me posted."

"Hold on!" Vivian shouted before Zoey hung up. "You need to keep me posted, too. Did you talk to Mama and her boys? Did they tell you anything new?"

"Yes. And no," Zoey said before she filled her nana in on everything that Mama, Bubba, and Tiny had told her. "There wasn't anyone else here tonight who was also at the LAW show last Saturday. So, no, I didn't really learn anything new."

Zoey hung up on Vivian and then checked the text message that Zack had just sent her. He'd arrived at the Emergency Room at the Hershey Medical Center. Quincy was already there, and the doctors were prepping him for surgery. Among other injuries—including extensive road rash—Quincy had broken the tibia in his left leg in two places. One of the breaks was a compound fracture. The doctors were planning to put a titanium rod in Quincy's leg during the surgery. They would then address his other injuries.

Zoey kept her eyes on the estimated time of arrival listed on Terry's GPS as she willed him to drive faster. Terry, who was always cautious about everything, stuck to the speed limit for the entire drive. It was almost two in the morning when he pulled into the parking lot at the enormous Hershey Medical Center.

"Thanks for the ride, Terry. I'll see you later."

After scrambling out of the SUV, Zoey slammed the door shut and then sprinted to the Emergency Room entrance. Inside, she found a nearly deserted waiting room. Zack along with Quincy's parents made up half of the people in the room. Zoey approached them with caution. She still got along with Quincy's dad, but his mom had never really forgiven her for breaking up with her oldest son. Carol Durand was aware that Quincy was attempting to get back together with Zoey, and she'd been pressuring Zoey to go out with her son. Zoey could only hope that Carol would knock off the badgering for the time being.

"How is he?" Zoey asked. "What happened?"

"He's alive," Zack said as he pulled Zoey down onto the chair next to him and gave her a hug. "The light turned red, but Quincy didn't stop. He didn't even hit the brakes. A car was pulling into the intersection, so he laid the bike down—"

"How bad is he hurt?" Zoey asked.

"His lower left leg is broken in two places," Teddy Durand said.

"The doctors are still operating on him," Carol added.

"His left shoulder and wrist looked messed up," Zack said. "But it was hard to tell around all the blood. He was wearing shorts and a t-shirt, so his left arm and leg got torn up. At least he was wearing a helmet. It could have been so much worse . . ."

Zoey, Zack, and the Durands sat around in silence for over two hours before a doctor came out to give them an update. Quincy was out of surgery for his leg, and he was now being treated for his various other injuries.

"The two of you may as well go home," Carol said to Zoey and Zack after the doctor left. She gave Zoey a dismissive, side-eye look. "There's no point in you sitting here the rest of the night. I'll let you know when Quincy is up for visitors."

"Yeah, all right." Zack ran his hands over his face. He then stood up and gestured for Zoey to follow him out of the waiting room. "I don't know what we're going to do. I don't want to sound callous . . . But Quincy is going to be out of action for a while, and that's going to hurt the shop. We need to keep the money coming in, or I will have to start charging you rent."

"I told you that you should have hired someone fulltime after Rick left."

Rick had been the fourth tattoo artist at 3 Count Tattoos until he had moved to Missouri in April. Zoey had urged Zack to hire someone else on a permanent basis, but, instead, he rented out the room to different artists who needed the space. The room had sat empty for almost a month now.

"I know. I know. And I should have listened," Zack led the way to where his car was parked in one of the garages. "Can you put some ads out that we're hiring? And reschedule Quincy's appointments for next week. Santino and I might be able to squeeze some of the smaller tattoos into our schedules, but the custom pieces will have to be bumped back until Quincy is healed up."

Zoey reached over and squeezed her brother's hand. "We'll get through this, Zack."

TWENTY-THREE

Friday August 31, 2018

ZOEY CRINGED AS SHE READ WHAT PASSED for a resume. This candidate had no formal training, and admitted to teaching himself how to tattoo by using his friends as guinea pigs. The pictures that he'd sent of his work showed he had no idea what he was doing—and led Zoey to assume that these friends were no longer associating with him after the permanent messes he had left on their bodies. Somehow, though, this was not the worst applicant. That "award" went to the guy who'd sent sample pictures of other artists' work—including a picture of a neo-traditional style velociraptor that Zack had tattooed just last month.

After deleting the email, Zoey turned her attention back to the schedule. Since Monday, she had spent most of her time calling all of Quincy's appointments to inform them of his accident. Except for a handful of clients with custom pieces, most were willing to be tattooed by the new hire. That's if Zack hired a new person. He'd interviewed three artists, but decided not to hire any of them. Zoey hoped he found a worthy applicant and hired him or her before she was forced to reschedule any more of Quincy's appointments.

The sound of the front door opening distracted her.

"Welcome to . . ." Zoey trailed off when she saw who it was that had entered the tattoo shop. She could only come up with a couple reasons why Chief Coleman and Detective Gates would visit the shop—and none of them were good. "What are you doing here?"

"Where's Zack?" Jim asked. With his slumped shoulders and drawn expression, the police chief appeared defeated. "We need to talk to him."

"He's . . . he's with a client," Zoey said. She broke out in a cold sweat and her hands trembled. "You can't . . . He's almost done."

Detective Gates turned towards the foyer, but Jim placed his hand on the younger man's arm. "Let him finish."

"What's . . . what's going on?"

Detective Gates held up a folded piece of paper. "We have a warrant for Zack's arrest."

"No." Zoey shot to her feet, sending her chair crashing into the wall behind her. "You can't do this. Zack didn't—"

"Zoey, there's evidence," Jim said.

"Are you kidding me, Jim? You can't actually believe Zack killed Devon." Zoey turned back to the detective and said, "To hell with your evidence. It's wrong."

"It's more than just Devon," Jim said. He reached across the desk and patted Zoey on the arm. She recoiled from him. "It's also Quincy—"

"What about Quincy? What does he have to do with this?" Zoey pressed her palms against the desk and leaned forward. "Let me guess, you think Zack and Quincy worked together to kill Devon? Did Quincy make some kind of confession? Because he's on some serious pain medications. You can't really believe anything he's saying right now. I mean, two days ago he was telling the nurses that he was the reincarnation of Napoleon."

Quincy was still in the hospital nearly a week after his accident. Aside from the broken lower left leg and the considerable road rash, Quincy had suffered a number of injuries. His left shoulder had been dislocated. He'd also broken his left wrist and shredded the skin and tissue on his elbow down to the bone. Three of his ribs also cracked when he hit the pavement, and a small piece of bone had been chipped away from his hip.

"No, we don't think Quincy worked with Zack," Jim said. "We think . . . We think Zack caused Quincy's accident."

"What?" Zoey collapsed into her chair. "What are you talking about. What happened to Quincy was an accident. I saw him yesterday and he told me that he crashed because the bike's brakes wouldn't work. It was about the only coherent thing he said when I was with him. But he said it at least a dozen times. How can you possibly think . . ."

"Miss Wilde, the reason the brakes didn't work is because the brake line was cut," Gates said. "And it was done cleanly with a knife or some other sharp object."

"And you think Zack . . ." Zoey shook her head in disbelief. "Why would he do that? He and Quincy have been best friends since middle school. They're business partners."

"And the business has been having some problems lately because of Quincy," Jim said. "Maybe no one told you—"

"Told me what?" Zoey asked. "What has Quincy been up to?"

"Gambling," Zack said as he walked into the office. "Quincy had a gambling addiction."

"Don't say anything else, Zack," Jim warned his son-in-law.

"What does it matter?" Zack waved Jim off and then turned to Zoey. "Quincy started gambling after he and Elena split up. He wound up getting addicted. And he started losing a lot of money. I've been trying to help him out and get him some help, but Quincy just won't stop. The other week, I gave him enough money to cover his rent, and then I told him I was done bailing him out."

"Why didn't you tell me about any of this?" Zoey asked. She'd noticed some tension between Zack and Quincy on occasion, but she thought it had to do with Quincy's laidback attitude more than anything else. Even though Quincy owned half of 3 Count Tattoos, he had very little to do with managing the business.

"Quincy didn't want you to know. He was afraid you'd think less of him if you knew about his problem," Zack sneered. "I tried to tell him it didn't matter because you had no interest in getting back together with him. He didn't want to hear it. I also told him to stop pestering you. We got into an argument—"

"Zack! That's enough," Jim barked.

"Why? What's going on?" Zack asked. "Oh my God, did Quincy die from his injuries?"

"No," Detective Gates said as he held up the arrest warrant. "But you are under arrest for Quincy Durand's attempted murder as well as the murder of Devon Isler."

"Attempted murder?" Zack's eyes darted between Zoey, his father-in-law, and the detective. "It was an accident. I saw the whole thing. Quincy didn't stop at the red light and he laid his bike down in the intersection to avoid hitting a car."

"We can talk more about this down at the station," Detective Gates said as he fastened a pair of handcuffs around Zack's wrists and then steered him to the front door.

"Zack, don't say anything else without a lawyer," Jim said.

"Zoey . . ." Zack glanced over his shoulder and gave his sister a wide-eyed look. "I didn't do this. I swear I didn't."

"I know, Zack. And I'll take care of it," Zoey said. She watched as Detective Gates forced Zack out through the front door. She then turned to Jim and asked, "What do I do?"

"Call Zack's lawyer. That's about the only thing you can do."

"What about Arielle? And my parents?"

"I'll go break the news to them." Jim kicked the front of Zoey's desk and swore. "I don't know how Arielle is going to handle this—"

"Not very well," Zoey said. "There has got to be something I can do."

"There isn't, Zoey. There isn't anything you can do."

"WE NEED TO DO SOMETHING."

"I know, Nana," Zoey said as she unlocked the door to her apartment. They had spent the past few hours at Zack's house trying to get Arielle and Roxanne calmed down. Zoey knew she'd done little to comfort either of them. Her anxiety was on overdrive, and it was all she could do to hold herself together. She felt so useless. For years, Arielle had been her rock. Now, when Arielle needed her, Zoey was about as solid as a marshmallow. "But I did the only thing I could do. I called Pasqual. Besides that, there is nothing we can do."

"We can find the real killer." Vivian stomped over to Zoey's desk, shoved the cardboard cutout of Shawn Michaels out of the way, and grabbed the corkboard. She then slammed the corkboard down on top of the desk. "Come on, Zoey. It's up to us."

"Nana . . . Give it a rest."

"No. We can do this," Vivian snapped. "Someone bashed Devon over the head with a sledgehammer. And someone cut Quincy's brake line. And we both know that person was not your brother."

"You can't possibly think the same person is responsible for both."

"Why couldn't they be connected?"

"Because . . . because Devon and Quincy have nothing in common."

"Aside from the fact that they are your ex-boyfriends."

"Well, yeah. Aside from that."

"It's really not a good time to be one of your exes," Vivian said. "It's probably for the best that you weren't in any other serious relationships."

"But why would someone be after my ex-boyfriends?" Zoey asked as she walked over to join her nana at the desk. "I mean . . . Unless I have a homicidal secret admirer."

"Well . . . You did have those three stalkers. One of them might be back."

Zoey tugged on her hair in frustration. "We have to take into account that Quincy had some serious gambling debts. A loan shark or a bookie could have had one of their guys cut Quincy's brake line to send him a message."

"Kind of an extreme message," Vivian pointed out. "What if Quincy had died? He can't pay back his debts if he's dead."

"True . . ." Zoey leaned over the desk and examined the three remaining suspects. "Well, we know Chelsea couldn't have cut Quincy's brake line. She was in police custody all day last Friday and Saturday. She also couldn't have left the threatening notes. I still think she could have killed Devon though."

"But how did she get the sledgehammer from backstage?"

"That's the million-dollar question," Zoey said. She tapped the picture of Leland. "Uncle Leland had access to the sledgehammer. He even admitted to removing it from the wall."

"He also has a motive and no alibi."

"But why Quincy?" Zoey asked. "What did Quincy ever do to him?"

Vivian shrugged. "Maybe Leland is trying to frame Zack."

"Okay . . . But why? It doesn't make any sense." Zoey moved on to the remaining suspect. "That just leaves Quincy. He had a motive to kill Devon. It's not a great motive. But it's still a motive. And he has no alibi."

"But we have the same problem with him that we do with Chelsea . . . How would he have gotten the sledgehammer?"

"And why would Quincy have cut his own brake line?"

"Because . . ." Vivian drummed her fingers on the edge of the desk. "He's also trying to frame Zack?"

"This is crazy."

Zoey headed into the living room. Laying down on the couch, she pulled a blanket over her head and concentrated on breathing. She was barely keeping the mounting anxiety attack at bay. She had to keep it together or else she would be overwhelmed by a breakdown. She couldn't let that happen—not when Zack needed her.

The sound of the window and then the screen being pushed open caused Zoey to sit up. She shoved the blanket off her head just in time to see Vivian climb out the window and onto the narrow porch roof.

"Nana!" Zoey sprang off the couch and rushed to the window. She grabbed Vivian by the shirt and hauled her back inside. "What the heck are you doing?"

"I'm trying to see what's going on up at the VFW Hall."

Zoey squeezed her eyes shut and suppressed the urge to scream. "It's the last Friday of the month. It's bingo night."

Vivian clapped her hands together. "We should go."

"Zack's under arrest, and you want to play bingo."

"No, I don't want to play bingo." Vivian smacked Zoey on the arm. "I want to take another look at the crime scene. Are you coming with me?"

"What other choice do I have?"

After making sure that the window was shut—the last thing she needed was Lita to get out—Zoey ran out the door after Vivian. Even though the VFW Hall was only a few blocks up the street from Zoey's apartment, Vivian insisted on driving. They passed through the intersection where Quincy had crashed and then turned into the VFW Hall's parking lot. After examining the parking lot around where Devon was killed, they headed around to the front of the building.

"B-four," blasted out of the speakers as Vivian and Zoey walked inside. Passing the table where two middle-aged women were selling bingo cards, Vivian headed towards the concession stand where her brother, Elwood, was selling snacks. "B-four."

"We heard about Zack getting arrested," Elwood said as he handed Zoey a chocolate chip cookie. Elwood, as well as two other brothers, was a veteran of the Vietnam War. He was also a huge fan of pro wrestling. "It's a damn shame."

"Yeah, it is." Zoey ripped the plastic wrapper off the cookie and took a bite. She was dismayed that word of her brother's arrest had gotten out. "Zack didn't do it."

"Of course not," Elwood said.

"Did that drywall ever get fixed?" Vivian asked.

"Nah." Elwood patted his hands on his stomach. "One of our Gulf War vets said he'd patch it up, but he hasn't gotten around to it yet. If he doesn't take care of it by the end of next week, I'll give Marlon a call."

"Mind if we go backstage and take a look at it?" Vivian asked.

"Knock yourselves out," Elwood said as he shooed them away from the concession stand. "But it ain't that interesting."

Zoey and Vivian made their way across the banquet hall and then slipped through the doors that were to the left of the stage. A narrow hallway ran along the side of the stage and connected with the hallway around back.

"Elwood's right. It's not that interesting," Zoey said as she examined the jagged hole in the drywall. The hole, which was right next to the door to the men's bathroom, was roughly a foot wide by a foot tall. "We had to see this because . . ."

"Because . . . why not?" Vivian looked around the deserted hallway and then walked over to the women's bathroom. "I need to pee."

"You have the bladder of a squirrel," Zoey muttered.

To keep herself occupied while she waited for Vivian, Zoey decided to have a look in the storage room. Leland claimed that after he finished yelling at Justin, he'd gone into the storage room to calm down and smoke a cigarette. It was while he was in the storage room that he overheard Zack arguing with Devon in the parking lot.

Zoey had just barely stepped through the door when she came face-to-face with the smashed in nose of a plastic Santa Claus. Piled up around the life-size blow mold were other holiday decorations including four artificial Christmas trees and a wooden cutout of a witch.

Picking her way around the teetering stacks of boxes, discarded backdrops and props, and the rest of the junk that had found its way into the storage room, Zoey examined the four-foot-tall, opaque awning windows. There were eight windows on the side wall and five along the back. A countertop ran along the side wall, and the boxes that had been stacked on top of it obstructed access to the eight windows. Four of the five windows along the back wall were blocked by a crudely-made plywood backdrop that was painted to resemble either a primeval forest or an alien planet.

Zoey pushed a vintage popcorn machine out of the way so she had better access to the only unobstructed window. She then unlocked the window and shoved it open. The window only opened a few inches before it got stuck. Zoey put some muscle into it, but she couldn't get it to open any farther. Because the glass was frosted, she was unable to see anything through the window, but she could hear the muffled sound of a car driving through the parking lot.

"I guess Leland could have snuck out the back door, bashed Devon over the head with the sledgehammer, and then snuck back in . . ." Zoey muttered as she pulled the window closed. She continued talking to herself. "But there were too many people hanging out in the hallway. Surely one of them would have seen him going out or coming back in . . . Unless Leland actually brought the sledgehammer in here with him. But then how would he have gotten outside?"

Pressing her cheek against the dirty glass, Zoey peered behind the forest backdrop and realized that what she'd thought was the middle window was actually a door. Grabbing the heavy plywood backdrop, she pulled it out from the wall far enough for her to squeeze through.

Zoey pushed open the door and then waited for an emergency alarm to sound. When nothing happened, she stepped outside and fought her way through the boxwoods on either side of the door. The overgrown shrubs were taller than her and almost completely blocked the door.

Breaking free of the boxwoods, Zoey stepped into the parking lot. From where she stood, she could see the Linville Community Park office building at the back of the lot.

"All Leland had to do was wait until Zack walked away and then he could have slipped outside and killed Devon. He then reentered the building through the storage room with no one ever knowing he'd been outside." Spinning around, Zoey reached between the two bushes and grabbed the doorhandle. The door had locked behind her. "Plenty of things in the storage room that Leland could have used to keep the door propped open."

Zoey walked over to the back door that opened up into the hallway behind the stage. That door was also locked. She pounded on it until Vivian opened it.

"What are you doing out there?" Vivian asked.

"It was Leland!" Zoey grabbed Vivian's arm and dragged her into the storage room. She showed her nana the exterior door and then explained her theory. "Leland killed Devon, and then he pointed the finger at Zack."

Vivian swore. "I always knew that man was scum. When I get my hands on him . . ."

"I need to call Jim." Zoey pulled her phone out of her shorts' pocket and called Chief Coleman. He didn't answer, so she left a voicemail. It was the same with Detective Gates. She also tried calling Pasqual. "Let's go over to the police department and see if Jim and the detective are there. This can't wait."

Zoey and Vivian made their way outside and then over to where Vivian had parked her Cadillac. Pulling out of the parking lot, Vivian turned right onto Market Street.

"Wrong way, Nana," Zoey pointed out as Vivian drove through downtown Linville. "The police department is in the other direction."

"We aren't going to the police department." Vivian took a right onto East Willow Street. "We're going to confront Leland."

"But Kim kicked him out," Zoey said as Vivian turned left onto North Hanover Street. Kim and Leland lived in a one-story rancher halfway down the block. "What makes you think Leland will be at the house?"

"Because Kim is in Richmond with her sister until Monday." Vivian pulled up behind Leland's enclosed trailer that was parked along the curb in front of the house. He used the trailer to haul the wrestling ring and other paraphernalia to the LAW events every month. Instead of the wrestling equipment, the trailer was full of various boxes and precariously stacked pieces of furniture. "She told Leland he needs to have all of his stuff out of the house before she gets back."

"There aren't any lights on in the house," Zoey said as she sent a text to Jim to let her know where she and Vivian were. She then climbed out of the car. "And where's Leland's truck?"

"The lights are on in the garage." Vivian pointed to the detached two-car garage that was at the back of the property. "Maybe he's back there loading stuff in the truck."

Zoey jogged across the backyard towards the garage. As she reached for the door handle, she glanced through the window and saw Leland's truck. The engine was running, but the garage doors were closed. Leland sat slumped behind the wheel.

"Hang on, Leland!"

Zoey shoved open the door and then stepped into the garage long enough to hit the garage door button that was mounted on the wall near the door. Both garage doors slowly crept upward. Once both doors were open and oxygen was flowing into the garage, Zoey hustled over to the passenger side door and tried to open it. The door was locked.

"Use this," Vivian said as she handed Zoey a hammer. "We've got to shut the engine off and get him out of here."

Zoey raised the hammer and swung it at the passenger side window. She had to hit the glass multiple times before the glass shattered. She then reached inside the truck and unlocked the doors.

Careful to avoid the broken glass, Zoey climbed over the passenger seat and shut off the engine so that they would no longer need to worry about the carbon monoxide filling the garage. She then pressed her fingers to the side of Leland's neck to check for a pulse.

"He's alive. But his pulse is thready." Zoey backed out of the truck. "Help me get him out of the truck. Then call 911."

As Zoey rounded the front of the truck, Terry came barreling through the open garage door and slammed into her. He pushed her away from the truck and sent her sprawling into the open garage stall where Kim usually parked. As Zoey hit the ground, her shoulder slammed into the concrete. The wind was also knocked out of her.

Vivian dropped to her knees next to her granddaughter. "Zoey! Are you all right?"

"I think so." Zoey rolled over and looked up at Terry. "What was that for?"

"You two aren't supposed to be here." Terry pounded his fists on the hood of the truck. "You've messed up everything. Leland needs to die. For cheating on my mom. And for what he put you through. Now you've screwed it all up."

"What did we mess up? We just stopped Leland from killing himself," Zoey said. With Vivian's help, she sat up. She then gently pressed her hand against her throbbing shoulder. "Leland killed Devon. If he dies, he can't confess. And I need him to confess so the police will let Zack go."

"No, you don't need him alive." Terry pulled a crumpled piece of paper out of the cargo pocket on his shorts. "Leland left a note. I found it—"

"Let me see that." Vivian ripped the note out of Terry's hand and read it over. "'*Kim, I'm sorry I cheated on you. And for all the other stupid stuff I did*' . . . What stupid stuff? Does he mean killing Devon? Then he should come out and say it. Like Zoey said, we need Leland alive to confess."

As Vivian took a step towards the truck's driver side door, Terry reached out and wrapped his arm around her shoulders. He then hauled Vivian closer to him and held her pinned against his chest. With his free hand, Terry reached into his pocket and pulled out the utility knife that he always carried.

"We're going to turn the truck back on, shut up the garage, and let Leland die from carbon monoxide poisoning," Terry said as he pressed the tip of the blade against Vivian's throat. She stopped struggling. "He deserves to die."

"But I need him to confess!" Zoey inched towards Terry. "Zack's life is on the line!"

"Stop right there." Terry pointed the knife at Zoey and gestured for her to stay back. "Leland has to die. Otherwise . . . I mean, there is no otherwise. Leland killed Devon. But he couldn't live with what he did, so he killed himself. Or he would have if you two hadn't shown up and ruined everything."

Zoey glanced past Terry to the truck and, through the driver's side window, noticed that Leland was moving around a bit. He was no longer unconscious.

Turning her attention back to Terry, Zoey wondered when he had become so heartless. She'd known him since they were kids, and he had never shown this ruthlessness before. Sure, he and Leland hadn't always gotten along over the past few years. And she could understand why Terry would be angry at Leland for cheating on Kim. But there had to be more to it than that, and Zoey could only come up with one explanation.

"It was you . . ." Turning back to Terry, Zoey whispered, "You killed Devon. And now you're trying to pin it on Leland. But how . . . And why?"

"You know how, Zoey," Terry said. He used the knife to gesture for Zoey to leave the garage. Instead, Zoey backed towards the far wall. "I bashed Devon over the head with the sledgehammer while he was kneeling on the ground next to Justin's Jeep. I saw what he did to your car, and I knew he'd mess with Justin's tires, too. Devon heard me walking up. And he saw I had the sledgehammer. He laughed at me. He said I was too much of a wimp to do anything. He said he was going to get you back. But I showed him."

"You told us you were in the bathroom . . ."

Terry laughed. "And you believed me. You and Vivi were so busy checking everyone else's alibis. But did you bother to check mine? Of course not. Did you try to figure out if anyone else had been in the bathroom at the same time as me? Nope. And you know why you didn't? Because you barely notice that I'm alive."

Overcoming the initial shock, Zoey asked, "So what . . . You just picked up the sledgehammer and followed Devon out the back door?"

"No," Terry said shaking his head. "I picked up the sledgehammer and went into the bathroom. I then went out through the exterior door that's in the bathroom. There isn't a security camera there. I left the door propped open with someone's bag so that I could get back in."

Zoey had forgotten about the exterior door in the women's bathroom. Now she recalled how Hannah had propped open the door to get air into the stuffy women's bathroom. She should have known that there was an exterior door in the men's bathroom as well.

"It never crossed my mind that you would kill Devon. Or lie to us about what you were doing," Zoey said. "You had no reason—"

"I had lots of reasons!" Terry shouted. "Years ago, Devon bullied me. He picked on me for being fat. And for not being athletic enough to be a wrestler. And for having a crush on you. He always rubbed it in my face that he was dating you and that I would never have a chance. He started bullying me again that night for all the same reasons. And he kept going on about how you would be dumb enough to get back together with him and that he could ruin your life. I didn't think you'd get back with him, but . . . but . . . I saw what my dad did to my mom. She thinks I was too young to remember. But I remember enough. I remember how he used to verbally abuse her all the time. How he would smack her around. She'd kick him out and tell him she was done with him. Later, he'd come crawling back full of false apologies. He'd beg Mom to take him back. He'd swear he was a changed man and that he'd never do it again. And every single time, Mom was dumb enough to take him back. And every time, he pulled the same shit. Until the time he hit me. Then Mom finally wised up and kicked him out for good."

"So you killed Devon because he reminded you of your dad?"

Terry nodded. "I couldn't let you make the same mistake over and over again like my mom. Devon almost killed you last time. Next time—"

"There was not going to be a next time," Zoey said. "I'm not your mom. I was not going to get back together with Devon."

"You say that . . . But I had to make sure. I had to save you from him." Terry's eyes darted around the garage. "Plus, he had those pictures of Leland and that slut—"

"You already knew that Leland was messing around with Beverly?"

Terry nodded. "Devon threatened to post the pictures on Facebook. My mom would have been humiliated. I had to stop him. I had to protect my mom."

"You set all this up. You forced Leland to write the note—"

"No, he wrote that himself. I found it stuck to the fridge. I was going to put it in the truck and hope everyone thought it was a suicide note. I also used his phone to send texts to my mom confessing that he killed Devon."

Zoey shook her head. "Okay, Leland wrote the note. But you forced him to get in the truck and then turned on the engine. And you sent those texts to your mom so that way he would be blamed for Devon's murder. And you would get revenge against him for cheating on your mom," Zoey said as she took a step towards Terry. He took a step backwards, dragging Vivian with him as he pressed the blade against her throat. Over Terry's shoulder, Zoey noticed Chief Coleman and Detective Gates rounding the side of the house. They both had their guns drawn. Zoey assumed that Jim had seen the text message she'd sent to let him know she and Vivian were at Leland's house.

Worried that Jim or Gates might do something that would startle Terry and cause him to turn around, Zoey loudly said, "Put the knife down, Terry. Maybe I am secretly grateful that you killed Devon. But you know I'll never forgive you if you slit my nana's throat."

Jim and the detective both froze.

"You're not grateful." Terry pressed the knife closer to Vivian's neck, drawing a few drops of blood. He forced Vivian along with him as he backed out of the garage and into the driveway. "You told me I was cold-hearted for being glad Devon's dead."

"Of course, I said that," Zoey said as she followed Terry. For once, she wasn't feeling anxious. In fact, she felt strangely calm. "I couldn't risk word getting back to the detective that I was happy Devon was dead. He already suspected I played a role in the murder."

"So . . . You are grateful?" Terry asked.

"Extremely. You're my hero, Terry." Zoey raised her hands in a placating gesture. "Now how about you put the knife down—"

"How do I know you aren't trying to trick me?"

"Why would I do that?" Zoey asked.

"Because now that you know what I did, you'll tell the police to save Zack."

"They'll see Leland's texts—"

"And they'll drop the charges against Zack for Devon's murder," Terry said. "But what about Quincy?"

"I don't . . ." Zoey took a step backwards. She kept her eye on Vivian as the older woman dug around in her purse. Behind Terry, Jim motioned for her to keep Terry distracted. "You cut Quincy's brake line?"

"I did it for you! You kept complaining about how annoying Quincy was. How you were sick of his pestering you about getting back together. So I decided to get rid of him for you. I cut his brake line. But I messed up. He was supposed to die. And the police were supposed to think a loan shark had Quincy's bike messed with because of his debts," Terry screamed. More blood ran down Vivian's neck as Terry pressed the blade against her wrinkled skin. "Don't you get it, Zoey? Everything I do is for you! But you don't see any of it. You barely even see me. The same way Devon barely saw Chelsea. She did everything for him, and he didn't care. The same way you don't care about me!"

"I care about you."

"No! I'm just another brother to you. Except I'm the 'brother' you never questioned. Why can't you see me as something other than a brother? Why can't you appreciate everything I've done for you. All the flowers and the gifts—"

"That was you?" Zoey asked. "You sent me all that stuff? I thought it was some creep—"

"So now I'm a creep?"

"Well, those letters you sent with the flowers and other stuff were pretty damn creepy."

"Borderline psychotic," Vivian muttered.

"Nana!" Zoey turned her attention back to Terry. "What about the person who sent me all those anonymous emails? And the texts from the burner phones? Was that you, too?"

"Yes. I was trying to get your attention, but nothing seemed to work."

Zoey shook her head. "For all that time I was terrified that some nutcase was stalking me. But, all along, it was just you? What was the point?"

"For God's sake, Zoey, do you think I go to all those shows with you and do everything you ask of me because I have nothing better to do with my life?" Terry screamed. "No, I do it because I love you. And I've been in love—"

"That's enough, Terry!" Zoey's head was swirling and all she could think about was how Mama had referred to Terry as her "boy toy," and Tiny insisting that Terry wanted out of the "friend zone." Zoey thought Terry had gotten over his crush years ago. Turns out that he had just gotten better at hiding it, or she turned a blind eye to it because she saw him as nothing more than another brother. "Put the knife down and let Nana go. You do that, and I'll play along. I'll never say a word it was you—"

"Bullshit. You'll throw me to the police to save Zack. And I can't—"

Behind Zoey, the truck's horn blared.

Startled, Terry moved the knife away from Vivian's neck. With a sharp object no longer pressed near her jugular vein, the elderly woman finally took her chance. As she pushed away from Terry, Vivian pulled a knitting needle out of her purse and stabbed him in the thigh. Terry howled in pain as he dropped the knife and grabbed the knitting needle that stuck out of the side of his leg.

"You have a lot of nerve threatening an old lady." Vivian walloped Terry with her purse. She then looked over to where Jim and the detective stood just a few feet away. "'Bout time you two got here."

"We'll take it from here," Gates said as he holstered his gun and then unclipped a pair of handcuffs from his belt.

While Gates placed Terry under arrest, Zoey helped Jim get Leland out of the truck. Leland was conscious but woozy. He also had no memory of how he'd gotten into the truck. The last thing he remembered was packing up his belongings inside the house.

Within minutes, the backyard was overrun with police officers and EMTs. Leland was given oxygen and then rushed to the hospital. Terry was also taken to the hospital to have the knitting needle removed from his leg while Zoey and Vivian were both treated for their injuries on site. Vivian only needed a Band-Aid for the small cut on her neck, and Zoey was given an icepack for her bruised shoulder. While both had breathed in some carbon monoxide before Zoey opened the garage doors and shut off the truck's engine, neither of them seemed to have suffered any negative effects aside from minor headaches. It was Leland who'd spent several minutes in the garage while the truck's engine was running.

"I told you to stay out of it, Miss Wilde," Detective Gates said as he sat down next to her on the rear bumper of an ambulance.

"If I had left it up to you, Leland would be dead. And my brother would still be in jail."

"Technically, Zack is still in police custody." Gates held up his hands and gestured for Zoey not to interrupt. "I will release him as soon as I get back to the police department."

"Good." Zoey chugged from the water bottle that one of the medics had given her. "After the day I've had, I need something stronger than this."

"My offer for a drink still stands."

Zoey glanced at Detective Gates out of the corner of her eye as she thought about what Bernadette had said a few days earlier. Her therapist would encourage her to go out on a date with the detective. She needed to get out of the safe, roped off shallow end of the pool and take some risks. Her life would remain in neutral otherwise. There was no denying that she was attracted to Gates. But she was also angry at him. She knew she had to get past the anger before taking him up on the offer.

"You accused me of murder and arrested my twin brother," Zoey said. "It's going to take me a while to get past that."

"I'll wait." Gates grinned at her. "You know how to find me when you're ready."

TWENTY-FOUR

Saturday September 18, 2018

"Y ou're here!" Leland shoved aside Sasquatch and hustled over to where Zoey stood just inside the back door of the VFW Hall's banquet room. Vivian and Hannah were with her. "I wasn't sure if you were coming tonight. You didn't return any of my calls—"

"That's because I have nothing to say to you, Leland." Zoey pushed her sunglasses on top of her head so that she could glare at the man she had always considered as her uncle. She then hefted the rhinestone studded, hot pink title belt higher up on her shoulder. The darn thing was heavy. "But I'm the LAW Women's Champion, and I previously made a commitment to be here for this show."

Zoey genuinely felt bad for Leland, and she was glad to see that he had not suffered any permanent damage following his nearly fatal carbon monoxide poisoning. She knew that Leland had brought it onto himself by cheating on Kim and then playing along with Devon's blackmail game, but that didn't mean that he deserved to die. Luckily, Zoey and Vivian had found him within minutes of Terry shutting him up in the garage with the truck's engine running.

Despite his repeated attempts to reach out to them, none of the Wildes had seen or talked to Leland since the night Zoey had shown up at Kim's house to accuse him of murdering Devon and wound up saving his life. None of them were quite ready to forgive Leland and resume their friendships.

Zoey had talked to Bernadette a few times during the past two weeks. She also had several therapy sessions scheduled in advance over the next month. Now that the killer was in custody—and she and her brothers were no longer suspects—Zoey was finally ready to talk about what had happened to Devon. She was ready to put all of this behind her. She'd even tried to make peace with Paula Isler, but Devon's mother was clinging to her anger and hatred of the entire Wilde family. Zoey hoped that someday Paula would be able to find some peace. The same went for Chelsea.

"I . . . uh . . . Since I didn't know if you'd be here or not, I didn't schedule a match for you," Leland said to Zoey as he tugged on the ends of his handlebar mustache. "I did book four women to compete in a Fatal Four Way Match to become the number one contender for the Women's—"

"Yeah, I saw that on Facebook."

Zoey might have ignored all of Leland's phone calls and messages, but she had kept up with announcements on the Linville Association of Wrestling's Facebook page. A week earlier, Leland had announced the Fatal Four Way match between Jasmine de la Cour, Persephone, Brunhilda the Warrior Queen, and Beverly Hill.

"Are you still doing the nasty with Beverly?" Vivian asked Leland.

"Doing the nasty . . ." Leland chuckled. "No. No, that's over. I broke things off—"

Interrupting, Hannah said, "That's not what Beverly told me. She said she dumped you."

"I . . . uh . . . Beverly didn't take the break up very well and is . . . uh . . ." Leland tugged at his collar as a flush crept up his neck and stained his cheeks pink. "I think I'm going to take a break from the dating scene. Thanks to Kim . . . I can't believe she knew Terry killed Devon and tried to help him cover it up."

Zoey wasn't surprised by that revelation. She hadn't really thought about it at the time, but, now that she'd had time to look at the bigger picture, she knew it couldn't have been a coincidence that Kim was out in the parking lot at the same time she discovered Devon's body. From past experiences, Zoey knew that Kim would never shut down the concession stand while the show was still going on. Nor would she be taking leftover snacks out to her car until after the show ended. Terry had refused to implicate his mother, but their phone records showed that Terry called Kim around the same time that Devon was murdered. Zoey assumed that Terry had told Kim what he'd done, and Kim had rushed outside to try to help him cover it up. She also assumed that Terry, who had still been lingering around the crime scene, took off when he heard Zoey approaching with the air pump. He'd had no idea that Zoey was out in the parking lot at the time. He tried to call Kim to warn her, but Kim had ignored the call and continued to the back of the parking lot where she found Zoey standing over Devon's body. It had been Kim's idea to leave the three notes warning her to stop sticking her nose where it didn't belong. Zoey also suspected that Kim had encouraged Terry to pin the murder on Leland and also stage his death to look like a suicide. A few days after Terry was arrested, Kim was charged with being an accessory to murder.

"What about tonight, Zoey? Since I don't have you on the card, how 'bout you be the ref for the Fatal Four Way? We could use it to set up the storyline going into next month's show. Or you could take the night off and just sit on the stage during the match. Maybe confront the winner afterwards . . . By the way, I have Jasmine slated to win since she is the only one available for the October show."

"What if I want to wrestle tonight?" Zoey asked.

"Oh, well, yeah . . . I can probably squeeze in another match," Leland said. He pulled his phone out of his jacket pocket and began playing around on it. "I can shorten up a couple matches and . . . Do you want me to pull one of the women from the Fatal Four Way for you to wrestle? Make that match a Triple Threat . . . It's whatever you want, Zoey. I owe you for saving my life. And for what I put you through. I know I should have told you about Devon—"

"Yes, you should have. And you're right, you do owe me. The most important thing you owe me is an apology—"

"But we know that won't happen," Vivian said as she shook her fist under Leland's nose. "In all the years I've known you, I've never heard you sincerely apologize for anything."

"I am sorry, Zoey. I—"

"Save it," Zoey said to Leland. She held up the title belt. "You also owe me a new belt. This one is a joke."

"I have a new title belt on order. It will be here for the show in October. It'll be just like the men's title and the tag titles, except it will have a purple leather strap."

"No rhinestones?" Zoey asked.

"No rhinestones," Leland said. "Now what about tonight's match?"

"Let me think . . ." Zoey tapped her finger against her chin as she ran through the possibilities that Leland mentioned. None of them really appealed to her. She also thought about the four women who Leland had hired. She'd wrestled them all before. She knew how skilled they were and what they were capable of. "Cancel the Fatal Four Way. We're having a ladder match . . . No, a tables, ladders, and chairs match for the Women's Championship."

"A TLC match?" Leland's eyes bugged out. "You've got to be kidding me. You want to have a TLC match? Don't you remember what happened last time we had a ladder match? There is no way the people who own the VFW Hall will agree to a TLC match. Not after what Justin did during that ladder match."

"You told me it's whatever I want. And I want a TLC match. Besides, none of us women are as dumb as Justin," Zoey said, earning herself a glare from Hannah.

Six months earlier, during a ladder match for the LAW Heavyweight Championship, Justin had the bright idea to dangle from one of the banquet hall's three elaborate chandeliers when the ladder he'd been climbing was knocked out from under him. No one bothered to check beforehand if the chandelier could support Justin's weight. Turns out that it could not. Justin, luckily, only suffered bumps, bruises, and various shallow cuts from the broken glass.

"All right. All right," Leland said. "So the five—"

"Six!" Hannah bounced up and down. "I want in on this."

"Okay, so the six of you women will have a TLC match," Leland said. "I have the Fatal Four Way scheduled for right before intermission. I'll keep—"

"No, you're giving us the main event," Zoey said.

Leland's shoulders slumped beneath the jacket's fringed epaulettes. "Okay, you can have the main event. I assume you'll be winning the match."

"Of course." Zoey glanced over at Vivian and was struck with an idea.

"Actually, no, I won't be winning. The title is changing hands tonight. There is also going to be a seventh competitor in the match. And she's going to win the title."

"Who are you talking about?" Leland asked. "There aren't any other women here tonight. Not even a valet."

Zoey put her arm around her nana's shoulders. "Vivacious Vivian is going to make a comeback for one night only. And she's going to win the title."

"Yes!" Vivian pumped her arms in the air and shuffled her feet around in a jig. "I'm going to win a title! I'm going to win a title!"

"No. Absolutely not," Leland said. "I can't have an eighty—"

"Excuse me," Vivian screeched. "I'm only seventy-nine."

Leland pressed his hands over his eyes. "I can't have a senior citizen get in the ring. Especially not in a TLC match. Not in *any* match. My God, she could fall off a ladder and break a hip."

"Don't worry, Leland," Zoey said as she patted him on the arm. "Nana isn't really going to be in the match. Yeah, she'll start out in the ring with the rest of us. But, as soon as the match starts, Nana will . . . I don't know . . . Hide under the ring. She'll only come out again at the very end when the rest of us are down. She can then climb the ladder and grab the title."

"I want to hit someone with a chair," Vivian said.

"Okay . . . Someone other than me can be climbing the ladder and you can knock her off with a chair shot," Zoey said.

"And then what?" Leland asked. "Vivi defends the title at next month's show?"

"No, Nana *surrenders* the title," Zoey said. She held up the current title belt. "You then retire this monstrosity. Personally, I think you should burn it. But I don't think rhinestones are flammable."

"No!" Vivian grabbed the belt and yanked it away from Zoey. "I'm keeping it. I don't care if it's ugly. It's my title, and I'm keeping it."

"Fine, you can keep the title after it's retired," Zoey said to Vivian. She then turned to Leland and said, "You then reveal the new and improved Women's Championship. There is then a match for it. Make it a Triple Threat between me, Hannah, and Jasmine. Or find another woman and make it a Fatal Four Way. I then win the match and regain the title."

"Yeah, all right." Leland nodded a few times and then twirled the ends of his mustache. "I can make that work. But, Vivi, you need to promise me right now that you will not sue me if you get hurt tonight."

"Deal." Vivian shook Leland's hand and handed him the title. She then headed out the door. "I need to go home and grab my ring gear."

As the door swung shut behind Vivian, Leland said, "Zoey, if your crazy grandmother comes back wearing that red two-piece bathing suit, I will never forgive you."

"Brace yourself," Zoey said as she let go of the title belt that she was attempting to unhook from one of the arms of the repaired chandelier. She grasped the top step of the ten-foot-tall ladder as it teetered to the side. "I hate this part."

"Remember, it was your idea," Brunhilda the Warrior Queen said. Her blonde hair was held back by a leather headband, and her fur-trimmed leather and wool outfit was supposed to resemble that of a Viking shield maiden. "You're the one who wanted a TLC match. Here's your ladder. And down there is your table . . ."

"And you're the one who volunteered to go through the table along with me," Zoey said as the ladder finally tipped over. "Here we go."

Pushing off the ladder, Zoey and Brunhilda cleared the top rope. Sitting at ringside was a cheap wooden table. As they fell, both women rotated their bodies so that they crashed back-first onto the table. Beneath their combined weight, the table snapped in half across the middle and both ends popped up. Zoey took an elbow to the ribs and just narrowly missed being struck in the face by the corner of the table as her back slammed into the floor. A thinly padded gym mat did little to cushion the fall.

"Oofff," Zoey wheezed as the wind was knocked out of her. Pain radiated from her back and out to her arms and legs. She would be feeling this bump for days to come. "What was I thinking?"

"Am I dead?" Brunhilda muttered as she shoved a piece of the table away from her.

"You're talking and moving. And so am I," Zoey muttered. "Pretty sure we're alive."

Zoey pushed herself up onto her elbows and watched as Vivian crawled out from underneath the wrestling ring. Her and Brunhilda crashing through the table was Vivian's cue to come out of hiding and reenter the match. Vivian—who was dressed in stretchy, black pleather pants and a sparkly, red tank top—had been hanging out under the ring since the match started almost ten minutes earlier.

After grabbing a steel chair, Vivian climbed into the ring and then crept up behind Hannah as the younger woman slowly climbed up the ladder. Once she'd gotten rid of Zoey and Brunhilda, Hannah had set the ladder back up in the middle of the ring. Believing that she was the only woman left standing—Beverly, Jasmine, and Persephone had already been taken out and were lying motionless either in the ring or on the floor—Hannah took her time as she played up to the jeering audience.

Swinging the chair over her head, Vivian brought it down across Hannah's back. Hannah screamed in pain and then fell from the ladder. Vivian struck Hannah with the chair a second time before she tossed it aside.

Zoey pushed herself up and crawled back into the ring as Vivian climbed to the top of the ladder and grabbed the hot pink title belt that hung from the chandelier. The crowd of over four-hundred people went wild cheering on the septuagenarian. The ring bell sounded as Vivian held the title above her head.

"The winner of the match . . . And your new LAW Women's Champion . . . Vivacious Vivian Wilde!"

RANDEE GREEN IS THE AUTHOR OF THE Carrie Shatner Mystery series and the Zoey Wilde Mystery series. Her passion for reading began in grade school with *Little House in the Big Woods* by Laura Ingalls Wilder. She has a bachelor's degree in English Literature, as well as an MA and an MFA in Creative Writing. When not writing, she's usually reading, indulging in her passion for Texas country music, traveling, or hanging out with her dog, Daisy.